C000274138

THE PROPHECY

J.B.LIQUORISH

BALBOA.PRESS

A DIVISION OF HAY HOUSE

Copyright © 2021 J.B.Liquorish.

All rights reserved. No part of this book may be used or reproduced by
any means, graphic, electronic, or mechanical, including photocopying,
recording, taping or by any information storage retrieval system
without the written permission of the author except in the case of
brief quotations embodied in critical articles and reviews.

Balboa Press books may be ordered through booksellers or by contacting:

Balboa Press
A Division of Hay House
1663 Liberty Drive
Bloomington, IN 47403
www.balboapress.co.uk
UK TFN: 0800 0148647 (Toll Free inside the UK)
UK Local: 02036 956325 (+44 20 3695 6325 from outside the UK)

Because of the dynamic nature of the Internet, any web addresses or
links contained in this book may have changed since publication and may
no longer be valid. The views expressed in this work are solely those
of the author and do not necessarily reflect the views of the publisher,
and the publisher hereby disclaims any responsibility for them.

The author of this book does not dispense medical advice or prescribe the use
of any technique as a form of treatment for physical, emotional, or medical
problems without the advice of a physician, either directly or indirectly. The
intent of the author is only to offer information of a general nature to help
you in your quest for emotional and spiritual well-being. In the event you use
any of the information in this book for yourself, which is your constitutional
right, the author and the publisher assume no responsibility for your actions.

Any people depicted in stock imagery provided by Getty Images are
models, and such images are being used for illustrative purposes only.
Certain stock imagery © Getty Images.

Print information available on the last page.

ISBN: 978-1-9822-8291-2 (sc)
ISBN: 978-1-9822-8293-6 (hc)
ISBN: 978-1-9822-8292-9 (e)

Balboa Press rev. date: 07/19/2021

For Ross, who helped me to write

CHAPTER 1

DRAGON SLAYERS OF OLD

The year was 2000 BC, and times were dark. War had suffocated the world, and all sense of peace had been lost. Foe after foe came, deadly foes, the like of which had never before emerged in the world. But they never walked upon the earth; they ruled the skies and struck down from the high winds like a thunderstorm with powers that seemed endless. Wherever these foes struck, only death, destruction, and fire would remain. Hope for the survival of civilisation waned; however, when humanity is threatened, humanity fights back!

Amongst those who would challenge the tyranny, one strong enough to be a commander emerged, and his name was Drake. He chose Aillig and Alec, who were great friends to him as well as fierce warriors, to lead at his side. Under their leadership, a small amount of hope stirred within the city walls and small villages; farmers, peasants, and humble village folk took up arms. But no matter how many rallied to the call, it would not lift any of the leaders' secretly crushed hopes. Their enemy came from the darkest places of time and legend and was unmatched in every way imaginable. What hope was there against such fearsome demons, the storm breakers, the devil's harvesters, the dragons from up on high? Over time, the dragons had moved far and wide, but for unknown reasons, they always returned to one place: Scotland! Their immense shadows swamped cities, and they blanketed the skies in giant ash clouds and smoke like fog on a cold December morning. For many years, Scotland was suffocated and buried under an ash age! The once-great civilisation of fishing peoples was no more. Fear and war had shaken the very foundations of Scotland.

Spring arose early in Cill Chuimein. The sun broke above the city walls, piercing through the narrow, roughly hewn windows of Drake's small stone house, disturbing him from his slumber. He rose from his bed, stretching his stiff body and caressing an old battle wound on his arm. It was a nice change to have been woken by the sun for once, he thought; most of the time the light never made it in through his little window or anybody else's, with the air so full of ash. Most windows were boarded up to keep the ash out. Sleep was something that was only spoken about, never truly had. How could you sleep under such a threat and with the near-constant ringing of the warning bells? During the little sleep Drake did get, he never took off his chainmail, and his sword leant against the bedpost.

There was a loud knock on his door. His two friends Aillig and Alec stood breathless at his door.

"The king calls for our urgent presence!" Aillig said, panting.

Drake grabbed his sword and ran with Aillig and Alec without a further word to the keep. Within minutes, they stood before King Ennis upon his throne in the high keep of Cill Chuimein.

"What service do you require of us, sire?" Drake asked.

"Victory! That is what I require."

"But that's not possible!" Aillig's words spilled from his mouth before he realised the reaction they would cause.

"Enough! I will not have my command questioned. You will bring me victory."

For Drake, Aillig, and Alec, three great swords, each with a large, bright, scarlet ruby set within the hilt, had been forged by the great seers and impregnated with their blood in the hope that their powers would make the blades strong enough to pierce the hide of a dragon without shattering. In truth, it was a complete mystery as to what they could do, since they were the only blades with powers that had ever been forged.

After what seemed a brief second in the chamber, they left with the orders to march upon Srath Pheofhair at first light. When the time came, the gates were opened, and they rode out on three black warhorses to stand before a huge army at least ten thousand strong. But all these men did nothing to lift Drake's heart, as this was not going to be a victory.

Drake drew himself back and let his voice bellow. "Men of Scotland, we are united under one banner to face the dragons head-on. Blood will be spilled, but it will not be ours! No more shall people suffocate in the ash clouds or look up into the sky and not see the sun. Today the dark veil will be torn, and light will flood the dragon-defiled mountains. March with me to Srath Pheofhair, to the dragons' end!"

The march began, and loud horns were blown from the city walls. They feared they would not get to Srath Pheofhair before the dragons struck; an army of this size would not go unmissed for long. The slight breeze that blew was carrying the sound of their movement. By midday, they were deep in the valleys of Srath Pheofhair, luckily without casualty and with no sign of any dragon.

Their eyes fixed upon the snow-capped peaks. Drake kept the army advancing slowly right up to the slopes of the tallest mountain. A dragon would have stood out against the white as clear as day. Where were they? Was it a trap? Had the dragons been hunting them whilst they marched? An entire army stood now with weapons drawn on the slopes of the tallest mountain. The three leaders dismounted and removed provisions from the horses. As horses would be no use in fighting against dragons, Drake set them free. Drake, Aillig, and Alec walked up the slopes to look over the heads of the army. Seconds later, there was an enormous thud on the mountainside, causing a landslide. The tremors from the crash shook the ground under the soldiers' feet, causing them to stumble. It seemed clear that it must be a dragon.

Drake was not going to be scared by this or let his army be weakened. "Do not let your fear get the best of you." His voice broke the air like a crack of thunder. "Are you not the king's army? On this field, we will show no fear and no mercy. The ground will be painted

3

red with the blood of the enemy. We fight for our freedom, our land, our homes, and our families. Stand with me as men of Scotland." Roars of cheering echoed across the glen, and now Drake believed they were ready.

They could hear a heavy beating sound echoing like a giant drum, and a great shadow was cast across the whole valley, blocking nearly all the light for a brief moment. The dragon emerged from the peaks of the mountains, circling like an eagle. Without any warning, the dragon tipped its head back and bellowed forth an ear-piercing roar. More monstrous beating sounds and roars came in reply from all round, and moments later a great flurry of giant wings soared into the valley. The force of such a mass of wings gave the effect of a hurricane. Immediate panic set in. The men were circled by no fewer than nine dragons, all watching, all waiting, with great protruding teeth bared. A couple of men tried to run from the fierce, penetrating gaze of the dragons' blood-red eyes, but it was obvious that the dragons were not going to let anyone go. A flash of bright light, intense heat, and a smell of burning flesh, and nothing was left of the deserters.

Drake could only watch his army and shout at the top of his voice as morale crumpled into cinders. His voice was never going to be loud enough to be heard, and the air was rent with panic and fury. Alec and Aillig seemed to be the only ones still waiting for orders.

"Alec, you take the left flank, and Aillig, you take the right. Circle the valley. We attack from all angles."

The positive movements from Drake, Alec, and Aillig were not unnoticed. Big groups of men broke free to join the assault, and quickly the army began to separate into three. It didn't take long for the vast numbers of men moving to dwindle. The air was superheated by the dragons' foul, hot breath, and smoke hung in thick clouds. Fireballs and tails smote men lifeless, strewn like ragdolls on a bed of nails. Their attacks were effortless, almost lazily given.

The formation was broken, and the men scattered themselves widely. But it was not arrows they were trying to dodge this time—it was winged beasts as big as large houses. The talons alone were sharper than any arrow that had ever been forged, and worst of all, they never missed a target. It seemed an impossible enemy. Blades, arrows, spears broke like twigs on the dragons' thick, ironlike scales. The number of men who had died already from rebounding volleys of arrows was uncountable. The air was filled with raining arrows, broken or whole. The dragons could have killed them all in seconds, but they flew effortlessly over their heads, mocking their pathetic attempts. Drake could at least be grateful that it was daylight, since a dragon at night was invisible death; their black bodies were as dark as the night sky.

Over their heads, the soldiers formed a dome of shields, but no sooner had it been created than it fell apart. It was like holding a bonfire in your hands, the skin instantly blistering as the dragons torched the shields. A few of the dragons dived down on the three armies, striking with more ferocity. Their tails cracked like whips, and with every strike came death. Faith lay in tatters, and none of the three could command. They were all fighting for themselves, and not just against the dragons—they were fighting one another for a way out. But those who tried to flee were the next to die.

The dragons dived through the smoke, torching everything in their path. The remaining flanking positions fell. The dragons soared overhead with not a scratch on them. Nearly half the army had retreated to their deaths. Drake had to make his move. His blown horn rang with ferocity across the valley, but only a few rallied. Drake's only intention was to find Alec and Aillig now. He kept on sounding the horn again and again till he didn't have enough strength in his lungs. Many heard the call, and only a few answered. Those who came to rally looked beyond the fight ahead. Their swords were limp in their hands, and most were hunched over in agony. Despite their state, Drake would only look at them with loyalty for answering the call and would not have had any other army.

The rallying troops had caught the interest of one dragon especially. It seemed bigger than the rest and also older, its scales rough and scarred. It landed on the far side of the valley and bellowed a warning blast of flames. The rest of the dragons spiralled overhead, watching the conflict unfold below. The weight of every eye was on Drake; the time to prove his sword was now. He gripped the hilt so tightly that it cut into his red, raw hands, and his teeth ground together so forcefully he could feel them chipping. Drake charged, and the rest followed in a wedge formation. They got ever closer, but the dragon didn't even twitch, its eyes, blood-red, pinned on them. Its chest began to glow molten orange, and only when they were right on top of the dragon did it rear up. It flicked its tail in a low sweeping motion and brought much of the army to the floor, but not Drake. Drake darted underneath the dragon as it swung its tail, and with all his strength, he drove his blade deep into its belly. The dragon gave a shrieking cry and crashed like a sack of potatoes to the ground.

The other dragons circling above dived with great fury, their roars splitting eardrums. Drake's successful blow had restored some hope amongst the men, but how long could it last? Drake felt the pressure pounding on him as ice presses upon stone. His fear told him the truth: the dragons would easily dominate. The first dragon had been old, but these looked much younger and faster. Drake stood lost in thought with his eyes following each dragon's movement. Their new rage tore through men like a hot knife through butter. Drake stood frozen as the dragons attacked. Tears splashed his face. It was only when he heard cries of pain close to him that he came back to his senses. His heart raged as fierce as the dragons gaze, and he raised his sword to charge. Aillig and Alec united their swords with his and a small army joined the charge.

The ground shook as the dragons thudded down to meet the soldiers. Both sides began to charge towards each other. As they got close, the anger that drove Drake was thwarted, by a tsunami of fear, as he realised how big a mistake the charge was. Drake and Aillig retreated from the wall to avoid the head-on attack, and many followed. But Alec was just too slow to turn in time. Drake and Aillig fled up the slopes whilst a few dragons attacked. They caught a final glimpse of Alec before his company shattered. The company was lost under the dragons' feet. Everything seemed to almost come to a stop round Drake and Aillig, the tortured screams dying away, bodies thrown far and wide. It was a slaughter, four dragons against three hundred men.

Searing hot tears splashed Drake's and Allig's faces as they charged to Alec's aid. In those brief moments, everything died—the land, the trees, the birds, the whole world. From a distance, as the final bodies began to fall, they saw Alec. His sword flashed in the sunlight as he swung with all his might, but it was not enough. The reaction of the dragon was far too quick, and Alec missed. He recovered in time to avoid the jet of flames, but his back was turned. A heavy blow from behind smote him to his knees with his entire weight resting on the hilt of his sword. The sword sunk into the ground as he tried to stand, and he could not free it. The second strike came to his chest. His body left the ground, broken and mutilated, flying high into the air. For Drake, it was as if life had stopped; the pain of what he was seeing was too much. Alec's body almost seemed to float through the air before it hit the mountainside. His friend, who was more like a brother to him, had walked the final path, and the veil was closed.

The last few ghostly cries died away like a howling wind. The army, once ten thousand strong, was reduced to a couple of hundred. The wounds that many had sustained would soon kill them. They had failed each other. Drake and Aillig only intended now to get the rest to safety if they could. This could not be achieved without fighting. The dragons were on top of them now, and soon they would join Alec. Together they struck upon the rear flank of a dragon. The blood that oozed was thick and looked almost black. The dragon did not turn and strike as they expected. With great speed, it fled from the attack, but soon its pace began to slow; an effect like poison brought it down upon the mountainside, still and lifeless.

The power of the swords had not gone unnoticed by the dragons. All their attention was focused on Drake. Every chest glowed with molten fire, and the air was growing intensely hot, the stench of rotten flesh overpowering. The dragons moved with such speed, anger burning like acid in their eyes, as they tore through man after man. Drake and Aillig were the only two who did not flee. No matter what, death would take them eventually; their last act would not be running away. They shook with fear as they charged head-on towards the body of dragons. With every effort, they swung together and missed. It seemed like Alec's death would replay itself. The swords hit a jagged rock but surprisingly did not break or buckle. From the force of the hit, the rock split, and a powerful blast of energy released at the same time. Whatever it was, the dragons tried and failed to evade it; they crashed into the ground all over the valley, half crumpled. They couldn't move, no matter how hard they tried. The sound of their cries and rasping breath was fading. Drake and Aillig could only stand and watch, confused and speechless. The final cries faded away. Drake prodded a few of the dragons with his sword, and they seemed to be dead. All the strength he needed to hold his sword was gone, and he dropped it. Many men still on the battlefield had seen what happened and began to return, looking for friends amongst the dead. Waves of shock at their unexpected victory passed through Drake and Aillig, and it was some time before they joined the men to look for Alec. It did not take them long to find him. They pressed their lips upon his forehead; it was the last time they would ever touch him. A torn flagbearer's colours were draped over his body. Together they said, "Goodbye."

CHAPTER 2

THE SUCCESSFUL HUNT

Time passed on. Now it was 500 BC, and history had been forgotten. The scarred ground was healed, flowers grew anew, birds sung once again, and the sweet scent of heather and pollen had filled the air for many years. Scotland had lived in peace for over five hundred years now. Trade was booming again, and a way of life had been renewed. Where once had been wildlands, there were now small communities. As the communities expanded, homes began to pop up right into the mountains—little ones built of stone and thatch, set into the earth. High up the slopes of a valley stood a solitary stone house. It was by no means a big house; it only had three rooms, barely big enough to stand up straight. It was here that a young boy lived. Warwick was his name. Small and underfed, he often appeared tired. Even now that the dragons had gone, life was still just as hard for those of little wealth. A lot of families like his never survived the harsh winters; those that did often spent months repairing walls and roofs. His father, Deal, was extremely resourceful and worked tirelessly every day to provide for his family. Having served in the king's army had taught Deal how to survive in the harshest of conditions. In the warm months, he gathered straw and grass so it would be dry for use during the winter. Then, through the cold months, he spent a lot of time stuffing that straw and grass into what clothing they had. If they were lucky enough, they may have an animal hide for extra warmth. This would mean hunting, though, and hunting at that time of year proved a real challenge. On the off chance, you saw a deer or a hare, it would be high in the mountains and often too quick to catch. It was not just the wildlife that ran short; all the berries, nuts, seeds, and fungi would be buried deep under a pearl-white blanket of snow. That's if the bitter coldness hadn't killed them first. At the first sign of winter's fall, a mass harvest would be gathered. It would be stored under animal skins and straw to keep it dry and prevent it from freezing solid. They began every new year without a single gold piece left, since at the time of mass harvest, all would be spent on thick clothing or materials to repair damage to houses. As soon as the weather began to warm up in the new year, trade bustled, with everyone heading to the market to sell their expertise, desperate to make as much money as they could to survive the next winter.

Warwick was sixteen. As he was under eighteen years of age, he still had a plait hanging down from the back of his thick, black, matted hair. Only once he had passed the trials of manhood at the age of eighteen would it be removed, and then he would be allowed to step forward into the world alone. Each year couldn't go by quick enough for Warwick. In the meantime, his mother, Helena, kept him busy. Every morning he would climb high into the mountains to a well he and his father had dug, bringing back a large pail of water. At first, he would lose a lot of water on the rough terrain, but now that he had been doing it for years, it was second nature to him. Had he been well fed, he would have been very muscular and tall. Since he hadn't, though, his heels were cracked with many scars from cuts and blisters, his arms and legs were skinny with raised veins, his neck was thin, looking almost too weak to support his head, and his face was long and bony but not pale. His eyes were quite striking to behold. They were deep blue, standing out against his skin like diamonds in the moonlight.

Deal, his father, had had to rebuild most of their home. It had once been the home of their ancestors, who were goat farmers. Money had been hard for them as well, and they'd had no option but to slaughter their goats to survive. After their lifetimes, the house lay abandoned for many years till the time when Deal could no longer serve the king, being too beaten and old to fight. It was then that he returned and rebuilt the pile of rubble that was his ancestors' home. Shortly after, he met Helena, Warwick's mother. Since Deal no longer fought, he spent most of his days darning torn fishing nets and hunting. It was very rare that he successfully caught anything big. He always said to himself that he would catch a deer one day. At times he would be gone for over half a day, doing all he could to catch even the smallest thing, and when he would come back, he would be covered in mud, his clothes torn. It was the drive to catch a deer and the fear of disappointing his family without a catch that made him work tirelessly and relentlessly.

Helena often spent her days sitting by a fire darning threadbare clothing or cooking. She mostly made soups and broths from scraps she could find; they weren't really all that tasty. Keeping herself busy—not that she had a choice—had the benefit of keeping her worry at bay. Every day when Deal returned from hunting, she always had the same deeply relieved expression, like a heavy weight had been lifted from her shoulders.

So Warwick did not spend much time with his parents. He was forever busy being sent (within the limits the law would allow till he was eighteen) for water, food, and young green saplings, the latter of which were very useful for darning nets and sheets. From the moment he could walk and talk, this had been his life. He'd never known what it was like to have a childhood. But he was quiet and never asked why; he just did what he was told. It was the only way to survive.

Everything in Warwick's life had changed at the age of fifteen, but they didn't know it yet.

ONE YEAR BEFORE

It was a clear day and not so cold. The birds were singing, and the scent of heather came in through the windows. Helena, though, seemed agitated. She came into Warwick's room holding something wrapped up in her hands.

"This is for you. Do not lose it!" she said.

Once Warwick had hold of it, she left the room, looking slightly nervous. She took the pail with her, which she had never done before, and went to get the water. Curiosity and concern stung Warwick. The parcel in his hand felt weighty and hard. Not being able to bear the suspense of what had just come to light, he opened it quickly. What he saw sitting on the cloth confused him greatly, but had he known what would become of it, he would not have been confused but scared. Why had he been given a key? he kept asking himself. It was the most unusual key you would ever see. Most were made of wood, if you were lucky enough to own a lock, but this was forged steel and very long, about seven inches. Normally metal keys were only forged for castles and places of high importance. *Why should I have one?* he thought to himself. Jagged teeth protruded from both sides of the shaft. But what caught his eye most was a glistening scarlet ruby set into the handle. Somehow its shine, an almost unnatural glow, seemed entrancing. Someone had clearly gone to a lot of effort to forge it, but what was it for? A thousand thoughts crashed into one another in his head.

The key would be a source of much confusion for nearly the next twelve months. Warwick tried to talk about it, but Helena always hushed the topic. All the nights thinking about it seemed a terrible waste, but it ruled his mind from the first day. He could not stop thinking about it, no matter how hard he tried. Helena eventually grew tired of his behaviour and forbade him from speaking about it.

PRESENT TIME

Warwick woke early on a particularly cold November morning. His whole body was numb to the bone, and his breath fogged his vision. Winter was well on its way. The first snowfalls could be seen on the highest peaks, glistening brilliant white in the low sun. Round his neck he wore the key, but if it weren't for his mother's insistence that he keep it safe, he definitely would have taken it off, as the coldness of the metal on his skin was boring into him like a needle. Mostly to keep himself warm—though undoubtedly his clothes would get wet in the deep snow—he grabbed the pail and set off up the mountain path. He enjoyed the walk more these days. It gave him time to think about the key. His mother and father had got up long before Warwick had. Deal was off hunting, and Helena, having already got the fire going, was preparing food. The hope for something tasty clawed at his stomach. With his mind focused heavily on food and the key, it seemed a short journey. When he got back, he was shocked to see a stag sprawled on the floor with a clear arrow wound to its chest. He let the pail of water slip and nearly spill at the sight of it. The stag was young and tender, and such rich meat would last them months. Even with that said, it did not stop Warwick fantasising about all the different meals it would make. The earthy, bitter mushrooms and sharp, sour berries he ate regularly had grown thin, so a change as good as this was like having all his dreams come true at once. However, not all the food he usually ate was bad; he greatly enjoyed the few fish he got, their skins crispy and soot-blackened and the flesh inside succulent, moist, and dripping with juices. In recent years, though, the number of fish they consumed had lessened. More and more fish were being sent to the market as it became harder to make money.

Deal's hunt had not been a complete success. His trousers were torn from ankle to knee, and a trickle of blood ran down his leg. From head to toe, he was scratched and covered in stinking wet mud. The once-black boots that had served him through many battles were finally broken. Matted hair thick with mud covered his eyes. Helena took the pail of water from Warwick and shoved it forcefully into Deal's arms. With the orders to wash himself down outside, he left Helena and Warwick to prepare the meat. It was a long time before he came back, the pail of water in his hand refilled and his clothes soaking wet. He hung his clothes in front of the fire and changed into his only spare pair of clothes. As a rule, he would always try to avoid wearing his spare clothes, not because they were badly fitting or uncomfortable but because they reminded him of war. A tatty leather cuirass, broken and repaired several times, had sat untouched in a small chest for years along with his black trousers.

Warwick's eagerness to ask his father about the hunt would not abate. When Deal took a seat by the fire to dry off, Warwick went and sat by his father keen and hopeful. "How did you catch it, Father? How did you get it home? It's magnificent."

Deal was overjoyed to see how happy his son was. "You know I can't teach you until you come of age. I know how annoyed you must be. It would help me out a great deal if you could hunt too. Think of this, though: you only need to wait two more years. Then you can take the test to become a man, and I will gladly hand you my bow. It is this bow that saved my life in battle many times. I would give you my sword if it were mine to give. You must not attempt to go hunting yourself until you're of age. It's not that you're not trusted, so please don't let your tongue speak with evil. The wilds are dangerous to wander alone. The reason the law stands as it does is because of a young prince. The tales say that once, a very long time ago, a young prince no older than you was drunk on his own power, knowing that the throne would one day be his. He would not listen to his father and one day took his father's sword and walked into the wilderness. People scoured the landscape for years, but he never was found. That is why you shouldn't go off by yourself!"

"Father, I have no intention of wandering the wilds by myself. I want to know how you caught the stag. I don't want to hunt."

Deal met Warwick's eyes with a deep penetrating gaze. "Alright." There was a note of agitation in his voice. "The hunt took me high onto the mountain ridges. I set off at night, as most beasts hunt then. The only downside was that the wind was high and icy cold. Within minutes of leaving, I lost all feeling in my hands. How I was going to draw my bow I knew not. Clouds descended as I climbed. Visibility was almost lost, and my clothes clung to me like bandages to a bloody wound. It was only getting worse, but I would not go home without a catch. After several hours of hiking, I found a small alcove. It took a great effort to get into it, but at least I had protection from the weather. In the dark of the alcove, I waited and waited until I'd almost fallen into a terminal sleep. When, finally, I saw something move not too far away, I wondered if I would be able to even raise my bow. In the poor visibility, I could see the outline of something big and knew that it was a stag. With a chance of catching something really impressive, I felt a new strength in me. I was able to raise and draw my bow. The arrow found its mark." He pointed to the arrow wound on the chest of the stag. "I tracked the beast for a while as it walked away limping. Slowly its life force drained from the wound, and it collapsed. I was quick to heave it along. Didn't want to get caught out by wolves. I had no option but to drag it and just hope that the meat wouldn't spoil. The journey was long, and by the time I got back, I was exhausted. Still, it is my best catch ever, and I couldn't be happier."

No part of the animal was wasted. The hide they stripped of hair, stuffing clothing with it for extra warmth. They stripped the meat from the bones and put some into a cooking pot; the rest they salted and added to the food store. They made water skins from the bladder. While Warwick and Helena were doing this, Deal nailed the antlers onto the wall to hang things from, mostly fish.

Evening came. Tiredness was deep in all of them. Hands, feet, everything hurt. When the meal finally came, it was most welcome. A steaming bowl of venison stew went down a treat. Deal's gratitude at seeing how happy his wife and son were beamed across his face. They reflected his smiles back like a mirror. Warwick felt that night like he had been taught a valuable lesson on motivation, and now he could not wait till he was of age.

CHAPTER 3

THE BREAKING OF LOVED ONES

Warwick woke afresh, smiling. The dawning sun had peeked above the horizon and crept silently through his window. He almost wanted to run to get the water. It was hard to remember the last time he'd felt this content and full. Warwick grabbed the pail, but as he went to leave, Helena stopped him, pulling him back into his room.

"Mother, what is it?"

Helena ignored him. Something seemed to preoccupy her at the minute, keeping her from talking. Her gaze was fixed on Warwick's chest. His eyes followed hers till he realised what she was at: the key! Helena seemed to be tense; her eyes were bloodshot and puffy. Her hand reached out and pulled back the collar of Warwick's grey tunic. She pulled the key off over his head.

"What … Mother … why are you …?"

Helena's gaze finally moved to Warwick's face. She was smiling, yet Warwick felt frightened by her actions.

"I have taken the key from you so that I will have your full attention, Warwick. I am not cross with you but more with myself."

"Why? I don't understand. What is wrong?"

"I have been thinking for a very long time. I do not need to say what about, as it sits right before my eyes. Much sleep I have lost because of this damn thing. Why it came to be so I doubt I will ever know. Yes, Warwick, as you might have guessed, I have had the key in my possession for a very long time. I cannot say what it does even after all this time. It is a weird thing, very unusual. Now

16

it is very important you listen. I am going to tell you how I came to have the key."

The hair on the back of Warwick's neck stood on end. Finally, he would be able to use it. But why did Helena hate it so much? What trouble could a key cause?

"I do not want you to use it!"

Warwick's excitement instantly sunk.

"I only tell you now because I trust you to be responsible for your actions. I do not, however, tell you lightly. There has been too much distress over this decision to tell you. Your father rather wished I had thrown it away; he does not understand. For nearly half my life I had that key. It was when I was fifteen it happened. I remember that day as if it were yesterday. I had gone to the market with my mother. She walked off to get what we came for and left me lost amongst many feet. Most people just bustled past me, barely acknowledging my existence—everyone except for one. A hooded person in black robes had been leaning up against a wall looking right at me. I could see him out of the corner of my eye. Whoever it was, I never saw his face, yet he was not making any attempt not to be seen. It was he who gave me the key. Someone knocked me to the floor, and the next I knew I was being hoisted to my feet as if I were a child. It was that hooded person, and it was clear then from his deep voice that he was a man. He asked me to come with him. I did not want to go, but his grip on my arm was tight. I was scared, but you see by acting like this, he had got my full attention. When he had taken me to a quiet street, he turned to face me, but never did he lower his hood. This was the moment I was given the key. He said 'Helena, you must take this! There will be a time when you have a son. It is imperative that you give this to him at the age of fifteen. Keep it safe till then. Be careful about how you use it!' That was the last I ever saw of that man. I looked for him, as I, like you, had so many questions I wanted to ask. This, I'm afraid, is all I can tell you about the key. It is as much a mystery to me as it is to you."

"Haven't you ever tried to figure out what it does?"

"Yes, son, I tried many times for years before you were born. Every time resulted in nothing. Whatever this thing is, I do not feel it is friendly. Those times I did try to use it, something odd happened with my brain. It was almost as if it fogged my memory, making me forget all about it. As far as I can tell, it was as if it did not want me to use it. Though I was not told it had a power, I do believe it has one. From the moment I first held it, I felt something different."

Warwick, ashamed as he was to admit it, was disappointed. For such a long time he had wished for this very conversation, so much so that he had even imagined it at night. Yet now that it had happened, he still knew nothing about the key and only had more questions he wanted to ask. *Who the hell was that man?* The very thought of him sent a shiver up Warwick's spine. *How did he know my mother, and how could he know about me before I was born? Was it possible to feel curiosity as well as anger for one person?*

The day drew into the afternoon very quickly. His father had been oblivious to the conversation they'd had, and Helena was going to keep it that way. She had warned Warwick to speak nothing of it, but upon seeing his father outside, Warwick began to wonder. Deal was swinging his axe with vengeance upon the logs. His jawline was tight, like his teeth were grinding against each other. Helena had noticed Deal too and kept Warwick busy for a while helping her, but the help Warwick provided was useless. More than ever before, his mind was focused on one thing only: the key. He played with it between his fingers, twisting and turning it. Helena's agitation would not hold. "Warwick, you are doing exactly what I told you not to. The way you look at it, the way you think about it—I know what that's like. I have experienced it. It drives you mad. Just focus on your work; it won't do you any good. This damn key was clearly meant for you to have, so I am sure that in time it will reveal itself. So please, can you just put it away and do some jobs."

Warwick took the key from round his neck and put it on the table. Helena at least seemed to be pleased about this, if nothing else. Whilst they worked to clean the kitchen, Warwick could not help but look over his shoulder from time to time. To see the key still on the table relaxed him, and a thin smile broke across his face. Now that his full attention was on the work, it was done in no time.

Deal had moved on from cutting the logs and seemed a lot calmer now. He sat now on an upturned pail darning his fishing net. The net was so patchy that it was hard to tell which bits had been repaired and which hadn't. The shallows of Loch Domhain were riddled with sharp stones. Often he would snag his net on them. It seemed impossible not to. A pile of long reeds lay at his feet. Piece by piece he wove till the hole was fixed. Warwick finished helping his mother and went to find his father.

"Ah, finally, son. Has Helena sent you to help?"

Warwick avoided his father's eyes. Seeing the disappointment in them would have been too much.

"I'm sorry, Warwick, I didn't mean to sound cross. You're here now, and that's what matters. Helena doesn't want me to know, but I am aware she spoke to you about the key this morning. ... I am sorry for my ill temperament. I only act like I do because I love you and I want the best for you. You are still so young in a mighty world, and I just don't want you wasting years of your life. Why don't you come fishing with me later at Loch Domhain? I am nearly finished here anyway. When I'm done, we can go."

Warwick hugged his father, and in that brief moment, much happiness was felt.

After dinner, they left. The sky was dark and the wind bitter. The grass hung wet with evening dew. It was not going to be a pleasant fish. They went weaving down a well-trodden path between trees into the valley. A while later, they climbed up the far banks of the valley. There at the bottom of the next valley, shimmering in the ghostly light of the moon, was Loch Domhain.

On the edge of the lake, they found some big boulders to shelter them from the wind. They cast out their nets and the wait began. After a while, Deal noticed that a thick mist was forming. The far bank slipped from view, and the lake's ghostly light vanished. They would have been in total darkness if it were not for the faint glow of the stars and the moon. The coldness was creeping into every limb as they sat there. In the hours of waiting that passed, Warwick slowly slid down the rock and became distracted yet again by his key, which was dangling freely round his neck. In the inky blackness, the ruby was emitting a faint glow, just strong enough to illuminate his hands and face. Deal had been staring fixedly out into the dark water to where the nets were for any sign of movement, which kept him from noticing the key. That was lucky for Warwick, as he was certain Deal wouldn't approve.

The fishing wasn't going well. After an hour, Deal began to pull the nets back in, cursing every time he felt them snag. He realised Warwick wasn't helping to pull the nets and turned to look at him. Warwick was curled up with his back to his father. Deal saw the outline of his face glowing. He grabbed Warwick's shoulder firmly, making Warwick jump. In the faint glow that now illuminated Deal's face, Warwick could see that agitation in his father's furrowed brow and bulging eyes.

"What did I say to you earlier? This key is more trouble than it's worth." Deal reached to grab the key and throw it in the lake, but as soon as he touched it, he let go with a sudden gasp of pain. "It burnt me." The anger that had made him want to throw it in the lake had been crushed by the shock of what had happened. It was the first time he had known the key to do anything. On his left hand was a raised, red burn that had already started to blister.

The fear and guilt that Warwick felt now were worse than the punishment he had imagined Deal would give him. He began to splutter as he rushed to find the words to explain. In the end, all he managed to say amongst sobs was "I … sorry … the key … glowing!"

Deal continued to look at Warwick, realising how upset he was, and decided just to pat him gently on his right arm. He was no longer angry with Warwick, understanding that it wasn't his fault. Though neither spoke, they were thinking the same thing: why did the key have to exist?

Stiff and exhausted with no reward for their effort, they traipsed home cold and wet. When Warwick finally settled down in his bed, tucked under a tatty sheep fleece, the key was still glowing. He held the key in the palm of his hand in the light of the moon, not wanting to put it down. The glow grew brighter, and the ruby seemed to shimmer almost as if fireflies were trapped within. He half wondered if he had fallen asleep and was dreaming vividly. Realising it wasn't a dream, he sat up, focusing even more on the key. What power was this? The rest of the night, Warwick sat bolt upright in his bed examining the key. He desperately hoped that he wasn't seeing things, and under his breath, he willed it to do more. Nothing else happened, to his disappointment, and soon he was walking out the door with the pail.

Upon his return, a bound piece of parchment lay on the table addressed to him. Helena and Deal had been waiting for him to return. Deal stood up and handed the parchment to Warwick.

Before Warwick could open it, Helena spoke up. "Who's it from? I found it first thing this morning, just outside. I noticed the seal was marked with an eagle."

Warwick's eyes moved from his mother back to the parchment. His hands trembled as he slit the seal.

To Warwick, son of Deal,

I write to you to warn you about the key. Last night, the key showed but a small fragment of the power we believe it to hold. I am warning you now that it should not be used until you fully understand what it is. Even though I am gifted with foresight, I cannot answer the questions you ponder. I do not see all. Things that are powerful but unknown should never be used. In opening yourself up to it, you have taken great risks. I cannot say to what effect this has had. I am drawn to its power, and if I am drawn myself, then others will be drawn as well. There are many perils in this world, and not one of them should be risked. Yes, you are its master;

that I do see. With time, I am certain it will reveal itself to you. Just because you're something's master, though, does not mean you should go using it. Close your mind to it and put it somewhere safe. I am watching you. Something is approaching!

Warwick was shocked. Never before had he felt fear like this. His trembling had become a violent shake, and a cold sweat broke out across his brow. "It c-can't be the same man wh-who gave you the key, could it? He would ha-have died years ago sur-surely?" stuttered Warwick.

"Yes, he would have?" replied Helena with a note of confusion.

At the bottom of the letter, there was an eagle eye marked in ink. Warwick stared at it so intently that he forgot his mother and father stood inches from him. He only became aware when Deal spoke, frightening the life out of him.

"What does it say?"

Warwick read aloud, steadying his nerves. As soon as he had finished, Deal took the letter from his hand with force to read himself. It was there, word for word, before him. Warwick knew he was in for some trouble now. This was proof that he looks at the key at night. Any second, his father's booming voice would shatter his eardrums. The temptation to run was strong. Warwick thought better of this, however. Running from his trouble would not help. When Deal did speak, his voice was surprisingly calm. He could only ask if it were true that Warwick used it. Warwick spoke so quickly that his reply was garbled, but after repeating it slowly, his parents didn't seem half as tense. After all, he had only been holding it at night.

Shortly after he left the room, Warwick heard raised voices. Helena and Deal had never agreed with each other when it came to the key, but never had they argued like this before. Warwick sat in his room, ears plugged. To hear his parents going at each other like this was too much. His guilty conscience kept building; this was his entire fault. He longed to examine the parchment again, but right now leaving his room felt like the hardest challenge. He pulled the key from his neck and threw it across the room with force. He hated it so much. To destroy it would bring him much joy.

The arguing ended badly. Deal took his fishing net and went without a word. When Warwick came out of his room, he noticed that Helena's eyes were red and puffy. A lump was in his throat. What had he done? Glancing round the room, he noticed that the parchment was torn in two on the floor. He had no thought for it, only for his mother. He put his arms round her, hugging her tightly. The lump in his throat burned searing hot, and his eyes spilled down his cheeks. His whole body shook. He wanted to tell Helena how sorry he was, but the words were lost. Everything ached, but nothing more so than his heart. Helena held him in her arms and kissed him softly on the cheek. She could not show any annoyance, ever. She loved her son, and nothing would change that, no matter what.

Warwick's feeling of guilt was greatly lessened in his mother's arms. His emotions had spoken the words he wanted to say, and Helena showed absolutely no anger towards him. He felt no guilt now in taking the torn parchment to his room. Pointlessly he re-read it. He knew nothing more could be got from the words, but still he looked. This only brought recurring thoughts. What had the key done? What had he done?

Helena came into Warwick's room. Her eyes were still puffy and red, but she at least looked slightly happier. Memories of the day she had been given the key ran strongly in her mind. Every word that that man had spoken she never forgot. Softly she put an arm round Warwick. "That letter, what do you know about it, Warwick?"

"Nothing that you don't. I had hoped I could ask you if you had seen that eye anywhere before?"

Helena moved from Warwick, having seen the key on the floor. She picked it up and handed it to him. As Warwick grabbed it, he felt something rough along its edge. He hadn't felt it before, though he had held the key many times. How could he have never felt this? He turned the key on its edge in the palm of his hand and saw a very small engraving of an eagle. It was the same eagle that had been on the seal. He could almost have sworn that it had not been there before. "Look here," he said.

Helena bent in close, and she too saw the engraved eagle. "I don't believe it. In all my years of having that in my possession, I have never seen that. I examined every inch of that key. How did it get there?" She paused briefly while deep in thought. "Tell me exactly what happened."

With the words on the parchment coursing through his head and a new fear of what might happen should he speak about the key, he found it hard to tell. Helena, however, could see the fear burning like a bush fire in his eyes and returned a very stern gaze. The commanding gaze was enough to tell Warwick that she was not going to stop until he had spoken. "I only held it in my hand in the beam of light from the moon. Whether the moon was its cause of glow I do not know. It looked like fireflies were trapped in the stone. I didn't think much of it. That was all that happened." Warwick had forgotten that it had been glowing down at Loch Domhain when the moon was eclipsed by fog, so the moon had nothing to do with its glowing.

"Well, I don't see how that could have caused any harm. Now that I think about that parchment, I am sure it is only a warning, not really anything to worry about. I am guessing the author, whoever it is, put the words in just to scare you from using it. Don't go worrying about it, Warwick." Helena breathed out a long sigh. It seemed an immense weight had been lifted off her shoulders.

The morning had almost gone when Deal returned with five giant salmon slung like sacks of potatoes over his shoulder. Paying no attention to the fish, Helena threw her arms round him as soon as he came in the door. He looked too as if he had been crying; his eyes were bloodshot. In that moment, Warwick smiled to see the love between his parents. As soon as Helena finished hugging him, Deal turned to Warwick and hugged him tightly. It seemed that finally the feud was over. Warwick was keen to help Deal and took the fish from him.

"Leave that," said Helena.

24

"Why?"

"I want us to spend some time together. Let's walk to Loch Domhain and take some food with us. We all need a break from this. Come on. Just leave the key and parchment here."

Warwick still had worries about the key. He knew in his heart that he should not leave it here, so he tucked it inside his clothing, well hidden from view. Helena had been too busy gathering the food together to notice. Warwick took the food from Helena, and they were off. The day was clear, and it wasn't so cold. The wind was still, and the grass and trees stood as still as stone. As they reached the lake, they could see a nice spot on the north side, an enclosed patch of moss surrounded by tall pine trees. Warwick slumped into a crook at the base of one of the trees, looking across the glasslike surface of the lake to the far shore. For the first time in months, he felt completely relaxed, weightless. All his worries, all his anger, all his upset washed away in the gentle lap of the water. He was almost asleep when he heard a thud on the ground. Deal had brought sticks. He built a fire to put a spit over and cooked three of the salmon he had caught gently over the fire till their skins were crispy and the flesh fell away from the bones.

The three of them sat huddled round the fire, watching the water gently lap at the banks late into the afternoon. Far across the lake, an osprey soared majestically, diving into the water and reappearing moments later with a brown trout clasped tightly in its talons, thrashing and fighting. It flew effortlessly overhead, ruling the skies, and settled in a nearby tree to eat its catch. It slammed the fish hard into the branch, killing it, and tore chunks of flesh off with its razor-sharp beak, tilting its head back with every mouthful. Warwick watched with avid interest, but with every tear the bird made, he cringed. It was truly a master of hunting, but its eating looked somewhat difficult.

The bird had momentarily distracted them, and the light would soon be gone. They had to leave. The days in the mountains were short especially at winter's fall. The mountains became a wall against the sun. So, the quickness of their departure was urgent.

Deal was used to wandering the wilds at night, but neither Helena nor Warwick had ever been allowed to. Should a wolf attack, they would have no chance.

They adopted a fast pace. Soon they would be able to see the edge of the trees and then the edge of the lake. Deal began to slow as they approached the edge of the trees, his ears pricked up like a cat. He had heard movement amongst the trees parallel to their own footsteps. His experience told him that it was most likely something hunting them. Luckily Deal never travelled without any protection. From his boot, he pulled out an iron dirk. But all sound of movement stopped. Deal prowled low through the trees and bushes till Warwick shouted. For a brief second, he had seen a person in black, hooded robes standing behind a tree, watching. But as Deal got closer, the figure bolted up the slopes and out of sight. Upon close examination of the tree the figure had hidden behind, they at first found nothing. But then Helena looked up. Whoever it had been had clearly been up the tree. Cut into the bark was a roughly carved eye. Could it possibly be …?

That night, Warwick pieced everything together, first the key, then the letter, and now this carving. They had to be related. The only question that wanted answering was, Who was it? They were scaring him and his family; he wanted them gone. He had been happy before the key came into his possession. For the first time, he felt sorry for Helena for having had it all that time without a single answer. She must have been driven mad to the point of breaking. Did this person wish them harm?

Warwick was so restless that he crept outside and went where he had desired to go for the past few weeks: the old watchtower on the hill at Melfort. Really, it was just a ruin that had been there for hundreds of years, but to Warwick, it was his chance for escape. Often, on clear days, the ruined tower in the distance would look like a tombstone.

He did not think of the trouble he would get into should Deal and Helena find out. He just desired to be away from home and alone to think in peace. As he walked, the wind blew his long hair across his face and numbed his body. He ran for a while to warm himself up. His pace slowed as his path began to climb, and soon he was walking slowly. When he finally made it, it was the middle of the night. For a few hours, he sat against a low part of the remaining outer wall of the ruined watchtower, looking out across the sheet of deep-indigo glass to a far horizon beyond sight. Just as he had began to vent his built-up emotions, he felt with a sudden dread the key beneath his collar begin to vibrate, gently at first but with steadily growing violence. He pulled the key out and saw that the key was glowing. It was becoming very hot to the touch. Suddenly, the faint glow exploded into a blinding white light erupting from the heart of the ruby. With a sudden shriek of pain and fright, he dropped the burning key and covered his eyes. Even with his hands drawn across his eyes, the light still reached them. Then, as quickly as it had happened, the light had completely gone, and the key lay on the cold earth smoking. Having noticed the instant darkness between his fingers, he lowered his hands and cautiously picked up the key, expecting it to be really hot. But he found it was quite cool to his touch. In that brief moment as he held it, a sudden worried feeling came over him. His instincts told him to get home quickly; he did not wait to think. He got to his feet, with the key safely round his neck again, and ran like he had never run before. Against the black of night, he could see smoke rising blacker than black, higher than the clouds, and on the horizon, a fiery orange glow was lighting the sky like a beacon.

Over hill and peat bog he ran, covered from head to toe in thick mud. Now he could smell the smell of burning wood and soot. On the last ridge before his house, he froze in complete horror. Flames adorned his home, rising like twisting serpents high into the air. He could see no signs of movement. He started to run again. Without one thought of being burnt, he ran straight through the flames into what remained of the house. The heat of the flames licked at his body, asphyxiating every breath he wheezed. He was brought to his knees, drenched head to toe in sweat. The air was slightly more breathable below the thick cloud of smoke. But even crawling became an exhausted drag within seconds. The fire formed a cage round him. He was blinded by the smoke and felt his way with his hands, clenching his teeth and closing his stinging eyes with the agony of crawling over red hot timbers and stone. It felt as if he had been in the flames for hours, and he didn't even know if anyone was amongst them. There were no shouts or screams. Right at the back of the rubble, his hands fell upon a body. The burns on his body were fairly extensive now, so it was very hard for him to open his eyes. When he finally managed to do so, his sight was unfocused, but he could make out the hazy outline of his mother. Her burned, blackened body was almost unrecognisable. Tears streaked his cheeks, and pain burned deep inside so strong that he could not feel the burning heat round him. He leant over her and kissed her cheek, and as he did, a hand grabbed him. She wasn't dead! Was it only her love for her son that kept her alive? With all his remaining strength, he dragged her from the rubble, and on the grass, away from the flames, he laid her down. He had lost his voice. She grabbed his arm again and pulled Warwick towards her. Her voice was barely audible. Amongst the coughing and wheezing, Warwick heard "P-please ... g-go! There's n-nothing you can do!" Hastily he wiped his tears away, trying to look strong. His guilt was eating away at him for going up to the watchtower, so he wasn't about to disobey his mother. He leant over his mother again and kissed her on the lips. At this, she closed her eyes and muttered with her remaining strength, "I love you." Her arm fell limp, and her last breath faded away.

Warwick's grief choked him as he hugged his mother. With difficulty, he pulled himself to his feet and turned his back on his mother's body. He walked as fast as he could, scared to look back. If he had looked back, he would have fallen there and then. As he skirted the flames, he fell upon what he knew was the burnt corpse of his father, though the body was completely unrecognisable. Warwick was too close to the flames to say goodbye properly. All he managed amongst the choking tears was to lower his head. He could not speak. His respect for his mother was the only thing that kept him alive. But how could he go on when his family had been stolen from him?

He'd not even had a chance to say goodbye. He could not bear to look at his father's body and staggered off towards Loch Domhain. He had heard of the town of Loch Domhain. Maybe there he could find shelter. His pace was nothing but a stagger. At the bottom of the valley, he collapsed, overcome with grief.

CHAPTER 4

ALONE IN THE WILD?

A day? A month? A year? how long he had lain there seemed of no significance. His legs seemed barely strong enough to support him, and in truth, he didn't want to move. As he looked back to where thick black smoke still rose, he wished he could go back, that this had all been a horrid dream. The dawn of realisation was seeping into him as his injuries throbbed. As much as he wanted to go back, he knew deep down there was nothing there for him. Anyway, he could not go back if he was to honour his mother's last wish. Warwick stumbled when he stood up as his legs tried to give way. His mind was set on survival, and the longer he stayed, the harder it would become to leave. Whether he would ever return had not crossed his mind.

At the shores of Loch Domhain, he collapsed, exhausted from the effort it took to keep going. His legs had pretty much dragged all the way, making a short journey seem extensively long. The burns on his body had blistered and were throbbing worse than ever. They were also smelling rather foul. At once he began to bathe his wounds in the ice-cold water. The moment the water touched his burns and wounds, he shut his eyes tight, crying out in sheer pain. By the time he had finished, pools of deep-red water had dispersed far from the shoreline.

He sat back, stinging all over, reflecting upon the silence that was seeping into his heart at the sound of the gentle lap of the water. A hard lump was rising from deep down and was burning in his throat. Tears burst from his eyes, bringing him to his hands and knees, his sorrow washing away in the gentle current. His hands clasped the mud banks and dug deep grooves as he dragged his fingers. Looking down at the grooves, an impulse of anger burnt hot deep down inside. It began to eat at him. Vengeance! Who could he blame? It had to be someone's fault. Had to be. Where were they? In his anger, he screamed out across the water and threw a large rock at the same time. It flew far and disappeared deep below the surface of the water with a mighty *splosh!* The ripples rushed back to the bank, breaking on his outstretched hands. He soon turned his anger on his parents. Why did they have to leave him like this with nothing but a useless key? He was not even of age yet! They could have waited until then! His breath fell heavy, and with every bad thought, he chucked a stone in anger. As the remaining anger burst from within, the fear it masked rose from a deep cell of his heart. For the first time in his life, he was completely alone, with the daunting prospect of the unknown stretching out before him like a vast maze with walls a hundred feet high. The wet mud dripped sluggishly from his hands as he sat back, looking towards the water's end and the mountain ridges.

The dawning fear brought about an eagerness to move on. Except when Warwick managed to stand up, he raised a hand to his forehead, feeling dizzy, and wobbled precariously on his feet. He hadn't drunk or eaten since before the fire. The only thing for it was to drink from the lake's calm waters, but every instinct he had warned against this action. His thirst was so bad, though, that he ignored this and plunged his head into the deep water, drinking deeply. A taste of dirt and grit filled his mouth, and he had to shut his eyes in full concentration to swallow it. Staggering to his feet with great effort, he began to slowly move. Every muscle screamed and burnt as he dragged himself along.

The place where he had sat not twenty-four hours ago with his parents, enjoying a meal, loomed close. Seeing it brought back the memories of the last happy time, and his eyes burned with searing-hot tears. He refused to stop, even with all this pain and exhaustion. Stopping now would be the end. Slowly, one foot at a time, he dragged on into unknown grounds, stopping for a breather every twenty minutes. He did not dare stray from the water's edge and followed it to the end.

He was not alone at the far end of the lake. Cloaked and stooped was a tall figure dressed in black, every feature of its skin covered. Not even the light of its eyes shone out from under the darkness of the hood. It would have seemed almost lifeless as a statue if it were not for the wind whipping at the cloak. Warwick suddenly realised he had seen this person before. Only the other day, when he was with his parents just west of here, this person had fled away from them. Anger at whoever this was burned hard inside Warwick, and the sight of the figure brought the key back to his mind. Warwick expected the figure to run again, but instead it walked towards him, stopping at his feet. Slowly the hood slid back, and at first, Warwick could only see a matted mass of black hair tinged with grey. A couple of long bony-fingered hands drew back the hair, and Warwick saw a man's heavily worn, sorrowful face lined deeply with weariness. Despite this weariness, a corner of the man's mouth was twitching higher in what could only be considered an attempt at smiling, though his deep-set grey eyes were shining with tears. Warwick's guard was raised; this man's tearful deep grey eyes pierced into him with a knowing look. At the sight of the tears, a burning desire came over Warwick to hurt the man. *Why should he show emotion?* Warwick thought to himself. His insides were clenched in a knot of anger. The sight of the man made him seethe. The words he had been holding back burst from him. "Why are you so tearful? It was *you* who sent that letter, *you* who have been following my family!" Warwick yelled. "You're the reason my family is dead ... murderer!" The words did not properly sink in till a minute later. He was standing there, his parent's killer, right before him, ready to kill him. Fear erupted to the surface with the power of a volcano. Warwick attempted to run, to get as far away from this man, but his burns and injuries prevented any quick movement. The man simply reached out and clasped a tight hand round Warwick's wrist. Warwick's heart beat at twice its normal rate, and his brow was bathed in a cold sweat. However, he tried to remain strong and fight his opponent.

"Let go of me!" He had intended to sound angry, but his voice lost its aggressive tone as it trembled.

"No! Not until I have had my say. If you still want to run once I have spoken, then I won't stop you." The man's voice was deep and hoarse and strangely commanding.

"I don't care about anything you have got to say. Now let go of me!" Warwick's voice shook less this time, but his heart rate if anything had intensified to the point that he felt he would be sick. He jerked his hand, trying to free himself, but the man wrenched him back towards him, holding even tighter.

"Not until I have spoken." The man attempted to keep his voice calm.

"I will kill you if I have to! Let go!"

"No!"

Bang! Warwick had brought his free hand back and with all his strength aimed a hard punch at the man's stomach. With a sickening groan, the man relinquished his grip and fell to the floor on hands and knees, clenching his stomach. Warwick did not hesitate. Moving as fast as he could, he staggered swiftly into the tall pine forest lining the far end of Loch Domhain and to the feet of the mountains. Desperately he fought branches and brambles threatening to hinder his process; the deeper he went, the thicker the forest canopy became, almost blocking out all the light. The ground was rapidly ascending through a course of rugged rocks and loose stones, which slipped beneath his feet. Only fear kept him going as the slope increased. His clothes were torn, and blood oozed thickly from deep gouges in his hands and legs from where he had fallen several times. He reached a point where he could climb no farther and collapsed on the steep slope. He was level with the top of the canopy of the forest, but the trees were too thick for him to see movement below them.

Whilst Warwick searched for a hiding place, the man darted amongst the trees, snagging his cloak on bramble thickets and low branches. In his search, he lost Warwick's footprints amongst thick undergrowth. He couldn't even trace a trail of broken branches and crushed foliage; the ground was too thick with growth. This way and that way he searched hopelessly. Meanwhile, Warwick lay as still and quiet as a still breeze. Unfortunately for Warwick, the dense canopy absorbed the sound of the man's movement.

Warwick searched for a cave or a deep dark hollow, but every hollow he found was too shallow or too exposed, and caves were few, if there were any at all in the hard rock. Every spring was nothing more than a gentle bubbling, splashing over the rock through a small crack. For Warwick, the search was disastrous. Whilst he had been moving on the steep slope, rocks had slipped, creating large, suspended dust clouds that did not disperse for a long time. The man reached the base of the slope, and although he could not see Warwick, the dust clouds provided a map to his location.

Warwick threw himself into one of the hollows he had previously seen, gritting his teeth as he crashed down upon the hard stone. The hollow was lined with a couple of boulders, hiding it from immediate view. Warwick pushed himself hard up against one of these boulders, ignoring his pounding heart and his throbbing pains. His ears were pricked for the slightest sound of movement. He thought he could hear the distant movement of stones. This was it. No escape!

The man scrambled over the ridge of the hollow right to Warwick's side, where he crouched down. Fear pounded like drums in Warwick, making his eyes bulge. He closed his eyes and clasped his arms tightly round his knees. The touch upon his shoulder was surprising. Its softness spread unexpected warmth through him. Something then happened that Warwick could not explain. His body relaxed, and his eyes slowly opened. He saw an aged man smiling at him with tears in his eyes. No restraint was forced upon Warwick neither did he show any sign of anger. It was unnatural. "Please listen. My name is Rowan. I am sorry that I frightened you, but you need not be scared of me. As you rightly said, I am the one who has been watching you and your family, the one who sent the letter."

Warwick, finding his voice, cut Rowan off. "Why then have you waited till now to reveal yourself? Why did you run when I saw you before?"

"Please, just let me finish. Then you may ask any question you like, and I shall not hesitate to answer." His tone was warm, and as he stood there, he seemed to relax, knowing that the heavy burden could finally be revealed to Warwick.

Warwick now listened intently, torn between worry and shock, his mouth gaping slightly.

"This is hard for me to say, but I shall tell you, as it is crucial you know. A destiny ... an ancient and lost prophecy ..." He sighed and closed his eyes briefly "OK ... ever since you were born, your life has been written for you. A long, long time ago, well before our time, a prophecy was made; it was so long ago, in fact, that it has almost been completely forgotten from history. Only those of us gifted have knowledge of it, and even that is very basic. All we know is that the prophecy was made about you and had something to do with the key you carry, so when the time was right, I passed it on to your mother and gave her instructions to give it to you when I thought the time would be right. I took it upon myself to watch over you and your family until you were ready, though as you might have guessed by now, not everything has gone as intended. My downfall was that I knew very little of the key and so could not understand truly what hold it had on you. The letter I sent was meant to discourage you, but now I realise I only made things worse. I followed you to Loch Domhain and watched you and your family from a distance to let you see me but not talk to me. I am certain that if your father had caught me, it would have made keeping a watch much harder. If I had only known what was going to happen later that night. ... I am so sorry, Warwick." Tears rolled down Rowan's cheeks.

Warwick's mouth gaped even wider, and his eyes were shining with tears. *Was this a confession, the truth at last? This man, Rowan, if that was his name, was responsible for his parents' death? All this suffering was because of him? And how did he know all this? Who was he?* The thoughts raced through his mind quicker than his heart was beating. All of a sudden, he felt his fists clenching once again whilst he fought back the lump rising swiftly in his throat.

No sooner had Warwick thought all this than Rowan replied,

"Warwick, I am a seer. This is how I know about your destiny. You should not blame me for what happened. I don't know what or who is responsible, but it was not me." Rowan's voice had become that of an old man, and his stoop had become more pronounced as all the colour washed out of his waxy skin.

Warwick, finding his voice now, spoke his thoughts. "But if you are a seer, how did you not see what was coming? How come you don't know this full prophecy?"

"I did not expect you to understand the true meaning of being a seer, Warwick. To be a seer is to be blessed and cursed. We can see the past, present, and future, yes, as you have thought, however, we cannot choose what we see. That is why it is a curse."

Warwick thought for a moment, taking in what this man had just said. "Well, why weren't you watching them? From what you say, you have barely stopped following my family, but when they were in danger, you were nowhere. Why didn't you help?" The last words were very difficult to say as the lump grew bigger in his throat.

Rowan ran a hand round the neck of his robes and hesitated at the clasp in thought. "When I risked myself to be seen, the cost of such a move was that I had to lay low for a while, as I knew your father's guard would be up. That would have made it hard to move unseen. I had planned to wait till early morning, when I could catch you alone on your walk into the hills." At the look on Warwick's face, Rowan lowered his head and let a tear fall. "Please ..." He begged now, almost completely defeated. "Trust me ... I am not your enemy. I know I have made some mistakes, but I have only ever tried to protect you. If you cannot overcome your anger and believe my words, then perhaps this will help you understand who I am." His reasoning for fumbling with the clasp at his neck suddenly became clear. He pulled open the front of his robes, revealing the body of an old, starved man. But it was not this that shocked Warwick; it was the tattoos. The centre of his chest was filled with a huge, black, triangular eye from which veins snaked like branches. Around these branches, many stars of all sizes stretched across his whole chest.

When Warwick had looked at it for a while and looked past the stars and veins, he realised the eye was the same eye he had seen in the letter. "This, Warwick, is the mark of the seer. When we are young, we are marked individually with different marks that tell us who we are. No two seers will have the same marks. This eye is known as the 'Eye of Foresight' or the 'Mind's Eye', from which we see. The branches resemble the 'Tree of the World', which is the foundation of this earth, the roots of stone. The stars round it are my family members, who are also seers. All the seers who have ever lived are related. When a seer dies, another star is added. Where you can see empty spaces, which are sadly very few, that is for those of us who have not yet passed on. It is another reminder of our curse. To be a seer is to be often alone, so we are marked as such to draw the spirits of our family to keep us company. Now do you see why I must stay secret? Why I pass as mere shadow amongst the darkest of forests? Why I veil myself from the world? Why I could only watch and deliver secret messages?"

Warwick was silent, drowned by the heavy weight that had been thrown upon him. Memory and thoughts coursed through his mind so fast that he could not form one sentence. In truth, he was confused, unable to make sense of the words.

Rowan watched patiently but could quite clearly see the look of puzzlement upon Warwick's face. "I see my words have not helped. Let me tell you this, then." He thought how to phrase it for a second. "Once there were five of us living in a small wooden hut far to the north. Soon people began to learn of our powers and feared them to be witchcraft, so they massed and burnt our hut to the ground. Two of us died that day, and not a day goes by where I don't think about it. It's just me, Seth, and Robin that are left. We travelled for decades after that day till we found one place we could safely return to. I have told you this against my own will, for it pains me greatly. Please don't make me have to say more."

Finally, Warwick understood as Rowan hung limp and exhausted with grief. It was uncomfortable for Warwick to say what he must, but slowly and quietly he spoke. "You stayed away because you still fear people finding out who you are. So you showed yourself that time to let me know you were always watching, but I guess you had hoped you might slip my father's gaze?"

Rowan raised his head and looked at Warwick with a smile. Warwick had been exactly right. For the first time, they finally understood one another. This was the happiest Warwick had seen Rowan, and suddenly, somehow, he looked a young man again. Although Rowan seemed to be happier, Warwick swiftly became very depressed. His heart was heavy, and his body heaved with deep, sickening sighs. Rowan was innocent and completely alone, yet he, Warwick, had just punched this man and accused him of murder. Without question, Rowan had shown forgiveness, but Warwick felt he did not deserve it. The pain was fierce, searing like hot lava in the pit of his stomach.

"Don't do this to yourself. There is no reason to feel guilt. I hold no grudge against you for the way you acted. You acted the way anyone would have in a situation like that. I am pleased just as much as I am relieved that I finally got to talk to you. Come on." Rowan extended an arm to Warwick and pulled him to his feet.

For a moment they looked just at the sheer state of each other. Their clothes were torn, muddy, and Warwick was covered in burns. Warwick began to climb out of the hollow, but Rowan stopped him. "Just wait a minute. You should know"—Rowan shifted slightly nervously, and Warwick looked worried—"I did try to help. When I saw your house ablaze, I ran to find you and your family. When I saw your mother and father, I feared you had joined them. I laid them to rest, buried under a stone cairn, and then came to find you."

Warwick closed his eyes, and a tear splashed his cheek. He did not need to say thank you, as Rowan could feel his gratitude.

"I hoped in my heart that you were alive, that you would have the sense to head for the nearest civilisation, the town of Loch Domhain. For now, I will guide you there. It's just north of here in the next valley."

Their perilously narrow path took them high up into the

mountains, climbing ever higher, ever steeper, through streaming gullies and over shifting stone. It was strewn with slippery, wet grass tussocks as high as straw. The burden of the key felt considerably lighter to Warwick compared to his pained, exhausted body. It was swiftly becoming evident that he could do very little more. He leant heavily on a crooked branch, moving slowly upwards, using any remaining energy to keep his balance. Unfortunately, Rowan could do no more than walk behind him on such a narrow, eroded path.

"If I had a choice, Warwick, I would not take you on such perilous paths through the mountains."

"Is there no other way?" Warwick hung, almost bent double in renewed pain, gritting his teeth.

"Yes, Warwick, there are other paths, though none short enough to bear in your condition."

Warwick looked up from the ground, staring hopelessly up into the mountains for the path's hidden end. "How long are they?"

Rowan spoke with an air of foreboding. "Miles and miles to the valley mouth. You have done well to make it this far, but I fear those roads would finish you."

On they climbed now, past grass tussocks and streaming gullies, till nothing but the naked earth lay in their wake. Every step, every drag seemed endless as the rugged path snaked ever upwards. Warwick rested his full weight on the staff, the rough wood like sandpaper against the palm of his hands. In half a day, they had moved less than five miles. Behind them, still, a sliver of Loch Domhain could be seen between mountain peaks.

Several gruelling hours later, they stood upon the summit of the pass. Warwick had collapsed twice on the assent, and just before the summit, his staff had snapped. The energy was bled from him, and he lay crumpled and pale, with his head against a large, flat rock, his chest rising and falling rapidly. The small supply of water and berries Rowan had gathered were gone. However, hope had not failed them yet; just poking out between crests was the most rewarding sight Warwick had seen in all his life: civilisation. Rowan hoisted Warwick to his feet, spurred on by the sight of the town of Loch Domhain. Warwick's legs shook, and if it weren't for the support of Rowan, he would have collapsed. With great unease, they began to make their descent into the valley, snaking back and forth.

By late evening, they walked amongst the foothills, feeling exhausted but elated to see their destination less than a mile away. They followed the path of a river to the edge of the town, where a small bridge of bound logs stretched across the water.

Warped and twisted rickety timber buildings lined either side of the narrow street like sentinels. At their feet, shoehorned in, were market stalls and wagons selling bits of cloth, fish, and swords and knives for the wealthy, though none were well stocked. This way and that Warwick looked as they wove up the narrow path, squeezing round oxen carts carrying manure and avoiding fresh dung on the path. By the looks of things, it had been a long time since the market had seen any great trade. The garments the few farmers, fishermen, and other traders wore were in tatters. Off the main road that ran through town was a small inn, to which Rowan led Warwick. Once inside, they were greeted by the sight of a blazing fire dancing merrily in a pit in the centre of a long, timber-framed hall. When they stepped into the light of the fire, an air of discomfort fell over them like a veil. At the far end of the hall, a barman frozen in cleaning a tankard stared right at them with a slightly furrowed brow.

"Outsiders!" boomed the barman's deep, gravelly voice. "You look like you have come far to be here. And by the looks of you, I would say your journey was not without unwanted trouble."

Rowan cut across him before he could say anything else, stepping in front of Warwick as he did so. "We seek a bed for the night. Do you have any?"

"That depends on whether the trouble you faced has followed you here. I would like to know a few things before I consider letting you sleep here. What reason do you have to come to such a small place of little importance? Or are you just here to rest before going farther? Strange folk do not often wander in our mist, and when they do, I want to know I can trust them."

Rowan took a step backwards, allowing the barman to see Warwick. "Please, we do not bring any trouble. Our journey is of little concern. We travel far to the east and north to join our family on the trading caravans, but we cannot go farther without rest, which is why we have graced your doorstep." Rowan spoke with a tone that he hoped would be convincing.

"Well, if that is the case, then you are welcome to shelter under my roof. However, be warned: people will be curious about your presence here, so it would probably be best to either remain hidden or leave just before first light."

Rowan and Warwick's silence was a prompt to the barman to show them their rooms. At the door to the room, Rowan paid the barman all the money he had, which was just enough for a couple of nights. He did not admit this to Warwick, though. All that mattered was that Warwick rested and ate well. Rowan waited till the barman had disappeared. He closed the door softly before turning to Warwick. "I am so relieved that the lie worked. I take it I don't need to tell you why I lied? The key, your journey, is too dangerous, and as long as it can stay quiet, it should."

"I hate this blasted key. You're sure it has to be me? I know nothing of the wilds. How am I even going to find evidence of something that has nearly been entirely forgotten?" With all the troubles of meeting Rowan and the journey so far, he hadn't thought about the key in a while, but now it swam in the pool of his thoughts. So intense was his anger, but also curiosity, that he found himself twiddling the key between his fingers.

Rowan's face sank into the expression that Warwick knew to mean grief. He need not have spoken to give him his answer.

Soon the food arrived, which briefly distracted them from the situation they faced. Rowan ate quickly, eager to carry on with the conversation. "Something deeply worries me, Warwick. We would do best not to linger here, I feel. As soon as you're rested, it would be wise to move on."

"What is it that troubles you?"

"It is just a feeling I have?"

"But where will we go from here? I've never gone farther than this."

"I have been thinking, even though it has been very long since I have seen my family, as I call them, I think it could be wise to seek them out. They are very wise in the gift of foresight. It is about the only thing I can think to do for now. Sorry, Warwick."

"Where do the others live?"

"Good question. When we were being hunted, we moved a lot. We did settle deep underground for a while in some very ancient caves on Sgitheanach, far, far to the north and west of here. I have not been to the caves in a very long time, so I don't know if we will find anything at all. But right now, I think it is our best chance of finding answers. It will be a very long journey, so we will need plenty of supplies. I will take you past An Gearasdan. Hopefully, we can get some supplies and treatment for your wounds there."

"How far is An Gearasdan?"

Rowan sighed. "At best three days, but with your injuries, it could take us six days by my reckoning."

"Six days!" Warwick exclaimed. He sighed and slumped down in his seat, feeling guilty.

"If there were any other option, any easier way, I would not hesitate to take it, if only to prevent you from further pain. But you must continue on your journey, if only to seek serenity in the truth of your parents' death."

"I cannot understand any of it. How do you know I am the one if this prophecy has been lost for hundreds of years? Why do I have to undertake this journey?"

"Nothing is ever totally lost, Warwick. There are always traces. I have no doubt now that my foresight was correct. You must have noticed how strongly the key responds round you! As for this journey, you don't have to go. The choice is yours whether you follow it or not, but you must follow your heart."

Warwick sat hunched in silence, thinking through everything that had happened and been said, imagining what could be yet to come. In reality, though, it did not matter how hard he imagined. How could he imagine something like this? Not even Rowan could see the road ahead. Once more, and certainly not for the last time, he wanted to throw the key, but as he tried to, he found his hand clenching tight round it. Maybe it was his heart's deep desire to find recompense in the truth of what happened that stopped him. All he knew was that he could not let go of the key. It was like it had become the missing part of his heart, like it was the key to the door at the end of an ever-darkening tunnel. His grief choked his voice, and without further ado, he lay upon his bed and turned his back upon Rowan. Rowan knew he was not asleep and for a while sat quietly watching, though he never spoke or disturbed him out of respect.

When morning came after what had seemed an endless night, Rowan was nowhere to be seen, and his bed didn't look like it had been slept in at all. Warwick sat bolt upright with sudden fear, hastening to get up as fast as he was able to look for Rowan. Upon searching the building, he found that Rowan was not there. He did not dare to search the streets with the words of the barman ringing in his ears. Rapidly, he returned to the bedroom to think. As time went past, his fear only grew stronger, and he began to pace up and down the small room.

It was a couple of hours before Rowan finally made an appearance in the room. Hanging loosely from his hands were two enormous salmon. However angry Warwick had been with him, it could not displace the feeling of relief he felt at the sight of Rowan, dishevelled and cold. Warwick could not help but notice, though, that despite catching the salmon, Rowan did not seem very happy.

"What is it?" Warwick asked, unable to take the suspense. A sense of due dread filled every inch of his body.

"Something deeply worries me, Warwick, I have felt it in the air. I know that you are far from ready to travel, but we would do best not to linger here, I feel."

"Wait … what? What has happened?"

"Not here. We cannot delay any longer." Rowan gathered all his things hastily from round the room, trying to avoid eye contact with Warwick.

Within the hour, they left, having scavenged as many provisions as they could, and set off up the valley to the north, turning east at its far end. Warwick followed Rowan, completely lost in thought about the abruptness of the change of plan. He was like a lamb that follows its mother with no knowledge of the destination. For miles, he shadowed Rowan, his annoyance building all the time. Never did Rowan speak or look back. He moved at a speed that was painful and impossible for Warwick. It wasn't until darkness fell that they finally stopped, their feet raw and bloody. Warwick collapsed upon the ground, his legs unable to take anymore.

They had been forced far north from their path by the twisting valleys towards the vast water's edge. The delay this caused, along with Warwick's wounds, would add at least a day to their journey. For this reason, Rowan was quick to be off again whilst Warwick struggled to comprehend how he ever stood up. His legs wobbled, and he worked desperately to keep them from buckling. Till he could get proper rest, he could not hope for any more than a drag.

After a short way, having realised the state of Warwick, Rowan finally came to a stop and turned to look upon the boy. Rowan did not see a young man anymore but an old man barely able to stand, his body weak and broken with grief and physical pains. Swiftly, with the agility of a young child, Rowan moved to catch Warwick as his legs finally gave way. He set Warwick down on the soft, heather-strewn grassland. He was certain that the guilt he felt on the inside was just as visible upon the outside of his flesh as he sat down next to Warwick. "My dear Warwick, you must forgive an old man's blindness. Like you with your key, I have let my worries take control. I would be telling a lie if I said that the journey hasn't got me worried, and I know that you have noticed my odd behaviour." For a moment he closed his eyes and sighed, and from under his closed eyes, a tear fell, to the surprise of Warwick. "I have been cruel to you, Warwick, crueller than you know. I hope that in time you will realise why I did what I did and forgive me. Out of my will to save you from more pain, I have withheld information from you that should never have been kept secret." Warwick sat up much straighter, and his eyes widened as he stared at Rowan, confused. "What I said before about not knowing how your parents died wasn't true. I didn't tell you this to spare you pain, but I can't see any way round telling you now. The night your parents died, I was close by watching, having seen you leaving the house. Had I only sensed or seen with my mind's eye what was to come moments later, I swear I would have done everything to get your parents to safety. What I saw has been haunting my mind and stopping me from sleeping. From high up in the dark sky, I saw a gigantic shadow, blacker than night, diving towards the ground at a speed I didn't know was possible. The wind it created roared and blew me over. Then I saw it, and I couldn't believe what I saw. Your parents' death came at the hands of a dragon. There is no other explanation for what I saw. Flames shot from its mouth and lit the whole of its giant body clear as day. I have been pondering where it came from ever since, and I am scared. No one has seen a dragon in hundreds of years. This is why I barely stop, why I walk with such vigour, why I often look to the sky night and day. I am so sorry." Rowan looked away too ashamed to face Warwick.

The shock stayed Warwick's tongue. He just stared blankly at Rowan as if he had misheard, or as if it were a dream that he would shortly wake up from and find himself still at the town of Loch Domhain. Eventually, though, it dawned upon him what Rowan had just said. Immediately, whilst his grief spilled from his eyes, he felt inclined to hit Rowan till his body was broken or to bellow till his voice could no longer be heard. When he tried to shout, his voice broke in great wails of sorrow.

Rowan, to his great distress, realised the pain he had caused by prolonging Warwick's ignorance; so much did he understand that he could feel Warwick's pain inside himself, dragging him down. It was with this that he left Warwick's side for a while.

Warwick did not care that Rowan had left. Right now he didn't even care if he ever saw him again. With Rowan gone, the full extent of the pain he felt overcame him. There he lay for the whole night, too weak to move. He grasped the key at his neck for comfort, drifting in and out of restless sleep. The key, in some respect, had now become something new: a way to remember the past with his parents.

Before first light broke, Warwick came to, his eyes puffy and red and his clothes and flesh dirty with wet mud. To his surprise, a fire gently crackled and popped close by, but there was no one else to be seen close to it. The warmth brought some strength to his body, taking away some of his external pain. He suspected Rowan was behind the fire, trying to make amends. In some respects, it had. Warwick began to wonder where he was and was soon upon his feet, looking for Rowan.

Sheltered behind some rocks just a short way ahead, Rowan was slumped uncomfortably with his head resting in his lap. He too had drifted in and out of restless sleep, but at least had made a fire for himself as well. The sound of movement disturbed Rowan, causing him to sit up straight. He was not sure what to expect, but from underneath the tatty garment, he drew an iron short-sword from a tatty leather scabbard. When Warwick appeared, a little hesitantly, the glint of the blade caught his eye, and he stopped in his tracks. Not once since meeting Rowan had he seen a sword or heard it clanking at his side. *Does he point it at me?* Warwick thought to himself. Warwick's question was answered swiftly, as Rowan sheathed the sword. Warwick breathed out a heavy sigh as the sword withdrew. "Sorry, Warwick, I wasn't sure what to expect when I heard movement. Will you sit down please?" Rowan asked pleadingly. Warwick sat down, wincing at first for the pain in his legs. "I am pleased beyond hope that you have appeared, Warwick. I have desperately wanted to speak with you."

Warwick was unsure that he would be able to speak, that he could say the words he wanted to say. Not only this, but he was feeling very two-faced towards Rowan. To control it was going to take a great deal of effort. He wanted to forgive Rowan, at least for the sake of the journey ahead. He had decided he was going to seek to find this prophecy, if only to find all the answers his wounded heart desired and to avenge his parents' untimely end.

"What I did to you, Warwick, is unforgivable, I know. When I look back at what I did, I realise I made the greatest mistake of my life. You had the right to know. It should have been the first thing I told you once I had gained your trust. I weep for your sorrow. If I can, I want to help your pain and help you upon your journey more than I have. I don't wish this to be the end of our friendship." Rowan had never looked as old as he did then. His skin was pale, creased, and sagging, and his body was hunched over.

Warwick could not help but feel pity for Rowan. It wasn't as if he hadn't understood why Rowan did it in the first place. As he sat there reflecting upon what had happened, he saw himself doing the exact same thing in Rowan's shoes, because in truth he knew he would never have had the heart to tell Rowan. "I am sorry." Warwick extended his arms and hugged him.

Rowan was flustered by Warwick's willing forgiveness. He could not have dreamt of more, and the tears welled in great pools beneath his heavy eyelids. With peace having been made, he left Warwick there briefly to search for food.

Warwick waited round the fire, nursing his stiff, smarting body in an attempt to prepare for a long trek. A dark, solid wall extending across the land was just visible as he looked ahead to the far horizon. He guessed they were headed for it, since they had been travelling this way for miles and miles.

Rowan finally returned about an hour later, having given up on trying to catch anything; all he had for his reward was some berries and mushrooms. So, after a small breakfast, and not a nice one by any means, Rowan helped Warwick to his feet. They trod over moors and wide glades of heather, often climbing along ridges to avoid the sodden marches at the valley's floor, and forded the fast-flowing mountain streams. Every mile, every step, was just as painful as the last. It was becoming clear to Warwick that his wounds would not heal without proper help. Out here, though, where would they find medical help close at hand? Only the great cities would have trained physicians, and the cities were few and far off. The thought that An Gearasdan lay on their path was of little comfort, because he had to get there first, a task which was nearly impossible.

A haze of light smeared the sky as they descended the final slopes towards the dark forest canopy. What had looked like a giant wall from a long way off was a magnificent, ancient forest. In the gloom, he could see the trees at its borders stretching ever upwards like great pillars into the sky.

Under the dense canopy, mighty Scots pines grew close in a terrible battle for space and those few precious shafts of light. The smell of earth and pine oil grew heavy as they walked farther into the damp, mossy forest. Their path was riddled with slippery roots thick as trunks, which constantly threatened to injure one of them further. Not until they had penetrated deep within the forest did Rowan risk stopping, but only under the condition that they light no fire. He chose to rest in a small parting of the trees just large enough for them to sit with backs pressed against tree trunks. He dared not go to see whether there were better places they could have stopped. His orientation under the canopy was being tested, so he refused to leave the straight path on which they travelled.

They ate the rest of the berries and mushrooms Rowan had found earlier. Warwick found it hard to eat, so he imagined it was a nice cut of venison. It did nothing to suppress his hunger. In the end, thinking of days past was the only thing that would take the edge of his pained hunger for a while; memories played like a film reel. Amongst the visions he saw, the key was always the clearest. It was no new thought that the key was almost completely responsible for everything that had happened.

That night, whilst they attempted to sleep as much as they could, cramped up against rough trees, Rowan was awoken sharply by the sound of Warwick talking in his sleep. "Warwick … Warwick …wake up." Rowan shook him firmly. Eventually, Warwick stirred, bleary-eyed and confused.

"What's the matter?" Warwick sounded worried.

"You were talking in your sleep."

"What!"

"You kept mentioning the key very clearly."

A guilty look spread across Warwick as he hunched down. "It's just everything. It all seems like one big nightmare that I am going to wake up from any moment. Can you blame me for thinking of the key when out of the blue I was handed a key with unknown magic powers? When a dragon mysteriously appears after hundreds of years and kills my parents? Now I am in a position where I must seek a prophecy that is apparently tied to me with no clue where to start. It feels all this is happening because of the key."

Rowan rested a hand on Warwick's shoulder. "I know things are hard right now, and for that I am sorry. This pain will get better with time, and your mother and father will always remain inside you. Never forget that. Now you must forgive me, but I sense that something you haven't spoken about is bothering you?"

This question caused Warwick a lot of discomfort, but he knew it would prove useless attempting to hide it. "Wh-when I left ... left my house the night when ..." Warwick closed his eyes tight at the pain of reliving the memory. "Well, when I went up upon the ruins at Melfort ... all I did was sit thinking about everything that had happened regarding the key. It was then that I felt the key vibrating and growing in heat beneath my clothing, so I took it out to look at it. A blinding light exploded from it like nothing I had ever seen before, and I had to let it go, for it was burning hot. But no sooner had it happened than the light was gone, and the key lay smoking upon the ground. As I picked it up, though, it was cold. That's when I felt something sickening inside me, telling me to hurry home immediately. Since I learnt the truth of what happened, I haven't been able to stop thinking about it. What if it was the key that caused the dragon to come and to attack?"

"Well, I can understand why you would be worried. I myself have been giving that dragon a lot of thought. I just can't understand how it could be, where it came from. They have been dead for so long that I can't even see back far enough?" For a moment Rowan was silent, deep in thought. "What you said happened with the key does, however, shed some light on some of my thoughts. I believe that it could be that the key and the possible return of the dragons are related. When I warned you not to use the key, I was only going on what I sensed. There was no knowledge behind the it. Now I wonder if the prophecy itself has to do with the dragons; their appearance now is surely not a coincidence. Now I must answer your question. This is going to be hard. I think that it both causes and warns, this key. What I think you saw was a warning of what was about to happen, but I also think that it was the key's power that drew the dragon to come. I do not, however, feel that you are responsible, so don't blame yourself. I think the key reacts when extreme danger is near, whether you're thinking about it or not. Don't blame yourself. The guilt would devour you. I am sorry."

The pain of watching Warwick crumple under the weight of the possible truth broke Rowan's heart. Warwick did not want to acknowledge it and rolled over so he did not have to see Rowan. They both slept once more. It was another restless night, whether because of all the horrific thoughts or because they heard the sound of movement all round them in the bushes and trees.

They both woke in the early hours of the morning to the sound of rain and the dawn chorus high in the canopy and the occasional drip on their foreheads. Their clothing hung heavy and soaked, doing nothing to keep them warm. They were not aware how long it had been raining. Warwick seemed in better spirits, now that his pain was out in the open, however that did not last long, as Rowan informed him of the long journey they must make that day without any food, unless they managed to find anything during the day's trek.

Just as much of the forest lay behind as lay ahead of them. Because they were later in getting started, Rowan forged through the trees as the crow flies with great speed. You would not have thought he had been travelling for days with much pain burdening him if you had seen him. Of course, this did not please Warwick.

Just trying to keep up caused him to trip and stumble over the tussle of the forest floor. Every so often, Rowan halted, grasping the hilt of his sword at the sound of movement in the undergrowth, but it always came to no nothing. After a while, their path began to descend into a steep hollow where no trees grew. At the very bottom loomed a deep bog. Rowan had some experience with bogs, but to his eye, there was no obvious route across its glutinous, muddy surface. Only when they had tried and found no way across would Rowan turn back and risk getting lost trying to find another path.

They tried the ground in many places but could not find a spot of ground firm enough to walk upon. The only other option they could think of was the tree's long branches, which reached far out. Warwick made his way over to the nearest tree with the longest branch, but Rowan pulled him back and went himself. In truth, Warwick knew as he watched that he never would have made it up that tree in his state. Rowan shimmied along a long branch right out over the bog till the branch began to bend, creak, and splinter. Eventually, after he pushed down upon it hard and nearly fell from the tree, it finally broke free, falling with a heavy thud and splattering mud. Warwick grabbed the end of the branch and rotated it round to span the bog. At first the branch sank slightly as it settled on the bog. Rowan scrambled down the tree and began to observe with Warwick the strength of the bridge. "I don't think I have ever seen a bog quite this glutinous in all my years, Warwick. I should think it will only take one at a time." The unmistaken note of worry in Rowan's voice was not helping Warwick to feel confident. "Well, it's now or never. I will go first. It is the least I can do after what I have put you through." Gingerly Rowan took the first step and felt the branch sink more under his weight. The branch was just holding. It had sunk to the point that about only half was left above the surface. With his arms wide, he edged slowly along the branch. Where the branch creaked, he took a long step, scared it might splinter and break. Eventually, with a sigh of relief, he stepped off the end of the branch, having only just kept his balance. The ground was firm, and it was just a short climb out of the hollow ahead. He held his breath when Warwick took his first steps, and he became tenser than when he had done it himself. Slowly Warwick made his way, his eyes focused on Rowan, teetering on the branch like a sword resting just beyond the point of balance on a finger. Unfortunately for Warwick, a lot of the branch had sunk to the point that only a narrow strip remained visible. If this weren't bad enough, it had also been greatly weakened by Rowan. Nearly every step rang across the forest as the branch cracked and creaked. It seemed a long time of very tense breathing before he made it across, wiping the cold sweat from his brow.

When they reached the top of the slope, their moods suddenly improved, for they now saw what had been hidden before by the dense trees. The edge of the forest was well within sight. The trees grew a greater distance from each other, and light seeped in through the canopy in great shafts. After a short, slow stagger, they stood upon the very edge, looking out upon vast plains of heather and hills growing ever taller as they approached the roots of snow-capped mountains. Heavy black clouds were rising out of the east, shadowing the land up to the feet of the trees. Without a doubt, it was going to be a difficult journey. Warwick took the first steps from under the edge of the trees, but Rowan pulled him back. "We stand upon the edge of a vast wilderness with nothing between here and An Gearasdan. Out here, I will only stop when it is not possible to go on without rest, and when we rest, we will rest hidden amongst rocks and trees without fire. So I must ask you to move as quickly as you can, Warwick. My lack of knowledge of dragons scares me just as much as I know it does you."

"I understand, but where do we go from here?"

"Well, I happen to know these lands a little better. Unfortunately, if we keep going as the crow flies, we will come to an unpassable river running to the southeast. However, this will provide an opportunity to find some shelter, as we will follow that river into the deep valley of Loch Eite, which is lined with mountains that should provide cover. From there, I plan to lead you past Gleann Comhann."

They headed towards the distant spine of ridges, which grew like some monstrous dinosaur towering ever higher in the sky. It was not long before they came upon the unpassable river. The banks dropped away steeply, disappearing beneath dark, foaming water. The blackness and width of the river was a sure indicator of it being too deep to ford. Here they turned south and hung to the water's edge.

Warwick found the going much easier after the forest. In truth, the ground in the forest had been so hard on his legs that walking on mossy grasslands felt like a sponge. His rising hope was very short-lived, however. Their path was barred by the beginnings of steep dales, rolling ever higher to the slopes of mountains amongst which the valley of Loch Eite was nestled. They followed the river until it snaked away. The river had brought them to the foot of the first of many loose, treacherously high, shingled slopes. *Could we go round?* Warwick wondered. *Even if I knew how to get round it, would my leg make it? It could be miles, days even! Anyway, Rowan would object. Remember what he said about being in the open when we left An t-Òban Forest. Hell, he probably even knows what I am thinking.* Warwick stood looking at the first hill and then to the next and the ones after, imagining just how many there would be before they descended the final ridge into the valley.

As they climbed, they kicked hard on every step to try to reduce their slip, gritting their teeth in agonising pain. It was a useless effort, as the slopes were far too loose to climb without slipping. For every two steps they took, they slipped back one step. Before they had even started, Warwick had known it would eventually hurt and be tiresome. He just wasn't prepared for how quickly the pain and exhaustion would set in. Rowan put his arm round Warwick, and together they just managed to scramble forward, almost bent double.

The slow pace was grating on Rowan. It was still the first hill! Even though they had not seen any sign of a dragon, Rowan's fears had taken control of his will. When finally they reached the top, Rowan immediately looked for a way round the ridges. He could see quite clearly the great spine of mountains that lined the valley of

Loch Eite but no quick way round. The only way round would add miles onto their journey.

They descended, climbed, and then descended and climbed again. It should not have seemed so long, as in truth it was only a few miles, but neither knew this. The problem was the loose surface, which very tiring, and the fact that Warwick had to stop frequently to rest. These factors made the journey seem to drag on.

On their final descent into the valley, the ground began to tremble beneath their feet. Small rocks began to tumble past them, steadily growing in size and number. All of a sudden, the slope sheared away in a torrent of rock, cascading like a stampede. The sound was like roaring thunder. Warwick struggled to move out of the way, but the mass of rocks was too quick upon him. Head over heels he tumbled like a ragdoll. Rowan was lucky to have just been out of the path of the landslide. Everything seemed to happen in slow motion for him as he glimpsed Warwick being dragged away by the torrent of rock. Warwick didn't stop till he reached the very bottom. There he lay, caught between rocks, thistles, and brambles. Rowan half ran, half slipped down the slope, his heart in his mouth. Falling to the floor, he pulled Warwick's torn sleeve back, frantically searching for a pulse. If there was a pulse, he could not feel it. He cleared the rocks from round Warwick and felt his neck for a pulse. Twice he tried, with eyes screwed shut in concentration. Eventually, he felt the slightest of beats against the pressure of his fingers. Warwick was alive! Rowan collapsed in shock, crying harder than ever and grasping Warwick's arm firmly. Warwick was stronger than he thought. The fall had knocked him unconscious, but still, on the very edge of death he clung on. As he thought this, he knew he shouldn't have been surprised. For Warwick to have come this far must have meant he was strong.

Long after dark had fallen, Warwick finally began to come round. Dazed and confused, he tried to move his left arm to feel the sheer pain on the right-hand side of his chest. But when he did so, he found it far too painful to move. He then noticed a bit of ripped black cloth bound round his left arm, holding it in place. He was lying on a bed of thick heather, covered with a thick blanket, against a wall of stone. A blazing fire crackled away close by. He had no recollection of how he had got there, and all he could see when he tried to think was falling rock. Having not seen Rowan, he tried to turn to look round, but that pain he felt kept him in one place. He felt all his pained parts now and clenched his teeth. There was a large sticky patch on his head, and his hair felt matted. He guessed this was blood.

Rowan had been dozing, huddled close to the fire on the other side, for he had given up his cloak to keep Warwick warm. When he realised that Warwick had woken, he sprang to his side. Immediately he began to look at all Warwick's wounds and bruising. His left arm in its sling was luckily not broken, just dislocated. Unfortunately, it seemed a few of his ribs on his right side were broken. Rowan had deeply feared that Warwick's legs were broken—if they were, that would be the end of their journey—but upon checking his legs, it only seemed his left ankle was sprained. So once Warwick's wounds were cleaned, his arm set, and his ankle bandaged in a torn garment, he was at least able to sit up with extreme difficulty. With no real choice, they stayed there for the rest of the day and night. Warwick couldn't even stand, let alone walk.

They had made it to Loch Eite, but despite this, Rowan did not feel any more comfortable. The air was deathly silent. The flat water stretching far into the darkness loomed almost as if it lay in wait of something. It was like the suspense at the edge of a battle. Rowan jumped at every shadow, expecting the worst. Warwick's condition had set his teeth on edge. He knew that the journey ahead was going to be much slower than he liked and did not sleep that night.

They arose in the morning to heavy winds and thick, swirling mists drifting across the surface of Loch Eite. Under the cover of the mist, Rowan helped Warwick muster his strength for the journey. Whilst Rowan had not slept last night, he had busied himself carving a wooden ankle brace for Warwick. The brace, at least, allowed him to put some weight on it and hobble forward. It was better than nothing, anyway. Warwick winced with every step, leaning on a long stick shaped like a giant wishbone that was braced under his left armpit. His bruised body and the agonising pain in his chest made it hard to breathe.

Their path snaked before them for miles at the foot of the mist shrouded mountains amongst the trees. Their pace was only broken by the fast-flowing mountain streams, which sometimes rose above their knees. The icy water came as a relief for Warwick, numbing the pain in his ankle. It at least brought freedom from one of his many pains for a brief moment. They continued under an endless canopy of trees, being forced closer to the water's edge by cliffs. By late afternoon, when they were completely exhausted, they made camp with still at least ten miles to go.

The temperature plummeted in the early evening. As they were hidden under the trees, they decided to risk it and make a fire, huddling close beside it. The night was still and passed quietly. By next morning, the mists and winds had lessened, but even so, they were still strong enough to impede progress. It seemed the valley of Loch Eite was home to a constant funnel of wind. Not long after first light, they were staggering forward, Warwick mustering his strength at the back with all his determination. Ever since he learned the dreadful truth of his parents, his will had turned to revenge. With each day that passed, the key crossed his mind more and more. He felt strongly that the only way to avenge his parents' untimely end was to go after this prophecy, wherever this unforged road might take him.

Daylight didn't seem to last as long in the mountains. The mountain ridges were like a drawn curtain in the sky. Darkness came in the early afternoon, by which time they had only reached the end of the loch. If Rowan could have carried Warwick he would have. Warwick looked hopeless walking with such a prominent limp at such a slow speed. It seemed a wonder he had made it this far. Since he had been placing all his weight on the walking stick, the base of it had begun to split. "Come on, Warwick, just another mile. Then we can rest."

"I can't go any farther. My ankle is done. I can't walk another step. I need to rest!" Rowan stood looking at him, trying to hide his disappointment and fear. "I did not think I would come so far on this ankle and with this aching body. I strongly doubt I will be right again. I wish for a damn horse. I would even take a donkey if it meant my legs should not have to walk another mile."

"If I could have, Warwick, I would have given you a horse days ago. I should think we will not see a horse till An Gearasdan, though. Even then, I don't think it possible that we will be allowed to take one, especially since we can't afford one. I'm sorry, but we must brace ourselves for another long march. For now, if you really can't go any farther, then we will have to find a good spot to shelter. There's a spot up behind those big rocks that should at least give us some shelter from the bitter winds. I will remain on watch whilst you sleep. I think it would be wise not to light a fire."

Together they limped over to the spot and settled down, pushing themselves between the rocks as much as possible for warmth. The winds funnelled through the gaps in the rocks with a ghostly whistle, which echoed long into the night.

Rowan had been growing more fearful with every day that passed. There was still no sign of any dragon, and that terrified him. He was always trying to push Warwick for that extra mile. The more ground they covered each day, the more his mind was at ease. He didn't even seem to sleep anymore, especially if they had to make camp in the open. If he did, it was only for about half an hour, after which time he would awaken in panic. The whole night he sat with his back against the rock close to Warwick with his eyes fixed upon the near horizon.

As soon as it was light enough to see, Rowan had Warwick on his feet, dragging on up the slopes at the far end of the glen. The mists and winds had receded a little, and the moon could be seen shining, casting its long gaze across the loch behind them, mirrored in the lap of the water. Ahead of them, they could see a dark ribbon winding between the foothills. For now, they could follow this. Within the next hour, they descended to the water's side and began twisting and turning their way over pebbled banks. A couple of hours later, they reached Dalness. They turned north, away from the river, and then headed through a copse of pine trees round the northern arm of the mountain. Straight away, Rowan knew his plan of forging a straight path was going to be beaten. From the high place, they could see twisting glens riddled with foaming blue veins, rushing out of the mountains to far places unseen.

Even on the move, Rowan tried to stick to a path where plenty of trees grew. Warwick could only limp on behind, baring his teeth and rubbing his aching muscles and ribs. At least he could replace his splintering walking stick amongst trees.

Warwick called from behind as Rowan slowly crept ahead. "How far is it now?"

"I should think twenty-nine miles at least, if we travel as straight as the mountains will allow. If possible, I would like to do this in two days. ... I know you can't see how this is possible. I won't lie, it will be difficult for me also. But when we reach An Gearasdan, we can get you some proper rest and treatment."

"How can such a small item like this key cause all this pain? I have barely made it to this point, and our journey hasn't even really started, has it? Yet I have no other choice than to keep going endlessly on. Nothing waits for me back there now. Can we even be sure that we will discover the purpose of this key?"

"Gifted I might be, but the key is beyond my gifts, Warwick. It consists of a far greater power, which I think was designed to be concealed from all but you. I am sorry, but I cannot give an answer to the torment of your mind and heart. The strength we find in each other is the greatest ally we will have now. Just for now, let us concentrate on getting to An Gearasdan. Help may come yet!"

CHAPTER 5

AN GEARASDAN

Progress was very slow on that day as they navigated round peat bogs and gushing waters. By sunfall, they were nestled deep within the soft heather amongst the many rivers and streams. Whilst they could, they drank deeply from the mountain springs. Although a little peaty, the water tasted quite pleasant and refreshing to Warwick. They had hardly covered half the distance Rowan had hoped for, and by now Warwick just wanted to get there. They were going to push on late into the night until they couldn't see their hands in front of their faces. It was the only way they would make An Gearasdan by the second day.

Long into the night, they climbed through heather and onto rocky ledges. In the early morning, high up on the ridges, they could just see distant walls jutting out at the edge of a wide stretch of water. By the end of that day, they had descended, twisting amongst the low hills and rocky cliffs into a glen, and had only a couple of miles left. The towering peaks of Beinn Nibheis led them to the gates of An Gearasdan.

Under the shadow of the towering walls, built closely together, stood row upon row of wooden huts. Everywhere they looked, they could see ragged people farming, building, and repairing. Some, Warwick thought, looked worse than he did, and yet their sleepless efforts did not give them the right to live within the walls. Warwick's dislike of the great city was rapidly increasing the more he saw. When they reached the foot of the gate, a watchman leaned over the ramparts, and seconds later the gates began to creak and swing inwards. However, they could not attempt to move through as soon as they opened, for their path was obstructed by town guard clad head to toe in mail. "Halt! Speak your purpose quickly!" boomed one guard in a deep, gravelly voice.

Warwick looked towards Rowan and caught his eye, but Rowan shook his head and turned towards the guards. In that brief moment, Warwick saw fear in Rowan's eyes.

"Speak!"

Rowan hadn't planned for this and stood nervously, trying to raise himself to full height. "We come seeking food and shelter. My friend needs urgent help from a physician."

One of the guards moved round them, looking very intently at the state of Warwick and searching the both of them. Rowan felt his heart in his mouth, but it sank slowly back down as the guard nodded in approval of their story.

"Before we let you past you must give us your names."

"I am Rowan, and my friend here is Warwick."

"You may pass, but any trouble and you will be spending your time in An Gearasdan in a cell!"

The guards stood aside. Rowan braced Warwick under the arm with his shoulder and moved as quickly as possible under the gatehouse, through the gates, and into a maze of streets lined with tall, stone-and-timber-framed, white-walled buildings with many windows. They twisted and turned through the streets till they reached the keep. A wash of fine-coloured silks and cotton struck Warwick's eye in particular, for he had never seen such wealth. Now he knew the reason why all those people were trapped outside the walls and why their arrival was less than welcome. People from afar, even from overseas, filled the streets, conducting a rich trade. Cattle and horses were herded back and forth in rapid succession to be sold, and merchants pushed carts filled with heavy loads of silks, foods, timber, straw, and much more. It was a difficult task to walk. Both of them were toiled and bumped about wherever they went. The only times when the main cobbled streets weren't blocked by the mass of people were when guards or important messengers rode through on horseback.

Rowan pulled Warwick away down a narrow, shadowed street towards an inn. The inn was called The Drunken Sailor. Compared to the streets, it was fairly quiet. An old man sat in a shadowed corner, just visible in the flicker of the sputtering and coughing flames. Few others were there, unless they were hidden in the deep shadows. The fire in the centre of the room danced and crackled happily, its heat filling every corner of the building. At the very end of the long hall was the barman, who was polishing pewter tankards. He stopped and put the tankard he was holding down forcefully as Rowan and Warwick approached. "Have you a room? We only need one," said Rowan.

Silence remained while the barman looked them up and down. "You're not from round here, strangers? What're your names?" His voice was rough and, it seemed to Warwick and Rowan, angry.

"I am Rowan, and this is Warwick."

The barman grunted his acknowledgment. "Can't he speak for himself?"

Rowan ignored his comment and asked again with a little more force if he had a room.

"Take the room up the stairs, just on the left."

The barman stepped out from behind the bar and led them to a small door that concealed a rickety staircase. They passed by quickly, and the barman slammed the door behind them. At the top of the stairs was a narrow corridor, barely shoulders' width, and just a little way on was their room. The tiny door creaked and wrenched open. It seemed as if the room hadn't been used for a long time. Thick dust hung on every surface, there were no candles in the brackets, and the only light came through cracks in the timber walls like pinpricks. Two shabby beds and a rickety table were the only items in the room. "Well, it's better than nothing. We will stay here till you're well enough to travel again."

"But are we safe? You have been agitated for days."

"That, I cannot answer. The forces at work are greater than the power I wield. My judgement is being clouded by fear that grows with every day that passes. Whilst the dragons rule, I don't think there is a safe place left."

A sharp knock rattled the bedroom door. Rowan quickly got to his feet just as the door swung inwards. "Been sitting in the dark, have we? Not wanting to be seen, are we? I just came to see if you require any food." As the barman spoke, he walked over to the sconces, put a candle in each, and lit them.

"Please. We would be most grateful for some bread, a pail of water, and maybe a little cheese."

The barman left the room without a word and came back shortly carrying a large wooden platter with everything they'd asked for on it. Once he was gone, they devoured the food, not thinking that they might need to ration it.

"We rest tonight, and then early tomorrow I will venture to the keep. You're welcome to come, but I want to make sure you get plenty of rest. I want to see if I can take counsel and get aid for our journey."

The morning came, bitter and icy. It was the major first sign of winter. The fire had burnt out, and the inn was empty. Warwick decided to come with Rowan, and they headed towards the door with their clothes wrapped tight round them. As they opened the door, they were instantly blinded by a thick blanket of pure white snow. It had fallen heavily in the night and looked to be a good couple of feet. Warwick gave his feet a glance, thinking of how cold and wet they would get. "Rowan, I cannot go out there in this weather. Look how poorly dressed I am, and my feet … well, I should think I would get frostbite and lose them."

Rowan looked at Warwick's feet and did not quarrel. Rowan shut the door and headed to the bar.

Out of a dark corner, the barman appeared. "What is it?"

"Do you have any clothing, shoes we may borrow? We can't go outside like this with all that snow that there is."

"Come with me."

The barman did not smile, but Warwick was starting to see that he was a nice person after all. The barman turned and walked with his big-booted feet into a side room. It was dark and dusty. The only light visible came through gaps in the timber-framed walls. It shone ghostly on cobwebs and oddments littering the floor. The barman leaned over a dusty, old, plain wooden chest and rubbed his hand over it, brushing the dust and cobwebs away. Then he felt for the latch and raised the lid with a slight creak. Inside the chest was mainly linen, which didn't look well used. As he pulled the linen out of the chest, Warwick moved a bit closer to get a better look. At the bottom lay some stable-boy clothing: a leather waistcoat that looked very old and worn but that was better than what Warwick had, black trousers with a torn seam at the bottom on the left leg, a white tunic with long sleeves, and a brown leather belt with a big buckle. Warwick did not complain at the quality nor at the fact that when he put them on they were a little baggy. The barman looked down at him with a flicker of a smile when he had them on. "Now, you wanted some boots, am I right?"

"Yes," replied Warwick with growing confidence.

The barman gave him a quick smile, turned, and started moving small boxes out of the way. Eventually, he stopped at a smaller chest and lifted it open. Warwick saw five pairs of decent leather boots. "Just pick a pair that fits."

Warwick moved to the box and reached in to grab the smallest pair. To his relief, they fitted and were comfortable. "Thank you."

The barman nodded his gratitude. "I … I am sorry for the way I have been … for the way I have treated you. Please … will you forgive me? It is the norm to treat outsiders in an ill manner. Often those who come a-wandering bring trouble. I have no doubt now that both of you are decent folk. Please take these items of clothing as a token of goodwill. I do not require any payment for them. My name is Abhainn. It means river, if you wondered. My mother gave me that name after giving birth to me on the Abhainn Lòchaidh."

There was a false calm in which they all shook hands. Then Rowan and Warwick headed towards the door, doing all they could to remain calm. Just before they reached it, Abhainn's voice drifted towards them. "Be careful out there. I have heard that some terrible winged demon stalks the skies!"

Warwick and Rowan froze for a split second, Rowan's hand hesitating on the door handle, before leaving quickly.

"Big trouble will come of this I'm afraid, Warwick. I am very scared and worried. Everything about our journey smells strongly of danger. You heard what Abhainn said about outsiders; I don't think the city has faced any greater peril than it faces now."

"But can you be sure that we do in fact bring trouble? We barely know anything about this key or this ancient prophecy. I don't think it would be wise to act in a hurry. People might be suspicious. We can't afford to risk people knowing about our true journey, can we?"

"My senses speak of danger, Warwick. We must leave quickly, but I appreciate that you cannot walk far. We must look for an alternative method—a boat or maybe a horse. Hasten now to the keep. Time is heavily against us, and I fear the shadow of night. They are closer than I had hoped, most likely attracted to the cities to feast. I doubt even these walls would keep those black menaces at bay. It is most unlikely that dragons fear city defences. We must seek counsel with great urgency or not at all and flee far from here."

"Don't you think there will be defences already in place if they have heard or seen these beasts?"

"It is unlikely. Powerful men can often be blind to rumour and myth. Remember that. It is likely that even if they do believe, they will think they are already strong enough to take down a dragon. We must convince them otherwise."

The sky was heavy with a roof of clouds, dark and low, and the air was so icy it pierced exposed skin like razor-sharp knives. Every street and building was barred by great drifts of snow. They sank into the cold, wet snow with every step. It soaked their clothes and bit at their ankles. A few streets later, they entered the central market. Clear above all else stood the towering walls of the keep, its imposing turrets, battlements, arrow loops, and thick, bold walls like a warning over the whole city.

Before the gates to the keep, they were met by guards barring the path. The captain of the guard, clad head to toe in mail and iron, broke from the ranks and closed the few feet between them. "You citizens have no business here. Be on your way now!"

Rowan did not move. "We've travelled far with great urgency to speak with the lord of the city. Please … will you not send forth a messenger with our request?"

As the guard looked at them in irritation, he seemed to grow in height. "The lord is busy. I do not see the wisdom in bothering him at this time. Turnabout and return to whence you came. Trouble will come of those who do not heed warnings!" His voice had continued to grow till almost a shout.

Even despite the bitter weather, Rowan's forehead began to shine with beads of sweat. Still, he stood his ground. Warwick only looked upon this as foolish, and he was already beginning to back down. "We do not come intent on trouble or on wasting the lord's time. From far we have come, through wood and mountain pass, to the doors of your keep. We cannot go back!"

"What errand could be so important to prompt a swift flight over many leagues to the doors of the lord of An Gearasdan?" The guard's eyes stared menacingly and unblinkingly at the both of them.

Warwick was shaking. He had no control left, and Rowan was not far behind him. "We must speak with your lord, or else many, many lives may be lost. Please, it is vital that you do the right thing and let us speak with him."

A dozen swords were pulled from their scabbards, and a dozen guards advanced upon them, surrounding them.

"Arrest them!"

Their arms were forced behind their backs and heavily shackled. Warwick winced at the pain this caused in his whole body and would have fallen if the guards had not been holding him up. They went round the outside of the keep and through a small arch. Warwick struggled, weeping when he saw the hangman's noose beyond the arch. Yet they carried on straight past this and entered a dark, dingy tunnel leading down. At the bottom was a small, thick black door adorned with a very big and heavy lock. It was a door that was not designed to be opened often once shut. It took two of the three guards to wrench it open. A pitch-black, narrow tunnel lay beyond, leading far back. They were marched down it, and all they could hear was the thump of their hearts, the sound of echoing footsteps, and a steady drip of water splashing down on a hard floor. Suddenly they were brought to a halt and could hear the sound of something being unlocked followed by something creaking as it opened. The next thing they knew, they were stumbling forcefully forward as a very heavy metal door slammed behind them. The last thing they heard was the sound of fading footsteps and the distant bang of a door.

"Are you alright, Warwick?"

Warwick groaned his reply.

"What a mess I have got us into." This was spoken as if to himself.

"What are we to do now? Is this it? Is it all over before it has begun? I did not think it would be anything like this when I set out to avenge my parents."

"I ... I don't know, to tell you the truth, but don't lose hope yet, not whilst we both still live."

"I don't think I am going to be getting any treatment now. I am in so much pain and am so cold and damp. I wish I had perished with my parents. I suppose it's lucky that the guards didn't take or find the key."

For two days they lay in the dark. The only change in their circumstances came whenever food was shoved in with them, but it was only ever stale bread and water. On the eve of the second night—not that they had any sense of time in the darkness—the doors opened, and hands grabbed hold of them and dragged them back up the tunnel. Even though it was dark outside, the snow left them almost blind as they stepped out of the tunnel mouth. Once their eyes had adjusted, they saw a tall man in fine garments of black lined with fine, red silk. "Follow me," he said.

They were led along the long torchlit halls and passages of the keep, climbing higher and deeper all the time. To Rowan, the whole place had a feel of having been erected very quickly. The walls were devoid of pictures, the floors had no carpets, and very little design could be seen in the walls and doors. The air was thick and smelt of burning oil. They ascended two flights of stairs until they came to a door. The messenger knocked on the door loudly, and a big, booming man's voice beckoned them to enter. They entered into a high chamber that was full of much sweeter air, as well as being much lighter. On the walls were pictures with intricate designs of slain wild beasts. The lord sat high and proud on his throne of oak at the head of a long table surrounded by many an empty seat. The splendour of the throne made him look more like a mighty king. It was etched with grand carvings of man dominating all, and above his head were the words *Unita sicut unum verum Deum et hominem, vincere princeps in terra ista daemonia conspirata*. Rowan translated the text for Warwick quietly as they skirted round the table to the throne. "It is written in the old tongue, Warwick. Latin. It hasn't been used as the common language for hundreds of years, but there are those who stick by the old ways and believe that there is power in the words. It translates in the common tongue to 'God and man united as the one true ruler to vanquish the demons of earth.'"

Warwick did not dare to reply or show his interest in its meaning now that they stood before the throne. The messenger bowed low before his lordship. "My lord, I bring before you one Rowan and one Warwick as requested."

"Very good. You may leave."

Giving a low bow and turning sharply, the messenger marched from the room. At this, Lord Exihainn stood up with his chest raised, and the power of might could clearly be seen in his tight, muscular face and dark-grey eyes. His long, dark hair draped across a fine coat of deer hide, which extended down to his calves. A fine, jewelled hilt could be seen glinting in the light at his hip. Glimpses of a red silken tunic could be seen through small gaps in his deer hide. Rowan and Warwick addressed the lord with a very pronounced bow.

"Do you know why I have ordered you here?"

"No, my lord." Rowan tried to keep his voice steady.

"It came to my attention that two travellers in my dungeons by the names of Rowan and Warwick caused a disturbance at the doors to my keep, requesting an audience with myself. I brought you here from my dungeons because I am interested in hearing what you have to say and finding out why it was so urgent."

"Yes, your lordship. We have travelled from afar with great urgency, through wood and mountain pass, to your doors in the hope of aid. But we also bring with us news of a matter of great concern that should not be thrown aside lightly. We implore you to take heed of our words, for the fate of your great city rests on your immediate action."

"Speak more of your peril and be swift, for I am greatly troubled by the threat of war in the south."

"Dragons, your lordship. We were attacked by one far to the south and west. Till recently, we hoped that there was only the one dragon, but it does not seem likely that this is the case, for we have heard word since our arrival of a winged demon haunting the skies. Doubtless you have heard of or seen this devilry?"

The lord sat back in his throne, troubled and deep in thought.

"I cannot say anything more on the subject of dragons," said Rowan, "for I did not think they existed outside of children's tales. However, I am a learned man and would be humbly at your service if you could enlighten me on the matter."

"Folly! I cannot offer you what you ask. I have heard of this winged menace, and yet no word of fire and death has come to my ear. Should such a menace exist, then action would already have been taken. Myths do not walk upon the earth."

"But your lordship, forgive me, if they don't exist, then how do you explain the beast that attacked us? Never have I seen a bird the size of a building that can breathe fire. What say you of that?"

Agitated by Rowan's retort, the lord's fists clenched round the arms of the throne. "I would remind you to whom you speak, unless you want to spend an eternity in my cells! And I would have thought ones who claimed to have been attacked by a dragon would look much worse than you do, if they weren't dead. How did you happen to escape the will of something so evil?"

All this time Warwick had not spoken, but anger was awakening inside him, anger that would not hold its tongue. He limped forward, seeming to rise in height. "You speak ill of us and our hardship. You know nothing of my suffering. You sit here safe in your walls making people grovel before you like peasants, not heeding their warnings of this menace that they have seen. My family was burnt to death by a dragon, and we escaped while it burnt my house to the ground, fleeing here in the hope that action might be taken against such beasts." Tears streaked his face.

Mingled fear and fondness could be seen in the eyes and contorted lines of Rowan's face. However, the lord released his grip upon the arms of the throne and slumped deeply, worried and abashed. The guards on either side of the door had taken a few steps forward but stopped when the lord limply raised his hand. "I have been a fool. It is clear that it took a lot of courage to say that, and I can see the pain. You may have spoken boldly, which would normally be punishable, but for once it was not out of turn. You have opened my eyes to the truth. You must forgive me, but it is never easy to believe in something that until recently had only been a myth. The danger I have put my city in through my blindness sickens me. I shall summon the council of lords. Come back tomorrow just as the sun rises above the walls, and we shall discuss the actions that must be taken as well as the aid you require. In the meantime, as a gesture of goodwill and friendship, I invite you to feast in my halls come sundown. You may address me as Lord Exihainn."

"Thank you, your lordship," Rowan and Warwick said together, both bowing deeply.

CHAPTER 6

THE STORM BEGINS

Outside the keep, the sun blazed low over the walls, blinding them. They had only been a couple of days in the cell, but they could not help but feel like it had been a lifetime since they had seen the sun. Whilst they were imprisoned, the main streets had been cleared of snow so the market could continue. Citizens had draped themselves with bulky animal hides till their skin was barely visible.

"I don't want to be here too long," said Rowan. "If possible, we leave tomorrow. I can't help but see danger. I hope you are prepared to travel. We must now collect whatever we can get for the journey ahead. We should try the docks, I think, for a boat. That way you could at least get a good head start on your journey while your body heals."

"*My* journey! Are you not coming?"

"Warwick, no matter how much I help you, no matter how long I travel with you, this prophecy was made about you. I can guide you to the right path—how long that will take I do not know—but when the time comes, you must become a man and travel it alone. If it was made about you, then it was made about you because you are strong enough to see its end."

Warwick sighed and turned his head to look at the north wall. Masts of tall ships were just visible above parapets, and the sound of rigging clinking on masts could be heard faintly on the wind.

As they walked amongst the maze of icy jetties stretching far out, the sounds of hammers, shouting, running and general toil filling the air, what first became clear was the armada of vessels of all sizes. They kept walking till they found a few, very small rowing boats nestled far out on the edge of the jetties. Unfortunately, they seemed well used. Some were beyond being able to carry any weight, while others already had ankle-deep water in the bottom. However, not all were in ruin. Some would certainly carry some weight. They waited by one that was only really big enough for two people till they saw someone close by. A tall sailor stopped halfway up a gangplank and looked at them, squinting with suspicion. Rowan approached cautiously, trying not to slip and keep his eyes on the sailor.

"You best not be looking for trouble down here!"

Rowan ignored him. "The boat over there, is it for rent?"

For a moment the sailor said nothing and continued to stare with his piercing eyes. "Provided you have the gold, any can be rented. But dressed like that, I doubt you could afford anything that floated." Laughing, he moved on up the gangplank.

Rowan returned to the boat and sat on a mooring post next to Warwick. Someone else would have to come by, surely. The docks were busy enough. It was a long time before someone finally did, at which point they had become so cold that they could not feel a bone in their bodies. An older man staggered down the jetty straight for them. They could not see his expression, as his face was shrouded by a thick animal fur. He stopped right before them. "What would two people such as yourselves be doing down on the docks?" His voice was gravelly and deep.

"We are seeking passage to Sgitheanach."

"That is a long and dangerous journey. You won't find many down here willing, especially since you're landlubbers. Why the need anyway?"

"We are fully aware of the risks and perils of our journey. We travel to build a new homestead amongst our family on the west coast of Sgitheanach." Even though Rowan had just lied, there did not seem to be any sign that the old man had detected it.

"Why you are so far from family I shall never know, as it's not my business." The old man looked out across the waters, thinking. "Do you have the gold?"

"We have very little gold."

"It's as I thought, from the looks of you. I don't blame you for not having much. Times are hard. Only the other day I was sailing up Loch Iall, and I heard a monstrous cry of something giant. Then smoke, thick and black, plumed high into the air. Whatever it was, I did not feel it could be anything of this earth."

Both Rowan and Warwick went pale. It did not go unnoticed.

"I may be old, but my eyes do not deceive me. Something about what I have spoken disturbs you grievously. It is plain in your eyes! If I were to guess, I would say that you know something of what I speak? If you will tell me, I will take you when you are ready for free. I have wanted to know what it was since it happened."

Warwick was not going to speak, but he looked at Rowan. By the looks of it, Rowan was deep in thought. Warwick tried to stop him, but Rowan only held him back. "If it is what I think, then it was a dragon."

"Dragon! Surely not! They don't exist."

Rowan stared into the man's eyes with a look of knowing. A small nod was all that was needed.

"So you have actually seen one? Well, this is going to cause a lot of trouble for certain. The world really has come to an end when myths become real."

"We barely escaped with our lives," Rowan said.

"Well, I am glad you survived, even if it's just to warn others of the terror. But as I said, I will take you for nothing, friends. When you know when you will want to leave, come and find me at the docks. My name is Morogh." He smiled and walked with them back to the city gates.

For the next couple of hours, they walked all over the city, haggling and scrounging at market stalls and in doorways. All they had to show for their efforts was a stale loaf of bread frozen solid and half a dozen bruised apples. It was then that Rowan did something he hoped he would never have to do again. Using the crowds round the market to hide him, he made his way to a wooden barrel full of fish close by, and when he felt sure no one was looking, he grabbed a couple of the biggest salmon he could see, slipping them under his cloak.

Back at the inn, they dried off by the fire. Warwick spent the afternoon resting his pained, stiff, wounded body. Luckily for them, Abhainn had let them keep their room for free while they remained in An Gearasdan.

Come evening, they made their way to the keep and were let in without question by the guard. They were led into a great big hall just off to the right of Lord Exihainn's chamber. Laughter, music, and the banter of many voices bellowed through the great oaken doors, drawing them in. Lord Exihainn made his way swiftly over to them, pulling them into the centre of the room, where a huge oaken table ran the full length of the room. It groaned under the weight of a mountain of platters stuffed to the brim with the finest foods—a banquet fit for a king. There were spit-roasted meats in seemingly endless supply, stone-baked crusty breads piled high, and pies the size of small barrels filled with the richest game meat. Whole rounds of strong cheese perfumed the air, and ale, mead, and wine ran like water. The trouble was that all this food was simply too rich for Warwick compared to the food he was used to, and soon he felt very heavy and bloated. Rowan wasn't far behind him. Warwick noticed the amount of food Rowan had piled on his plate. He had eaten surprisingly little of it, yet his plate was clean. It wasn't until Warwick caught a glimpse of a sagging linen cloth hanging just under Rowan's cloak that he began to understand. By the time the eating had finished and almost everyone was drunk, the cloth looked in danger of splitting, so they slipped away quietly back to the inn.

The moment they crossed the threshold of the inn, Abhainn advanced from the shadows, filling three flagons with mead. "I have been waiting for you. You've been gone for days! Business clearly didn't proceed without trouble! I wish to talk in private … with both of you."

Warwick shot a nervous glance at Rowan, which was mirrored back at him. Together they followed Abhainn into the back room.

Now the room was free of cobwebbed chests and boxes. Instead, a round table sat in the centre with three chairs round it, and candles hung in brackets high up on the walls providing a soft, flickering light. They sat on opposite sides of the table, Warwick bringing his chair closer to Rowan.

"I don't like being lied to!"

They both frowned at this.

"When you left two days ago and I warned you of the rumour that has been spreading rapidly, there was a moment where you both froze exactly at the same time. You know something about these winged demons."

Rowan sighed. Already his plans to keep their journey quiet seemed in ruin. "We never intended to lie to you, though you are right. We were fearful at the news, because if my senses speak true, we know what these 'winged demons' are. They are something we hoped to never see again, something we know by another, more fearful name: dragons!"

Abhainn laughed raucously at them. "You don't expect me to believe that fairy tales told to little children are real!"

"So tell me, then, what do you know of these 'winged demons', if they're not dragons?" Rowan half-shouted in his anger.

Swallowing hard to silence his laughter, Abhainn responded, "They're probably nothing more than golden eagles getting a bit close to people, causing them to panic and exaggerate about what happened."

"These rumoured creatures are bigger than golden eagles. You know that! Rumours don't spread like wildfire about eagles. You're as scared as us. There's no shame in showing fear."

Something about the look of Warwick caught Abhainn's eye. As much as Warwick had been trying to hide what had happened, the talk of dragons had brought everything back like it was only yesterday. He wanted to keep things to himself, but his heart felt as if it would split. "You sit there laughing when you have no proof that dragons don't exist. I will tell you this only once, for the pain in my heart consumes me. The reason I look sad is that I lost everything to a dragon—my home, my family, all gone, consumed in dragon fire. So you tell me now that dragons don't exist!"

Rowan turned his attention from Abhainn to Warwick, shocked to silence. He had not expected Warwick even to speak up, let alone to talk about the attack.

Abhainn sat back in his chair, speechless. His eyes would not meet Warwick's or Rowan's. For a moment it looked as if Abhainn may have even shed a tear, hastily wiping it away. Even if it were truly to show remorse, Warwick had had enough of the sight of him, so he left without another word and went to their room. Rowan remained with Abhainn till he eventually slumped away into a room to the right of the bar.

Warwick sat in the room with his head in his hands, staring at the floor and shaking with grief. As far as he knew, it was the key's fault that his parents were dead, the key's fault he had no home, the key's fault he had to travel so far. He didn't want it anymore, except to destroy it.

Rowan walked into the room. He noticed the key on the far side of the room, where Warwick had chucked it forcefully against the wall. Foreboding hopelessness crept into Rowan's mind as he thought long and hard about what was best to do. In the end, he decided to leave Warwick to his thoughts and went to bed.

Warwick woke early in the ice-cold air. The room was still pitch black, but from the gentle snore, he knew Rowan was still asleep. Suddenly there was a loud knock on the door, waking Rowan and making Warwick jump. Warwick hesitated to open it, but the knock came again moments later. It was Abhainn. He stood there in his nightclothes with a lantern in his hand. "Sorry to disturb you so early. I had trouble sleeping."

Warwick let him in and shut the door after him.

"I couldn't stop thinking about what we had spoken about last night. Dragons! I just can't ... believe it!"

Rowan could see the danger and stepped in front of Warwick before Warwick could speak. "You're not alone."

Warwick glared at Rowan dangerously.

As much as Rowan didn't want to admit it to himself, he knew in his heart that the chances of succeeding today were not great. Even Warwick had realised that their chances were small, especially after seeing Abhainn's reaction to the truth. Rowan hadn't realised that his worry showed on his face, but it was too late to hide it, as Abhainn had seen. "I have seen that look of defeat on many a man's face before. I am truly sorry for what you went through, Warwick, but I know you're up to something. If it involves risking the lives of everyone in An Gearasdan, I am going to have to stop you!" Abhainn's eyes moved between Warwick and Rowan, searching them for any clues as to what they might be up to. Then he spotted the key still on the floor.

Rowan hadn't moved the key, as it was for Warwick to accept his quest and not have it handed to him. He saw where Abhainn was staring and intervened quickly before Abhainn could really be drawn to it. "Oh, you found my key. I have been looking for that. I dropped it last night and couldn't find it in the dark. Well, it isn't really a key, just a family heirloom. I wear it as a pendant." Warwick felt sick with worry, but Rowan managed to hold it together and convince Abhainn. They still had to tell Abhainn what they were doing, though. He knew they were up to something; there was no way round that. "You will not tell anyone this!" Rowan spoke with a stern voice. "We're going to the keep to counsel the lords about the dragon situation and urge them to increase the defences of the city, just in case there is a dragon attack."

"So once you have convinced the lords that dragons are real— good luck with that—you're just going to leave the city in a mad panic? The city will tear itself to pieces before it even sees a dragon!"

"Would you rather people didn't know and have no chance at all if one attacked? We have seen the destructive power they have. This city, the way it is, would be flattened! We are well aware that the truth could cause trouble, but that's the risk we must take to try to save hundreds."

"No, I suppose you are right, but I will not see the city crumble into disarray. Whatever you do, whatever you say, this *must* be handled with extreme care! I will be watching you while you remain in An Gearasdan." Abhainn took a step back, turned, and walked away.

They ate a little of the food they'd scavenged from the banquet for breakfast. Afterward, Warwick reluctantly put the key back round his neck, and they ventured to the keep. The whiteness of the snow against the black of the sky left them snow-blind for a while. They trudged through the new snow, which was ankle-deep, finding their way as best as possible. The ice-cold snow against their trousers stung like a thousand stabbing needles. They were glad to get inside the keep and dry off.

They were not led, as they expected, up the staircase to the council chamber but into a very small, dark, cold room. High up on a wall, a torch flickered, giving off a very dim light. It was only just bright enough to highlight a bench with someone sitting on it. Immediately, the man rose from the bench and stepped forward so they could see his face. It was Abhainn.

"Why are you here?" Warwick asked before Rowan could try to halt him or ask the question himself.

"After everything we discussed, how could I not come?" Abhainn's voice was calm, but his face did not give the same impression. His gaze pierced their flesh like daggers.

"I thought we were in agreement last night. This meeting has to go forward. If not, all these people will be unaware of the true danger out there and will have no chance. They must be warned or ... or gods help them!" Rowan stood firm.

"Who are you to say what is best for this city when you're not even a citizen? We have walls lined with archers at all times. They would bring down a dragon easily." Abhainn's arms were tightly folded, and he spoke in nearly a shout.

"I don't understand this change. You know full well that those who have heard the rumours don't believe they are dragons. Take yourself, for example. Only when Warwick lost his temper and spoke of his torment did you believe. So you're telling me archers are going to be ready and waiting when a dragon attacks? It is, in my eyes, only madness not to warn the city. Surely you don't want your home and the city burnt to the ground?"

"I would rather not have any trouble at all! I shall be coming with you to this council. Any trouble, and I will personally drag you out of the city!"

All three of them were led into the council chamber, where a great, long table had been placed in the centre of the room. Round the table sat many important members of the court in their finest garb. Lord Exihainn sat at the head of the table, and the conversation was already well underway. The voices blended into one in this vast echoing chamber, so it was hard to tell what any of them were saying. Silence fell the moment the three of them took their seats, and all eyes turned towards them.

Lord Exihainn raised his hand, and instantly all attention was on him. "I see there is a new face amongst us. Stand up! Who is this that willingly walks into a private council uninvited?"

Guards from round the edges of the room moved swiftly towards Abhainn and stood on either side of him, ready to drag him away.

"I am Abhainn, my lord. They have been sleeping in my inn in the city, and I wanted to be of help to them, my lord."

"And do you, Rowan and Warwick, vouch for this man?"

Rowan stood up promptly from his chair, and Warwick nervously did the same with a terrible tremble in his legs.

"Yes, we can both vouch for him, my lord."

"Very well ... were the circumstances different, you would be severely punished for walking in upon a private council uninvited! However, since the subject at hand is of a matter so unknown to us, and since Rowan and Warwick vouch for you, then this once I will be lenient. You may sit."

"Thank you, my lord." Abhainn bowed before taking his seat.

"Before we begin, should anyone publicly speak what is discussed in this room, the perpetrator will be punished! Now that we know who everyone is and matters of discretion are dealt with, I, Lord Exihainn, hereby announce that this council on the potential threat of dragons is in session. Rowan, Warwick, will you please stand and give forth to the court what you told me yesterday." Lord Exihainn's voice boomed across the table.

"The news we bring to you concerns the whole city. We arrived a few days ago in desperate need of aid, having fled here from far to the west in a flight of great fear. You may have heard talk in the streets of winged demons. It is our misfortune to be the bearers of ill news as to what these foes are: dragons! Till the attack, we hadn't even believed they were real, but there can be no mistaking what we saw. I know many of you here will find this hard to believe, but we speak nothing but the truth."

Lord Exihainn stood up and bowed to them to take their seats. "My lords, as I know that most of you will have endless questions ready to ask, I do not wish to waste time on the subject of believing what they bring before you. They have my full trust and belief, which should be enough for all of you. Please speak your questions." He raised his arms to the court, and they began to rise.

"I am Lord Cairn," said a tall, middle-aged man with jet-black hair and dark-brown eyes. He was dressed in the finest purple garments, which hung snug round him and trailed on the floor. "My question is why there was this need to travel so far. I can't help but wonder if there is another reason for your coming. If you were just looking for safety, you could have found somewhere closer, surely."

Heads turned between the three of them, Rowan, Warwick, and Lord Cairn. "Our home was destroyed by this dragon, and we travelled here to seek medical aid and safe passage to the north, where our other family members live. Also, warning one of the major cities in Scotland seemed quite an important thing to do. Perhaps within the city walls we might just have a fighting chance, if we all work together."

"Be that as it may, I would like to hear more about this attack," said Lord Cairn. "I want to know exactly what it was you saw."

Lord Exihainn, seeing the danger, rose at once, and almost as if a dark veil were thrown across the table, the other lords were swallowed in the shadow of his might. "I have heard the full story of what happened. If only to spare him pain, I do not ask for it to be spoken of again." The room had fallen deadly silent in response to Lord Exihainn's rage. He did not return to his seat, seeing that he would need to keep control.

Warwick sat in his chair, very agitated by the tension in the room and feeling like the weight of the whole room was crashing down on his shoulders. He slowly unclenched and shakily stood before the court, greatly surprising Rowan, who followed swiftly after. Warwick looked at Lord Exihainn with what he hoped was a smile and bowed slightly. Lord Exihainn closed his eyes briefly, knowing what was about to come. "I do not say this willingly, but I can see it is the only way you will all truly believe, and I think that my lord Exihainn knows it too deep down. My family and I lived far to the west near the town of Loch Domhain. It was there that the dragon came. It was larger than many of the buildings in this city. It burnt my home to the ground as if it were built of straw and burnt my family with it. I only escaped because I was outside at the time and managed to get away whilst it torched my house. If it had not been for Rowan finding me, I would not be here to warn you of the truth. Now you know why Lord Exihainn believes us. Now please, can we proceed with this council before it's too late!"

Another of the lords stood up, one who hadn't spoken yet. "I am Lord Achaius. I see you are deeply grieved, boy, and I believe now what you say about the dragon attack. But I still think there is something you're not telling us. Now tell us what the real purpose of your journey is. Why do you not want us to know? I do not believe you travel to see family. You have just told us he is not your father, so where is he leading you? Surely he wouldn't know where your family lives." Lord Achaius was tall, towering over Warwick. His voice sounded menacing and pounded into Warwick with the force of a swinging axe. The question was directed at Warwick; no one wanted to listen to Rowan because of his lies. Rowan sat there with complete shock on his face as Warwick stood again. He hadn't expected Warwick to speak at all, let alone tell them about his parents, and now it seemed certain he was going to tell of the key. Was this going to be the end of the quest?

"You may believe him, Lord Achaius, but I still do not believe this," Lord Cairn said with venom in his voice, spitting as he spoke. "I can see you have some injuries, but I personally think, based on the description of the dragon you gave, that you should have more wounds. And yes, I too want to hear about your real reason for coming here, as well as the full story of the dragon attack. What would suddenly have caused a dragon attack, when dragons have been dead so long that they have passed into myth? I want to know everything before I will even think of believing!"

"Lord Cairn, you will restrain yourself until it is your turn to speak. You may be a lord, but you will do well to remember your place at my table!" Lord Exihainn's eyes flashed red, and he slammed his fist upon the table. Then he turned calmly to Warwick. "Warwick, will you please stand and give your answer."

Warwick wiped the tears from his eyes as he stood there looking from lord to lord round the table. All eyes burrowed into him. There was no way out; he had to tell them the truth. "At the age of fifteen, my mother gave me a key. She was told I must be given this key at that age. The key has powers, and I was warned that some things are drawn to its power. The night the dragon attacked, the key shone with a blinding white light, which I think drew the dragon to attack, because the dragon came soon after and crushed my home. My father must have run outside to try to draw it away and perished. I found my mother trapped in the burning remains of my home. I dragged her from the flames. With her dying wish, I had no choice but to leave her and save myself. Rowan soon found me, and we journeyed here seeking aid. I have been told that I am an important part of a prophecy, but no one knows what this prophecy is, as it was written centuries ago. I hoped I might find some ancient documents that may give some leads about my journey and quest. I fear that I have something to do with the return of the dragons."

"Show us this key." Lord Exihainn fixed his eyes on Warwick's hands, watching carefully as Warwick lifted the chain from round his neck. Rowan closed his eyes. It was surely the end. Warwick placed the key on the table. Everyone was standing, leaning over it, and a quiet muttering filled the room. It was quite some time before everyone came to their senses.

Warwick ached with renewed grief. Anger boiled inside him looking at all the lords. "You have your proof now. I will not say any more about my family. If you think I have lied even after I showed you the key, then I do not care about your safety."

The whole room fell quiet, and the atmosphere in the room was one of pure fear. There was no doubt that they believed him about the dragon; all of them sat speechless in their chairs.

Lord Exihainn did not rise to speak and looked pale. "We will leave this meeting for this day and retire to the banquet. Rowan, Warwick, and Abhainn, as a gesture of my goodwill, will you please join us in our feasting?"

"Thank you, my lord," spoke Abhainn when neither Warwick or Rowan answered.

One by one, the lords left the room through two great big doors at the side of the room. Warwick and Rowan stood up as the last of the lords progressed into the banquet hall. They filled their bellies with succulent meat and bread and washed it all down with two flagons of mead. Warwick, not used to drinking, wobbled and spluttered. It was about mid-afternoon when they could finally slip away.

Outside the keep, the sun was blinding as it ever was this time of year, sitting low in the sky as if a lasso were pulling it closer. The three of them trudged through the freezing snow back to the inn, their clothing hanging heavy and sodden. For a good hour, they sat shivering close by the fire whilst their clothes gently steamed.

"I guess we were successful," said Abhainn, "at least in some ways."

"For now, perhaps you're right, Abhainn," said Rowan, "but I can't help but feel that in two days we have made no further progress beyond convincing them. There is still a lot to be done and very little time to do it in. I fear that if nothing is sorted soon, we will all face the wrath of dragons! I had hoped we could have got to the talk of defences today instead of being put in a position where we had to reveal Warwick's prophecy."

"You kept it from me as well!"

"You must understand that whatever it turns out to be, it is crucial that this prophecy happens. We both strongly feel that it has something to do with the dragons as well. For the key to have passed to Warwick at the same time that the dragons emerged is surely no coincidence. This is the reason we have tried to pass quietly, partly out of fear. We didn't want to risk it all ending before it began."

"Warwick, I am not angry with you," Rowan continued. "Please don't think that. You were put in a position where you had no choice. I don't think they would ever have believed us if you hadn't told them. We will just have to battle against them if they try to stop us."

Warwick sat quietly, not wanting to speak, so Rowan gave him what he hoped would be an encouraging smile and pat on the knee.

"Well, I can definitely see why you wanted to keep it quiet now," Abhainn said. "It's all a bit too complex to get my head round— prophecies, magic keys, and dragons. But now that I know, I am deeply sorry for the contempt I showed you. I only spoke ill to protect my home. I feared you would only make things worse, though now I see it's quite the opposite. I can't deny that I am scared. I think it is only a matter of time before a dragon comes, with or without you being here. We are a big city, and each day hundreds of people come and go selling their wares. I believe in what you say, that we need more defences, but what defences are there that can stop these airborne beasts? We are drawing far too much attention to ourselves. For your sakes, I hope that you are gone before an attack happens!" Abhainn tried to give them a smile to defuse the tension, but as much as he tried, he couldn't smile when the threat of dragons appearing any day was on his mind.

"You don't have to apologise," Rowan replied. "We understand. It is we who should apologise for possibly bringing danger here. I know we can't keep them out indefinitely, and none of our weapons are strong enough to even pierce their hides. We can give the people some feeling of safety and maybe forestall an attack long enough for people to escape. But unless we fortify where we can, the city will turn to ash. All the men who are able will need to fight! We must succeed tomorrow at the council. If we leave the meeting with no plan put in place, we will leave the city. I won't risk anyone's life longer than is needed."

"May I come with you again tomorrow? You're going to need all the help you can get."

"Yes, we would be glad of your help."

Warwick sighed.

"What is it?" Rowan asked looking directly at him.

"I had hoped I would have found some aid for my wounds whilst we were here," he replied. "It just seems as if I must carry on with the rest of the journey in pain."

"I'm sorry, Warwick," said Rowan. "Things haven't gone at all as I'd hoped they might. I haven't forgotten and will do what I can to help before we leave. The boat will aid us, and you can certainly rest as we sail." Rowan then turned and spoke quietly to Abhainn. "Is there anything at all you can do to help Warwick?"

"I have a few old bits of cloth to bandage him with, fresh water to clean any wounds, and alcohol to numb the pain. I am afraid that's the best I can do. I am no physician. The only physician I know serves the lord, and his treatment comes with great cost, a cost only affordable to the wealthy."

"Perhaps we shall discuss this at council tomorrow."

Rowan and Warwick got up from the fireside and climbed the stairs to their room. Abhainn briefly popped in carrying a bowl of fresh water in one hand and a bottle of strong wine in the other, with bits of frayed cloth draped over his arm. He washed and dressed Warwick's wounds and numbed his pain. Warwick could even walk a little without aid.

Night fell swiftly, but in the darkness, Rowan and Warwick could still hear each other moving restlessly. "Can't sleep?" Rowan's voice drifted out of the shadows.

"I'm too anxious to sleep. In a few hours, we could possibly have saved An Gearasdan, or we could be fleeing as fast as we can, hoping that in our search for aid we haven't brought destruction." Warwick clasped the key in his shaking hands. His gaze was focused on it, and he didn't turn away, even when speaking to Rowan.

Rowan got up and lit one of the candles, walking over to sit next to Warwick. He looked down at the key in Warwick's hands. The amount that Warwick's hands shook worried him. "I know what's going through your mind, but you must try to resist."

"This key makes me so angry. I see it as nothing but a curse. I only continue now to avenge my parents' death. It seems now that the weight of hundreds of lives rests on my shoulders, whether I like it or not."

Rowan placed a hand on Warwick's shoulder. "Just remember that through this all, no matter how lost or alone you may feel, you're not alone in this pain and struggle. Let's try to take it a day at a time. Come on, we will go and get some breakfast."

In the glow of the firelight, Abhainn's silhouette could just be seen at a table in the corner of the room. The sound of the creak of footsteps on the stairs made him jump up and run towards them. To Rowan and Warwick, he didn't look like he had slept either but had clearly sat waiting, dressed and booted, for council.

"Ah, Rowan and Warwick. Are you hungry? There's a pot of soup steaming away over by the fire. There are some bowls and bread on the table. Dig in." Abhainn raised a piece of bread to his mouth and then stopped immediately, his brow furrowed, clearly in deep thought. "Are you sure no one else knows about this prophecy? How do you even know where to go when you leave the city?"

"No, I don't believe they do. It is so old that it predates our language, and all knowledge of it has been lost, or so it seems. Look how much trouble we had convincing the lords that dragons exist! Something like this key wasn't forged in any city. It would have been forged in secret, possibly in a cave somewhere, which is why I am taking him to some very ancient caves on An t-Eilean Sgitheanach in the hope of finding some cave paintings that may give clues to this prophecy. The only trouble is we don't know if there are any paintings or, if there are, which cave they are in. All I know is that the caves I am taking him to are very ancient and may predate the key."

"That's a lot to put to chance. I wish you both the best of luck."

They finished their breakfasts, and by midday, they were trekking their way through the deep snow to the keep. The ground was covered in a thick, fresh layer of powdery snow that had fallen overnight. The journey was slow and exhausting, their feet sinking deep with every step. It took twice as long to reach the keep as usual. Their feet were numb and soaked, and their clothes were pulled tight round them.

As they walked into the council chamber, it was clear to them that all the lords sitting round the table had been in deep discussion. The groan of the heavy doors, however, had silenced them, and Lord Exihainn stood, inviting them to take their seats.

"Before you arrived we discussed whether we all believed you about the dragons, and we came to a conclusion. We all believe, after what Warwick said, that you are telling the truth, and we will not doubt what you say."

All the lords turned to look at them and smiled. Immediately Rowan stood up. "If I may speak, I would like to get straight to the point, my lords."

Lord Exihainn nodded his head in approval.

"My lords, the matter of the meeting today should be about what can be done to make safe the city from attacks. Against dragons, man has very little hope—we all know this—which is why we need to build stronger defences. If we can't fight a dragon, we should be thinking of how we can hold off an attack and preparing plans to get people out of the city to safety if all goes ill." In that moment, Rowan grew in stature. If it weren't for his tatty old clothes, he would have looked like a lord.

"There is a lot of wisdom in that," Lord Exihainn replied, "but what defences do you think we need to fight dragons? The cost of anything from troop movement to fortification will have to come from the war fund, as will the resources needed to get people to safety. The war fund is just not big enough to contend with our needs. Time worries me, too. How much time do we have to fortify a whole city?" There was a note in Lord Exihainn's voice they hadn't heard before, but if he was scared, he was hiding it well.

"Having seen a dragon, I would think we would need siege weapons on the walls capable of firing huge rocks and huge arrows. Pikes made of steel should be fixed to the outer walls to stop anything from landing there, and soldiers should have full-body armour and new, stronger bows, arrows, spears, and swords. With all that, I think we may stand a chance of defending the city from complete destruction. We do understand that cost would be a deep concern to you, but I believe this is your best chance of survival. Time is the reason we jump abruptly to the point, for we don't know how much there is. I hope my lords will forgive our boldness."

Abhainn suddenly stood up, which came as a surprise to the table. "My lords, what about the vast cellars that run beneath the keep? Couldn't we move the citizens there?" He looked round as all the lords looked from one to the other, nodding their approval.

A very tall, black-haired man stood up. He wore heavy robes of leaf green and a pendant round his neck with a silver star upon it. "My name is Lord Blane. On the matter of the protection of the city, I think that yes, it would be wise to move all the women and children into the cellars should the time come. We can at least try to protect the future people of An Gearasdan."

"I would certainly like to achieve at least that," replied Lord Achaius. "My problem is, what about all those who live on the outside of the walls? We don't have enough room for all of them, but we can't let them die. What about the local produce that is delivered every day from the farms and the docks? If we lose that, surely we will die of starvation."

"You raise important points, Lord Achaius," said Lord Exihainn, "but just moving the people is not going to be enough, I fear. Rowan, you say this dragon was about the size of a building and strong enough to destroy the walls round us. Would we then be like the shepherd who leads his sheep to the slaughter, Lord Blane, if we trap our citizens underground whilst a dragon brings the city down upon their heads?" Though Lord Exihainn addressed his question to Lord Blane, he looked curiously at Abhainn, Rowan, and Warwick at the same time.

"Yes, my lord," Rowan replied. "It was easily that size and easily strong enough. But I think the citizens would be better underground than above. There's no sense in trying to outrun a dragon. Surely the foundations are the strongest parts of the city with all the weight sitting upon them. It's not a big chance of survival, but it's bigger than being in the open."

"Thank you, Rowan, Warwick, and Abhainn." Lord Exihainn smiled and nodded at them to sit down again. "Are we all in agreement, then? If the time comes, we will move as many citizens as we can into the cellars?"

Everyone round the table nodded their approval.

"Anything in the cellars that can be moved will be moved to create more room," Lord Exihainn continued. "What harvest there is will be gathered and rationed to all. The kitchens can make bread and salt fish. We will do everything we can to save our people." He turned his attention to Abhainn. "Abhainn, you've heard of the rumours. Do you know where these beasts are said to have been seen? It is important we know this, as it might well tell us just how much time we have."

"Other than beyond the walls, I cannot say exactly where they were seen. Nor do I know anyone within the city who has seen the beasts, my lord."

The murmur from round the table settled into silence with everyone deep in thought. Lord Exihainn slumped a little in his seat with his hand resting upon his cheek.

Abhainn stood up and brought the attention back to the table. "My lords, if I may trouble you all from your thoughts, I would like to speak on behalf of Warwick. He is not yet eighteen. As the law stands, even in a time of crisis, Warwick is not a man. Would my lords be willing to bring the trials of manhood forward to give him some training so he has a better chance on his journey? And is there any medical aid you can give him for his many wounds?"

"Why should we let you carry on this quest?" Lord Exihainn said in reply. "How do we know you won't just make things worse?"

Rowan stood up with Warwick at his side. "My Lord Exihainn, this quest could mean the end of the dragons for good! We only ask that you trust us to see it done."

"The reason we wait to train boys till they're eighteen years of age", said Lord Exihainn, "is not because of their height or because they're not men yet. It is because of the physical demands of the challenges. I doubt Warwick would be strong enough to cope."

"He must be trained to stand any chance," Rowan replied. "The dragons could come any day. Surely you can put the law aside for something as small as this. When all of you were his age, I bet you were being taught the skills? Please, will you help him? He cannot go on without it."

The lords spoke in whispered voices amongst themselves. Abhainn stood up from his seat to stand at Rowan and Warwick's side. They tried to hide the feeling of defeat engraved upon all their faces.

"We will help. Please sit back down," said Lord Exihainn. "We should be more grateful to you. You have opened our eyes to a threat greater than any we have faced. Now that we know what we are dealing with, we have a small chance of preparing ourselves. If we hadn't known, I doubt a soul would soon be living in An Gearasdan. I grant you your request to undertake this journey, but should you discover what this prophecy is and find that it brings peril, then you are forbidden to come within my city again! I cannot put my people in danger, young Warwick. Now, Warwick, if you wouldn't mind standing up and following my guard, he will take you to see my physician." A guard hastened over to Warwick's side and escorted him from the room.

Lord Exihainn turned to Rowan and Abhainn. "We will not keep you from your own deeds for much longer. You can tell Warwick that his training will begin tomorrow evening, just as the sun dips below the horizon. He will be trained alone. You shall go with him and make sure he does everything he is instructed to do. If he does not, his training will stop. Now this key, you mentioned the dragons may be drawn to its power? If this is so, as soon as he has completed his training, you must leave the city. We wish you good luck on your journey. You may go."

CHAPTER 7

The Challenge of Warwick

Warwick sat outside the chamber waiting for them. He had had his wounds cleaned and dressed and could walk a great deal better. The three of them ventured back to the inn together and sat close to the fire, shivering in their wet clothes.

"We have some good news to tell you," said Rowan. "The lords agreed to have you trained. You will start at sunset tomorrow. I am allowed to watch you train. But I must ask that you give it your all, or they won't train you."

For a moment, both Warwick and Rowan saw a flicker of a smile on each other's faces; they couldn't begin to remember how long it had been since they had smiled. Abhainn sat watching with a smile upon his face. He coughed, clearing his throat. Both Warwick and Rowan turned to look at him. "I would just like to say thank you", Abhainn said, "for everything you've done to help the city, especially opening our eyes to the reality of dragons. When you leave, please always remember that you're welcome to stay here as my friends anytime. And Warwick, I wish you all the luck on your quest. You're incredibly brave to venture out there, and if I can do anything to help you before you leave, you only need ask. But remember, the wilds are dangerous. Do not stray from your path." He patted Warwick on the shoulder and then moved to the bar, coming back with three pints of ale. "To Warwick." He raised his tankard, and Rowan quickly followed suit.

The rest of that morning, they celebrated their victory sat round the fire, eating, and drinking. Afterward, Abhainn remained at the inn while Rowan took Warwick up the tallest mountain to do some training. The two passed through crags and frozen cascades and traversed ice slopes littered with boulders, the wind gnawing at their flesh. It took a very long time to reach the summit. Warwick ached all over and felt very tired, even with the much-needed support round his ankle. The height, they had hoped, might help them to look ahead or see any potential signs of a dragon. Though there was no sign of a dragon, Warwick took no pleasure in the view, knowing his time to journey out there was very swiftly approaching.

Abhainn had a thick broth ready for them when they returned. It bubbled away over the fire. Warwick and Rowan ate generous helpings. As they ate, they could feel the warmth of the broth slowly bringing feeling back to their numb limbs. Their feet were almost red-raw from the hike. Abhainn sat with them as they ate, listening to them tell of their adventures. Rowan suspected his interest was not in their venture; he seemed fixed upon trying to find the slightest hint of a dragon sighting.

That night, Warwick lay nervously in his bed with his hands clutching the key round his neck. What would his training involve? Thoughts of his schooling, possible dragon attacks, and the key caused him to break out in a nervous sweat. The key lay in the palm of his hand, and his gaze was fixed upon it. It had been dormant for a while and seemed like any other key. How much he wished it were! Its dormancy came as no comfort to him. His mind merely turned to wondering why it had been so dormant. Was it building up for something, just listening and waiting? His head swam with negative thoughts. Looking towards Rowan for help now was useless, unless Rowan could use his foresight in his sleep. Warwick felt sick with worry. He curled up tight in his bed, his head pounding like a drum with all these horrid thoughts. Suddenly, from the deep pools of his mind, a voice spoke. "Warwick."

It was Deal's voice. The voice echoed like a whisper on the wind, and Warwick sat bolt upright, hardly believing his ears. "Father? ... Is that you? Where are you?" he whispered with his ears pricked. But no answer came. Silent tears trickled down his face. Had he just imagined it? Should he tell Rowan? He decided to sit there and ponder the moment with happiness, and it brought strength to him.

Rowan was suspicious of Warwick's seemingly good mood the next morning but did not ask about it. Instinct told him that it was something personal. Leaving Warwick to his thoughts, Rowan made his way to the docks to make sure they still had passage. To his relief, he found that they did, and he came back to the inn soon after.

Warwick had lingered by the fire for him, jumping up the moment he saw him come through the door. "Do we still have passage?"

"Yes. Now that we have everything sorted, it's time to get our things ready to leave. I shall speak with Abhainn to see if he has any leather satchels."

By evening, they were packed, having managed to get some satchels from Abhainn. Warwick's nerves were in tatters once more as they strode through the snow. They walked to where they had earlier seen guards training. Their eyes were met with the sight of many lit torches hanging high up in their brackets. A guard waited with his sword in hand, sitting by a small fire burning in the middle of the floor. He was dressed head to foot in steel armour. He looked like a giant. In the glow of the fire, his armour looked golden. When they approached the guard, he turned his head briefly and then turned back. Confusion took over Warwick. Was this the man who was going to train him or not? A glance at Rowan told him that it was the right person. Rowan had a distinct look of anger. He could not subject himself to being ignored like this. Clearing his throat, Rowan spoke loud and boldly. "I believe, guard, that you have been instructed to train Warwick here." His eyes flared up dangerously like they were wreathed in flame.

Standing slowly, the guard moved towards Warwick. His armour clinked with every step, and it was quite a frightening sound. Rowan gave Warwick a small smile before turning to sit down close by on a low wall. The guard presented Warwick with a hunting bow and quiver, pointing towards the archery butt fifteen metres away. Warwick nervously drew an arrow from the quiver. His hands shook slightly, and several times the arrow fell as he tried to draw the bow. To him, the bow felt very strong. The poundage of the bow was better suited to soldiers and fully grown men, not boys of sixteen who have never drawn a bow. With great effort, he managed to lose an arrow on his fourth attempt. It wasn't a good shot, spearing into the snow a little way in front. The guard did not attempt to help. Rowan was growing even more impatient at the guard's lack of effort. Warwick shot a quick look at the guard and drew another arrow. This time he didn't drop it, and his shot just made the target. His arms were already beginning to hurt from the sheer strength of the bow. With each shot, the string whipped his unbraced right arm. He could feel his arm bruising as it turned red-raw. After a while, Rowan, seeing Warwick struggling, got up to help. Warwick had been at it for several hours now, and his knuckles were split and bleeding. It was pitch black, as the clouds blocked out the moon. The only light came from the torches in their brackets and the whiteness of the snow. Warwick had no energy left to fire the bow. Rowan thought for a second before seeing a small sword on top of a pile of straw. Rowan took the sword and carried it over to the sharpening stone. When he realised Warwick wasn't watching, he turned and saw that the key in Warwick's shaking hands was glowing. They could plainly see the fear in each other's eyes as they looked from the key to one another. Loud bells sounding from the keep cut the silence of night. The moment they had feared most had come. Rowan and Warwick knew it would happen at some point; they just didn't know when. No preparations had been made. The city couldn't be any more vulnerable. No one had been moved to safety, and the extra defences were nowhere to be seen. Warwick had tears in his eyes. Rowan grabbed him firmly by the shoulder. "We need to leave now!" he shouted.

Warwick's life was virtually sucked from him as the great shadow swept across the city. His face was pale, and he froze in complete fear. Rowan saw a look of death in his eyes. The thought of all these people falling from this world the same way his parents died weighed heavily on Warwick's mind. Everything went out of focus as if he had gone blind, and he didn't hear anything that Rowan shouted at him. He was lost in thought.

The dragon had come to feed. Swooping overhead, it knocked over a chimney stack with its tail. The stone fell to the ground, narrowly missing Warwick and bringing him back to his senses. They ran to the inn to save Abhainn, but their efforts were useless. The inn was ablaze and crumbling before their eyes. Against the night sky, the dragon was like a ghost, its dark scales blending into the sky. Screams came from many buildings as the dragon torched roof after roof, the flames illuminating the whole sky and the dragon's blood-red eyes. Its tail swung like a mace, smashing everything it hit. The town guard fired arrow after arrow from the walls, but each missed. With anger, the dragon turned on the wind and folded its wings back, diving headfirst, its chest glowing molten orange. The towers exploded, wreathed in flame. Rowan kept a firm hold of Warwick, and they ran for the nearest gate. Above them, the dragon rose high before diving like raining spears on the mass of fleeing people. Fire burst from its mouth, and the screams were gone in seconds.

Fires raged to the height of the city walls. Plumes of black smoke rose in great columns as if a volcano had erupted. The smell of death and burning was overwhelming, choking everyone who still breathed. The dragon landed hard on what remained of the stable roof, crushing it like it was made of sticks. Deadly shards of wood and burning straw rained down on the victims trapped inside the buildings. Phantom screams echoed on the wind across the whole city. Within minutes of the dragon's arrival, the whole city was ablaze. People jumped to their death from windows, enveloped in coats of flame. Every time the dragon roared, it shook the earth. The sound was deafening to all those who still lived. Warwick and Rowan ran, dodging falling debris and all the other people running for their lives. They managed to get to a city gate. To their luck, it was already open. Vast swarms of people fled through it, some falling over and getting trampled to death. Rowan grabbed hold of Warwick, pushing down the side of the crowds.

They ran high into the mountains without stopping once till they were safely out of sight. They found a shallow cave just big enough to squeeze into. They could see An Gearasdan still, burning as bright as day. The dragon was illuminated, making it look like a demon from the underworld circling above the city. All the farms, ships, livestock, and buildings, as well as most of the people, were gone. Both were speechless, unable to move. The very breath had virtually been sucked from their bodies. They were choked by their grief. Even from where Warwick and Rowan were, all they could hear were the dying cries drifting far on the wind. Warwick turned his head away so as not to look, but it made no difference. He could still hear the massacre. Tears streaked down his face for the loss of his parents and now for the loss of an entire city.

An unbearable silence came hours later, falling like a giant hammer. Their ears were left ringing. It was much harder to hear each other for quite a while. The dragon had gone, and most of the city had been reduced to a mountain of burning rubble. Smoke could be smelt and seen high in the air. Devastation like this would be heard of throughout the land for sure. At least when the air had been full of screams, they had the comfort of knowing people still breathed, even if they were breathing their last breaths in the wake of the dragon's filth and poison. Tomorrow, though, they somehow had to continue on their journey.

CHAPTER 8

KIELOCH PASS

Their night was plagued with visions and ghostly cries that haunted their minds, waking them in sweats and tears. Lingering here was possibly very dangerous, so before there was light in the sky, they moved on with as much speed as they could muster. They were tired, thirsty, and hungry, and all their supplies had been lost in the fire. They did not even have a change of clothes! Their pace slowed as they journeyed through mountain gorges. The cold was beginning to set in, their shoes and the clothes round their ankles were wet through. They had lost the feeling in much of their bodies. By the end of the day, their sense of direction and purpose had begun to wane, though they had barely covered five miles. Rowan didn't even feel connected to his foresight.

To make things worse, there was tension building between them. Warwick had taken to blaming the key once more. Why was he here? he frequently asked himself, putting the blame on Rowan for disturbing his quiet family life. If he had never given his mother the key, then possibly his parents and all these innocent people would still be alive. Warwick didn't speak his thoughts, but he didn't need to; Rowan could feel his anguish burrowing into his back.

For days they journeyed, covering very little ground. They foraged in the snow for small amounts of wild berries and ate snow to drink. They did not stop moving once, for if they did, death would surely get them. The journey did not become easier but only got worse as the snow fell again. A great white blanket fell from the sky, covering the icy snow with a fresh layer of soft, powdery snow. Their feet were sucked deep into it. In places, the snow had reached the height of their knees. Now they were soaked up to their waists as they trudged on in silence with the wind whipping their faces. The blizzard seemed a solid wall, almost impossible to see through. Faintly in front of him, Warwick could see the outline of Rowan trying to forge a path ahead. They had to get higher up out of the deep snow drifts.

The journey up the Muirshearlich pass took them over the pass of Kieloch. The climb was hard. The steep path wound its way along a very narrow cliff edge. To their left, cliffs rose up a thousand feet, and to their right were sheer drops and certain death. The wound in Warwick and Rowan's relationship started to heal as they traversed the pass, helping one another. The path was very icy, but at least it was not covered deeply in snow. It was sheltered by the overhanging cliff, which kept the wind and snow off but unfortunately not the ice. Many dangers lay ahead on this path. There was no knowing when an avalanche might happen.

The path grew thinner, and in some places it had fallen away. A big gap loomed ahead of them. For the first time, Warwick was hit with a wave of vertigo. He threw himself against the cliff wall with his eyes tight shut, breathing heavily. When he opened his eyes, Rowan was already standing on the other side waiting to catch him. Legs trembling, Warwick moved towards the edge, digging his feet hard into the ground to search for the smallest amount of grip. *One ... two ... three.* With pure fear in his eyes, he leapt forward into the air—his feet slipping backwards—and strait into Rowan. Rowan was bowled over, but to Warwick's surprise, he heard laughter. The two of them lay on the floor like sacks of potatoes. Warwick began to laugh as well as they pulled each other to their feet with difficulty.

After several more near-death moments, they reached the top of the pass. The sun could faintly be seen through the clouds, and the falling snow didn't seem nearly as heavy, even though the snow on the ground was deeper here. For the first time in a long while, they could see a little way ahead to the flatter lands that waited.

Finally, the descent began, but it was no easier than the climb. If anything, it felt harder. Their knees suffered great strain as they steadied themselves while scrabbling down the path. The ice nearly made it impossible to walk without slipping over the edge of the path. On several occasions, each time worse than the last, Rowan had to grab Warwick to save him. The descent was starting to level out slightly, and the path widened, but only enough for two children to walk abreast. Luckily for Warwick, his unexpected vertigo hadn't come back to haunt him yet. As they rounded a sharp hairpin in the path, they were brought to a halt. A huge avalanche had destroyed the path, leaving a huge, twenty-foot gap to get across. Warwick eased his way to the edge of the drop, unaware that hairline cracks were following his movement.

"Stop moving!" Rowan yelled. He had seen the cracks appearing in the nick of time and so pulled Warwick back.

"Thanks," Warwick said, panting. His heart was in his mouth as he watched the rock he had stood on fall away into the chasm. How were they to get round? The whole path would collapse if any weight were put upon it. The cliffs, meanwhile, were too high and too dangerous to climb down. They most certainly wouldn't make it going back. There was only one thing for it: to climb up the avalanche and round. Rowan went first. He stayed hard up against the wall to avoid the weak point in the path and made it to the edge of the snow mountain.

"Careful, Warwick." Rowan watched Warwick's every move as he edged his way towards him. They began to climb very slowly. Little bits were still moving occasionally, often from under their feet. The closer they got to the centre, the more the snow shifted. They tried to climb high up the snow as best they could but found themselves sliding towards the seemingly bottomless chasm behind them. Rowan nearly fell once, and Warwick had only just been able to reach him. With every step, their hearts pounded slightly more, and they did not look down. The avalanche was, in fact, much fresher than they had known. Half an hour later, they had made it to the other side.

After several long hours, they reached the bottom of the pass. They couldn't remember the last time they had eaten or slept, it had been so long. They couldn't go on, not like this. Warwick knew that were the numbing pain of the snow not dulling the pain of his ankle, he would be in agony. They walked under the shadow of the cliffs, looking for a cave or a dry crevice to rest in. It wasn't long before they found a cave just big enough to squeeze inside. The rock was cold, but at least it was dry to sleep on, and it sheltered them from the wind and snow.

CHAPTER 9

LORD EXIHAINN

L ord Exihainn was sitting in his study reading over the war manuscripts when a sudden feeling came over him. He felt drawn to the window. As he leaned out, his heart leapt into his mouth. High above, the bells of war began to ring in the towers, resonating through the entire building. He stared hard into the night for the flicker of advancing torches beyond the ramparts, but there was nothing. Suddenly there was a loud noise like thunder carried on strong winds that tore past the window, and an immense shadow as big as the gatehouse soared over the city. The figure became clearer as its chest started to glow molten orange. He fell back from the window as he saw a blinding flash and intense heat scarred the side of the building. A guard heard the commotion outside the lord's study and charged in with his blade drawn. A huge roar bellowed through the window, making everything shake. Lord Exihainn was on his hands and knees on the floor gasping for breath.

"Milord, what is it?"

"It's a ... d-dragon!" Lord Exihainn breathlessly spluttered his words.

The guard turned a ghostly white and completely froze. He had no idea what to do.

The dragon flew high, smashing its huge body into the bell towers and destroying the bells. Huge chunks of rubble and splintered timber fell, narrowly missing the guards far below. Crawling back to the window, Lord Exihainn saw great trails of fire erupting from the dragon's mouth, torching everything. The buildings blazed, and the flames reached forty feet high. Lord Exihainn stared unblinkingly as the immense beast landed on buildings, crushing them. How anyone would survive this he did not know. He had failed his city.

Smoke and a foul, rotting smell began to drift through the window, filling the room with thick, black smog. It filled their lungs and choked them of air. Then there was a hurricane-force wind as the dragon beat its wings and shot into the air quicker than anything Lord Exihainn had ever seen. For the first time, he could see the fierce, blood-red eyes coming towards him. Then a huge fireball shot through the window. Lord Exihainn dived out of the way just in time, yet he was trapped. Instantaneously, the flames spread across the ceiling and torched anything made of wood or fabric, raining down burning timber and bits of tapestry. The guard grabbed Lord Exihainn by the arm and pulled him through the flames to the door. But the dragon hadn't finished. It came back with speed and vengeance, smashing through the walls like a cannonball. Giant lumps of stone flew in all directions, and the whole building started to crumble. As the dragon took back to the air, the walls and the floor they stood on collapsed, and Lord Exihainn fell through to the floor below. He landed on a pile of burning roof timbers, his face and hands covered in blood and burns. He couldn't move. He was trapped, and his leg broken. The keep was destroyed. The wall had fallen, and from where Lord Exihainn lay, he could see right over the whole city.

The dragon continued its massacre from the air, torching everything that moved. The roar of the flames blocked out all other sounds, apart from the cry of the dragon. In his head, Lord Exihainn could hear the never-ending screams of the city, and his eyes slowly began to fog. Then suddenly, he felt his legs being pulled. Through his blurred eyes, he glimpsed whoever was dragging him and saw the figure was wearing metal. Perhaps it was one of the guards. Lord Exihainn's body was burnt badly, almost beyond recognition, yet he still breathed. The next thing he knew, he was being laid upon something soft.

Only when the city was flattened did the dragon fly off to the west. The few that survived had fled in all directions, looking for shelter and safety in small places. Lord Exihainn's unconscious body was amongst those who left the city, carried on a stretcher. Two days later, Lord Exihainn awoke. He found himself in a warm bed with a physician dabbing the burnt skin on his forehead. His vision remained blurred, but he could still see enough to make out what objects were. He raised a hand to his rough face, and the pain was agonising. Half his head was bound in blood-soaked cloth. He felt his body all over, wincing more so when he touched his right leg. It seemed to him it was already lost, his leg.

Days passed, and still Lord Exihainn lay in his bed. There was no strength in him even to try to speak, let alone to move. Night and day, serving girls came and re-dressed his wounds, making sure he was as warm and comfortable as possible. He seldom slept, as every time he closed his eyes, he was taken back to An Gearasdan. The physician made poultices of herbs to try to relax his mind, but nothing would stop the visions.

More days passed, and it was clear as day that he was improving very little. Lord Exihainn had only begun to get his voice back and feel a slight bit of movement in his legs. People in fine garb began to pass in and out of the room with important documents. It was unclear who they were. Many hushed words were spoken to the serving girls attending to Lord Exihainn. Eventually, one came and leant over his bed. "My lord, I hate to bring such a heavy burden upon you at such difficult times, but we have received word from Dùn Èideann that the English advance. News has spread fast of An Gearasdan, and they think we are weak and vulnerable. The king has been informed and deploys his army. Is there anything you would have me do, my lord?"

He managed to answer in a rough, quiet voice. "I will pray that the bastards are killed by the dragons. Why should we waste life over such a rabble as the English! They are weak and cowardly. There is no greater dishonour." He paused, catching his breath. "Yes … yes, you may do something for me. Send word throughout the kingdom that all those who survived the attack at An Gearasdan and fled shall be given a home wherever they find civilisation. Let the big cities know of the advance from the English. We will not be caught off guard. They will be crushed by forces they did not expect. Make sure all women and children are moved out of the endangered cities. I will not see any more die." The talking had put him in quite a bit of discomfort. His neck muscles felt stretched, and his throat felt like it was lined with broken glass. Drool trickled from the corner of his constantly open mouth.

"Very good, my lord, I shall see it is done." With a curtsey, she left the room quickly.

He spent the next couple of days without a single word passing his ear. He received no word from anyone—not to inform him about any responses to his message, not even to tell him that his assignment was done. Thoughts of Rowan and Warwick had started to stir in his mind. More than anything, he wanted to know if they were still alive. He had believed them at the meetings, but he had no idea how deadly or just how big the dragons were. A serving girl came with fresh bandages for his burns. As she dressed his wounds, he grabbed her arm, pulling her close. Quietly, he said, "Send word to any of my remaining guards. I want to know if Warwick and Rowan are still alive. And if so, where are they?"

The serving girl gave a small curtsey and then called to another to finish dressing his wounds. She ran from the room with the speed of a gazelle. As his wounds were being re-dressed, he lay there still, looking up at the ceiling. He hadn't realised how high the chamber was. With his blurred vision, the ceiling looked hundreds of miles away, stretching to the heavens. For a minute, he wondered if he were dreaming and would wake up in his bed in An Gearasdan.

Every day that passed without any news made him irritable. Had his messengers been killed? Had the word reached its destinations? His questions were shortly answered. The next day, he lay in his bed when he heard the clinking of armour coming towards him. The guard held a scroll in his hand. It was sealed in green wax inset with a badger. It was the mark of Lord Hades of Peairt. Breaking the seal, the guard read it to him.

From Lord Hades to Lord Exihainn,

We have received word that the English foul our
lands. Our defences have been fortified against any
siege. All women and children have been escorted by
a company of guards far north to Obar Dheathain.
Our army has risen and marches forth to join the
king's at Baile Chloichridh. Aid has been sent to the
survivors of the attack, and word has been passed
on to others close by. They are all trying to do the
same as us. The English may be strong in number,
but we will fight them nonetheless. Let's pray the
gods are vengeful upon them.

To Lord Exihainn's relief, it was good news. He nodded as best
he could to the guard, who then took his leave. Lord Exihainn had
been in the medical wing for five days now and was growing tired of
being abed. Even though he wanted to get up and walk, he knew he
would just collapse. At least he could just about sit up now without
help, though the sight of his leg made him not want to sit up. It was
heavily mangled beyond repair, and the smell ... not even smelling
salts masked it. When the news came to him that his leg would be
removed, it did not sadden him. He had suspected it for days now.
He was just surprised he hadn't been told days ago.

Evening came, and the king's private surgeon came to his
bedside. "It is time, my lord." A couple of servants followed at the
surgeon's heels to carry Lord Exihainn to the operating table. The
surgeon led them into a small, candlelit room. Lord Exihainn could
see with his bad vision all the metal tools laid carefully on the
surgeon's workbench. As they lay him on the table, he was suddenly
aware of how hard the table was. He sweated and twitched. His heart
was in his mouth as he thought of what was about to happen.

"Here, drink all of this." The surgeon gave him a large, full
leather wineskin.

Lord Exihainn downed it. The two servants held him down, and the surgeon began. He tied a leather belt tight round Lord Exihainn's leg, stemming the blood supply, and then he placed a chock of wood in Lord Exihainn's mouth. Lord Exihainn bit down so hard on the chock that he felt his teeth would shatter. At the sight of the razor-sharp blade, he retched. The wine did nothing for the pain when the blade came down like a guillotine, stopping when it hit his bone. The chock in his mouth did not stop the ear-piercing screams. Tears streamed from his eyes. He clenched the side of the table so hard that he could hear it groaning and feel rough splinters digging under his nails. Vomit spewed from Lord Exihainn's mouth as the surgeon brought out a saw. He pulled back the flesh to reveal the shiny bone before putting the saw to it. It took several strokes of sheer agony, but eventually, the bone broke clean. Lord Exihainn watched in complete shock as the surgeon pulled his mangled leg away and put it on the bench at the side of the room. But the pain hadn't finished yet. A cautery had been heating up in a small fire and was now white hot. The surgeon picked it up and touched it to the stump. The screams Lord Exihainn let out as it touched were sickening to anyone who heard. The cautery hissed as it touched the flesh, and instantly the flesh sealed itself. The throbbing pain continued for hours. Sweat ran in buckets from his brow, and he felt very sick, very weak, and very tired. The surgeon finally removed the leather strap, telling him it was done. The servants gave him all the wine he could drink to ease the pain and then carried him back to his bed.

The night was restless, and the pain would not ease. The thought of never being able to walk again on his own two legs saddened him greatly. He waited now for news of Rowan and Warwick. It was the only thing that would lighten his spirits. Two more days passed as he just lay in his bed, regaining his strength. He could still feel the pain. His temper got worse with every day that passed without any news. He started to fear that news would not come of Rowan or Warwick.

CHAPTER 10

WATERS OF ŁOCH ŞHUBHAIRNE

Warwick and Rowan travelled a long way from the pass of Kieloch. They passed Loch Arkaig, heading past it on the north side. Then they walked for days upon snow-topped ridges, sleeping in the driest places they could find. All round them were mountains that were higher than the clouds. There was no easier way round them. Some of them were so tall that they could see their destination faintly in the distance; it was how they mapped their journey.

They woke one day on a hard ridge of rock high up in the mountains. All knowledge of what day it was had left them. From the top of the mountains, they could clearly see a huge forest approaching, and just beyond that the sea. The forest looked too wide to go round, but they didn't want to be in a forest after night fall. The trees were home to many wild creatures, especially in a forest as large as this. What Rowan feared worst were the snow wolves. They would journey south in the winter to richer hunting grounds, and trees provided excellent shelter for them. Rowan, however, did not mention any of his growing worries to Warwick.

They walked on at early light, winding their way down the steep mountainside while fighting for grip and balance over the loose sliding stone. The trees loomed ever closer, looking tall and menacing. The only comforts the trees offered was shelter from the bitter winds and the chance that a greater abundance of food could be found amongst them. It was at times like this that Warwick wished he had a hunting bow. The miles rolled on, and Warwick and Rowan longed for flatter land. The constant climbing and descending was tiring them far too quickly. How they were to go on much farther without a proper meal or good rest they did not know. If by some miracle they made it to the other side of the forest before night fall, they still had no way of crossing the sea. Luck seemed to be against them. Not since An Gearasdan had they heard or seen sign of a dragon. Where were they? Rowan was certain there would be more than one, but this quietness scared him more than seeing one.

The wind picked up, and it felt bitter, as if icicles stabbed their flesh. It was still light, but they couldn't go any farther. They found a very small sheltered cave not too far away. It was a really tight squeeze to get inside, but once in, they were completely sheltered from the wind. For hours they sat listening to the wind screaming at the cave entrance, wishing for its subsidence. Not till the middle of the afternoon did the winds calm. As they headed from the cave, they found themselves struggling to walk through much deeper snow. To their right, an avalanche had fallen, barring their path. After what had happened the last time, they certainly weren't going to climb over it. But the alternative was to change their course and head south. At best they might make the entrance to the forest before dark, but the odds were looking slim. The snow was growing deeper by the hour. Several times Warwick slipped and fell face first in the deep snow. Rowan nearly followed him on occasions. Now they were faced with a big hill to climb. It looked more like a mountain. Beyond this, though was the forest. They were so close now, yet it would still take them a long while in the hard conditions. Straight ahead were lots of high cliffs with overhangs. They could not go up this way. Climbing diagonally, they headed for the lowest of the cliffs with the hope that it might lead to a small gap they could traverse, but the footing was rapidly getting worse the higher they got. What had started off as smooth snow had now become huge, frozen boulders with deep snow trapped between them that could potentially be covering up crevasses. Scrabbling over the boulders took forever, and it tired both of them rapidly. Warwick looked ahead endlessly. The white of the snow blended into the white sky.

Late afternoon came, and finally they reached the top. The light was beginning to fade. Rowan had been limping in pain for a while, so he removed his boot to rub his foot. His foot had turned purple, was covered in blisters, and smelt strongly of mould. Trails of clotted blood were all over his foot. Warwick took a look at Rowan's foot and imagined what his own must look like, but he dare not look. However, they couldn't stay here with the evening temperatures set to plummet to a level they would not survive. It was already much colder here than in the valleys. Looking for a way down the other side seemed impossible. Each side either was a sheer cliff or had a very steep slope that looked too steep to climb down. After some thought, they tried one of the steep slopes. Warwick took the lead. He lay on his back and slowly slid his way down, staying close to the rock to slow him down. Rowan was impressed by Warwick's thinking and how quickly he managed to get down the steep slope. Before long, they had both reached the bottom of this slope and could walk on more easily. There was a good five hundred feet to go, but the worst was behind them. They could clearly see the forest now straight ahead. It was relieving to see that it wasn't nearly as long as it was wide. They gritted their teeth as they quickened their pace to reach the shelter of the trees.

Mighty Scots pines stood sentinel over the land. Under the canopy, they found a small clearing in the gorse bushes and settled for the night, huddled by a warm fire. They ate what little berries they could find on nearby bushes, and soon sleep came over them. Sleep was very fleeting, as they woke at almost every crack or creak to make sure they weren't being watched. Their worst fear was wolves. All they could hope was that they weren't in their territory. All round them they heard shuffling in the bushes and the calls of many different animals echoing through the trees. It was very frightening, hearing the distant cries of wolves, so much so that before long neither of them could relax enough to even try to sleep.

Morning came later than usual under the canopy of the trees, but as soon as there was enough light to see clearly, they were on the move. They walked with as much haste as they could muster with their aches and pains. Rowan called to Warwick whilst on the move. "You may have guessed the danger that has arisen. Those were the cries of wolves last night, and wolves hunt day and night. We must move quickly and silently. We cannot stop till we're clear of the trees. From now on, we must remain silent."

"But what happens if we are hunted by them. What do we do then?"

"If such a situation arises … just concentrate on getting yourself—"

"I won't abandon you," Warwick interjected, cutting him off mid-sentence. "If you die, who is going to help me find my path?"

"Warwick, I thank you for you loyalty and friendship, but in the end, this prophecy was meant for you and you alone. I can only come with you for very little of your journey, and I fear that our friendship is nearing its end. Whether we will meet again remains unknown. You must promise you will get yourself to safety if we are attacked."

"But—"

"Promise me, Warwick. Whatever this prophecy is, we can bet it includes the dragons. That much is clear to me. As for the rest, that is for you to find out. I hope that our long and arduous journey together will not be in vain."

"Alright, I promise, but you must get yourself to safety as well. Don't risk your life for me!"

They carried on as silently as possible with their eyes constantly focused on all the bushes. The frozen ground was encrusted with a thin layer of snow, which crunched under foot. Animal prints were clearly visible in most places. There was evidence of deer, rabbits, foxes, and unfortunately wolves. The wolves had been closer than they thought, and these tracks were fresh. The only sound that they heard for a long way, though, was the canopy foliage swaying in the wind and the gentle crunch of snow and ice. They passed many deep pools of water, but they were covered in thick layers of ice. The ground was hard to walk on in places; it was riddled with roots. Many a time they followed in the tracks of wolves. They could only hope that they weren't walking into a trap. They tried to keep their path as straight as possible through the forest so they wouldn't get lost.

In the heart of the forest, it seemed like it was night. The trees grew so close together that the canopy blocked most of the light. It must have been into the afternoon now, and still, all things were quiet. It looked like their journey would pass safely. They stumbled on, knowing that they must be nearly on the other side; the light had started to creep back in, and the space between trees widened again. They were approaching the end. Hope was in their hearts, almost bringing smiles to their faces. But their situation had suddenly become very dangerous without them knowing. They heard a growling from behind a bush. Next they could see a pair of big, bright, yellow eyes staring at them out of the shadows. Before they knew it, five wolves had appeared before them, snarling, drawling, and hunched up ready to spring. Rowan felt his heart in his mouth, and the look on Warwick's face resembled that of someone who faced the hangman's noose. Rowan drew the sword he had taken from An Gearasdan, pointing it at each wolf in turn. "Back up very slowly. No sudden movements," Rowan whispered to Warwick. The wolves followed as they backed up, but the swishing blade seemed to keep them at bay. Not far through the bushes was a large, frozen pool. By accident they stumbled across it, and it seemed their only chance of escape. The wolves stopped at the edge of the ice, but Rowan and Warwick very carefully backed onto it, praying that the bitter cold meant that the ice was thick. As soon as they stepped onto the ice, though, it began cracking beneath them, and veins began shooting across the surface. They could feel it moving beneath their feet, and they stopped dead still, gently bending down to their hands and knees to spread their weight more. For a while, the wolves remained, snaking round the edge of the ice in hope of a big meal. The ice seemed to be holding out better now that Rowan and Warwick were on their hands and knees. Time seemed to slip past them. It could have been the middle of the night for all they knew. Only when they heard a large rustle of perhaps a deer close by did the wolves finally give up, charging off into the bushes after it. Rowan's and

Warwick's hearts pounded so much that Warwick threw up as they stepped off the ice. They both trembled and seem to have lost the use in their legs. But as soon as they could move again, they found some unknown strength and ran as fast as they could to the edge of the forest. They broke out of the trees, breathing heavily and in a lot of pain. Before them lay the shores of Loch Shubhairne, which stretched out toward the sea.

CHAPTER 11

DEEP WATERS

Loch Shubhairne was much longer than it was wide. They could well walk to the point it met the sea, but what would be the point without any means of crossing the water? Not a hint of civilisation could be seen anywhere. "We should not linger here into the night. The wolves might still catch our scent."

"What should we do?" Warwick turned to look back at the trees.

"We could go in search of some civilisation, but I think that could take days. Naturally, I would choose this option over staying here near these trees, however we cannot continue on foot for miles and miles without food. It won't be easy, but I think our best bet is to build a raft. There's plenty of wood, and I have a sword we can cut it down with."

They stood at the edge of the forest but were very fearful of entering it. The wood at its edge would be enough. Hopefully the falling trees would scare any predators away. Rowan made slash after slash after slash. Creating a notch took forever with a sword. Finally there was a loud crack, and the tree began to fall away from the other trees and away from them. Having just cut one down, Rowan doubted he had enough energy left to cut down another. The tree he had felled was big, however, so perhaps it would not be necessary to cut another down. The sword certainly wasn't as sharp now as it had been.

The branches were reasonably easy to cut off. Most weren't too thick, but they were thick enough, once bound together with young tender saplings, to make a raft. Instead of wasting the leaves, Warwick laid them across the raft for a bit of comfort. By the time he had finished, there was a thick layer. Rowan, meanwhile, had roughly split a few branches down the middle to make oars. Together they pushed the large raft into the shallow waters till it was almost floating. They climbed aboard with a feeling of relief, sat on the soft leaves, and pushed off hard from the bank with their oars. It was floating! It sat very low in the water with their weight aboard, though, and lapping water spilled over the edges, washing leaves away. Though this was a worry, they were definitely thankful that the knots were holding on such icy water. The temperature felt much colder and the wind much breezier on the water. They pulled their ragged clothing tight round them, but it made no difference. The bitter wind cut into them like daggers. Progress was slow with the makeshift oars and with how low the raft was sitting, but soon they could no longer see the forest behind them. They took it in turns to row at the helm whilst the other rested. They did so, however, on the condition that should something happen, the one at the helm would wake the other, not that they managed to get much sleep.

It didn't take long for their hands to become red-raw and blistered from using the rough oars. The much-needed rest Warwick had been dreaming of still didn't come. Rowan woke from his light slumber to see Warwick struggling to row any farther, so he joined him at the helm. "Rowan, we can't keep going on like this. I shall catch my death in this cold. There isn't a day that goes by when I don't ache in extreme pain. First it was my legs, and now it's my hands rubbed red-raw. It's a pity the key can't heal wounds or take the need for food away. At least then I would feel more positive." Warwick looked at Rowan with sorrowful eyes. He had grown very close to Rowan, seeing him as family. After everything that had happened, it was very hard for him to show any anger to Rowan. They had saved each other's lives several times. So when he spoke with doubt, Rowan just showed him sympathy with a small smile. Rowan's words about their friendship coming to an end had been weighing heavily on Warwick's mind for a few days now. He really didn't want Rowan to leave. He didn't want Rowan to know that, but he feared he might sense it with his foresight. As much as he didn't want to admit it, this was one of the reasons he wanted to stop, to forestall that cold fate.

Rowan agreed slightly reluctantly and turned the raft towards the shore to find a place to moor. Farther along the shore, close to the edge of sight, something stuck out from the land. From a distance it looked like perhaps a jetty, perhaps civilisation. They made for it, but it started to change shape the closer they got. Soon, long bits of wood could be seen coming out of its side, and things seemed to be hanging loosely from it. Then they realised what it was. It was the wreck of a merchant ship stranded on the shore. Still, they made for it, as there might be provisions still on board. It was quite big for a merchant ship, having two masts. It listed to the port side, revealing a green, slimy hull that was buckled, splintered, and peppered with big gaping holes. The decking was buckled and in pieces. The ship had clearly crashed at speed. On the ground round the boat were the remains of a camp. A patch of snow had melted clean away and was blackened from where a fire had been. Rowan put a hand to the ash. It was stone cold. "I think it must have been blown onto the rocks. By the looks of this fire pit, it only happened a few days ago. That would have been the day when we had the extreme winds that caused that avalanche. Come on, there might at least be some food on board."

The ceilings inside the hull were very low, and light flooded in through holes. It was hard to move about the ship with such a strong list. Using the walls to stabilise themselves was a bad idea, for the timber beams buckled and splintered. Warwick climbed down a very tight, almost vertical ladder to the very bottom of the hull. Half a dozen sealed barrels were still standing upright at the far end. As the barrels stood in shin-height water, things weren't looking good for their contents. Rowan came to join him to help search the barrels. They waded through the icy water, which bit at their ankles, but they found that the barrels were shut tight. There was no branding or anything else on the barrels to suggest what they contained. Rowan drew the sword and prised the lid off one barrel with immense difficulty, and in the process, the blade snapped. What looked like some ruined cloth was at the bottom.

Warwick went off and searched the cabins on the higher decks. In the captain's cabin, he found a couple of swords and warm clothing. When he shouted, Rowan came running, fearing that Warwick was in danger. Bursting into the room, he sighed with great relief. Warwick was sitting in a chair looking at a map. The map was of a faraway land to the west called America. He had never heard of the place before. The ship had sailed for a long time if it had come from there. Rowan looked at the map, worried. Why would a merchant ship have come so far? They expected they would never find out. By the looks of things, the sailors had been fairly thorough in removing anything of importance. Warwick stood up from his chair, passing the clothing to Rowan. It was sailor's clothing, but it was better than what they had. It consisted of heavy, black, woollen jackets, grey shirts, and heavy, black, woollen trousers. The clothing was a lot warmer than what they currently had. The shoes were black leather and definitely weren't designed for walking long distances but rather for climbing rigging. But before they put their new clothing on, they headed back down into the hull with their swords to search the rest of the barrels. Opening a few of the barrels revealed cotton. Others contained wine. Only one they could get to had food inside. There were a few salted fish at the bottom of the barrel. The fish looked past their best, but it would have to do. Rowan and Warwick each had a small leather pouch attached to his belts, so they filled them full of fish. They just managed to get the remains of the barrel into their pouches.

Back on the top deck, they sat down to eat a couple of fish. All the moisture had been sucked from the fish by the salt, and that was all they could taste. They grabbed a big handful of snow and ate that, feeling dehydrated from the fish. To take their mind off the almost inedible meal, they search the top deck. Strewn across the deck was broken decking, splintered and buckled; rigging and sails draped loosely across the deck from their broken masts. Warwick cut off a big section of rope to strengthen the raft. Soon after, Rowan disappeared into the hull of the ship again and brought back a couple of empty barrels, one at a time. He chucked them over the side into the water, and they floated well above water level. They bound them tightly to the raft. Then, before setting off, they went back to check the ship for any more food or clothing. Warwick took some of the sail to replace the leaves on the raft and a little more for extra warmth. Rowan scrabbled round the decks to the front of the ship. There was no more food or clothing, but he did find an oar. It was a bit long, awkward to use, and quite heavy. This was a small price to pay, though, compared to the oars they'd had before.

They laid the sail across the raft and climbed aboard. They pushed off hard from the bank, floating well above the water line. The retreating tide pulled them away from the shore. Rowan dug the oar in deep and was able to propel the raft much quicker without causing too much pain to the hands. While Rowan rowed, Warwick rested and finally got some sleep, now that he could feel some warmth. It was the first time he had slept properly since An Gearasdan.

Water began to splash over the decking as they got closer to the mouth of the loch. The raft rolled from side to side on the waves, waking Warwick abruptly. He immediately wished he hadn't woken. Closer to the mouth, where there was less shelter from the land, the winds were much stronger, and it felt a great deal colder too. It was almost impossible to row against the wind. They wrapped the sail round them as the icy spray fell on them like a monsoon. The sail kept the water off their clothes at least. The loch was growing very wide and deep. Their whole faith rested in a few knots in turbulent waters. Water this cold would be sure to kill them in a matter of a few minutes! The light was fading rapidly under such thick clouds. Soon it would be hard to navigate. There was only one thing for it: they had to find the north bank and follow it. There wasn't the light of a ship, of a lighthouse, or of any star or the moon. They steered the raft hard to the right, knowing the north bank was in that direction. This was the only way they could navigate. They tried to sail against the current, but it was dragging them sideways more than they were progressing forward. Both of them were pushing hard with the one oar, driving it deep as possible. They were exhausted, their hands red-raw and blistered once more. "How far do you think it is to Sgitheanach?" shouted Warwick so he would be heard.

"We are out of the narrows, I suspect, by the feel of the water. I think we should be sailing round the headland soon and on to the north part of our journey. I will have a better idea when we find the bank," shouted Rowan.

They pushed on hard. In this stormy water, it was impossible to keep dry. Faintly, like a smudge against the sky, the bank came into view. Close to the bank, the water settled down, and the wind blew less. It was well into the night when the bank began to turn north. But now it was so dark that it was a challenge to see a hand in front of your face. There was no option but to moor up and settle for the night. They brought the raft up onto the stony bank and huddled close together under a tree. The following morning revealed the damage caused to the raft. Several knots were dangerously loose, water was spurting out of a tiny hole in one of the barrels, and the rougher edges of the wood were splintered. They drained the flooded barrel, re-lashed the knots as tight as possible, and then launched from the bank. The waters were still choppy, and the wind conditions were no better, but at least they could see. Rowan kept the raft close to the bank, maintaining a slow and steady progress. Far across on the western shore was An t-Eilean Sgitheanach, its snow-capped mountains blending into the grey sky.

Close to shore, large outcrops of rock were starting to protrude more into the water. Left with no option, they sailed into deeper water. The current immediately started to pull against the raft. Together they pulled hard on the oar to keep moving forward, balancing carefully so the waves didn't roll them off the raft. On the horizon they could see the banks rapidly growing closer. Rowan smiled at the sight. "I know where we are, Warwick. The narrow flow ahead of us leads into Loch Aillse. There may even be a chance of smoother water, with the loch being much larger. Keep going. We can have a rest on the banks of Loch Aillse."

"Why can't we just go ashore on Sgitheanach here?"

"I am trying to save your legs, as there is still a good trek to the caves when we get to land. Come on, Warwick. We've come such a long way. Don't give up now."

Now past the rocky outcrop, they steered closer to the bank. Rowan took the oar for a while to give Warwick a break. Warwick sat cross legged on the raft with the key in the palm of his hand. He was worried. As he twisted and turned it, his thoughts were of the caves. What if there was nothing there? he thought. Where then would his journey lead? Where would he start? He knew the answer to his journey was locked inside the key, but how would he find that out when the key didn't work when you wanted it to?

Whilst Warwick was enveloped in the key, Rowan pushed on and was soon at the mouth of Loch Aillse. Sadly, the waters were no calmer, but now that they sailed west, the current wasn't dragging on the boat so much. They came ashore for a break, sitting down by a fire. Warwick dragged his hands through the dirt, feeling An t-Eilean Sgitheanach for the first time. Whilst they sat, a pod of dolphins was feeding in the middle of the loch, jumping well out of the water. They sat and watched for a while, enjoying the amazing sight, till they were toasty warm. Back on the water, they were soon near the mouth of An Lighe Rathairseach. An Lighe Rathairseach would prove to be the hardest part of their journey by water. It was the deepest part, extremely wide, and long too. The current funnelled round the small islands, seemingly hitting them in all directions. Rowan had his sights set on the larger of the small islands, Sgalpaigh, aiming for the small channel that ran between Sgitheanach and Sgalpaigh. Now together they pushed hard, as the light was waning. They reached the channel in almost complete darkness, and finally, Rowan steered the raft towards land. Warwick looked back at the raft with a sigh, from here it would be all on foot.

CHAPTER 12

The Sky Caves

Even though Warwick had had a chance to rest and allow his wounds to heal properly, he knew that walking on them again would soon bring the pain back. He really needed better shoes. These would not last long on the harsh ground. The worst of the journey was behind them, yet they still had a fair bit of climbing to do. They followed the course of an ancient road, which headed roughly in the right direction. At times, though, following the road seemed questionable. Warwick was heavily trusting Rowan, following his every move. Out this far, Rowan didn't expect to find any trouble, so they riskily followed it for a bit. Their pace was certainly quicker on the stone road. Roads often lead to civilisation, but after An Gearasdan, they couldn't face another city. Still, it looked like it had been long since anyone had travelled this road. It snaked its way through glens and traversed rivers. The terrain was growing ever steeper as the path climbed to plateaus on the mountainsides.

"Those mountains ahead of us, is that where the caves are?"

"Yes, Warwick."

"What's the matter?" Warwick couldn't help but notice that Rowan's reply sounded melancholy. He thought quietly to himself, looking towards the peaks and then back to Rowan. "Are those mountains where you came from?" Warwick guessed.

Rowan looked away, but Warwick knew the answer was yes. For the first time, Warwick felt he could be of help. Rowan sat down on a frozen rock, looking towards the mountains. Warwick approached and cautiously rested a hand on Rowan's shoulder. "It's alright to be sad, Rowan. There isn't a day when I don't miss my home and family. At first I didn't think I would cope, but then you came along. At first I was scared of you, however I now see you as a father."

Rowan turned to face him, and he was smiling. "Your kindness is a great gift, Warwick. I knew I was coming home, but actually seeing it ... I didn't realise it would hurt like this."

"Think of the happy memories."

Rowan turned to look at the mountains again with a smile. His voice sounded strong again, and he replied without even looking at Warwick. "I don't believe you had finished speaking. You need not say it, though. I know what you were thinking, because I thought the same."

Warwick knew exactly what he meant and just smiled.

They moved on steadily uphill towards the mountains, turning away from the road. It was very tiring walking in the soft, deep snow. The snow was much deeper here, banked up in great drifts by frequent storms. Warwick walked on what he thought was solid ground but soon found himself sunken up to his knees in snow. Rowan pulled him out with difficulty, falling over himself. Warwick was wet through and shivering. They had carried the sails from the raft with them. Rowan quickly ripped arm holes in one with his sword and wrapped it round Warwick tightly. They couldn't stop, Warwick especially. They had to keep moving. The peaks grew higher and higher as the foothills rose. The mountains all looked the same and impossible to climb. "How do you know where the entrance is in all this snow?"

"You are forgetting that these mountains are my home. If we can see Loch Snizort Beag to the east of us, then I will know we need to start to climb. The caves are very high up, and there is only one way to reach them. We must climb. It won't be easy. The caves all connect into one, but even I haven't been as deep into the caves as I think we might have to look. Whether we will find answers there I do not know, but I do have some little hope. I have been in many ancient caves, and most have had carvings on the walls. Those caves weren't half as old as these ones either. It is the best option I can think of to try."

The mountains loomed ever closer, towering over head, their peaks like razors. A strange, heavy energy hung in the air round the mountains. It was clear to Warwick that this wasn't a normal thing to feel. The wind completely died, and everything hung still as stone, as if a bubble encased the mountains. They reached the bottom of the cliff, and the loch was just in view to the east. Rowan took the lead up a narrow crag, turning his body almost sideways to squeeze between the sharp rocks. Warwick was close behind him, breathing heavily. He paid close attention to where Rowan put his feet and hands, shadowing his every move. Some of the ledges looked too far to reach, but somehow Rowan managed to grab them. Warwick seriously doubted he would make one particular ledge. He feared to look down. He could feel the weight of his body trying to pull him down. Reaching out nervously, his heart in his mouth, he slowly stretched for the ledge. Rowan was on his hands and knees guiding him. Warwick realised in the nick of time that it was just too far and pulled himself back. He closed his eyes and counted to ten. Then he threw himself into the air with his arms outstretched for the ledge. His hands missed. He was falling, desperately trying to grab hold of something. Rowan lunged right over the edge just in time to grab Warwick's wrist with an outstretched arm. The jolt nearly pulled Warwick's arm out of its socket, as well as almost breaking his wrist. "I've got you, Warwick. Keep your eyes on me. Now come on ... pull yourself up!" Rowan used most of his energy gripping Warwick so tight and pulling so hard, and he collapsed the moment he had pulled Warwick up.

They both lay on the narrow ledge, catching their breath. Warwick still felt like he was falling; his legs had turned to jelly. They were completely oblivious to how cold the ground was. As soon as Rowan caught his breath, he pulled Warwick to his feet. The light would soon be gone in the mountains. The caves were a short way above the cliff before them, riddling the mountain such that it looked like honeycomb. Unfortunately for Warwick, the hardest of the climbing was still to come. A treacherous overhang lay between them and the caves. Rowan climbed at Warwick's side, no more than half an arm's length away. Warwick was still in shock, and his body movement felt forced rather than natural. His fingers gripped the rock so tightly that blood was oozing from under his nails. But slowly, they proceeded up the cliff. They couldn't see the top, as the overhang blocked their view. Being this close to it made it look even more menacing. Warwick looked up at it, wondering how he was going to find the strength. The sharp crags were filled with ice, and good handholds were becoming scarce. They bashed their fists against the crags as hard as they could to dislodge the ice. They succeeded with the smaller crags, where the ice was thinner. They squeezed their hands into the crags against the sharp rock and pulled themselves higher. Even Rowan had vertigo at this point. Their feet were constantly trying to slip away; it felt like their full weight was hanging from their arms as they tried to pull themselves close to the overhanging wall. Rowan reached out for the ledge just above the overhang and pulled himself onto it. He could just see Warwick when he leaned back over to help him up the rest. His heart was in his mouth watching Warwick. He reached out a hand, and Warwick just managed to grasp it. Rowan pulled him up onto the ledge.

A small, dark cave entrance stood before them. It was so small that you wouldn't have believed it to be the entrance to a large cave system. For a while, they sat at the entrance, catching their breath. There was no way Warwick was going to scrabble and squeeze through a cave without having rested first. While resting, Warwick peered over the edge to see where they had just come from. He immediately wished he hadn't. "I can't believe we made that. I felt sure I would fall again. You surely can't have climbed that every time you left the caves?"

"No, I didn't climb that every time. But no matter which entrance you head for, you have to climb. The climb is what kept us safe here. Not many would attempt the climb. This cave entrance is the closest, which is why I brought you this way."

Warwick took the key from round his neck to look at it, as often he did. Rowan sat and looked at the key in Warwick's hand. He didn't say anything, which seemed odd to Warwick. Nor did he seem agitated.

"If there are answers here ... do you think the key might do something peculiar?"

"I hadn't thought of it," Rowan replied, "but it might do. We still know so little of it, so I can't really give you an answer. We shall soon see if there is any relation between this key and the caves."

"But if it does react, surely that would put us in great danger."

"That may be so. I have noticed, as I am sure you have, that it seems to react whenever you are in great danger. I think that is how it works. You said it glowed when the dragon attacked your home. Then at An Gearasdan, it glowed again, exactly like you had described before. To me, it seems like it's trying to protect you, maybe even guide you. If I am right, then I believe it will take you to where you need to go."

Warwick sat quietly in thought.

"Come on, Warwick. We should be moving on."

"How will we see inside the cave?" Till now Warwick hadn't thought about it.

Rowan looked round for a second and then drew his sword. He felt one of the sails and found that it was dry, so he ripped through the bottom of one and tore off a big strip. Just inside the cave were a lot of sharp, jagged rocks. Rowan neatly bundled the strip of sail on the ground by the rocks, and struck the blade of his sword against the rock. After a few attempts, the odd spark would leap from the blade with each strike, ebbing away quickly into the darkness. The more he struck, the more sparks showered, and a few started to hit the cloth. After a while, a wisp of smoke rose from the cloth, and with a little gentle blowing, it grew till flames spread across it. Rowan wrapped it quickly round the sword blade and held it at arm's length. "Come on." Rowan lay on his belly and reached inside the cave entrance with his free hand feeling for hand holds. Within seconds he had slid into the cave headfirst like a snake. Warwick was amazed at how easily he did it. There was no doubting now that he would fit. Laying on his front, he followed, gritting his teeth as he slid uncomfortably over sharp rocks. Even with the flicker of the light from Rowan's torch, he still couldn't see much from behind Rowan.

Soon the passage began to descend, and the walls and floor became smoother. Water trickled over the stone, which was covered in thick mud. With an effortless wiggle, his shoulders brushing the walls either side of him, Warwick slid forward, deep into the cave. The tunnel went on for a while before it levelled out at the entrance to a large cavern. Rowan was waiting for him by the entrance. Warwick looked ahead into the darkness to try to get a glimpse, but the darkness seemed almost to have a body. The light of the torch barely made a dent. It was by the echo of their feet that Warwick began to sense the cavern's true, gigantic scale. The constant sound of dripping on rock came from the ceiling. Rowan raised the sword above his head, and in the small light, they could see stalagmites and stalactites growing ever closer to each other in great numbers. "Not as bad as it looks, is it?" Rowan said to Warwick as they edged their way round the side of the cavern. Warwick looked on, mesmerised by the gleaming, crystal-white rock formations, like someone stepping forth into a new world.

The echoes started to dissipate more quickly, and in the faint light, a small passage appeared. It was tall but not very wide, like a vertical letterbox. Rowan held his hands high above his head, keeping the sword well away from his body, as he slid through the passage sideways. He deflated his lungs as the rock pressed firmly against him, and the passage started rapidly descending. The floor felt like ice; his feet were constantly trying to slip from underneath him. In the end, he slid down the passage on his side, Warwick close behind. They could hear the sound of water rushing over rocks not far away. At the end of the passage was a small drop into a fast-flowing river. They had enough light to be just able to see it. It seemed the only way down was to jump. Rowan went first, landing uncomfortably in the cold, clear water. The water was waist high, and the flow of it made it hard to balance. He stood at the bottom of the drop and caught Warwick when he jumped.

The river had cut deep into the rock, gouging a wide passage that you could fit several horses through. It looked as if the water had been much higher a long time ago. Their hands slid over polished rock above their heads as they steadied themselves against the current. The water seemed to be increasing in speed as it went round a bend a short way ahead. There a huge hole had appeared in the floor, carrying the water away into pitch blackness. They couldn't even hear the distant splash. Getting round it wasn't easy; the edges were thin and sat right up against the passage walls. Their toes protruded over the edge, and they had to jump the last few feet.

The tunnel narrowed, climbing gently towards what at first seemed a dead end. The light of the torch flashed across the far wall. At its foot was a small, black hole, the entrance of a passage that dropped down steeply under the great mass of rock where once water had run. Rowan knelt down to get a better look, shining the torch through it. The light didn't travel far enough; the rocks of the passage were illuminated in the faint glow. "Don't follow, Warwick. If I get through, I will shout up to you."

"I thought you knew all the caves and passages?"

"It's impossible to know them all. They run deeper than I dare to think. We did not explore this cave system so much, given how tight it is. We did not have the need. Anyway, our best chance to find what we are looking for is to explore the unknown places."

Before Warwick could reply, he was gone. Warwick sat fearful in the pitch dark, waiting to hear Rowan's voice. His voice didn't come as soon as Warwick would have liked. He began to think Rowan had fallen to his death or got stuck. If something had gone wrong, what would he do? He couldn't find his way back without light; even with light, it was doubtful he would remember the way. The time he sat there in the pressing darkness felt like hours, but in reality it was only a few minutes. Finally, a faint whisper echoed from a far off place, somewhere down the passage. Finding the entrance in the dark was enough of a challenge. He held his hands aloft in front, feeling round the wall. When his hands suddenly shot forward into a void, he knew he'd found it. He had no confidence. It felt like his heart was trying to burst out through his ribcage, yet he wriggled his way in with his hands glued to the walls on either side of him. As he descended down the polished passage, Rowan called to him. With every foot, Rowan's voice became louder, and eventually Warwick could see a faint glow of light, peeking through the darkness to dance on the walls. He could just start to make out a large rock in the tunnel. Somehow, he would have to rotate his body to squeeze past it. He put his hands round it, feeling for space. It was tight all round. He deflated his chest and sucked his stomach in, anchoring his hands round the rock as far as possible and pulling hard. The light rapidly grew as he tightly squeezed round it. On the other side, he could see Rowan on hands and knees, covered in mud and smiling at him. He pulled Warwick to his feet in the mouth of a large cavern. They were standing in what seemed to be a high-sided bowl. "Are you alright, Warwick?"

"That was terrifying in the complete darkness. I had no idea if I was following the right passage till I saw your light."

"I am sorry, Warwick, but I couldn't risk us both getting stuck." Rowan turned his attention to where they stood. All round them were steep banks. "This must have been a lake till the floor collapsed back there."

Warwick looked at himself in the light. He was encased in thick, coarse mud. Once he had wiped most of the mud off, he could see that his hands were covered in sores and red-raw. Rowan looked just as bad, and now the burning cloth was dying. Rowan cut more cloth from the sail and wrapped it round the sword. It was soon ablaze. They could distantly hear the sound of water again coming from the top of the bowl, but in the faint glow, it was impossible to tell where the echo emanated from. They wound their way through a boulder field, turning this way and that to cross the cavern. Steadily the sound of the water grew, and by the far wall they found a tunnel that dropped down in a vertical shaft. Not even the glow of the torch could pierce the darkness. The water they heard must have been down in the shaft, as the sound came clear as day out of it. Rowan grabbed a handful of small rocks from the side of the shaft and dropped them down it one at a time. A couple of seconds later, *splosh!* "Well, it seems to be quite a big drop, Warwick. Do you think there is any other way?"

There was none they could see in the light they had—well, at least none reachable. "I think we are going to have to go down this. Though once we do, we shan't have a light. I think there could be a lake down there."

"That's good thinking. Let's have a look." Rowan lit another piece of cloth and dropped it over the edge. They leant right over and watched the burning cloth plunge into the depths of the tunnel, illuminating the vertical, rough walls. Towards the bottom, the tunnel grew wider and wider. Then it must have opened up into a cavern, as the cloth only illuminated the air. Faintly, they saw a wide surface of water that looked very deep before the flames were doused on its surface. Warwick got up looking round and pushed the biggest boulder he could move over the edge. By the sound it made when it reached the bottom, it had clearly disappeared below the water's surface. "I am guessing we don't have enough sail to fashion a rope?"

"I doubt it, Warwick … but it was a good thought. I think we are going to have to jump!"

"How shall we know where the surface is? We won't have a light." Warwick felt sick.

Rowan tore off a large bit of sail and stuffed it down his clothing. "I will keep this under my clothing to try to keep it dry as possible. When we step from the edge, try to step into the middle and keep your arms in. We can do it together if you want."

Warwick trembled, and his skin was pale. The more he thought about it, the more he retched. The only way he was going to be able to do it was together. He nodded to Rowan. They stood sideways on the very edge face to face with their arms tight round each other. Warwick could feel Rowan's arms trembling as well as the heat from the sword close to his back. "One … two … three!" called Rowan. With their eyes screwed tight shut, they stepped far out into the void. Those few seconds that they plummeted, they felt weightless. It felt like they were falling to the centre of the earth. Then, the crushing weight of water swallowed them, flooding their nostrils and ears. Both of them opened their eyes, but it made no difference. They were deep under water. Kicking hard, still clinging to each other, they swam in the direction they thought was straight up. Their kicks became more frantic, and their eyes bulged. Then, just in time, they broke the surface, gasping deeply. There was a gentle current pushing them, but to where? They picked a route and swam following it, still holding one another. The expanse of water felt like a sea in the dark, but eventually they could feel rocks under foot. Before they knew it, they were on the shore.

They stood on the sharp, jagged rocks shaking, drenched head to toe in ice-cold water. Warwick refused to move and refused to let go of Rowan now that they had no light. When he couldn't even see his hand pressed against his face, he feared greatly that with any movement he would fall into the water and not find the bank. Not only this, but they were still both winded from jumping into such cold water from such a height. Rowan felt round for the neckline of his tunic and pulled out a sodden clump of torn sail. It was useless. They could feel nothing on any nearby wall that would burn—no moss, no roots. Rowan sat down with a thud on the rocks, finally defeated. Warwick only knew he had sat down because he felt Rowan slip from his grip and then heard the thud on the ground. So he sat down as well, hopefully at Rowan's side. "For the first time, Warwick, I don't know what to do. The longer we sit here, the colder we get. But we can't find our way without light."

"Give me the fabric." Warwick felt round in the darkness for the sodden clump, taking it from Rowan.

"What are you doing with that?"

"Trying to dry it out so we can get out of this place."

"How are you going to do that?"

"Somehow I will create friction, perhaps against a rock, and dry it that way." Sure enough, he hooked it tight round some dry rocks just in front of him and pulled it back and forth like a saw, though it wasn't long before he grew tired. Rowan then took over for a while. Several hours later, they were both completely exhausted, barely able to lift their arms. They could not feel the cold anymore, at least. But the material was still damp. In the darkness, all Rowan heard was a thud against the rocks.

"I know our situation is critical, but have faith, Warwick. The material is nearly dry enough to make fire."

Warwick slouched against the rocks. "Do you think there is any hope?"

"Hope for what, Warwick?"

"Hope for me to see this prophecy through?" He was surprised Rowan hadn't instantly made the connection.

"Hope is a friend and also an enemy. You shouldn't rely on hope. The time given to us will always be against us, but it's what you do with that time. The truth is in your heart. There is no better answer than what your heart can give you!"

"I am not sure I know what to believe anymore."

"Look, Warwick, I had pretty much given up until you took the sodden fabric from me. What you did was brilliant. More to the point, you kept me going. Don't give up now. We've faced much worse than this!"

Warwick turned at the sudden metallic screech of Rowan's sword being drawn. There was an echoing swish and then a much louder ring of steel echoing across the cavern. The faintest of glows appeared briefly before disappearing, followed by hundreds more. It took quite a while, and Rowan's hands hurt from the endless striking, but eventually a small part of the fabric began to smoulder. He blew on it gently, and it burst into flame. The sudden brightness was too much for their dilated eyes at first, and they shielded themselves with their hands. When finally they could see properly, Rowan wrapped the burning cloth round the sword, holding it aloft. They were in a huge, domed cavern filled mostly by the lake with just enough room round its edge to walk. There was no doubt about the depth of the water. It was super clear, and the rocky sides in a lot of places plunged straight down into the inky darkness of its depths beyond the light. High in the ceiling was the hole where they had jumped, and towards the edges of the cavern, there were a lot more tunnels and passages too high up to reach. A few of the passages they found that were reachable were too tight or didn't go anywhere. Deep under the water in the wall ahead of them, they could just see a big tunnel entrance, much wider than any of the other entrances. Was that their path? There was no way back up the sheer walls to where they had just come from. They were lost, even though Rowan refused to admit it. The only way forward didn't look possible. How long would they have to hold their breath to make it through? What if they got halfway through and found that it collapsed or that it flowed like this till it exited the mountain? How would they see? Rowan sighed and handed the sword to Warwick.

"What are you doing? You can't be serious." Warwick looked at Rowan, his eyes and mouth gaping.

Giving Warwick a pat on the shoulder, Rowan dived into the depths. Warwick watched as he grew smaller and smaller and then disappeared into the tunnel. Warwick didn't know if he should follow. What if he got stuck? The tension was unbearable. He sat down and watched the entrance of the tunnel without blinking, nervously curling his toes under his feet. Eventually he caught a glimpse of movement from the tunnel. He peered over at the water's edge on hands and knees to get a better look. Sure enough, it was Rowan, kicking and clawing frantically for the surface. He broke the surface with great speed, gasping heavily and struggling to where Warwick was. Warwick grabbed him by the arm as he got close enough, pulling him up on to the bank. Rowan couldn't speak. He was frozen to the core, looking petrified. Warwick held the flame close to him to try to warm him up. As his breathing returned to normal, Rowan managed to splutter a few words. "It comes out ... not too far ... if you get as much air into your lungs, it is just possible."

Warwick hadn't told him he was terrified, but it seemed that Rowan could sense his worries because he put an arm round him. "You can do this. I won't leave your side."

Holding onto Warwick, he led the way back into the water, keeping the torch above the surface. They swam as close to the far wall as possible to make it as easy as they could, then they dived, extinguishing the flame. Unable to see, Rowan worked his way to the tunnel entrance from memory and using his other senses. This was really the first time that his foresight had helped them, as he was able to guide them to the tunnel with his mind's eye. Their hands were like octopus tentacles clinging to the walls of the tunnel as they swam through. Then the tunnel swiftly started to rise before them, and they soon burst out of the water. They swam to the edge and rolled out, spluttering and coughing and shaking once more. The wet rag that had once been their torch flopped off the blade in a sodden heap. Warwick started once more to rub it against rocks he found in the darkness but shortly gave up. He drew his sword and lobbed it in anger. Rowan heard him draw the sword and heard the whoosh as it sailed through the air. But before he could lose his temper, he heard the impact. There wasn't a splosh of water or a clang of rock but, surprisingly, the ringing of metal on metal. Their anger immediately dissipated, and they began crawling in the direction from which the sound had emanated. What felt a hundred feet away, Rowan found the sword on the ground to the left of the metal object. Its sides were smooth and curved, both vertically and horizontally, the width growing as the sides reached a flat top. Could it be a cauldron? Feeling for the rim, Rowan pulled himself to his feet. Something was wet, and greasy to the touch inside the cauldron. It smelled heavily of rotten fish. Rowan smiled, knowing what it was. He lifted his sword and struck it against the cauldron, showering sparks in all directions. The oil burst immediately into flames almost burning him. Warwick jumped back as the flames roared up. The cauldron contained whale oil.

The cavern rose high to a splendid, glittering ceiling of stalactites falling like icicles hanging from a branch of a tree. A steady drip of water dropped from each to meet stalagmites slowly growing to meet their partners up above. The cavern was clearly very old based on the amount of stalactites and stalagmites there were. Some had grown so big that they were as fat as oak trees. The whole cavern shone like a crystal palace. At the back of the cavern, it looked like a big rock had been pushed in front of another tunnel. It seemed to have been there for many years without being moved. It was clear that the people who had been here did not want to be found easily, but why? The walls curved round to the right at the back to reveal what Rowan had hoped they would find. Straight away, Rowan knew the cave paintings were much older than the others he had seen. At some point they must have been vividly coloured, but time had taken its toll. Now that he and Warwick were here, they were in no hurry to leave, and before even trying to read the paintings, they stood round the cauldron as close as they could get without burning themselves till they were dry. They then moved back to the wall and took a proper look. The style was very simplistic, but the paintings seemed to depict a battle that took place a long time ago. Warwick let out a faint gasp at the sight and reached his hands towards the walls to feel the markings. Up close, the paintings were hard to read, so Rowan stood back against the opposite wall. He was shocked by what he saw, even though some bits had worn away too much and were impossible to see. Warwick went and joined him upon seeing Rowan's shocked face. "It depicts a huge battle, Warwick." He scanned the full length of the wall. "It seems they were fighting what looks like dragons, and many of them." He pointed to the bottom left at an army—painted very small—that was looking at a tall figure standing above them with his foot on a fallen dragon and his sword lodged in its head. "That must be their leader." They could faintly see that the ground was red and littered with the bodies of the leader's company. "It looks like the battle goes ill quickly." The next scene showed an army scattered with shields above their heads and broken arrows raining back down; above, seven dragons were raining down fire. At points, it all seemed a blur of colours merging into one another. "It's hard to tell what happens here, but from what I can tell, it looks like there was a final charge at the dragons, and the dragons seemingly fell."

"Does it not show how they fell?"

"Perhaps it did once, but sadly I can't see anything now."

Rowan hesitated for a second when out of the corner of his eye he caught a glimpse of some small lettering, which was carved below a painting of a hooded figure forging something above his head. It looked like the key! Something thick and black was seeping into it, filling the hole in the centre of the key. Warwick followed the trail of the substance, which led to a dragon. Something was being drawn out of the dragon and poured into the key as it was being made. Rowan turned his attention to the lettering below, getting as close as he could and squinting his eyes to try to read it. "The wording has worn away in places, but I think it says in the Latin tongue, 'Qui tenet velum Foekey sacro responsis invenietis'. If I am right, it translates to 'the one who holds the Foekey shall find his answers at the sacred vale'."

Warwick was hit hard by the words. It was like the thud a rock makes when it hits the bottom of an empty well. He still had no idea in which direction to travel or what he was looking for. How would he know when he found it? He paced back and forth in front of the wall with his arms folded muttering under his breath, "What is the sacred vale?" In some respects, he felt more confused now than he had before.

"I think you should worry more about where it is," said Rowan solemnly, bringing Warwick's pacing to a halt. He had searched the chamber head to toe for more answers, but it would seem that this was all of it.

"Well, obviously I need to think about that, but if it is secret, how will I ever learn where it is?" He chucked a rock at a wall, and it smashed into small pieces. Rowan was now smiling at him. "What?" Warwick said in a tone he had not intended.

"Don't you see? The paintings give us clues about the prophecy. It clearly shows a battle fought long ago against the dragons. A dragon fell, and its soul was poured into the key at the time of its forging. They managed to kill a dragon with a sword; perhaps this is what you must find."

No matter how hard Warwick looked, he did not see it. Some parts of him told him he didn't want to know the truth, but then there was the other side of him pushing him forward. He was in shock for a while. His head, once teeming with thoughts, now felt empty, as if a plug had been pulled and his thoughts had all drained away into never-ending darkness. Several minutes passed in complete silence before he managed to muster his voice. "Surely it can't be me. How am I supposed to slay the bloody dragons? I have barely lifted a blade, and they expect me to kill dragons!" Warwick's anger was only growing.

"I am sorry, but it is certain that it involves you, Warwick. But nowhere does it say that you are prophesied to kill the dragons!" Rowan paused for a moment. "Look at me, Warwick. You've grown so much since we first met. I am sorry I can't relieve you of this terrible burden. I know how hard this must be for you and know how scared you must feel, but that's alright. The greatest warriors would be scared of this. There is no shame."

Tears rolled over Warwick's cheeks, and Rowan rested a hand on his shoulder, looking into his eyes. Warwick spluttered a few words amongst his tears. "Do you think there's hope?"

"You have faced so many challenges so far—challenges a lot of men wouldn't have overcome. So there is always hope. You're stronger than you realise! I can't give you any more comfort than that. A power lingers over the land, and it is far greater than my powers. I am blind to your path. I cannot help you this time."

"I can't do this! Without you, I would already be dead!"

"You must trust in your heart to find the way. If you don't, you will lose yourself." Rowan's last words hung in the air like heavy storm clouds. Warwick slumped off and warmed himself by the fire, deep in thought. Rowan continued to study the paintings, even though he knew there was nothing left to find. Really his goal was just to give Warwick time alone.

Warwick was silently crying. Tears rolled off his cheeks in a continuous drip. His heart was heavy with grief knowing that this was the last night he would have company. His thoughts were strongly with his parents as he tried to think of happy memories. Although the memories brought a brief happiness, it would not overrule the worry and sickening feeling.

That night, they slept huddled round the cauldron. By the morning they were cold; the fire had burned almost all the oil up and flickered now at the bottom of the giant cauldron on the last couple of litres. They looked hesitantly at the water, wondering if they should pass back that way, but then they shortly remembered the impossible climb in the cavern at the other end. Rowan walked over to the boulder at the other side of the cavern they were in and felt all round it. A cold breeze blew across his hands from the edge of the rock. "Warwick, come and help me move this. I think there's a tunnel behind it, one that the seers used." They pushed and pulled as hard as they could till, eventually, it rolled out the way. A gust of fresh air rushed in, roughing their hair.

The now dim light from the cauldron was just strong enough for them to map the edges of the wide tunnel. Without hesitation, they walked into the darkness, following the passage with their hands on the walls. However, as they grew accustomed to the darkness, they realised they could faintly see their hands. The light was growing quickly, and round the next corner, they were blinded by the light of the exit. It was great relief to see the open air. They had no idea just how much they had missed the natural light till they stood in it. The air inside the cave had begun to feel claustrophobic.

Leading away from the mouth of the cave was a clear, man-made path. It was showing signs of its age, as the sides had eroded away in a lot of places. They progressed quite quickly on the path, as it rapidly descended into a tight gorge. The walls were high round them and seemed as if they were trying to close in on them. Rowan felt dizzy; he could sense an ancient power lingering over the gorge. Something was trying to push him into the ground. However, Warwick didn't feel anything, and he walked on normally, unaware of Rowan's struggle. The key must have been protecting Warwick. Rowan had just enough power to fight it and continue forward. The other side of the pass opened up onto a huge, flat shelf of rock: Rowan instantly thought this would act as a good observatory, as it looked over the great, flat lands between the mountains. From here they could see for miles, and in summer, they would be able to see even farther.

CHAPTER 13

†INAL †AREWELL

The path, in most places, was quite sheltered from the snow and ice. Rowan was becoming quite irritated; for years he and the other seers had lived up in these mountains and yet had not found this path. It all seemed very odd. How could he have not seen it before? Eventually, after many miles of snaking between the mountains, the path opened up onto the valley floor. However, the exit was blocked by trees, bushes, and brambles so tightly wound together like snakes that no light could be seen through them. The only way through was to crawl and fight past the snagging brambles. Once they were clear of the trees, Rowan turned to look back up the path, but to his shock, he couldn't see anything. It was like the mountains had swallowed the path. Now he understood why he had never found it before; it wasn't meant to be found.

They walked away together from the hidden path. Things had changed between them; Warwick couldn't hide it this time. Soon Rowan's pace slowed to a halt. Warwick carried on walking, however, even though he had heard him stop; he didn't want to stop and look at Rowan.

"It's time."

Warwick had never heard sympathy like this in Rowan's voice. The lump rapidly growing in Warwick's throat felt like lead, and it pulled him back like reins on a horse.

"We have come so far together, but now the time has come to go our separate ways. If I could, I would journey with you to the ends of the world." Rowan paused with a sigh. "It is now time for you to follow your path, to whatever end. I will always be helping from a distance, as much as I can."

Tears swam in Warwick's eyes. "I still don't understand why you can't journey with me."

Rowan sighed, closing his eyes as a tear leaked down his face. "When a prophecy is written, it is written for only those who are chosen. You were chosen to hold the Foekey. That is why I can't come with you. It was written for you alone, and if there is going to be any hope of fulfilling it, you must do it alone. I am sorry things have to be this way."

Warwick hung his head and wept. Rowan put both his hands on Warwick's shoulders and looked into his eyes. "The times ahead are going to be hard. You must stay true to your path. You've already come too far to give up. You are ready for this!" Rowan pulled Warwick into a tight, fatherly hug. Warwick could feel moisture on his shoulder and knew Rowan was crying as well. Amongst the tears, Rowan spluttered "good luck" and then released Warwick. Warwick turned slowly without a single smile and began to walk away. He could feel Rowan's gaze on the back of his head, so he walked as fast as he could. At the end of the valley, he took one final look back up the way he had come and saw that Rowan was still standing in the same spot. Warwick raised his hand high above his head and waved goodbye for the last time. With a deep breath of fresh morning air, he turned and began his journey.

He really had no idea where to start as he journeyed onwards and out of the valley. For miles his thoughts were still with Rowan, and right now he was walking with no heading. He needed a plan. The paintings showed an army, but where had the army come from? Was there still any place old enough in the world to date back to the battle? But then he remembered his father talking about his service to the king at Cill Chuimein. He knew that the lineage of the throne went back a long way; there must have been a king on the throne at the time. So it was decided. He would head for Cill Chuimein. The only problem now was that he did not know where it was. His father had never mentioned its location.

He was all alone in the snow, and suddenly it seemed much harder to keep moving. There was a slight relief as the sky was clear and he could see the sun climbing over the far horizon. The path they had taken to the cave lay on the other side of the range; the chances of finding it were small. If he kept on heading east, he knew he would eventually find the shore and perhaps civilisation. More than ever, he needed warmer clothing, as well as food supplies. The soft snow blended with the harder snow. It often took Warwick by surprise, and he would find himself all of sudden waist deep.

The shore soon appeared as a smudge on the horizon. Until he had seen the shore, he hadn't realised how far north from the raft he was—to far to reach it. Besides, he wouldn't be able to cope with the feeling of guilt if were to take it and leave Rowan stranded. He wondered if Rowan was already heading that way. When he reached the water, there were hardly any trees to build a raft, and as far as he could see, there wasn't a trace of a fisherman or port. He sat on a rock thinking, if only he had wings like a dragon. Then he remembered the dragon's soul inside the Foekey. He took the key from round his neck, and it sat like any other key in the palm of his hand. Really, he knew it was very silly to think the key would give him some power of flight, so he put it away. He walked on for several miles, following the shoreline to the north in the hope of finding a port. Thankfully, the snow wasn't so deep by the shore. If this land was populated, it wasn't populated by many. The only trace of civilisation had been that road too far to the south, and it headed in the wrong direction with no guarantee of finding anyone at the end. Warwick sat once more on a rock after a while of walking north. *If I had a fishing rod, I would at least be able to catch something*, he thought to himself. A brief moment of worry subdued his mind. *What happens if a dragon comes while I am sitting here?* He shook that out of his mind. Anyway, the dragons had seemed to be drawn to the more populated areas.

He had sat there for too long in his wet clothing. All his dried fish was gone, and he was starving. The only relief the snow provided was that he always had an endless supply of clean water to drink, even if it numbed his teeth at the touch. He walked on, slipping from time to time, till he found a few young pine trees. Within the hour, the trees were felled and lashed together with young saplings, and a raft was ready on the shoreline. A thick branch was all he had for an oar, but once he had stuffed some of the foliage inside his clothing for a sliver of warmth, he kicked off from the bank. The raft sat low, and rolling water frequently lapped over its surface. His stuffed clothing was doing nothing to keep him warm as the icy water splashed him.

An island lay in the way of his path to the mainland, and as he was closer to the northern point of it he sailed north fighting against the current. Soon he could see that the island was in fact two islands. A small channel ran between them, which would be no problem for his raft. However, he was rapidly tiring, and the closer he got to the northern point, the stronger the current felt. The water funnelled from a large source into two channels on either side of the island, compressing it. He kept paddling until he was in the sheltered, calmer waters of the narrow channel and then brought his raft ashore, unable to go any farther. He warmed himself by a fire and rested, trying to forget his hunger. Once he was warm enough, he launched himself hard into the water, his eyes fixed on the far bank as it crept closer. The raft rolled and drifted once more, but eventually the bottom grated on land. He climbed onto the bank, dragging the raft with him. He was frozen and exhausted, and darkness was approaching fast. He tilted the raft against some large rocks and crawled into the space underneath, building a fire just outside the entrance.

That night, he slept silently and untroubled. His sword was at his side and his key round his neck as normal. He kept the key even closer now that he knew the nature of the connection between it and the dragons. It made sense now why Rowan was so scared of it; he must have been able to sense the connection, even if he did not realise it. The constant worry was starting to make him feel sick, but then he remembered Rowan's last words telling him to keep going, that he was ready. The comfort of the words was enough to get him moving.

The day was young, and the rising sun cast pools of light across the water, breaking on every wave. The only sound he could hear was the gentle lapping of the water on the banks. He hoped to catch something to eat; his stomach felt like it was being tied in a knot. He still had no idea how to hunt, but at least had something to hunt with. He figured he should try to move unseen as quickly and quietly as possible. He remembered the forests, filled with the sounds of animals. This strategy would have been useful if there were any forests nearby. Whatever he thought of was no good. The rivers were abundant with fish, yet with only a sword and without rod or net, catching any seemed near impossible.

While he had been thinking, he had stumbled blindly upon a rutted road that seemed like it was leading to a farm. Someone had been this way not that long ago, too; the footprints revealed the dirt below. He smiled and followed in the direction of the tracks. At the side of the road, tall pine trees grew; their tops bowed with the weight of the snow. Occasionally, the odd bird took to the skies as he passed close. There was no way he was going to catch one. At least, if nothing else, the trees acted as a windbreak for a short while. The tracks were going on for miles. It must have been more than a road to a farm, more like an ancient road to a settlement. Even if it was ancient, people still came this way. Warwick's pace steadily quickened as he tried to catch up with whomever had made the tracks. The road turned a sharp corner, and before him, a gate barred his way. It was an unmanned gate and was only latched by a small hook going through a ring on the gate post. He unlatched it and passed through without further thought. The tracks were still leading this way. Before he knew it, the trees fell away, and before him stood a small village. His heart was filled with joy as he imagined hot, roasted meats and fish and as much mead as his belly could hold. However, his longing didn't last long. The people he saw walking about the village looked famished and tired themselves. Every eye was on him as he passed by. No sooner had he arrived than he wanted to leave. There was an inn on the far side of the village. Perhaps they had some food. He entered into the village inn, but tattered sheets covered the floor all round the central fire pit. They seemed to be beds. Something smelt bad, and he hoped he wouldn't find out what it was. On the far side of the fire, he noticed a couple of bodies. At a closer look, he almost froze to the spot—they were badly burned and not far from death. He trembled, fearing it was the result of a dragon attack. From a side room, a barmaid approached with a bucket of hot water and a tatty, blood-stained cloth. "Can I help you?" she asked.

Warwick was still in shock and didn't hear her the first time.

"If you're looking for a bed or food, then you're out of luck, my friend."

"Errr … no … sorry. Where am I?" He could not look away from the bodies as he spoke. He prayed to himself that his journey would not leave him looking like that.

"This is the village of Talladale." She sounded a bit taken aback and looked at him curiously. "You look awful young and pale. Have you travelled far?" She put the bucket down and put a hand to his cheek. Warwick was uncomfortable with her sudden move to touch him and backed away, slightly blushing. Her hand dropped slowly back to her side, but her face maintained the look of curiosity.

"I am fine," he lied. For a moment he stood in silence. "Could you tell me how to get to Cill Chuimein?"

She had a slight worried look now. "I hope you haven't travelled from An Gearasdan looking for Cill Chuimein! If you have, you have travelled completely in the wrong direction. Cill Chuimein is to the east of An Gearasdan." She sighed, looking round. "I hope you were not at An Gearasdan when the attack happened. If you were, you have been fortunate! All these here are from An Gearasdan. I can't believe it was a dragon! I grew up on stories of dragons, but I never thought for a second they were real!" She looked round again and then suddenly snapped back to Warwick. "What is your name?" she asked, looking curious.

Warwick stood a bit taken back for a while. "My name is Warwick." He nearly slipped and told her his reason for being here, but then he changed his words to ask why she wanted to know his name.

"I ask because, strangely, two armed guards marched through here with a message. They were looking for two people. Someone called Rowan and the other Warwick. They didn't stay. Is it you they look for?" She sounded quite worried.

Warwick looked puzzled. Why would guards be looking for him? Keeping calm, he thought it would be best to lie. "No, I don't think so. I don't know anyone called Rowan?" Gathering himself together, he thanked her and left. It was still early, and he wanted to make a good start south. He was thinking he would have to go back to An Gearasdan, the one place he had hoped not to see again.

The road he had followed into the village carried on east and eventually turned north. He turned from the road, using the sun as a compass to take him south. Soon as he turned off the road, he plunged into deep snow; some parts felt so deep and soft that he was sure he would sink under the snow. He had grown use to the feeling of the snow after having walked through it for so long, but the desire for dry ground still hung strongly in the back of his mind.

Mountains loomed round him once again; he was starting to grow sick of them. All they had done was slow him and Rowan down, making them change their path. His wish to have a map, or just to have knowledge of the land, was growing stronger by the hour. He had not even a remote idea of how close or far he was from An Gearasdan. His only hope was to find the path they had taken previously. Soon he met a wide stream covered with a thin layer of ice. He had no option but to wade across. A fallen branch lay close by. Using his sword, he stripped the smaller branches off. He then used the branch as a walking stick to help him across the water. As soon as he touched the ice with the branch, it fractured and floated on the current. Then he stepped into the water, and it instantly stole the breath from his body. He felt his way amongst the slippery rocks with the stick. When he came out, he couldn't feel his feet or ankles. Instead, all he could feel was a mighty, stabbing pain. He was wet through up to his shins; the thought of carrying on in more snow was worrying. As much as he wanted to build a fire, he couldn't. First, there was not enough wood, and second, he couldn't just keep stopping. Another dragon attack like at An Gearasdan would destroy the kingdom.

CHAPTER 14

The Journey South

It had been two days since he'd passed through Talladale. He had journeyed high into the mountains, traversing many steep slopes, in hope of finding a better view south from the mountain peaks, but most of the time, the clouds sat on the mountain tops. He resorted to walking round the foot of the mountains, snaking through the glens. The sun peeking through the cloud gave him his bearings. His hunting had been unsuccessful; there was hardly an animal or animal track to be seen. It was beginning to have a bad effect on his pace and the distance he was able to cover each day. The most food he found was a few berries clinging to a bush half-buried by snow. He had no idea if they were edible, but still, he ate them. They were unbearably sour, but they didn't seem to cause him harm. At rivers, he jabbed his sword through the ice like a spear trying to catch a fish. The odd fish he did see was too quick for his reflexes. Whenever he rested, he practised his sword swings against rocks, even though he knew this was not going to be any use if he came into real combat.

It was the fourth day of heading south, and still everything seemed unfamiliar. He had changed his route to veer slightly towards trees in the hope of finding something good to eat. His pace now had become barely a drag. There was a small group of trees growing along a small valley floor. As he entered the canopy, he was almost immediately shrouded in darkness. He could move quicker in the forest; the dense canopy kept the ground clear of snow. There was no sign of animal tracks even here, but his determination would not falter. He cast every thought out of his head so he could think clearly about how his father would have caught something. After half an hour of keeping quiet, he finally heard a rustle of something in the bushes. He gripped his sword so tightly that his knuckles were white. As low as possible, he moved in the direction of the rustling bushes. Inches away, he could just make out the body of a wolf. There was no sign of any other. Holding the sword aloft with the point aimed between the wolf's eyes, he trembled. With every little movement he made, the wolf growled and snarled. Its yellow eyes were fixed on Warwick as it crept towards him. Warwick began to back away. His whole face was pale and sweaty. He stepped on a stick, making a loud crack. He was frozen to the spot, his heart pounding and his body quivering all over, as the wolf leapt at him. He swung the sword at the air with his eyes closed and felt a huge, heavy jolt bowl him over. He lay on his back, waiting for the pain of teeth sinking into his neck, but it never came. Opening his eyes slowly, he saw a bloody wolf lying lifeless on top of him with his sword firmly through its stomach. At first he wondered if this were all a dream; he couldn't believe he had finally managed to kill something. He wished his father could see him now. Pushing the wolf off of him, he got up and yanked his sword out with a short squirt of blood. The blade was stained red. The smell coming from the guts was horrid. He decided he had walked far enough today, and it was late too. After dragging the carcass to the edge of the forest, he set to work gutting it. The blood ran all over his hands and the snow. Once the insides were cleaned with snow, he put the wolf on a spit made from a fallen branch. He built a fire and placed the spit over it. Provided that he didn't eat too much, he would have enough meat to make it to Cill Chuimein. The happiness he felt from the warmth and the prospect of a hearty meal outweighed his worry about the dragons. He wished more than anything that Rowan were there to enjoy the feast. The smell that met his nose made his mouth water; he longed so much to try the sweet meat. It was pitch black by the time it was cooked. He sliced off the meat with his sword. It tasted strong and smoky and was really tender; it was as good as it smelt. He managed to eat a couple of big slices before he felt full. Weariness was soon on him, and he fell fast asleep, feeling full.

The embers from the fire were still glowing in the morning. He took the wolf off the spit. The freezing-cold air would preserve it nicely, but he couldn't think of a way to carry it. He couldn't drag it, as the meat would be inedible, nor did he want to have to leave it here. He still had his piece of sail that Rowan had put arm holes in. He would feel colder if he took it off, but it would act as a great sling. The carcass would not fit in whole, so Warwick cut off its legs. It didn't feel quite as bulky cut up smaller and was easier to carry over his shoulder. He hoped today that he might make it to somewhere that was familiar. He had been thinking that he must be getting close, yet with every ridge he climbed over, he never saw anything familiar. Everywhere was starting to blend into one vast expanse. He had no idea how far the twisting glens were setting him off course. He prayed that he might just see the waters of Loch Shubhairne from the top of each ridge sparkling in the sunlight, but every new ridge just revealed more mountains and a maze of glens. It was hard to see which ones led south, as none were straight. To glide like an eagle over them was desirable. His thoughts were strongly with Rowan all the way.

Carrying the wolf started to tire his shoulders, but he did not let this slow his pace any more than the snow already did. That morning, he pushed on deep into the maze of valleys. He felt sure he was lost, but whenever he sighted a glimpse of the sun between the gaps in the mountains and clouds, it was always to the east. He had found that one valley often led into many, and it seemed an impossible task to choose between them. It wasn't till he had taken one and come to a dead end that he accepted that he was lost. He was probably miles off course, and thick clouds now sat across the sun. The options that lay ahead were few: either go back and find another path or climb out of the valleys and try to locate the mountain path. He chose the second of his options. The sides of the valley were very steep and slippery. He tried to get a hand to a rock to hold on to, but most of the time there weren't any suitable. The only way he could stay up was by leaning into the mountain. With every step, his feet slid back, nearly causing him to fall face first.

His shoes were heavily worn to the point of holes. He might just as well have climbed barefooted with how wet and cold his feet were. If anything, the shoes were slowing him down with their slippery soles. Soon, the slopes grew even steeper, forcing Warwick to climb diagonally. His left leg throbbed as he placed most of his weight on it to keep him balanced. He walked like this for an hour before finally the ridge peaked. Standing on the top, he could see clearly all round for the first time in days. That revealed that he was too far to the east of the sea and the original path. Then he looked back and could see the extent of the maze of valleys he was lost in. In front, the valleys looked fewer in number and easier. It seemed he had managed to cover the worst of it that morning, even if he did feel lost. All he could do was carry on south with absolutely no idea of how far it was.

By the time the sun had set, he had covered many miles and was chilled to the bone and exhausted. He collapsed into a small crevice in the cliff face after lighting a fire at its entrance; being in the middle of nowhere and as cold as he was, he didn't care about the risk of a fire. He sat as close as he could without burning himself, drying out and massaging his feet. Blood had seeped from blisters and congealed in great sticky patches all over them, and all sense of feeling in his toes had been lost. The smell that came from them made him feel sick, so he put his shoes back on once they were dry. Eating his fill and warming his insides with rich meat once again felt good. He was just beginning to doze when he heard the crunch of a footstep in the snow. It sounded close! His heart rate increased, his hand gripped the hilt of his sword tightly, and he stared unblinking into the darkness at the edge of the light from the fire. He got to his feet and moved a little closer for a better look. Coming towards him was a fully cloaked figure in black. For an instant, he thought it might be Rowan, but in the back of his mind, he knew that that was just wishful thinking. The person did not seem to be bothered by his gaze and came ever closer. "Who's there?" Warwick could hear his heartbeat in his ears. *Maybe the key will protect me*, he thought, grasping it tightly in his other hand.

The figure slowed to a stop right before him. "What would someone so young be doing out in the wilds at this time of year?"

Warwick kept his sword aloft and, avoiding the question, replied, "I might ask you the same! Who are you?"

The man's hood was pulled so far down that Warwick could hardly see his face glowing in the fire light. He did not seem to be bothered by the point of the sword or Warwick's tone of voice. "I am Robert, messenger to King Angus." Finally he lifted his hood and flicked his cloak to the side, revealing the stag-and-hunter crest of Cill Chuimein on his breast.

Warwick was not so nervous now that he could see the man's face and lowered his sword. Robert was a young lad, not much older than himself. He had a small moustache and beard. He looked very clean and well dressed in his fine silks of green, but he had to if he was the king's messenger. His hair was cut short and was black as coal. His brilliant green eyes shone like emeralds. "May I join you for some food and warmth? I am parched, having trekked far. I would give an arm and leg for a bite of that meat."

"Yes, come and sit down." Warwick sat down and put the sword away.

Robert smiled and came to join him in the small crevice. "Thank you, sir," he spluttered, shivering to the core. "May I know your name?"

Warwick thought for a moment, pondering whether it was safe to give his name, but then he decided it was. "My name is Warwick."

Robert stared curiously at him for a brief moment before turning his attention back to the wolf carcass warming at the side of the fire. "You must be a bloody good hunter to have caught that wolf. It's not something I would ever have attempted."

Warwick felt a sense of smugness and warmth inside as he sliced off a large piece of meat and handed it to him. Then he took a bite himself. "So why are you out here all on your own in this weather?" asked Robert.

Warwick still felt uncertain about telling the truth; his mind was firing faster than a flying arrow. "I am travelling to Cill Chuimein to see my family, but I have lost my way," he said, rapidly creating a story. It seemed Robert believed it without even a second glance. A sudden thought hit Warwick: Robert came from Cill Chuimein. "If you don't mind my saying, which way are you headed?"

"I am headed north to Inverchoran on the orders of the king. I cannot say more than that."

"Could you point me in the direction of Cill Chuimein?"

Robert smiled. "Head southeast. It will cut several days off your journey and will be easier going. If I am right, you are under the slopes of Carn Eige. The path will be a lot flatter very soon. All you need to do is keep going till you see the vast waters of Loch Nis, and then you will see Cill Chuimein." He pointed in the direction to head as he said this.

By morning, Warwick's food supply had diminished quite a bit—they had eaten more than he had intended—but what he had left looked like it would be just enough, luckily. If anything, he was thankful for the reduced weight, as he could travel slightly farther and faster.

Robert had gone but had left Warwick his black cloak. Warwick put it on and could instantly feel warmth from the thick and heavy material. He didn't mind the weight, as the soft, silk lining was really comfortable hugging his body. Robert was taller than Warwick, so the cloak trailed in the snow. He climbed a bit of the mountain till he was high enough to see his new direction and to behold the land, which was indeed much flatter a short way ahead. After climbing down the mountain on the east side, he began to work his way through the last couple of short valleys. The valleys descended rapidly as he walked. He could almost feel the land becoming flatter. The snow would still be deep at the bottom, but he was used to that now. Finally, after an hours walking, the valley opened out, and before him were the flatlands; flat land seemed almost as valuable as gold after so many mountains. His heart was now beating like he had never felt before. The temperature was warmer, and it was certainly a lot less windy. He made so much progress that day that when he finally stopped, he could see a smudge of water running far to the east. *That must be Loch Nis*, he thought.

He wanted to make it an early night to make an early start tomorrow. The next day, he woke to a feeling of slight worry. From what he knew, he feared he was in dragon territory. He walked as swiftly as he could. On occasion, he looked to the mountain peaks and then to the sky, but he never saw anything he thought could be a sign of a dragon. The land steadily dropped as it came close to the water, and streams began to block his path. Some of them were deep and far too wide to jump. He resorted to following those till he found a narrow enough point to jump across. He sat down in the mid-afternoon to eat his fill, taking the last meat from the carcass and dumping the bones in a bush. He trekked the last few miles, and by evening, he stood on the shores of Loch Nis. To the west, he could see the ramparts and towers of a great city. He followed alongside the shore, watching trading vessels sailing slowly towards Cill Chuimein, and faintly on the wind, he could hear the sound of the rigging clinking on the masts. Soon he was walking amongst the docks. It was a weird feeling to see so many people hurrying back and forth, unloading and loading ships. He had almost forgotten in his solitude what normal life was. A smile stretched across his face at seeing civilisation, even though he was concerned that he might cause another dragon attack. When he stood before the gates, he could see An Gearasdan as clear as day in his mind. He wasn't going to stay long. As soon as he had his answers, he would leave.

CHAPTER 15

ROWAN

R owan stood and watched until Warwick was out of sight. His heart felt empty, almost as if a part of him were missing. He had not realised just how lonely he had been before Warwick came along. The thought of Warwick's path would not leave his mind; a part of him wanted to chase after Warwick, while the other side warned him not to. Rowan attempted to distract his mind by turning towards the mountain peaks and thinking of where his brother seers were. They the closest thing to a family he would ever know. It had been years since they last saw each other. Rowan had spent most of his time travelling, while they had remained in the caves, studying ancient runes.

He began to walk up the valley the way he had just come to the caves where he had last seen them. The only problem was that his brothers never stayed in one part of the cave for too long. A lot of the time they moved into the almost-impossible-to-reach places of the caves. If he was to find them, these cave entrances were going to be his best bet. The path to the other caves was barely a path at all; really, it was the thinnest of cliff ledges you could possibly imagine. At several points, Rowan had to jump sideways over sheer drops that were over a hundred feet deep. At no point, though, did he feel he would fall. He had regularly walked this path in the past and could have walked with his eyes closed. The path was short and reached a number of small cave entrances that riddled the mountainside.

After just having left a very deep, challenging cave, he found it took a great effort to enter into another. Crawling along a very narrow tunnel, he entered into a lit chamber. They had clearly been studying some more cave paintings close to the entrance. Something felt wrong, though. A fire burned, and yet there was no sign of any of them. Looking in the dirt revealed no fresh tracks. Where were they? They clearly hadn't run at the sound of his coming. He found a couple of footprints that looked days old and put his hand to them. A brief vision shot into his head, but it wasn't enough. He saw fire filling the cavern, bellowing out of all the tunnels. He didn't see what happened to the others though. How deep did these caves go? If they were home to a dragon, then where had it entered? How long had it been there? Endless questions spilled into Rowan's mind. The only way to seek answers was to find the source of the fire, and if it was a dragon …

The tunnels at the back of the cavern were blackened with soot, and the stench coming from them smelt worse than a thousand rotting corpses. The heat from the flames must have been as hot as a furnace; the rock that formed the ceiling had cracked and still felt warm. It could only have been a dragon. Only dragons could produce fire that hot. He expected to see the scrape marks of talons as the passage widened, but there were none. The smell, however, was steadily growing more intense, hanging on the air like thick, black smoke. It felt hard to breathe, and the walls seemed to close in round him. He had never before travelled this far into the cave, but he was glad he hadn't. Twice he held his breath, but eventually he had to breathe, and it was poison to his lungs. And the deeper he went, the thicker the air became. The stench grew so strong that Rowan could feel his stomach in his mouth. He swallowed hard and looked back up the tunnel. The last of the light from the fire had just disappeared, and yet it was still light. Rowan turned back slowly with a feeling of dread inside him. As he advanced slowly forward, a cold breeze blew over him. *Dragon breath would have felt hot; it must be an exit*, he thought to himself. To his relief, the next tunnel opened out really wide into daylight. From this point, several massive tunnels went off in different directions. Carved into the floor of one of the tunnels were talon marks. He walked over to take a look at them, but as soon as he got near, a great wall of stench hit him, rising from deep within; the fresh air, even though bitterly cold, was quite welcome when it blew on his face.

A short way from the exit was a pool of blood. It was still warm. Small trails of blood led from the puddle, heading down the mountainside. There was no path, so whoever had made the trail would not have got far. He could not deny that a small part of him feared it was one of his brother seers. But the moment he saw the person, he knew straight away it was Seth.

Seth was lying with his head propped against a rock, clenching a wound on his chest desperately to try to stem the blood flow. Seth had managed to make it a little way down the mountain before collapsing. Rowan pulled Seth's hand away to take a look at the wound. Under the torn, bloodied clothing, a huge flap of skin flopped uselessly on Seth's chest, and a deep slash going right across his chest gushed blood. The skin round the gash had gone quite yellow, and an eye watering stench of death rose from it. Rowan looked aghast, surprised that Seth was still alive, as he held him in his arms. Seth choked as he lay there, coughing and spitting blood. His breathing was frantic and heavy; he was desperately trying to gulp air. In between breaths, he spoke a few words. "Robin's ... dead!" He wrenched with an extreme burst of pain. "I don't have long. ... You should not have left Warwick."

"I don't understand!"

"Just listen! The prophecy was for him, but what you think is not true. You can help!"

Rowan's mouth was wide open in shock. He was hardly able to contend with everything that was happening.

Seth took a deep breath. "I don't have time to explain. Trust me! Find Warwick. Get as far away from here as you can! An ancient power lingers here, and the dragons created it. These mountains are sacred to the dragons!" His words were strained and hard to hear amongst his spluttering. He took one final look at Rowan, attempted a smile, and spoke his name as his final breath drifted away with the wind. Seth lay limp like a ragdoll in Rowan's arms, and his blood had soaked into Rowan's clothing, making him feel sick with grief.

Now Rowan knew exactly what it was like to be Warwick. He sat alone, feeling empty. Why hadn't his foresight warned him of what was coming? he kept asking himself over and over again. He wanted to properly bury Seth, but in the mountains, it wasn't possible to dig a grave without striking rock. The only way was to build a stone cairn over Seth's body. He found a secluded little hollow and built the cairn there. "Farewell Brother," he cried.

Leaving Seth's body in dragon territory weighed heavily on his heart, but he got up with Seth's words still crisp in his mind and began to move down the mountain as quickly as he could. As to where Robin's body lay, he would probably never know. He paused to catch his breath at the bottom of the mountain, feeling sick with worry. *What have I done? I sent Warwick to his death. I did not listen to my own foolish heart,* he thought as he cried and fell on his knees in the snow. Once more he forced himself to move on as Seth's voice spoke inside his head. He had to find Warwick somehow, even if he was dead; the prophecy couldn't be completed without the key. *Perhaps Warwick headed back the same way looking for more answers,* he thought with more confidence.

Setting off south, he headed for the road they had docked next to many days ago. He cursed the snow under his feet as he walked. The snow was still soft and swallowed his feet with every step. He could see after a while the distant trees that lined the sides of the road. The journey to reach them felt endless, lifting his legs high to make as long strides as possible through the snow. His wet, bloodied clothes hung heavy on his shoulders, not really serving much purpose. He drifted slightly too far to the east and came across a river. The smell from the blood on his clothing by now was overwhelming. As much as he tried, he couldn't wash away the stench, but now he was frozen to the bone and couldn't continue. Very reluctantly, he built a fire and sat as close as he could to it without burning himself. His eyes were permanently fixed upon the sky whilst he dried by the fire. As soon as he could feel some warmth in his bones, he kicked the burning wood into the river and was off as quick as he could. He fell on his and Warwick's old tracks not too far from the river and followed them back to the road.

At last, the road was before him, and he was able to move quite quickly on it compared to the deep snow. He had slightly more hope in his heart now, as he knew the sea was not far away. The wind seemed to roar through the treeline, and in his mind it sounded like the beating of giant wings. It felt as if the trees were closing in round him, and the roaring sound was getting louder. He soon realised that it was in fact wings. He fled with great speed over the slippery stone. He could hear the sound of the wings getting closer beyond the trees. When he looked briefly back over his shoulder, it seemed the trees were following him. The tops of them were tipped with fire. Hot embers and burning branches rained down all round him, almost hitting him. He knew the dragon must be almost on top of him, as he could smell the familiar scent of rotting flesh, but he didn't dare look back. He knew he wouldn't shake the dragon off. It soared over his head, inches from touching him with its tail. The wind it created nearly bowled Rowan over. The water was within spitting distance when the dragon turned in mid-air and torched everything with a ball of flames. Rowan dived from the road out of the way of the flames, but the dragon whipped his tail, catching Rowan across the back and causing him agonising pain. He was launched through the air into the deep water. As Rowan disappeared below the surface, the dragon circled above, waiting for him to emerge. Rowan sank deep, barely conscious. When Rowan didn't emerge quickly, the dragon slowly flew off, but if it had waited a few moments more, it would have had an easy meal. The pressure on Rowan's ears felt crushing, and he clawed frantically at the water with the last of his breath, losing consciousness completely as he broke through the surface on his back. The current was strong, and it worked with the tide to wash Rowan out to sea.

CHAPTER 16

ϮRADERS ON THE ϞEA

Rowan floated like a log deep into the An Linne Rathairseach. A few fishing vessels and merchant ships were going about their business but seemed not to notice a man floating in the water. The coastline was like a razor blade, and it wasn't unusual to see broken timber from ships floating with the current. From afar, that's what Rowan must have looked like to them.

It wasn't till a small trading vessel sailed close by that he was noticed. "Man overboard!" Everyone on the deck ran to the starboard side of the bow. There was much shouting as they frantically tugged at nets. One sailor dived into the water, and as the nets were cast, he pulled Rowan into them. With great heaving, the sailors brought the nets aboard. Rowan rolled out of the nets, pale and limp. A tall, stocky man with long, grey hair dressed in a heavy grey jacket, white tunic, trousers, and black leather boots that went up to his knees shoved any sailor that was in his way to the side. He rolled Rowan over with his boot to see his face and stepped back quickly. The crew echoed his reaction. Rowan's clothing was torn, and his tattooed chest was visible.

"What are those markings, Captain?"

"I don't know, but I do not want them on my ship! Throw him to the orcas!"

"Stop!" From a cabin below deck, a tatty-looking young man came running onto deck. He shoved past the crew and saw Rowan lying on the ground. As he knelt down to feel for a pulse, the captain grabbed him firmly on the shoulder. "Is he dead, boy?"

"No, sir, and don't you throw him over board!" The young man was the only one who hadn't recoiled at the tattoos.

The lines on the captain's rough face contorted. "You will be punished for raising your voice to me, and if you do so again, I will throw you overboard!" He drew his sword and pointed it directly at the young man. "Now, take this filth out of my sight if you must heal him. As soon as he is healed, I want him off this ship. Is that clear?"

"Yes sir." The young man grabbed Rowan by the arms and dragged him hastily to his quarters below deck. The room was dark, damp, and very small. A stained hammock full of holes hung from the ceiling, and a rickety table sat in the corner laden with bandages, surgical equipment, and bottles of many different sizes containing medicine. The only light he had came from a few candles and a dirty lantern hanging from a nail. He checked to make sure none of the crew had followed and then rolled Rowan onto his back to look at his wounds. They were yellow and the smell nearly made him sick. From a satchel, he pulled a small bottle out and poured a little over a clean cloth. The moment it touched Rowan's wounds, Rowan regained consciousness and screamed in pain. "I wouldn't scream if you don't want to end up like me!" The young man looked nervously to the doorway with pricked ears, listening for the sound of booted footsteps.

"You're Irish! Who are you? Where am I?" Rowan was finally starting to see things clearly. He had very little feeling in his body; whatever the ointment was, it had numbed his whole body. He was suddenly aware of a deep, sickened feeling and realised that he was drenched in sweat. He tried to move to look round the cabin, but moving was too painful.

"My name is Faelan, and I am the physician. You're lucky to be alive. You were found floating in the water, and we brought you on board. Don't go expecting a warm welcome on this merchant ship." He glanced back over his shoulder and leaned in close. "The captain is an evil bastard," he whispered.

Rowan could see him properly now. He looked a tatty young man in an ill-fitted white cotton shirt, which was stained with grease and dirt. His black trousers looked like a patchwork quilt with all the repair marks, and they hung loosely above his ankles. Faelan looked like he had been beaten quite badly. His arms were exposed, which revealed many raised scars. A long scar stretched from the corner of his mouth, and his right cheek looked burned. He had a lot of uneven stubble, and his hair hung limp, shining with grease.

Faelan began to bandage Rowan's wounds, making sure the bandages were really tight. Then he put all the candles round Rowan to try to give him some warmth. "Take these." He passed Rowan his only spare pair of clothes. "You'll catch your death in those sodden rags."

"Why are you helping me when we are at war with your people?"

"Just because I am Irish doesn't mean I'm a cut-throat! I would rather not be at war but instead be friends with Scotland. Now put those dry clothes on."

"Thank you." Rowan struggled into them, enjoying the warmth of having dry clothes.

Faelan seemed to forget Rowan's incrimination straight away and looked curiously at him. "The rest of the crew seem to fear your tattoos. If you don't mind me asking, what are they?"

Rowan was still hesitant to reveal himself, but it seemed he had no choice. "My name is Rowan. I am a part of an ancient order of seers. The markings show who we are and how many we are."

"I thought seers were only myth. I've only heard of them before in books."

"I could well be the last one, so it's not surprising you thought us a myth."

"I can't begin to imagine what it must feel like to be the last." Faelan looked at him for a moment in thought, and then his voice became barely a whisper. "I am going to help us to get out of here. I am a slave on this ship. I was taken from my family because I was a physician. I have been on this vessel for at least two months, but I have lost track of time. I have been living on maggoty bread and fouled water since I was put here. Now that there's two of us, it should be easier to escape."

"I am afraid I will only hinder you, as I can hardly move."

"I cleaned your wounds and gave you some opium for the pain, which is why you can't move. When you're rested, we can think about our escape. I would like to know why you were drifting in the water."

The full truth still felt too risky. "I travel a lot and like to find ancient cave paintings. I heard the mountains on An t-Eilean Sgitheanach were very old, so I thought I might try them. I didn't have any luck, though. Afterward, I was hunted by a dragon and knocked into the water by its tail."

"A dragon, you say! I had heard the quickly spreading rumours of a great winged beast attacking An Gearasdan, but I didn't think for one moment it was that! Was that … a … dragon?"

"Yes!"

The fear was clear to see in Rowan's eyes and Faelan collapsed onto the floor.

"You shouldn't go any farther north, not unless you want to be—" Rowan was cut off by the captain barging into the cabin and fell instantly quiet.

"Has this rat spoken yet?" He grabbed Faelan by the scruff and hoisted him up so he could see his eyes.

Faelan glanced at Rowan out of the corner of his eye with a warning glance. "No … he hasn't, sir."

The captain glared sharply at Faelan and then at Rowan. "Well, make him talk and quickly. I don't care how you do it, just do it! When you're done, make sure to throw him overboard. Is that clear?"

"Yes sir!" Faelan wanted to close his eyes, expecting to feel the sharp smack of the captain's hand on his cheek, but he did not dare this close to the captain. Receiving a heavy blow to the stomach, Faelan fell to the floor. "That's to remind you that you don't give orders!" The captain left the room and went back up onto the deck.

Faelan checked to ensure that the coast was clear, clutching his stomach. "That was the captain, Leod. If he finds out we have spoken, he will kill us both!"

The words didn't come as a shock to Rowan.

"I thought we might have time to heal you, but it seems like we don't now. You will be weak for days, and there's still a high chance you could die." Faelan paused, thinking. "There is one way we could escape, but it wouldn't be easy and would require the lightest hands!"

"What is it?" Rowan was concerned at the look on Faelan's face and his tone of voice.

"At the stern of the ship, behind the captain's cabin, is a long boat. All we would need to do is winch it into the water and cast off. It would have to be done under the cover of darkness, but even at night, the deck is patrolled by a couple of lookouts. Any sign of movement and they will raise the alarm. It will take great skill and unbelievable amounts of courage. They all carry short-swords; we have nothing. I think we are going to have to poison the crew!"

Rowan tried to feel round for his sword, looking confused. "Where is my sword?"

"There was no sword in your possession when you were brought aboard. You must have lost it in the water."

Rowan thumped the floor. "Well, we don't have a choice. We can wait here for the captain to kill us, or we can die trying to escape! Faelan, I don't care how weak I am. Make that poison. We escape tonight!"

They both spoke quietly; outside the cabin, they could hear many footsteps close by. Faelan gave Rowan a pat on the shoulder and began to make the poison. He planned to mix it into their evening wine. A small amount of hope remained, since having been aboard for so long, he had memorised their daily routines down to the letter. He spoke quietly to himself while mixing the poison, planning his attack.

Soon the poison was finished, and he helped Rowan to get as ready as he could. "We wait till first dark; that's when the captain eats. He always eats alone in his cabin. Once he has eaten, the crew are allowed to eat and are invited into the cabin to dine. We somehow have to poison the wine before they sit down to eat." Faelan's brow was creased as he sat deep in thought.

"Surely the source of their drink is stowed away in the hull?"

"Yes, of course, but it is always kept under lock and key. The captain keeps the key on him at all times."

"Couldn't you pick the lock? Surely your surgical knifes are fine enough to get inside the locks?"

"I suppose I could try, but it won't be easy. I reckon there will be about an hour to do this while everyone is on deck. You wait here, and I will come back to you when I am done. If I don't return, presume I am dead and jump from the ship!" Faelan gave Rowan a nervous glance and vanished from sight.

In the depths of the ship, it was jet black, but Faelan daren't take a candle or his lantern. Luckily he knew the ship, so he only need follow the rough walls with his hands. He descended as quickly and quietly as he could, gritting his teeth every time a plank creaked. He had to duck most of the way, as the ceilings were really low. Eventually he found the locked door, having felt round for quite a while in the dark for the handle. Frantically, he felt round with his knife in search of the lock. There was a click of metal on metal, and he knew he had found it. He didn't care about ruining his knife and jammed it hard into the lock. Luckily, it fit. He listened with his ear close to the lock as he turned the knife. One by one, he heard soft metallic clicks, and slowly the lock began to move. Then there was a loud click, and the door swung open. Fortunately there was a small hole in the side of the ship well clear of the waterline, and the beam of light coming through illuminated one of the barrels. In total, there was six barrels, and just visible in the light was their grape-shaped brand. A bung sealed each barrel, and when they were turned on their sides, the bungs came out easily. He poured the poison sparingly into each barrel, put the bungs back in, stood them up, and made his quick exit, locking the door behind him with his knife.

Rowan sat waiting in the cabin, anxiously twitching his fingers, his eyes constantly flitting towards the dark opening that was the doorway. It was like being trapped in a cage with a sleeping dragon, not knowing when it would suddenly wake and create hell. To his relief, Faelan burst into the cabin out of breath. "It is set. The poison will take at least a couple of hours to kill them for sure. If we don't time our move perfectly, we will be caught," he said, panting. The thought of what they were doing weighed heavy on Rowan's mind; the news that the plan was ready did not bring him any joy. He chose not to think about it but to get it over and done with as fast as possible.

They waited about eight and half hours without food and water in Faelan's cabin till the sun was setting. Faelan had cleaned and redressed Rowan's wounds and helped him to stand on his wobbly legs. He had used all his bandages and odd bits of cloth on Rowan, and there was nothing more he could do to help him.

Faelan sat by the door, sweating, whilst he watched through a small slit for the crew to bring the barrels up on deck. Eventually, he did see them and just hoped with a due sense of dread that he had got to all the barrels. Soon, first dark was upon them, and the deck above went quiet as the sailors went into the cabin to eat. Still they waited. It was early morning before all sound on deck disappeared and they figured that it was safe to move. When they crept onto to deck, it was still dark; it must have been about one o'clock. The full moon was shining high, glistening on the water. Faelan quickly checked a few of the bodies scattered over the deck and saw that they were dead. He came back to Rowan, put his arm round him, and helped him into the boat. By himself, Faelan struggled to winch the boat off the deck, and by the time he had lowered it to the water, he was exhausted. Faelan grabbed a couple of swords, a joint of meat, and some cloth and extra clothing for warmth. He slid down the ropes into the boat and cast away.

CHAPTER 17

†ORD ЄXIHAINN

Lord Exihainn had spent a good week resting in his bed and was bitterly agitated. For the first time, he felt he had just as much power as common folk. He didn't like this feeling and took to shouting at people, much to their dislike. He still acted like he had power, but here he was barely a lord. He still had heard no news that meant anything to him. It wasn't till a small serving boy came with a scroll in his hand that he felt joy. He shouted at the boy to open it and read it aloud.

> To Lord Exihainn of An Gearasdan,
>
> We have received the message with your request to take on any injured. Our halls are already full of the ill and dead, and we cannot take anymore. We have no food or water here at Talledale. All the extra people we have taken in are attracting a lot of attention. We have seen the dragons getting closer. We have not yet been attacked, but it won't be long. We have no defences nor anyone fit to fight. All the farmers are coming down with fever, and some of the people who have tended to the ill are now dead. We have had no choice but to place a quarantine on the village. We are plagued by the sick. With every breath they breathe, they pollute our air, and they foul our waters. We shall carry on to the bitter end, though. We also received word

that you were looking for certain people. A young boy passed through here not two days ago matching the description of one of them. A young serving girl spoke to him, and he said his name was Warwick. No one else was with him, though. He was heading south for Cill Chuimein. That is all we know.

We offer you much sympathy for the loss of your good people and city.

—Aymon of the tavern.

Lord Exihainn forgot his pain and the fact that he only had one leg in his sudden burst of happiness. He went to stand up but fell crashing back into his bed. He was laughing. He ripped the parchment from the young boy's hands and read it aloud again to himself. When he had read it again, even though the letter was filled with ill news, he still laughed and shouted "He's alive!" at the top of his voice several times. He hadn't thought about the fact, though, that Rowan wasn't with him. That night he was woken by that thought. He had put the scroll under his pillow. After being gravely wounded in the dragon attack, he could remember very little of the council he'd held with Rowan and Warwick. He feared, though, that Rowan was dead and Warwick was lost in the wild. The rest of the night he spent re-reading the parchment endlessly. He couldn't sleep, and the thoughts in his head brought him out in a nervous sweat.

When the serving girl brought his breakfast, she was shocked to see him awake and looking troubled with a scroll in his hands. She gave a small curtsey and went to put the silver tray down. Lord Exihainn swiped it from her arms with the back of his right hand, and it clattered with a heavy thud onto the floor. The serving girl bent down to pick it up, but Lord Exihainn grabbed her arm and wrenched her away from it.

"I have no hunger for food! Send for my messenger. Do it quickly!"

The serving girl looked almost scared by his tone of voice and without a second glance dashed at full speed from the room. Moments later, his messenger came charging into the room. "You called for me, my lord."

"Send a unit of men north. Give the order. They must find Warwick and bring him to me. They are not to return till he is found. See that it is done quickly!"

"Very good, my lord." With a short bow, the messenger moved swiftly from the room, and within the hour, a unit was sent forth. The messenger then came back to report that the orders had been carried out. Lord Exihainn was sitting deep in thought once more. "My lord, what troubles you?"

"I want an audience with the king. It is important that he knows of this prophecy—as much as I know and can remember. Warwick is going to need a lot of help."

"Is that wise, my lord? You could be putting Warwick in danger."

"Maybe so, but it is a risk I am willing to take!"

"Very well. I will see it done, my lord." With a short bow he vacated the room once more.

Lord Exihainn's wait was longer than he had expected. His answer came the next morning at the hands of one of the king's private messengers, dressed in fine, green silks emblazoned with the king's sigil. "Your audience with the king has been granted. At sun down, you will dine with the king." With a sharp bow, he left.

The chamber felt awfully quiet now. All round him were empty beds. He wondered if this was heaven. The white walls seemed misty and very distant, and the shafts of light radiating through the windows looked heavenly and danced on the walls. Looking up at the ceiling brought him back to his senses, though, as he saw the solid, oaken beams. He was beginning to feel tired after being up all last night, and he drifted off to sleep. He slept soundly for the first time since he had arrived in Cill Chuimein. Even though neither Rowan nor Warwick had been found, he felt sure in his heart that at least Warwick still lived.

When he woke, the light of day was fading. Torches burned in their sconces, and the shadows danced on the walls. A serving girl sat by the door, waiting to take him to the king's chambers. She lifted him from the bed with difficulty when he was awake and staggered to the king's chamber. He did not much like being carried like a baby and felt mocked as eyes turned.

The doors to the king's chamber were solid oak and twenty feet high. The sigil of the king could be seen plated in gold high up on the doors in a huge circle. The doors swung open as they approached, groaning heavily. The king's throne room was before them. Its ceilings seemed to stretch into the clouds. Great heads of animals hung from the walls. They were the king's trophies from his hunts. A big band of marble stretched almost round the whole room and was deeply engraved with words in the old tongue. At the back of the huge chamber, stretching from floor to ceiling, were the portraits of the king's predecessors, painted onto the smooth, stone walls. Before the throne was a huge banqueting table laden with sweet, sticky meats and silver bowls piled high with the sweetest, plumpest fruit from faraway lands. Endless jugs of wine and mead sat on the table waiting to be drunk. The air was heavy and thick with smoke from the burning torches all round the room and the scent of the hot meats. Towards the back of the room were two smaller doors, and serving girls and boys waited by them to attend to the king. In this huge room, it felt quite chilly, but he knew the king would not feel so, dressed in his entire garb. Lord Exihainn looked back as they approached the throne and saw two knights standing sentinel on either side of the door in full suits of armour with twelve-foot-long silver-tipped halberds at their sides. A serving boy pulled a chair before the throne, and Lord Exihainn was lowered into it. The serving girl who had put him in the chair gave a curtsey to the king with a polite smile and then moved swiftly to stand in wait with the other servants.

Lord Exihainn smiled up at the king and called out loudly, filling the room with his voice. "All hail King Angus, son of Mull the Great, ruler of all Scotland."

The cry was echoed throughout the room as all the others who were present hailed the king in response. The king smiled back at him, looking down from his huge throne of oak. The arms of the throne had been carved into two lion's heads, and above the king's head was carved a sun god casting beams of light upon the king's head.

The king had thick, black hair, which fell to his shoulders. A long, black beard covered his chin and rested on his chest. Round him hung a magnificent animal hide, fastened into a cape. It would have dragged on the floor had he been standing. A heavy gold chain hung round his neck with a heavy pendant encrusted with rubies attached. A crown of silver sat upon his head. It was inset with nine diamonds representing all the kings to have worn the crown. The rest of his clothing was made from the finest leathers and silks in rich greens and dark browns.

The king's hands grasped and flexed on the arms of his throne. "Speak quickly, as I have more important matters to deal with."

"Yes ... your grace." Lord Exihainn thought carefully; to be successful, he would have to be very tactful. "Before An Gearasdan was destroyed, I was in council with two strangers from the wilds, though it seems now they were a lot more than just strangers. It was they who convinced us of the existence of the dragons, but we were too late to defend the city. They spoke of a prophecy they had to fulfil, but they needed help, which they never got. When the dragon came, they disappeared into the wilds, and we didn't know where or even whether they lived. All we knew about this prophecy was that it had something to do with the dragons. Recently, I heard that at least one of the two was heading this way. May they seek protection and get help here, my liege?" Lord Exihainn gritted his teeth as he waited for the reply.

The king sat deep in thought, his brow deeply furrowed. "Very well ... but only on my conditions! When you find them, you bring them straight to me! I want to hear from them about this prophecy, and I want to know more about the dragons. I cannot vouch for their safety, though, even as king. I have very little time for matters other than the advance of the English."

"Thank you, your grace." Lord Exihainn smiled widely and bowed low, as much as he could in his chair.

"Come, let's eat." The king stood up from his throne and clapped his hands. The serving girls and boys rushed to either side of the long table and waited ready with the flasks. Two serving girls lifted Lord Exihainn's chair with him in it to the table. Soon the table was full with lords, and the king sat at the end of the table. Much laughter and talk filled the room. Lord Exihainn listened but did not know the subject, so he kept quiet. He still had to remember that he was here by invitation only and things could still go against him. As soon as the king had downed one tankard of mead or beaker of wine, a serving girl would be ready to fill his glass again. Music was played while they dined. A young boy stood at the back of the room with a lute, playing soothing tunes soft to the ear. King Angus grabbed a leg of lamb and took a great chunk from it, filling his mouth with hot, sticky meat. The juices ran down his chin, but he did not care. "Tell me about the dragons, Lord Exihainn." His words sounded muffled with his mouth full of food, and Lord Exihainn had to strain to hear what he said.

"Surely such subjects are not fit for the king's dinner table, my liege. Nor should they be spoken of in front of servants!" said one of the king's pages.

"Very well," said the king.

"May I be so bold as to say that I would not be able to give you much more on the dragons, my liege! I swear that when either Warwick or Rowan is found, they will be able to give a much better account of the dragons."

All the lords looked at Lord Exihainn with confusion. To them, Rowan and Warwick were completely unknown, but they dared not speak their thoughts in front of the king.

The king sat there staring at Lord Exihainn for a while. "I shall hold you to your word. You'd best make sure they talk!" There was a note of fire in the king's voice. Anyone who was caught wasting his time would suffer.

They dined heavily the rest of the night and drank till all the flagons had gone. Any scraps of food that were left were given to his guards and servants. Lord Exihainn was carried back to his bed drunk. He was even ruder to the servants when drunk, but they still willingly attended to his needs. He lay in his bed asking for a woman to take his aches and pains away. He was in utmost anger when the serving girl did not fetch him a woman. The serving girl hung her head low, avoiding Lord Exihainn's eyes. "I could not find a woman of your stature. May I offer my body instead and take care of your needs, my lord?"

"How dare you talk to me like that. I shall see you punished for talking to a lord in such manner!" He brought his hand heavy to the girl's face, smacking her across the cheek.

The girl ran from the room sobbing while caressing her throbbing, red cheek where his hand had struck. From then on, it was a young boy who attended to his needs.

Once Lord Exihainn fell asleep, he didn't wake till the early hours of the afternoon. He woke grouchy but more his normal self. A pageboy sat at his bedside with a sealed piece of parchment held tightly in his grasp. Lord Exihainn looked at him for a minute, and the pageboy opened his hands and passed the parchment to him. "It is for your eyes only, my lord." With one final glance towards the page boy, Lord Exihainn broke the seal.

To Lord Exihainn,

A company of nine rode north from Cill Chuimein with greatest haste. They found the remains of a fire not three days old at the foot of Carn Eige. Further information about Warwick has come to light from one of the king's messengers. The messenger informed me that he met Warwick at Carn Eige and ate with him. He aided Warwick in his journey to Cill Chuimein. There have been no more signs since. Two men were lost in the high passes during the search. We seek permission to return to Cill Chuimein. Send your reply to the camp at Cougie.

—Captain Manius

"Parchment please," Lord Exihainn said to the pageboy. He wrote his reply swiftly and shortly.

To Captain Manius,

I received your request to withdraw. Given the state of the search and having lost men, you may do so. I expect you on your return to keep close watch for Warwick or any sign of opposing threat.

Deepest sympathy for your loss. May their spirits be at peace.

—Lord Exihainn

He rolled the letter up tight and sealed it with green wax from a candle, marking the wax seal with his ring. "Send this with haste to Captain Manius. You will find him camped at Cougie."

"Very good my lord."

The pageboy left the room with the scroll tight in his grasp, and the rest of the day passed by quietly without a disturbance or even a whisper of dragons or the English. Lord Exihainn could not remember a time when he had been as tense as he was now. Even the walls seemed to resonate with the tension. He doubted that even a knife blade would cut the tension.

CHAPTER 18

WARWICK

Warwick passed into Cill Chuimein without too much trouble from the guards. They stopped him, but he was careful not to tell them his real reason for coming here. He'd thought Cill Chuimein would look similar to An Gearasdan on the inside, but to his shock, it was different. Where An Gearasdan had been tight and winding, Cill Chuimein was huge, and each street was wide enough for ten manned horses to ride abreast. The buildings leaned over the streets, tall and grand. A higher class of people lived in Cill Chuimein; that was clear from the cleanliness of the streets and the quality of the silks people wore. It seemed everyone wore fine silks of vibrant, rich colours. Even the stables seemed clean and didn't smell. Warwick looked round at all the guards, and they were clad in the finest silver-plated armour, shining like stars in the bright sun. Warwick had no money, so he could not stay in the warm inns. This was a heavy blow to his heart, as the inns seemed so welcoming—warmth radiated from them, and the smells of ale and hot meat hung thick in the air. In his search, he passed the blacksmith's forge, and even that looked grand and clean. Everything seemed to glow with wealth. He soon stood in the centre of the market, lost in the massive swarms of people. Merchants went back and forth endlessly, carrying barrels on their shoulders or pulling small wagons heavily laden with silks or meat. The sound of everyone talking was overpowering to Warwick; it was the first time he had been alone in such big crowds, and he struggled to hear himself think.

While he stood in the market, seven heavily armoured knights rode through. Warwick happened to notice one looking his way curiously with his visor up. The knight raised his arm, brought his company to a halt, and dismounted with a heavy thud of metal on stone. The knight was walking right towards him, and Warwick didn't know what to do. He felt scared, not knowing why the knight approached. The crowds split, forming a path, and fell silent as they watched the knight march towards Warwick. The light of the sun hit his armour, and everyone raised a hand to his or her face to block the reflection. The knight stopped right before Warwick, looking down. To Warwick, this man seemed a giant. Warwick could feel his heart beat in his mouth and lowered his head as the knight stood before him. "I am captain Manius. Do not be scared. You might be the person we look for. Are you Warwick? Did you travel with another by the name of Rowan?"

Warwick was completely stunned and struggled to find his voice. Eventually he managed to splutter a word. "Y-yes ..."

The knight gave him a short smile, kneeling down to his height. "You match the description of the person we are looking for. Come with us to the keep; there is someone who wants to see you."

Without another word, Warwick followed the knight, who lifted Warwick onto the back of his horse. They rode up to the keep. He hoped in his heart it was Rowan who waited. He wanted to see him again more than anything; he had felt lost without Rowan's company and guidance. The horse stopped right before the drawbridge. As they dismounted, a stable boy came and took all their horses one by one.

The guards at the door instantly opened it as Warwick and the knights approached and stood aside, each looking tall and proud, like a stag before his herd. The light was dim inside most of the passages they passed through. Warwick had no idea where he was being taken. He found the smoke from the torches on the walls too much; the smoggy air made him feel claustrophobic. The knight stopped before a big door and pushed it wide open. Warwick saw before him a huge, cavernous chamber full of beds. The knight led the way inside. *Was this is a hospital? Was Rowan hurt?* He thought with a sickening feeling. Warwick looked round the white, high-ceilinged room searching, expecting to see Rowan lying in a bed. All he saw, though, was a mutilated man, scarred heavily by burns and wounds and missing a leg. He looked dead, but he was just asleep; Warwick could hear raspy breathing sounds when he was led close to the man's bedside. Warwick stood a little behind the knight, a little scared and freaked out by the man in the bed. Clearing his throat, the knight called out loudly, "My lord!" The man twitched in his bed and began to open his eyes slowly. The knight pushed Warwick towards the bed. "You may address him as Lord Exihainn of An Gearasdan."

As much as Warwick tried to keep his mouth from falling open with astonishment, he could not. He stood there gaping while Lord Exihainn's eyes adjusted. As soon as Lord Exihainn saw who stood at the side of the bed, he grabbed Warwick and pulled him towards him so he could hug him. He was laughing with joy as he squeezed him tight. "Young Warwick, I feared you had died at An Gearasdan. My men were sent to look for you. Where did they find you?"

"In the market of Cill Chuimein, my lord."

Lord Exihainn smiled back at him. "So I need not have sent my men after all," he said, laughing. "Come, there are many important matters to attend to. The king is waiting for your council, and afterwards I would very much like to dine and talk with you!" He called to his guard by the door, who lifted him from the bed and led the way to the king's chambers. Warwick felt a sadness in his heart knowing he would be made to talk about his parents' deaths and risk the whole quest.

The doors of the king's chambers were pushed open. Warwick felt queasy looking up at the king high on his throne. The guard put Lord Exihainn in a chair in front of the throne, and Warwick stood beside him. Lord Exihainn addressed the king with a bow. "My king, as promised, I bring before you Warwick."

The king looked at Warwick suspiciously, like he knew him. "Tell me, young Warwick, who is your father?"

Warwick felt a tear well in his eye. "He was Deal, my lord."

The king chuckled. "I thought I recognised something about you. Deal was one of my best men." His smile suddenly changed. "You said he *was* your father? What happened? I wish to know all." He turned to a servant and shouted, "You, bring Warwick a chair."

The servant ran over with a chair, and Warwick sat down in the chair with haste and wiped a tear away. "My parents were killed trying to protect me. It was a dragon attack." He tried to sound strong, as he feared to show his emotions in front of the king.

The king seemed to slump in his throne at the words. "That weighs heavily on my heart, young Warwick. I feel your pain. Your father was a great man, even though he had no wealth. I wished I had seen him one more time before his demise."

Warwick had a momentary feeling of pride; the king had just respected his family. They may have not been wealthy in money, but they were sure wealthy in respect. Warwick hadn't realised that till now. "My father spoke fondly of you, my liege" was all he could think to say.

The king gave him a nod of approval. "Will you now tell me the whole business of your prophecy? I want to know everything you know, especially about the dragons!"

Warwick closed his eyes briefly, taking a gulp of air to relax him. "It started back when my mother was fifteen years of age. She had travelled to the town of Loch Domhain, where she met a man who gave her an unusual key. She was also told to give it to me when I reached the age of fifteen, though I was not yet born at the time. When I received the key, I was soon aware it held a form of power but had no idea about the source of its power. I found the key very curious and kept looking at it. One time it began to glow. I did not realise at that time that it was a warning of what was coming. After this, little signs began to come into my life where ever I went. One day, though, the key glowed again, but this time it glowed blindingly. That was when the dragon attacked. I fled with great haste and found Rowan. It turned out that Rowan was the one who had given my mother the key in the first place and had been the one leaving the signs for me. We travelled together then to An Gearasdan, and he informed me that the key was tied to a prophecy. The only problem was that no one knew what this prophecy was, as it had been written a long, long time ago. Rowan told me he was a seer and had travelled the lands for many years and lived in caves. He had seen many cave paintings, and he found that those in the older caves were very old. His plan was to pass by An Gearasdan seeking aid and then head north to Sgitheanach to the sky caves where he had once lived. He knew that those caves were the oldest in all Scotland and would be our best chance to find a clue about the prophecy. We made it to An Gearasdan and stayed there a while, not knowing the danger that waited. When the dragon attacked, we fled. We did eventually make it to the sky caves, but it nearly cost us our lives. In the caves, we found what we had come for. The cave paintings showed a great battle fought long ago against the dragons. It showed that somehow the dragons were defeated. It was hard to tell what happened, as some parts were worn away with age. The paintings also showed the key being forged and a dragon soul being poured into the heart of it, which is its source of power. I was instructed to find something called the sacred vale. My answers will be made clear there. I soon left Rowan after that, as he could not come with me, and I have not seen him since. I decided to head here in search of more answers, hoping to find records that dated back to the battle.

The king looked straight through him as if searching for further detail. "And where is this key?"

Warwick swallowed nervously and reached inside his clothes. Nervously he pulled the key out and showed it to the king. The king looked at it closely, his brow furrowed. The whole room had fallen silent as people looked upon the key. It was like this for a while, but finally, the king slumped back in his throne and smiled, pleased by the level of detail Warwick had given. "You explained your quest very well, and I see fit to grant you your aid. But first, tell me more about the dragons so I can hope to defend my city against the tyranny."

Warwick thought for a moment, uncertain of what to say. "From the experiences I have had, the dragons can't be harmed by any normal weapon. Their hides are too thick and strong, and normal blades shatter. The dragons are drawn to certain powerful things, such as the key, so I must not stay here long, else I will put you in grave danger. No matter what defences you put in place, the dragons will cut through them like butter. Their bodies are the size of large buildings. Their fire melts flesh and stone. Their tails crack like whips. They like to attack from the air, raining fire down, and then waft the flames with their giant wings to blanket everything. Their cries are deafening to anyone who hears them. The only chance you would have of stopping them, my liege, would be to build walls a mile thick and pray the dragons hit them. I doubt that would kill them, though, only anger them! I am sorry, my liege, I cannot give any better advice than that." He bowed to the king, feeling more confident.

The king gave another nod of approval. "You have spoken enough, young Warwick. I thank you for your council and truth, even if your news is ill." He smiled and clapped his hands. His servants were immediately at his side to take Warwick and Lord Exihainn back to their chamber. "I shall send my personal scribe to you at sundown. He shall take you to my personal library and help you try to find what it is you look for. You may leave now." With a smile, the king gave a courteous bow to them both, and they bowed back, smiling. The servants lifted Lord Exihainn and carried him whilst Warwick followed. As they exited the chamber, the king's booming voice chased after them. "See that they are given a banquet they will not forget. I cannot think of anyone who deserves it more."

The doors closed behind them, and soon they were in another chamber—but not the hospital wing. The chamber was well lit with torches, and a great table was before them. The king's servants waited to attend to them. When they had sat down at the table, the servants rushed to their sides with flagons of hot mead and sweet honeyed wines. Being waited on by servants who were not allowed to eat made Warwick feel guilty; there was enough food to feed a small village. He wondered if this was what it was like to be a wealthy man. He'd thought the previous feasts had been big, but this one looked like the cooks had prepared the whole of the king's larder. Warwick kept glancing at Lord Exihainn and instantly saw how comfortable he looked in the lap of servants. The whole experience made him feel a little sick. Why were these servants any different from them? They were still human. Warwick proceeded through the meal without looking up anymore and ate quickly. He wanted to leave as quickly as possible. Lord Exihainn continuously shouted orders to the servants. Even though it was clear they hated doing the work, they had no other option. If they failed to do the work or even attempted to sit, the punishment would be certain death. Lord Exihainn drank heavily, and as he drank more and more, it began to dribble down his chin. In truth, he only did this because when sober he could feel the pain in his leg. He was very violent when drunk; he knocked several flagons over, and they smashed with a loud crack on the floor. When the end of the meal came, Warwick quickly left the room. He had felt like he couldn't breathe.

Lord Exihainn ordered the servants to carry him faster in the hope of catching Warwick. They found him round the next corner looking lost in thought. "You look lost, Warwick. I was hoping to talk with you some more."

"I would just like to rest, my lord," he diverted from the truth.

"I hope we may speak soon, Warwick," said Lord Exihainn smiling. "Please take him to his chamber," he spoke to one of the servants.

Warwick bowed to Lord Exihainn, a slightly forced smile on his face. He quickly left with the servant. The long corridors were hot and stuffy, filled with smoke, and the ceiling seemed close round them. Warwick was taken to a small chamber in a tower, not far from the hospital wing.

There was a strong sense of power that came with having a room overlooking a city, almost like the power of a king. No dragon could possibly slip past his gaze now. Warwick sat on the windowsill with a jug of wine close at hand for a couple of hours. He was finally alone to reflect upon his thoughts. He hoped the aches in his body would soon ease after rest; his body felt as if it were an archery butt. A gentle breeze blew in through the window, landing softly on Warwick's face. The smells of the city followed with it. He couldn't tell what he smelt, as all the smells massed together in a giant cloud. The sounds of the market and the harbour echoed on the wind. He thought with a sense of heaviness about his path ahead. *I can't rest here, but I can't leave without answers*, he thought to himself. His thoughts soon turned to grief as he thought back to his parents. He was determined to avenge their deaths. He had realised that was the only thing that kept him going. Now that he was alone, the tears would not stop falling. He cried for a good hour or so; he could not tell how long he had been in his room.

That afternoon, he left his chambers. He remembered that Lord Exihainn had wanted to speak to him, but why hadn't he spoken at the meal? It clearly regarded a matter he wished not to be overheard speaking about. When Warwick entered the hospital wing, Lord Exihainn was sitting up in his bed with several scrolls on his lap. It took Lord Exihainn a while to focus his eyes; his vision was still bad. As he realised it was Warwick, he smiled. "I wondered when I would see you. I am sorry we did not speak at the meal, but I would rather not be overheard."

Warwick did not know how to reply, so just gave him a little smile. He sat in a bedside chair and leant towards Lord Exihainn. "There is something I wish to ask you. At An Gearasdan, just before the dragon attacked, where were you? Did the key react to the danger?" Lord Exihainn spoke in barely a whisper, so quietly that Warwick could hardly hear him over his breathing.

Warwick's reply was quiet, and before he spoke, he looked back over his shoulder to make sure no one was within earshot. "When the dragon came, Rowan and I were at the practise range. I was receiving the beginning of my training, however, I didn't get far before the dragon came. When the dragon came, the key shone blindingly bright. I do not know fully whether the dragon came because of the key or because it could smell all the people in the city. For everyone's safety, it's best I don't linger in the cities. I hope to be gone by tomorrow, even if I have no more answers. The dragons must be close. I wonder if that battle fought long ago ever really ended. I believe a time will come when the dragons come out of their hiding places in the shadows of the world and amass once more."

Lord Exihainn tried to show his support, but he could not hide the fact that he was scared. "I had wondered whether the key had shone again. At least we now know what it means when it shines like that. I shall do everything I can to help. I have witnessed enough now to see how urgent your quest is. I won't stop you! Tell me though ... where is Rowan? What did the cave paintings actually show? Why are you really in Cill Chuimein?"

Warwick thought for a moment, feeling swamped from being bombarded with questions. "I do not know Rowan's whereabouts. It is as I said to the king. I left him because I had to. The prophecy was written for me; that means I must complete it alone. That was what Rowan told me shortly after we escaped from An Gearasdan. I suspect he has gone to find his brother seers. They are as closest to family he has. In the cave paintings, there was a knight high upon a hill standing proud over the body of a dead dragon. The paintings showed at least nine dragons attacking from above, but it was hard to tell exactly how many there were. The next bit was worn away and hard to decipher, but it looked as if a final charge was led against the dragons and the dragons fell. It was unclear how the dragons were defeated. The last paintings showed the key being forged and the dragon soul being poured into it. Below the final painting of the key was some very old Latin. It read, 'The one who holds the Foekey shall find his answers at the sacred vale.' That is why I am here. I need to find the location of the sacred vale."

"You have come so far, Warwick. I am amazed. I just wish I could help in these difficult times, but I understand you must do it alone. I hope you find what you're looking for. You are going to need as much time as you can get in the libraries. I will send one of the servants to the king. Hopefully he can be persuaded to grant you a longer time in his library."

Warwick smiled widely at Lord Exihainn's attempts to help. The servants came to Lord Exihainn's bedside as he commanded them and were sent away immediately with the message for the king. They weren't gone long before they came rushing back. "My lord, the king is in a good mood. He has granted you your request. His scribe will be with you, Warwick, within the hour. The servant gave a sharp bow and left the room at a swift pace.

Warwick felt slightly relieved and was very grateful. His like of Lord Exihainn was growing. But as nice as this company was, the dawning realisation of the lonely journey ahead grew on his mind. He was going to miss the comfort of these walls. As he thought about leaving his surroundings, he considered perhaps getting better clothing and better travelling gear. He sat back in his chair quietly in thought at Lord Exihainn's bedside. Eventually, after what felt a very long time, an elderly man appeared wearing fine, red silks. He had a grey beard and was balding on top. "Master Warwick, I have come to take you to the libraries. Follow me, and do not fall behind." The scribe's voice was deeper than Warwick had expected and sounded hoarse.

Warwick stood up and followed him out of the room. He noticed that the scribe had a hunched back, almost unnaturally hunched. Still he moved pretty quickly. On the walls of the passage to the library were maps. Warwick looked from one to another in quick succession. He noticed that one was of Scotland, but there was nothing about a sacred vale on it. Ahead, two heavy doors were pushed open, and the library stood before them. The shelves reached high, the top ones well out of reach. Small windows were scattered round the room, casting beams of light on the dusty book spines. A fire burned at the back of the room in its grate and filled the room with warmth. The dust spiralled upwards in the heat and danced in the rays of light like fireflies. There were eight rows of bookshelves, all running parallel to one another. Tables round the edges of the room were laden with scrolls. Warwick headed for the oldest looking scrolls and instructed the scribe on what to look for. Warwick sat at a table, carefully unbinding scroll after scroll but finding nothing that was old enough. He could only guess, though, at how old the prophecy was. Hours passed with no evidence, and not once had the scribe brought anything to him.

The light coming in through the windows had turned from yellow to orange, and the shadows were slowly creeping into the corners of the room. The fire had almost burnt to ash, and there was a distinct chill in the air. A serving girl came in with a jug of wine for him and poured him a glass, blushing with a sweet smile. He drained the goblet in one gulp, and she instantly refilled it to the brim. Round his feet were dozens of scrolls he had cast away. He knew that if the scribe couldn't find anything, his attempts would be useless. The serving girl waited by his side till the jug was empty. Upon leaving, she curtsied and smiled at Warwick. Warwick took no notice of her attempts and carried on. It was late into the evening when the scribe came to Warwick. To Warwick's disappointment, the scribe carried nothing and looked puzzled. In all his long years, he'd always found an answer to whatever questions he had. This was the first time he hadn't found anything. The scribe offered his apology and gave Warwick a bow.

Warwick called to him as he began to walk away. "Is there anywhere else I could look?"

The scribe stood still for a moment, clearly in thought. When he turned back to look towards Warwick, his face was furrowed and concerned. "There are ancient vaults deep within the earth under the keep. They are seldom opened. The king is the only one permitted to enter, and he keeps the keys. For anyone else to be granted access, the matter would have to be of the utmost importance!"

"Go to the king at once and seek his permission!" Warwick's reply was sharp and came without delay.

"Warwick, may I persuade you to think differently? The king is not likely to take such a request kindly."

"You were sent to serve me, yes?"

"Yes!"

"Well, see that it is done."

The scribe bowed, closing his eyes, and took off at great haste. Alone, Warwick felt uneasy; a deathly silence seemed to close in round him. Not even the crackling of the smouldering fire could be heard. A feeling of being watched stirred in the shadows in the corners of the room; he longed for the scribes swift return. He was sure a sinister presence was with him. He had not even felt like this when a dragon had attacked. A loud bang came from behind one of the bookshelves cutting through the deathly silence in an instant. Warwick leapt in fright and began to slowly move towards the sound. He found that a book had fallen from the shelf. It was leather bound and tied up with string. It had no title but was marked with the number XVI. Curious, Warwick untied the string and opened it. A cloud of dust floated from the pages. Skimming through it, he found nothing about the prophecy. It couldn't have been old enough, as it was written in the modern tongue. As he put the book back on the shelf, the sound of returning footsteps greeted his ears. The scribe came to him wheezing, deeply troubled, and sweaty. "The king wants to see you. He is not happy! You'd best come immediately. Choose your words carefully!"

They were soon back in the throne room standing before the king. The king's expression showed straight away that he was in a foul mood. Warwick bowed low, and the scribe hastily exited. "I am troubled to hear you want access to my vaults. My scribe should not have told you about them, and I shall see that he pays. Tell me what you exactly want to know."

Warwick did not hesitate and spoke clearly, trying to keep himself from stuttering. "My prophecy speaks of a sacred vale, and I must travel to it. I do not know if I will find an answer here, but my best chance to find what and where the sacred vale is lies here in the oldest city in Scotland, under the throne. Without this information, I cannot hope to achieve what I must!"

The king sat and pondered his words for a moment. "What makes you think your answers will be here?"

"The cave paintings showed a battle of immense scale and an army I believe was big enough to be a king's army. I also thought that such a battle could only have been commanded by a king. That was what made me think of Cill Chuimein. I knew the line of kings ran for hundreds of years, and I only knew of one city to have a throne. And surely after the battle, scribes would have written accounts of it and of the years after. I do believe in my heart my answers are here."

King Angus had a slight smile upon his face. "You thought wisely, Warwick, and yes, you are right to have come here. I doubt I can help, though. It seems clear to us all that this battle happened long before our times, and I highly doubt there would be any written evidence that still remained. My vaults have not been opened for well over a decade; I could not speak to the state of them. You have put me in a difficult position, Warwick." He stood up from his throne and walked to a window, his gown trailing on the floor. "I understand the importance of what you are doing. You're a very brave young man. It is rare indeed that one should be able to change my mind. Just this once I will allow you access, but at all times, you will be kept under watch by my guard. My scribe will be at your service. Be warned! If you try to conceal anything from me or take anything you shouldn't, the punishment will be death." The king looked at Warwick with a ferocity that could kill. He then called for his guard and the scribe, and they led Warwick out of the room.

The sun had long since set now, and the passages they walked were scarcely lit and very tight. They walked down a winding spiral turret barely wide enough for two people to walk abreast. It seemed to spiral forever. Round each corner, Warwick expected to see a door, but he never did. Progress on the stairs was slow; they were very steep and worn heavily at the edges, sloping forward. Some of the steps had big cracks running the length of them. Warwick caught himself from falling several times. There was a small door at the bottom of the stairs, so small that Warwick had to duck to pass through it. The door opened onto a long, narrow passageway extending into darkness, the far end lost from view. The air smelt damp and was very claustrophobic. As it wasn't lit, Warwick used his hands on the walls for guidance. He followed close behind the scribe. The red of his robes was just visible. The passageway came to an end sooner than Warwick had expected. A heavily locked door was before them. The guard removed the king's keys from his belt and unlocked the door. None of them knew what they were going to see. They pushed the door, but it didn't move. It had welded itself shut with age. The guard pushed Warwick and the scribe aside with a heavy shove and kicked the door hard. The wood splintered where he kicked it, and with an ear-piercing scrape, the door burst open. A great cloud of dust bellowed forth from within, and a foul smell followed it.

Light had not entered into the room for a long time; a great wall of black hung in the doorway like a cloak. The walls seemed to radiate blackness. It seemed so dark that the darkness actually had mass. All of them were a little hesitant to step into the darkness; they could not help but feel scared of it. The guard was the first to take a step, and the scribe swiftly followed. Warwick had no choice but to go after them. He took a breath to steady his nerves and then walked in. The darkness instantly closed round him; it was as if he wore a blindfold. As Warwick walked, he stared hard into the darkness. Whether it was his mind playing tricks on him or not, he thought he could see shadows darting round the room. He did not know how this could be possible. There was no light source. He couldn't even see the scribe or guard in front of him. The only reassurance he had that he was still following them came from the sound of the guard's metal boots clinking on the flagstones. Warwick put his hands out, feeling round him, and several times he felt shelves laden with objects of all different sizes. A few of the objects wobbled as his hands brushed against them, but luckily nothing fell. He didn't know why he carried on into the darkness at this point. He wouldn't find anything without light. He wasn't even sure the guard and scribe had any idea where they were going. They continued to walk until they met a wall. The wall was roughly hewn and disappeared to the right, lost from view. They changed direction and followed this wall, feeling for sconces at the same time. They felt nothing for several feet, but then something jutted out of the wall. Even standing right in front of it they couldn't see what it was. The guard moved his hands over it and found that it felt strangely like rings. It moved and felt very heavy, and as it clinked against the wall, it became clear it was a heavy chain. Nothing seemed to be attached to it.

They followed all the walls right back round to the doorway. The air was very thick, so they stopped to take a breath. The cold of the room had made Warwick and the scribe feel numb; they felt envious of the guard in his heavy, warm armour. The guard marched back up the corridor and took one of the few torches from its sconce. He entered back into the room first, and they followed close behind. The light from the torch made very little difference in the darkness, but at least now they could start to see the faint outlines of objects. They headed towards the centre of the room, passing by many shelves of books and glass vials. At the centre of the room, they could faintly see the remains of an old firepit with some old logs piled in the centre. The fire had clearly been lain a very long time ago; most of the wood turned to dust when touched. There was a broken chair nearby, so they chucked it into the fire pit. Soon the fire was roaring away, and light filled the room.

The room had a low, vaulted ceiling and was longer than it was wide. Aisles of shelves ran the length of the room and were stacked high. Dust lay in thick blankets over everything. Warwick was quick to start looking and had to brush thick, sticky webs and dust away to read titles of books. After looking at several shelves, he had found nothing of use. He looked round and noticed a table positioned between two shelves and stacked high with scrolls. Many spiders seemed to think that these scrolls were a nice home, and their webs formed a thick blanket over the entire table, down to the floor. Warwick used his sword to clear the webs; he wasn't a fan of spiders and their enormous webs. As he started unravelling the scrolls, he soon realised to his annoyance that nothing seemed to be organised in any form. The scrolls were a complete mix, coming from all ages, and they took nearly two hours to search. By the time he finished with those, the fire had almost burnt out.

The scribe had been searching amongst other shelves at the far end of the room and hadn't come to Warwick with anything. The guard had taken up position by the fire, watching Warwick's every move. The scribe found several chests full with the trophies of war—moth-eaten clothing, old money, and armour. All of it was useless. There were half a dozen chests, all the same. He also found a load of scrolls under a cloth and began to read them. His concentration was often disrupted, though, by the sounds of scurrying. It sounded like rats, but he never saw one. The spiders were also distracting him. There were huge numbers of them, and they were on virtually everything he touched. All the shelves, scrolls, and chests were covered in webs. Parts of the floor seemed to crawl. While the scribe searched through the scrolls, Warwick joined him and began to move sheets, flicking the spiders off. With every sheet he moved, he revealed seemingly endless piles of scrolls and odd assortments of objects, such as bowls and broken furniture, that had been left to rot. All the scrolls he found looked the same. Warwick had already read so many like these that he knew they were most likely going to be rubbish. He swiped away the scrolls in one pile, looking for any old ones underneath, but as the scrolls fell, they revealed a small chest buried beneath. The scribe turned to look and helped Warwick get the chest out. Even though it was small, it still felt heavy. A thick layer of dust covered the chest and hid the markings upon it. The scribe brushed it clean with his hand, and the markings he revealed were breathtaking. On the lid of the chest was a dragon, carved in very fine detail. The sight of it made Warwick smile. Warwick tried to open it, but a big iron lock kept it locked. Where would he even begin to look for the key? They had not seen any keys in this room, and with a matter as important as this, they doubted the key would have just been left for anyone to find. While they tried to get the chest open, the guard came behind them and stood watching, looking slightly curious. He saw them struggling and drew his sword. He pushed them aside and rammed the sword point hard into the lock. There was an awful scraping and a clicking sound of metal breaking. He pulled his sword out, and the point was dulled. It had broken the lock, though, and the chest opened. Inside were six scrolls, all in Latin. The scribe read them. Most spoke of the battle against the dragons but didn't bring to light anything Warwick didn't already know. Only one was of use. The scribe pulled a corked inkwell and a quill from his robes and translated what it said onto a piece of blank parchment he found. Warwick was stunned into silence as he read.

Accounts XI of the War

The battle is drawing to an end. We have suffered many casualties—the price of one dead dragon. A final charge was ordered and ended with the fall of the dragons. Our visions have come true. The weapons were not powerful enough. The dragons live! The armies leave, but so do the dragons depart to places deep and unknown. Ten days have passed since. We have seen a new vision of the dragons returning and of a young boy long in the future. It is time to write the prophecy. The Foekey is forged and the soul of the dead dragon poured into it. The three swords created for Drake, Aillig, and Alec have been recovered and melted down. The boy who holds the Foekey must travel to the valleys where the battle was fought. There he will find the sacred vale and the rest of the answers he seeks hidden where no other man can enter.

—Raghnall, lord of the seers

Warwick reread the parchment time and time again, searching for any more information. *Surely it must give some clue about where to go*, he thought to himself. He pestered the scribe, thinking perhaps he had translated it wrong, but he hadn't. Even the guard helped when they started to look through the remaining scrolls in the chest. The other scrolls all spoke of the war but said nothing about the prophecy or a location. It seemed like the precise location was deliberately left out. Warwick searched the bookshelves and found a book called *Ancient Lost Places of Scotland, Volume 1*. The book was big and very heavy. He dropped it on a table and opened it; inside it were pages and pages of maps and research. Some of the pages fell out as he turned them. A lot of the colours had faded, making it very tricky to read the maps. From what he could see, there was no evidence of the sacred vale. The chance of finding a surviving map that showed its location was looking slim, if such a map had ever been drawn. The scribe found nothing either. He searched endless scrolls and books, but none were old enough. There was so much rubbish in the room burying everything. If their answer was in there, it was going to take more than a day to find it.

They had spent hours searching, and having to admit defeat was a heavy blow. Warwick doubted the king would know where to find answers. He hadn't shown any sign of knowing anything about the battle before. Warwick, remembering his promise to the king, took the scroll with him. The king seemed to be very agitated when they walked into his throne room. King Angus had expected them back hours ago and did not like to be kept waiting. Warwick approached his throne and bowed low.

"Well?" The king's booming voice broke the silence of the room and startled Warwick.

Warwick passed him the scroll and took a step back. King Angus gave Warwick a quick glance before reading it. He read it aloud and then looked back to Warwick. "Is this all you found?"

"Yes, my lord. May I ask if you know anything about where the battle was fought?"

"I cannot give you your answer. The battle was long before my time and has been long unspoken of. I know nothing of this battle. If it helps, you may go with my scribe to my record room. If your answer is not there, then it doesn't exist. Make sure to return with haste!"

His scribe rushed to Warwick's side and didn't wait a minute to take Warwick. Warwick only had the time for a swift bow before he was marched from the room into another long, low passage. This passage took them to a large spiral staircase, which led to a very solid door of carven oak. It was locked tight with heavy chains and huge iron locks. From his belt, the scribe took a set of keys and began to unlock the chains that spanned the width of the door and then finally unlocked the big lock holding the door closed. The door groaned under its own weight as the scribe put his full force into opening it, and slowly it moved inwards.

This tower room was clearly used much more often; the air didn't smell, the whole room felt airy and clean, and torches burned in sconces on the walls. They were clearly at the top of the tower, as roof trusses spanned the tapered ceiling. Once again, the room was filled with aisles of shelves, all crammed with the record books. Each book looked as if it had been dusted. Warwick was relieved to have the scribe with him; the number of books was daunting. The scribe wasted no time and went searching aisles. Warwick took a handful of books, and weighed down, he staggered to a table at the back of the room and sat in a chair. He buried his head in them. After hours of reading, none of them had given him any answers. The scribe had sat at another table and had not had any luck himself. Mountains of books were stacking up slowly on each table, but still they found no answer.

The scribe went for more books, and Warwick followed him. The aisle they walked down had the oldest books, by the looks of things. The covers were worn and dog eared at the edges. Also, the dyed leather in which the books were bound had gone a motley colour as the dye faded unevenly. Warwick reached up to grab a book from a high shelf, but the scribe pulled him back. Only the scribe was allowed to handle those books. Warwick thought this odd, since the whole reason for him being there was to find evidence of the battle. He felt an annoyance but was careful to keep it hidden. Any hostility now could cast him from the room and end his search. The scribe grabbed several books, each one as thick as the last, and took them to a table. Warwick pulled up a chair next to him. Looking over his shoulder, Warwick instantly saw that the first book was written in the old tongue. If this book was not it, then at least they were looking at books from round the right time.

The scribe was incredibly quick at reading. Warwick could just hear the words merging together on his tongue. He began to skim through big chunks and soon closed the first book. The next book he grabbed was the same and spoke of the time just after the war; it contained nothing that would help. There were five books still untouched. It wasn't till the scribe reached the last book that Warwick's answer came. Warwick sat watching the scribe read. When the scribe found the answer, he pulled Warwick close. "It says, 'The army has been sent forth from Cill Chuimein. Tensions are high amongst the men. The soldiers grow disheartened, knowing most are marching to their death. No such battle has ever been fought. Nor can we see how it shall be won. Our only hope lies in the hands of Drake, Aillig, and Alec and the secret weapons they bear. The armies march upon Srath Pheofhair with great haste. Drake is doing his best to keep his armies strong but is struggling under the pressure. The armies march right into the dragons' home and let the horses go. It is now that the dragons attack. The battle is going ill, and many have fled. One dragon is dead, but its death came at great cost. We have lost thousands of men. The battle is over."

Warwick did not care that it spoke very little of the battle. He had found out what he wanted to know and now had a heading. He had never heard of Srath Pheofhair before, but surely all he would need to do was ask. He didn't realise it, but a tear rolled down his cheek. The strain of his journey and his tiredness had overcome him. Yet a small part of him felt happy now that he had the tools to avenge his parents, and if it weren't for the thought of the coming journey and certain danger, his happiness would have lasted.

The scribe had been looking up at him from the chair with a look of worry on his face. "Master Warwick, are you alright? If you are done here, then we must take this book to the king. He doesn't like to be kept waiting!"

Warwick had completely forgotten that the king waited for his return. Quickly, he wiped his tears away, and they made haste back to the king's chamber with the book. Warwick hoped this would be the last time he would have to prove his purpose. These delays were making him very fidgety. Once more they bowed before the king and presented the book to him, but the king ordered the scribe to read it aloud. Before the whole room, the scribe puffed himself up and pronounced every word sharply and loud. Suddenly the doors to the chamber burst open, breaking the atmosphere and stopping the scribe from speaking. It was Lord Exihainn, being carried by two serving boys. He had come to see about Warwick's progress, as it had been quite a while since he'd had any news. Once the commotion had settled in the room, the scribe read aloud again. Lord Exihainn looked towards Warwick, smiling the entire time the scribe was speaking. Warwick could see Lord Exihainn out of the corner of his eye and gave a quick smile from the side of his mouth in his direction. Warwick's smile was interrupted by the king. "So you have found your answer, Warwick. I see fit to give you your aid as I promised, now that I know your business and where you're headed. I shall see that you are given some suitable clothing and food, and at first light, you will leave the city. On your way out of the city, head to the armoury. I shall inform my squire to wait for you and arm you for the journey. This is all the aid I can afford to give, with the war and the dragons approaching! I wish you luck in these hard times. We are all grateful for what you are doing, even if my hospitality has seemed wanting. You may leave now and prepare."

Warwick bowed and tried to remain strong. It was finally hitting him that this was it: the calm before the war. The war that had never ended was coming to light again. He wondered if he would ever see any of these people again. He walked slowly from the room and towards his tower. In his room, he slumped onto his bed. He felt a bit sick thinking of the key, Rowan, and the journey to come. He still didn't know where he was going, as he'd never got a chance to speak.

Sleep that night was fleeting and frequently interrupted by haunting visions of dragons. It seemed not five minutes before he was being woken. A young boy stood at the side of his bed with a platter of bread and meat and a goblet of wine. Warwick ate it quickly, desperate for energy after the poor sleep. He looked out the window. There wasn't the faintest smudge of light in the sky. The air felt ice cold blowing in through the window. The young boy went and lit a torch and put it in a sconce on the wall. The light revealed a satchel stuffed with food and clothing for his journey leaning against the wall in the corner of his room. As soon as he was dressed in his warm clothing, after having taken a little extra time to make sure the key was safely round his neck, he marched through the passages to the main doors. The main road through the city had been cleared of snow, and within no time he was at the doors of the armoury. He nervously stepped inside. A few guards on night watch brushed past him, their heavy armour clinking loudly. They glared at him. They were huge men and looked like they had seen one or two battles. Warwick found the squire sitting alone by a fire, waiting. "I was sent here with the promise of aid from the king."

The squire looked at him with a furrowed brow. "You must be Warwick. I have been waiting. I have had your gear ready for hours! Come with me." The scribe stood and led Warwick into a darker room. The walls were laden with racks full of swords, pikes, spears, war hammers, and axes. Neatly placed out on a table in the centre was all his stuff. "Take your clothes off."

Warwick hesitantly did as instructed and stood cold in the room. The squire lowered a white tunic over his head and gave him a pair of black trousers to put on. The trousers were just like the ones his father had had, and he began to smile as he thought of his father. Both the trousers and tunic fitted well and felt warm and well made. The squire then lowered a vest of chainmail over his head. Warwick briefly slumped under its weight on his shoulders. A leather belt was strapped round him with his scabbard and steel sword attached. He noticed that on the other side of his belt he had a smaller scabbard with a razor-sharp steel dagger inside. The squire gave him a pair of strong, brown leather boots, and they fitted well. Warwick thought the scribe had finished, but then he fastened a leather chest plate to Warwick's torso and gave him a thick, black, padded jacket that draped down to his knees. He then passed Warwick his satchel and patted him on the back, leading him outside. From that moment onwards, Warwick knew that his time had truly come and that he must see things through to whatever end.

As he approached the gates, he could see the outline of something high in the air being held up by two columns. He soon realised it was in fact Lord Exihainn. He had been waiting by the main gates for him. Warwick was shocked to see him. His servants had carried him all this way. He grabbed Warwick as he got close enough. "I couldn't let you go without saying goodbye. I had hoped we would get chance to speak last night." He looked at Warwick in his armour, smiling. "So it has finally come. I can't believe what you have managed to achieve; I remember a frightened and injured boy standing before me at An Gearasdan. Now look at you, standing before me like a true man, like a soldier. I am so proud of you, as your parents and Rowan would be too. As far as I am concerned, you have passed the trials of manhood, and more importantly, you have opened the world up to the truth of the dragons. It is now, though, that I struggle for the right words to say. How does one truly say goodbye? Remember me as a friend, Warwick, not as a lord, and remember this: don't think of what is bad; think of what is good. Your heart will lead you. Take this map, it will lead you to Srath Pheofhair. Goodbye, Warwick. I hope you find what you need to find."

Warwick took the map, hugged Lord Exihainn, and then walked out through the gates.

CHAPTER 19

SAILS GOING SOUTH

The winds were bitter on their first day south. Rowan was still very weak and spent most of the time resting under a thick layer of blankets to keep warm. Whilst he rested, he desperately tried to focus his foresight to find Warwick, but it wouldn't work. He wondered if it was just because of his weakened state.

Faelan steered them into the deep margins of An Lighe Rathairseach, rowing like a man possessed to get away. Not even the struggle to fight the current slowed him. Normally a longboat of this size would be manned by at least sixteen men. With every stroke of the oars, he dug deep, putting his full weight behind them. His hands were sore and red from the effort. The pain made it hard to grip the oars, but nonetheless, Faelan continued, gritting his teeth through the pain and occasionally wiping his brow with the back of his hand. Not once had either of them thought about where they would land, but wherever they made port, it would have to be close to civilisation. Rowan couldn't walk far. Both he and Faelan knew that. His body was weak, and his wounds kept opening up and weeping blood.

The swells were getting pretty big as the wind grew. In the deeper waters, the boat tossed and turned, and it was almost impossible to control its direction. Several times, Faelan was almost cast from the boat. Eventually he stopped rowing all together, pulling the oars in to the boat. His attempts to row were just turning them on the waves. He let the boat drift with the current and took some rest next to Rowan. When they woke, it was the next day. It was bitterly cold, even with blankets over them. A thick mist had descended and hovered just above the surface of the water. A distant landmass was just a ghostly outline in the mist. They had lost track of where they were. The last place that they'd recognised was the tip of Longaigh. They were just thankful that the waters had calmed and that they had escaped the notice of the dragons so far. But that didn't lessen their worry any. Rowan moved himself with difficulty to the front of the boat and watched from the bow, squinting to see any landmarks faintly in the distance. Faelan sat in the middle of the boat rowing. He had changed course and was heading towards where he thought the bank was. Rowan called back to him at any sight of land. Eventually they were close enough to follow the shore and turned south. It wasn't long after finding the shoreline that the opposite bank came into view. Realising that it was fast narrowing, Rowan knew where they were. They had reached the gap of Caol Loch Aillse. The waters were often strong, but compared to what they had sailed through before, they seemed easy.

Rowan took a break from watch and began to think of Warwick, as usual; since his meeting with Seth, he had not been able to stop thinking of Warwick. He wanted to know more than anything where Warwick was. He was starting to doubt he would see him again. He refused to think of what his heart told him: that Warwick was dead. *Why can't this boat go faster,* he kept thinking. For a short while, he stared at Faelan with an anguished glint in his eyes, yet deep down, he knew Faelen was working flat out. If anything was responsible for their hindered progress, it was nature for causing the boat to rock from side to side and threatening to push them onto razor-sharp rocks just below the surface of the shoreline.

The waters widened again, and in the distance it was plain to see that it split in two directions. "Faelan, hang to the right-hand bank," Rowan shouted over the wind.

Faelan steered to the right and stuck to the bank like glue. For hours they sailed, but it only felt like they covered a few miles. They passed Caol Reatha and Glinn Eilg and finally reached Loch Shubhairne, just as the light was beginning to ebb away. The fog still hung in the air, and it would soon be impossible to see. They could not continue. On the north banks of Loch Shubhairne, they moored, dragging the boat far onto the bank. They turned the boat over next to a pine tree and crawled underneath to shelter for the night. For Rowan, rest was becoming more and more infrequent; his mind was stuck in a constant spin, as if a tornado were charging through his mind, leaving only two thoughts in its wake: Warwick and the dragons. *How are the dragons, as big as they are, moving almost unseen? And where are they? We hide under a wooden boat; is this our coffin? Have we not seen the dragons because they have found Warwick?* These and many more questions played on a constant loop in Rowan's head. His throbbing wounds, which smelled rancid from the days-old bandages, only added to his torment.

As soon as a smudge of light dawned on the horizon, they turned the boat over and launched from the bank. However, from the moment they set off, Faelan knew they wouldn't be able to go far with the discomfort Rowan was in. Rowan's wounds had turned yellow round the edges and oozed pus and small amounts of blood. They were a lot uglier than the day before. "We cannot go any farther south, Rowan. I would have taken you as far as you wanted, but it seems we must find port. Your wounds need treatment beyond what I can give. We will dock at the next port, wherever that may be."

Rowan did not deny that his wounds grew in pain and needed treatment.

The land slowly passed by for miles without a sign of any civilisation. Faelan was starting to panic at how much farther they might have to go. At least Rowan managed to sleep buried under a pile of blankets in the bottom of the boat. It was at the last light of the day that they saw a flicker of fire, which seemed to float high in the air over the shoreline. Of course this was a lighthouse, and they steered towards it. Soon they were at the port in Malaig. It was a small port but had obviously been deemed to be important for trade, since it had a lighthouse. Boats littered the docks. Many were merchant ships not dissimilar to the one they had been prisoners on. They tied the boat up at a mooring and headed for what looked like an inn. They walked between big, stone warehouses and old barns filled with barrels and fishing nets. In all that time, they did not see a single person on a ship or on land. They went inside the inn and staggered up to the barman behind the counter, enjoying the searing heat from the fire in the centre of the room.

"Can I help you?" the barman asked with a furrowed brow, looking them up and down. "What's wrong with him?" He had noticed how pale Rowan was and knew straight away he must be sick.

"Please, can you help my friend Rowan? He was injured and needs medicine," pleaded Faelan.

"And how is it that he became injured?" The barman moved from behind the counter and was speaking with a very stern tone in his voice.

Fear flickered in Faelan's eyes, but Rowan, in his weakened, state drew himself up. "I slipped on ice and fell backwards onto sharp rocks a few days ago. My friend here did all he could with his limited supplies."

The barman came closer and took a better look at Rowan, glancing at his wounds. "Well, we do have medical supplies that come in frequently from sea, but it will cost you if you want to use them. What moneys do you carry?"

Rowan and Faelan glanced at each other, realising that neither carried any money. "We have a boat you could sell for money?"

"Come with me," the barman gestured for them to follow with a wave of his hand. In a small side room, he placed a bowl on a table and filled it with water from a jug, placing a cloth and a towel next to the bowl. From a chest, he brought out fresh bandages and a corked glass bottle. "This is all I have, but it should clean his wounds."

They thanked the barman, and he left the room. Faelan washed the wounds with cold water, and Rowan winced, gritting his teeth. Faelan then applied the ointment, which upon closer inspection he saw was an antiseptic. Rowan cried, as it stung like his wounds were on fire. It didn't take long for the cloth to turn a brownish colour. Soon Rowan's wounds were re-dressed. They thanked the barman and left the inn.

Now that they had no transport, they didn't have a plan. Even with treatment, Rowan was still too weak to walk any distance. From the side of the inn, they heard the sound of a snorting horse. They had a look and saw three horses tethered to a gatepost beside an old cart. "Rowan, those horses … do you think we could take them?" Faelan spoke in barely a whisper in case anyone lurked in the shadows.

Rowan considered how urgent their need was for a moment. "It would be very hard on these people, but we have no transport. Do we have enough food to get far? I doubt we will find much on the road. I have considered the idea myself and don't see any other way. After a moment's hesitation, he said, "OK, we take the horses, but we must ride fast."

Faelan gave a small nod of agreement and headed for the horses. They untied them, mounted, and were off. They galloped down an old road, which didn't look very well used, based on the fact that it was blanketed in snow. Luckily for them, the road ran southeast. They followed it until it came to an unpassable ford. They had no choice but to turn off the road and follow the course of the river south. The deep snow off the road brought the horses to a slow, almost clumsy walk. It was hard work encouraging them to go faster, but now that they were well clear of Malaig, they didn't push the horses so much. Neither of them spoke for miles; they each suspected the other was troubled by his own guilt.

They made steady progress. In the distance, after passing over several big hills, they could see water stretching far beyond their sight. They headed towards it, looking to feed the horses. The hills grew steeper as they descended towards the water's edge. The far shores were lined with mountains, their peaks almost lost in clouds. All round the loch was a thick pine forest. They made their way through to a small clearing in the trees. The horses sank their heads deep into the loch and drank deeply, snorting at the same time. The horses were difficult when it came time to leave again. They became very skittish walking back up the steep edge of the clearing.

The hills became smaller as they followed the loch west towards its end. On the better, flatter ground, the horses could move a little faster, but the snow still held them back. They followed a river at the loch's head round the edge of an ancient forest and on to a small fishing port. A few men, looking like bears with their thick, woollen clothing and muscular bodies, busied themselves, going to and fro from several moored fishing boats with baskets and giant nets slung over their shoulders. "Excuse me, where am I?" called Rowan in nearly a shout to catch their attention.

One of them put down the basket he was carrying and wandered over to the side of Rowan's horse. "This is Airgead na gaineamh An Bá. Don't normally get people passing through on foot or horse back. Where is it that you're headed?" He looked at them both with wonder, seeing their ill-suited clothing and the tiredness on their face.

"We are heading to An Gearasdan," said Rowan.

"You have a long way to go. You need to turn south here and follow the course of the mountains till you can turn southeast. Malaig is much nearer if you want a place to rest."

"Thank you," replied Rowan, and they trotted south, keeping their business secret. They trotted on for miles at the shore's edge, unable to turn inland. The good news was that the ground was so much flatter. For a short while, Rowan, enjoying the peace, closed his eyes and thought he was riding with Warwick. The happiness only lasted a brief time; Faelan rode closer to Rowan, disturbing his peace and glancing continuously at the peaks, which were growing higher as they began to steer from the shore. "Do you think the dragons will be near?" Faelan asked inquisitively.

"They could be, but even if they were, I doubt we would know about it until it was too late. I would rather not continue this conversation further!" Rowan looked directly into Faelan's eyes with a hard stare. Silence fell between them, but it wasn't peaceful. It was the noisiest silence either had experienced. The hills continued to grow closer and higher until they were forced to climb. The horses unwillingly trotted forward, stamping their feet as it got steeper and snorting impatiently. The ride was becoming so hard that it nearly unseated them both. The view ahead was only getting worse—it was a long way to the top, and boulders were strewn like scree across the entire hill. After an hour's scramble and stumble, they found the top of the ridge. They could see far from the summit. Below was a small coastal town, and just beyond that was a small loch running east. Something in the back of Rowan's mind rang clear as a bell. He turned towards Faelan, remembering finally at last where they were. "That is the town of An Garbh Criochan. We can stay there for the night."

"How do you know this place when for miles we have been blind?"

"I had forgotten that I had been to An Garbh Criochan when I was a child with my mother, but seeing the small town and the loch stretching beyond it made me remember." He was smiling at Faelan. It was the first time he had smiled since meeting Faelan.

They made their way down the slopes towards the town as the light waned, guided by the small lights from windows. The horses liked the descent even less than the assent. They restlessly slipped and stumbled, fighting for a footing and nearly unseating Rowan and Faelan several times. Rowan and Faelan increasingly worried that one might break a leg if it fell. At the bottom of the slopes, they dismounted with a sigh of relief.

It was only a couple of miles to An Garbh Criochan, but the horses wouldn't move for anyone. But after resting the horses, they could finally move on. When they were on the move again, they quickened their pace and soon were in An Garbh Criochan. From up on the mountain ridge, it had seemed calm, but now that they were here, they could clearly see that the town was in fear. People rushed between buildings shouting and didn't even notice their presence. It was impossible to tell what anyone said, as their voices merged together like the gabble of geese. Rowan began to sniff the air as the smell of something burning drifted towards them. Faelan turned to look at Rowan as he heard his breathing increase. His eyes were wide, his face pale, and his hands trembling in his lap, clasped tight together. "Faelan, we cannot stay here! The way these people dash about reminds me of An Gearasdan. If a dragon has not yet attacked, it has been seen and close by!"

Faelan watched in shock, having never seen such panic. "Where do we head now?"

Rowan was about to speak when he saw a glimpse of movement in the sky. "Faelan we must go now. Ride hard!"

Rowan turned his head as they galloped through the town and could see the dragon in the distance. He encouraged his horse to ride faster. Faelan shot a brief glance over his shoulder as well and saw the dragon for the first time. He was scared by the size of it and kicked his horse to go faster to catch up with Rowan. They galloped through the narrow streets, their ears filled with the sounds of screaming people. Behind them they could hear the dragon's roar growing ever louder. The thought of leaving these people to die by dragon fire was sickening, but they couldn't do anything to help. Whilst the dragon destroyed the town, they made their escape. They galloped over a small wooden bridge, which nearly collapsed with the speed of the horses. The bridge led to an old traders' road heading east. Miles later, they could still hear the cries and roars and could still smell smoke. They came across a small pine forest and led the horses deep into its heart. Without lighting a fire, they made camp for the night hidden amongst the thick undergrowth, hoping the canopy would protect them from view if the dragon came their way. Faelan tied up the horses and watched with a puzzled look as Rowan struggled into the nearest tree. "There could be wolves," whispered Rowan in response to the look upon Faelan's face. Faelan climbed into the next tree and found a good spot to sleep.

In the early light, they crept from their trees with eyes peeled and ears pricked. It was plain to see from the dark bags under their eyes that they had slept very little. Faelan seemed very anxious, glancing continuously at Rowan. "What is it?" Rowan asked in a quiet but sharp tone, having noticed the irritating glances.

"I can't get it out of my head—the sheer size of the beast, the speed, the terror, the destruction. I didn't want to ask, but I can't contain myself. How on earth did you escape when you were attacked?" He shifted nervously.

"Don't talk so loud! It was luck that saved me."

"But you've escaped them more than once? I could tell when I mentioned An Gearasdan being destroyed on the ship." Faelan had lowered his voice but remained so focused that he could only see Rowan in front of him.

"An Gearasdan was different. There were lots of people and lots to keep the dragon's focus, which gave me enough time to escape."

"I am glad I am with someone who is experienced and knows what to do." Faelan tried to smile.

Rowan smiled back. "I do not believe that there is such a thing as experience in the face of dragons. Still, I am glad to have your company also."

"May I ask why we travel to An Gearasdan when it was destroyed? Till now I had been happy just to follow in your footsteps and be free, but having seen what haunts your mind, I cannot help but wonder about your intentions."

"I am surprised you haven't asked before now. I travelled with a friend for a while from An Gearasdan. We went our separate ways when we got to An t-Eilean Sgitheanach. Ever since I was attacked by the dragon, I have been hell-bent on finding him. I go back to An Gearasdan in the hope that he came back the way we came."

"Well, I have nowhere to go now and no responsibilities, so I would like to help you find your friend. It's the least I can do for a friend."

Rowan beamed at him as a sense of true loyalty swelled in his heart. "Thank you. I am really glad I have you by my side, my friend. I think we are about two days away from An Gearasdan."

From the edge of the trees, they checked the sky and hills. When they were sure everything was clear, they broke from the cover of the trees, heading east as fast as the horses would carry them in the deep snow. They followed a river, a rope of blue, that ran in the direction of their path. Soon the river was a loch, and they hung as close to the shore as they possibly could to avoid having to find a path through the dense forests and then climb the peaks. By no means was the progress quick at the shore's edge—the banks were a bed of large, unstable, slippery rocks. The horses stumbled and slipped, moving at walking pace. By the end of that day, though, they had made it to Gleann Fhionnain and made camp on the shores of Loch Seile.

There was an unusual sound of distant banging and clinking echoing through the glens that night. Gleann Fhionnain was a completely unpopulated place, so Rowan sat bolt upright with widened eyes, trying to focus on the sound. Faelan wasn't far behind him. With the way the wind whipped and swirled, the sound seemed to change direction within a fraction of a second. "What if it is the dragon still destroying An Garbh Criochan? Or worse, following our trail?" whispered Faelan.

"It won't be the dragon destroying An Garbh Criochan."

"How do you know that?"

"With how easily An Gearasdan fell, An Garbh Criochan will be nothing but scattered ash by now." Rowan hung his head and sighed as he spoke.

Faelan's heart started to race. "So then you think it is the dragon hunting us?"

"Again, I am not certain. If the dragon hunted us, it would have caught us ages ago. I had thought myself we might be close to a bandit cave."

"A bandit cave!" Even with some reassurance that it wasn't a dragon, Faelan's heart still raced faster and faster. He suspected that Rowan was keeping something from him or not telling him the full truth.

The sounds continued to circle them. Rowan got to his feet and began walking towards the mountains, trying to find where the sound was loudest. As far as he looked, he saw no sign: not a light or anything.

"We should leave now! I feel more comfortable travelling under the cover of darkness." Rowan didn't even wait for Faelan to reply but began untying his horse. Faelan quickly scanned the ground, checking they hadn't forgotten anything, and then followed quickly after Rowan. The river that had been such an ally in their journey had now faulted, turning deep into a forest. It was clear to see that the forest was massive, as it grew up the slopes ahead of them and disappeared down the other side. It seemed they had no other choice than to go through the trees. They trotted forward, hugging the river bank until the river flowed into a gorge and its banks became sheer rocky cliffs. There was nothing for it but to face the darkness of the trees. Low branches whipped against their arms and faces, and a few watery eyes later, they were forced to dismount and walk. They squeezed between trees through the few gaps they could find, completely blind to their direction. The horses stomped and flicked their heads impatiently in the confined darkness. The deeper they went, the denser the pine trees became. Where the river crashed against rocks, they could faintly hear it rushing a long way to the right. Having only the faintest of leads, they turned towards it in the hope that the path might be better. All they found was a steep precipice with the thinnest of ledges between the edge and the trees. Even if they could have scrambled along it, the horses wouldn't. They turned back into the trees but never strayed out of hearing distance of the river. A short while later, they were climbing through the trees over rocky ground. At their feet, the roots snaked all over the rock like blood veins, trying to trip them up. The mass of rock started to divide the trees, and the going became a little easier. Before long, they were standing on the summit, trying to peer through the branches ahead to see over the top of the forest. The branches grew so close that they only caught the faintest glimpses of the tops of trees against the rising sun. They descended over the rock into the dense mass ahead of them. As long as they were heading downhill, they weren't straying too far from their path. When they finally emerged from the trees, they found themselves on a flat plain in broad daylight. The river was much farther away than they had thought, snaking a long way to the west.

The horses neighed happily in the open air, kicking the snow away to get at the young shoots buried beneath. After a rest, the horses managed to find more speed in the snow. It seemed they were thankful for the flatter ground. The plain opened onto the shores of Loch Iall, and to Rowan's delight, he knew exactly where they were and could almost see the walls of An Gearasdan. However, in the back of his mind, he was fearful to see the ruined walls. Not once had he mentioned to Faelan that he had doubts that they would find Warwick there.

The water of Loch Iall rippled at the shore peacefully. The sound was comforting, and to feel the breeze rising from the water was almost welcome, even if it was bitterly cold. They trotted the last few miles. At the first sight of the walls, Rowan froze and shut his eyes. Faelan drew his horse up next to Rowan and looked with concern at his face, which was scrunched up as if he fought to stop something. "Are you alright?" Rowan didn't reply, so Faelan gently shook his shoulder. He opened his eyes, and Faelan saw they were bloodshot. "What is it, Rowan?"

"I can still hear the voices screaming like it was only yesterday."

"Try to think of your friend and finding him. We are so close now." For the first time, Faelan road in front, and Rowan followed very half-heartedly. Before they knew it, they stood before the barely recognisable charred city walls.

CHAPTER 20

CHOICES IN THE DARK

The light was almost gone, and the silence that hung over An Gearasdan was oppressively heavy. It would have sickened someone with the strongest of will. The black, cracked, and crumbling scorched walls radiated the poison of the dragon. The air seemed to be permanently fouled by a lingering stench like burnt, rotten meat, making them heave. A tear ran down Rowan's face, and he sat down on a mound of rubble, grieving intensely. Faelan sat by his side speechless, looking at the rubble and the jagged buildings reduced to their foundations. *How could anything cause this much destruction in such a short time?* he thought to himself. His heart felt fit to burst with grief; now he realised just how much pain Rowan was in coming back here and just how much Rowan's friend must have meant to him.

Rowan appreciated Faelan's look of sympathy but was desperate to be alone. The pain had been made all the worse by finding the city abandoned; no one searched through the rubble for belongings, and no one had started to rebuild. The city seemed to have been permanently forsaken. All round the city was a mound of rubble piled three stories high, and poking from between the rocks were the remnants of the farming community just outside the walls. What once had been cultivated land, was now a scorched wasteland run through with deep cracks like crevasses. He got up and pushed the barely hanging city gates open and instantly froze. The remaining walls had acted as a barrier from the wind that carried the stench, but now that he was inside the walls, he got hit with its full magnitude. He'd thought the sight of the destruction couldn't get any worse, but what he saw now was beyond anything he could have imagined. No houses stood, their only remains being the mountains of blackened stone piled four stories high. He tried to identify any little bits of walls that still stood, but all was beyond recognition. He strolled to where he thought the inn had once been, turning his head away when he caught a glimpse of several bodies crushed under the rubble. It was almost impossible to tell which mound of rubble was the inn. The formerly snug, secluded little street was now wide open, and he could see a large mound of rubble and one wall that looked like it was being held up by the rubble. That was all that remained of the keep. *Not even the lords survived*, he thought, shaking his head.

After a while, Faelan dared to accompany Rowan. When he saw the mangled bodies, he wished he hadn't. "I am sorry to disturb your solitude, but we came to find your friend, and it doesn't seem he is here." Faelan tried his hardest to bring Rowan to his senses.

Rowan sat back down on the rubble. "No, it doesn't seem he is here."

"What do we do now?"

"I don't know. Finding him here was my only thought. But I am glad he is not here after seeing all this. It hurts more than I can say."

"I am sorry I couldn't be of any more help to you," Faelan said in a quieter tone.

"I will understand if you choose to leave. Thank you for your help and friendship."

"Seeing all this destruction and death ... I can't handle it. I hope more than anything you find your friend."

"Where will you go?"

"I think I might try to find my way back to Ireland and find my family."

"Good luck. I won't forget the help you gave."

They walked to what remained of the gate, where the horses waited. Faelan hugged Rowan and mounted his horse. Rowan stood watching as he rode away into the gloom.

In one last attempt to find Warwick, Rowan went to check the docks. When he didn't find him, he wasn't surprised. There wasn't a single boat that remained, and An Linne Dhubh was covered by a carpet of drifting timbers as far as the eye could see. Nothing but the blackened rock the dock once stood on remained. As he wiped away a tear, he was suddenly struck with a vision of a sickness born of the attack running wild through the wounded survivors. It had been so long since he had last had a vision that he couldn't remember when it was. But what did this new vision mean? He thought long and hard but came to no definitive answer. Was it a warning to stay away from the city? If disease was spreading, though, the walls wouldn't trap it. If the vision was true, then there was nothing he could do about it, so he did not think anything of it. He walked on slowly while tears leaked from his eyes.

Most of the night, he lay in a crumbling corner of a building outside the walls, which just gave him enough shelter. He woke frequently in a cold sweat having seen images of Warwick, burning buildings, and dragons. When he woke for what seemed like the sixth time, he wasn't alone. Sitting on a mound of rubble nearby, much to his surprise, was Faelan. He had never been more pleased to see someone. Rowan looked closely at Faelan; he could see the same sorrow and terror he felt mirrored in Faelan's eyes. It was clear that Faelan was trying to smile. "I am sorry I left," he blurted out, unable to contend with the weight of the guilt.

Rowan cracked a little smile. "I understand why you did what you did. I don't feel any anger towards you. I only wonder what it was that made you return and so quickly."

Faelan finally smiled, as the weight on his shoulders lifted. "I came back because you are my friend and I shouldn't have given up and left you. And even if I had made it back to Ireland, I doubt I would be able to find my family."

"I am glad you're with me."

"Do you have a plan for where to go next?" Faelan asked.

"No."

"We might have a better idea after some rest."

They settled back down in the corner that Rowan had been sleeping in, but Rowan didn't sleep. He couldn't sleep. Wide awake, he lay looking up at the starry night sky; the stars seemed brighter now than ever. It had long been believed that stars were the souls of the dead on their journey to a better world. A particularly bright star caught his eye. It looked much bigger and closer than the rest. He stared at it for so long that it seemed to move, and he wondered if it were Warwick watching over him. It brought warmth to his heart and a smile to his lips feeling that Warwick was finally free of pain and safe with his family again. His head felt clearer, and he felt he knew what to do.

Faelan woke at first light to see Rowan wide awake and ready for the off. Strangely, Rowan seemed to be smiling and acting really confidently.

"What's happening?"

"I am heading to Cill Chuimein." Rowan spoke quickly, as if he were trying to hurry Faelan to get ready.

"Just … just wait a second. Is there something you haven't told me? Last night you didn't have any idea where to go, and now suddenly you do. Who exactly is your friend? You never told me."

Rowan stopped what he was doing and looked at Faelan. "Yes … I believe my friend Warwick may be in Cill Chuimein. I didn't tell you straight away to protect him, but I see I can no longer keep it quiet. We didn't travel together just to look at cave paintings. The reason I am so desperate to find him is because of a prophecy—"

"A prophecy!"

"Please let me finish. Warwick is not an ordinary person. Centuries ago, there was a war against the dragons. The dragons lost, but from what I have come to understand, weren't killed. They disappeared after the battle, and no one knows what happened to them. This was when the prophecy was written. The prophecy was almost completely lost over the centuries, but now it has started to come to light as the dragons return. We seers were given a vision many years ago, after which I knew that this prophecy was tied to my dearest friend, Warwick. We travelled to An t-Eilean Sgitheanach looking for answers about the prophecy in cave paintings. The vision we seers had received was very basic. We found some answers, but it was still very unclear what he must do. After that, we went our separate ways, as I believed I couldn't interfere, since the prophecy was written only for him. But I was wrong. I could help him. Now I fear he may be dead because of me. I must at least find his body and bring him home. He carries the hearts of many who have died."

Faelan stood aghast for a moment before he returned to his senses. "Why did you not tell me of this before?"

"I feared for Warwick's safety, and I feared your reaction."

"Surely you could have used his name rather than calling him 'my friend'."

"I am sorry" was all Rowan could find to say.

"Come on, let's go and find Warwick." Faelan sat on his horse with not a single flicker of anger as if the conversation had never happened. Side by side they rode away from An Gearasdan.

Just to the north of the city was the trading road. Rowan recalled that it ran east for a while before turning north. For a good while, it would head directly where they needed to go. The road hugged the bank of the River Lòchaidh for several miles until it came to a derelict village. There it turned north, so they left the road. Since the land by the bank had been quite flat, they decided to continue following the river. It twisted and turned for miles, and the constant snaking slowed them down. To their relief, though, the snow wasn't as deep the closer they came to the water.

They came to a forest at Strone, but things took a turn for the worst. Bandits had made camp in the forest and preyed on any who dared enter. Rowan and Faelan had ridden right into their lair before they realised it. Turning back wasn't an option. The pine trees kept the snow from falling to the floor, but they also left no room to turn the horses round. Shouts and the sounds of twigs breaking loudly came from all round them. Then something whistled past Rowan's head, followed by more and more objects. One hit a tree close to Faelan and stuck straight out, vibrating violently. It was a spear! The trees were as much friends as they were enemies; slowly weaving between them, Rowan and Faelan were effectively protected by a never-ending shield wall of trees that the spears and bandits

J.B.LIQUORISH

had to fight their way through. Nonetheless, Rowan and Faelan lay flat on the backs of their horses, kicking hard at their sides to spur them on as fast as they could go. The bandits needed no horses to lay chase; snaking, ducking, and stumbling amongst the trees, it was impossible to gather any speed. In fact, it seemed the bandits were gaining ground and tightening the circle round them. Fortunately, the trees were also serving as allies once more—the thick, nearly impenetrable clumps of pine trees kept the bandits from coming too close and blocking every exit. For a brief moment, Rowan's racing heart relaxed a little as he began to think they might get out of this. Suddenly, one of the bandits broke from cover, charging as quickly as he could towards them. Rowan's and Faelan's hearts leapt into their mouths, and before they knew it, they had split apart and lost sight of each other, narrowly missing the bandit and his spear. The darkness looked endless ahead of them, and as hard as they listened for the sound of each other's horses, it was impossible to say where they were. They hadn't the slightest glimpse of one another. A short while farther on, Rowan burst out of the trees back at the riverside. He could no longer hear the sound of running or the angry shouts. He immediately turned his horse to look directly into the trees. His heels quivered at the horse's side as he stayed ready to gallop off with or without Faelan. His ears were pricked like a fox's. *How far did Faelan stray from his path?* he kept thinking, growing more nervous with every second he remained still. Rowan wondered if he had lost the bandits when they split. It seemed that way till Faelan burst from the trees higher up the slopes at such a speed you would think the forest burned. The air round him was filled with a vast swarm of arrows and spears, but free of the trees, Faelan mustered all the speed he could, and the volley fell short of its target. Rowan kicked his horse hard and lay flat on its back as he galloped after Faelan and away from the bandits. Faelan clung to the reins of his horse, his face pale and bloody. He didn't even realise Rowan was just behind him. They continued at full speed long after they had lost sight of the forest and the bandits had turned back defeated. Only when the horses tired of the hard running in the deep snow did they slow. It was a great surprise to Faelan to see Rowan pull up beside him.

They hoped to make it to Cill Chuimein before nightfall, but the days were very short, and it was still a long way. For almost an hour, the horses would not budge as they drank deeply from the icy water and dug deep for the young, tender saplings poking through the soil. Once the horses were ready, they were quickly on the move and soon at the end of the river, as its banks rapidly broadened into the huge waters of Loch Lòchaidh. They left deep tracks behind them in the deep, pebbled shore as they touched the water to avoid the snow and the band of trees running for miles.

Many forests lay ahead, much to their chagrin. They decided to try to avoid them if possible. The chances that the bandits they had encountered were the only ones in these parts were very slim. The shore soon became very rocky and began to climb up to high cliffs. Their pace was reduced as the horses scrambled up onto the ridges. The cliff ledges were very thin, and it was miles before they descended. But by being high up, they could get a view of the path ahead and of the loch. Though far off, they could faintly see the shores coming together at the far end. The cliffs to their left towered over them, which made them a little cautious. Their fear of the mountains and sky was growing stronger every day. No one knew where a dragon might be or when it would decide to attack, and this caused them many sleepless nights and much paranoia.

Quite a few fishing boats were making their way up to Cill Chuimein. Loch Lòchaidh was a vital source of food for Cill Chuimein. A lot of people used to fish on Loch Nis, but that stopped when they started getting very few catches. It was an odd circumstance, as that used to be the main place to fish. Some say it was simply overfished, but the older fisherman said different. They thought something had scared the fish away but didn't know what. So Cill Chuimein now relied heavily on Loch Lòchaidh for business. None of the boats were big, for the rivers that fed into the lochs were all narrow and shallow with sharp meanders.

Rowan quickened the pace as soon as he could. They had travelled almost halfway round the north end of Loch Lòchaidh. They were a bit more settled now that they were sure they weren't being followed, and the sound of the birds in the gorse bushes gave them comfort and a feeling that they were safe for the moment. Rowan often looked upon the ground, looking for any sign of wolves nearby, but all he saw from his horse were deer tracks heading into the trees.

The cliffs were falling slowly once more down to the water's edge. All along their path, the cliffs had been rising and falling, deeply upsetting the pace of the horses. They finally came to the bottom of a slippery slope and passed under a small canopy of trees, coming out onto a rocky shore. The water was lapping at the horse's feet. The horses were not too keen on this, as the water was ice cold. Several times they tried to turn into the trees, but Rowan and Faelan were desperate to avoid them for fear of having another close run-in.

The day became afternoon, and the miles slowly rolled on. They made it past the loch uneventfully and watched the boats as they struggled in the shallows of the River Ceann, trying to find the deeper, faster waters. Oarsmen were pushing off from the banks, using oars where they could. Rowan and Faelan saw this happening for miles before the river became lined thickly with trees. When the two of them came to these trees, they altered their route to skirt round them. They weren't going to take any risks, and the trees would only slow them down.

It was nearing mid-afternoon, and the light was beginning to fade behind the mountains. They still had Loch Omhaich to cover, and at night it could be too dangerous. With that in mind, they spurred the horses on faster. Soon they could see the river's end and the start of Loch Omhaich. "Faelan, come on. It's not far now." Rowan could sense that Faelan was not happy.

To Faelan, the lochs seemed endless, and the thought of another loch put a very heavy weight upon him. The cold was not helping. On horseback, he was having to do very little work and couldn't warm up. What was worse, the winds were stronger here and hit them from the side. If night fell whilst they were still riding, the horses would stop in the low temperatures and not go on. It was too much of a risk in the wilds now to have fires. Danger was growing every day.

They climbed up once more but higher this time, and they could see the whole of Loch Omhaich stretching to an end before them. Still, they couldn't see Cill Chuimein yet. Many forests were in between it and them. The light was setting quickly, but on these narrow ledges, they could not risk pushing the horses. It was too dangerous. At the foot of the cliffs were sharp rocks and deep, deep water. If one of them should fall, death would be certain. They came to the edge of a forest with very little room between it and the water. It was hard, but they managed to skirt round the edge. As Rowan looked in, he saw that under the trees, the light had already gone. The light would soon be the same round them outside the forest.

The bottoms of their trousers were getting wet. The horses were cantering through the water along the edge. But it was either get wet or get caught up in the trees. The water was making them very cold, but speed was with them. A joining river flowed into Loch Omhaich not far ahead, and they could see no sign of a bridge to cross it. They rode up and down its bank for a while, looking for the shallowest place to ford it. The current looked fairly strong, but they had no choice. It was Rowan who went first. Instantly his horse began to slip and slide on the rocks of the river bed. The horse whinnied frantically in the cold waters. At the point they chose to cross, the water came up to the top of the horses' legs. There was a lot of splashing, and Rowan ended up soaked by the time he finally clambered up the other bank. Faelan had waited on the other bank till Rowan was across. He was already miserably unhappy, and the cold water made his mood twice as bad.

No word was spoken the rest of the way. They gained a little relief, though, at the end of the last loch. All that was left was a few miles at the side of the River Obhaich. Trees lined its banks, but the ground was flatter here, which was some comfort. The number of boats was growing, and the river was looking clogged. They snaked the last few miles, and finally Cill Chuimein came into sight, sticking out from behind the trees. The river widened slowly as it approached

Cill Chuimein. The docks were built along the riverbanks, jutting out into the deepest water. Beyond this, the shores of Loch Nis stretched on for miles, far beyond sight. Rowan and Faelan turned from the river and headed away from the port to the city walls.

CHAPTER 21

THE MESSENGER

Rowan and Faelan dismounted at the gates when city guard approached. "Halt!" cried one of the guards with his hand resting on the hilt of his sword.

Faelan turned white when the guard's blazing fierce eyes met his. "Under order of the king, all outsiders must state their purpose before entering the city."

Having glanced at the look of fear on Faelan's face, Rowan stepped forward. "We are looking for a friend who may have travelled here."

"Your names?"

"Rowan and Faelan."

"Your friend's name?"

"Warwick."

"Wait here!" Whilst the guard marched into the city, the other guards stuck fast to Rowan and Faelan's side, keeping hold of the reins of their horses. The time that elapsed while they waited under the pressure of the watchful guard felt a lot longer than it actually was. Finally the guard returned. "The captain of the guard grants you entry. Be warned, you will find the discipline hard should you seek trouble!"

Rowan and Faelan's horses were led away and tied up outside the stables. Then the guards opened the gates and allowed them both to pass. Just out of sight of the guards, Faelan exhaled as if he had held his breath the entire time they were being interrogated.

"You'd better hold your nerve better in here, Faelan!" said Rowan before immediately turning down a side street and starting to search high and low for any sign that Warwick may be there. Faelan followed but still refused to speak.

They asked what seemed like most of the city's civilians about Warwick but received only silence and head shakes in response, which put a lot of doubt in their minds that they would find Warwick here. They started to look for an inn to get out of the cold. At least they could find a bed for the night. However, they never made it to an inn. They were waylaid first. At first they thought the man before them was a guard until they noticed he didn't have a sword. Instead, he had a leather satchel strung across his shoulder stuffed with scrolls. He stared at them both with a look of curiosity. "I hear you are looking for someone called Warwick."

Surprise stilled Rowan's tongue, and he struggled to speak straight away. "How do you know?"

"I am a messenger, and you have been asking all over the city. I was curious to find out who was asking?"

"My name is Rowan—"

He was cut short by the messenger. "Please wait here." The messenger hastened away, leaving them both dumbstruck. He returned a short while later and asked them to follow. He led them away from the narrow streets, past the market, and past the armoury. The whole time, Rowan and Faelan glanced nervously at each other. When they entered the keep, they couldn't help but feel fear in their hearts. Several flights of stairs and many corridors later, the messenger finally stopped outside a door. A cold sweat glistened on both their heads. He knocked loudly, and a voice beckoned them to enter. The door opened, and in a corner of the large room in a large wooden armchair sat, to Rowan's great shock, Lord Exihainn— though not like he had last seen him. Lord Exihainn's leg was missing, and he appeared to be heavily scarred. Nonetheless he beamed at the sight of Rowan and pointed to two seats in his room for them to sit. Rowan did not waste any time, now that hope was flooding back into his heart. "Have you seen Warwick, my lord?" He was sitting forward in his seat, and his hands clenched the arms of the chair tightly.

"Yes, he was here, and what a surprise it was to see him. It probably won't come as a shock to you, but we thought you dead. I cannot tell you how much it pleases me to see you alive." His grin spread right across his face, and his eyes started to glisten.

"He is alive!" Rowan was now standing, and Faelan had a hand round Rowan's wrist trying to pull him back into the seat.

"Yes, when last I saw him three days ago, he was alive. I couldn't believe just how much he had grown into a man since An Gearasdan."

"All this time travelling, I thought I would be looking for a body. I can't believe he made it all by himself." Tears leaked from Rowan's eyes. "Do you know where he is, where he is going?"

"I do! I shall tell you all that I know."

"Thank you!" Rowan sat back down, focusing as hard as he could so as not to miss a single word.

"I was hospitalised and couldn't move from bed. I had been ordering servants daily to send riders out looking for you both after An Gearasdan. I started to presume you were dead until I received a message several days later saying that a travelling messenger had given a young boy he'd met at Carn Eige by the name of Warwick directions to Cill Chuimein. My excitement, I can tell you, had never been so high in all my life. I did then wonder what had happened to you. A few days later, Warwick showed up in the city looking like he had faced an army single handed. He was brought to me and the king, who waited impatiently for word of Warwick's business. I had no option but to tell the king about you both. Warwick spoke before the court about his travels since An Gearasdan, the cave paintings, and the reason he had come to Cill Chuimein. He revealed all he knew of the prophecy. The king allowed him to search his private vaults and libraries for answers about where he needed to go. It took a long while, but eventually, he found enough evidence to point him in the right direction. He said the sacred vale was at Srath Pheofhair, and before he left, I showed him on a map where he needed to go. I am afraid I cannot show you what he found, as the king has locked it away in his vault."

Rowan gaped in amazement as he listened to the stories of Warwick's accomplishments. Then he thought about what Warwick must have faced on his journey from An t-Eilean Sgitheanach to harden him this much. "I must leave now and find him," Rowan said.

"I am afraid you won't be leaving just yet."

"What do you mean?" Rowan was already halfway to his feet, ready to dash for the door.

"All news that I receive is also shared with the king. You see, the messengers that have served me are actually the king's messengers. The king will want to see you. I should also like to hear your story."

Reluctantly, Rowan sat back down, looking rather agitated. Even Faelan looked agitated. So far, Rowan had drawn Lord Exihainn's full attention, and that had kept him from being interested in Faelan. But now his attention was focused on both of them.

"Who is this that you have travelled with?"

"This is Faelan. I was brought onto the deck of a merchant ship after having been found floating in the water unconscious off the coast of An t-Eilean Sgitheanach. I had been attacked by a dragon. That is when I met Faelan, who saved my life. But then I learnt that Faelan had been taken from his home for his skills as a physician and was being kept prisoner onboard the ship—the crew were corrupt. Soon as we could, we hatched a plan and escaped, taking one of the long boats on the ship. Since then, Faelan has been a friend to me. He decided to travel with me to help me find Warwick."

"Why are you speaking for him, Rowan?" Lord Exihainn's eyes had been fixed on Faelan the entire time Rowan spoke.

Rowan shut his eyes, but it was Faelan who answered. "I am Irish!"

Lord Exihainn shifted uncomfortably in his seat.

"Please," Rowan interjected quickly, "you can trust him. He is a very loyal friend to me and wishes no harm to anyone."

"I trust you, Rowan, with my life, and as you very determinedly vouch for him, I shall trust him too. Perhaps a friendship could bring about a peace between us and Ireland." Lord Exihainn relaxed in his seat and smiled at Faelan. He then looked suddenly at Rowan with a furrowed brow. "Tell me, why do you so desperately seek to find Warwick? He spoke of your separation on An t-Eilean Sgitheanach."

"I was wrong ..." He put a hand to his face, shaking his head. "Prophecies are written for specific people, and with my lack of knowledge, I believed that I couldn't offer him any more assistance than to point him, hopefully, in the right direction. If I interfered too much, I believed, then I endangered Warwick's quest. My vision regarding this prophecy had always been too basic. I learnt how wrong I was shortly after I left Warwick. I found one of my brother seers by a cave, but he was gravely injured by a dragon that had been living in secret deep within the tunnels. With his last breath, he told me I was mistaken and that I should make haste to find Warwick."

Lord Exihainn slumped a little in his chair. "I am sorry. It seems your journey has been just as hard as Warwick's. How did you know to come here?"

"The cave paintings showed a huge army, which I realised could only be a king's army. There is also the nearest civilisation to An Gearasdan, and I figured Warwick probably would have tried to retrace the route we had taken from An Gearasdan to An t-Eilean Sgitheanach, as he didn't know the land well. His father was also a soldier for the king, so Warwick must have heard of Cill Chuimein. It seemed a good bet."

Suddenly there was a knock on the door, killing all conversation. A messenger entered the room. "The king demands your immediate presence."

As he had addressed no one in particular, they all went with the messenger, Lord Exihainn being carried by servants as normal. Rowan clenched his fingers, impatient at yet another delay, as they made their way towards the throne room.

The king sat high on his throne in obvious agitation at their slow arrival. They stopped close to the throne, and all except Lord Exihainn bowed deeply. "Which one of you is the one who travelled with Warwick?"

"I did. My name is Rowan, sire."

"Ah, yes, he did mention your name. Why have you come? Warwick is no longer here."

"I came because I was wrong to leave him. I hoped I might find him here."

"Why were you wrong?"

"I believed from my knowledge of prophecies and my visions that I could only guide him through the first steps of his journey and then point him in the right direction. If I intervened too much, I thought, I could cause him to fail in his quest. I was proven wrong on An t-Eilean Sgitheanach when I found a brother seer badly wounded by a dragon. He told me the truth of what was missing from my visions. He told me that I should never have left Warwick. From that moment, I have been hell-bent on finding him, even if I was looking for a corpse." Rowan's agitation kept on growing every time he had to repeat himself. "Sire, please, may we leave so we can go and find him?" There was clearly desperation in Rowan's voice.

"Not yet! Who is this that accompanies you?" The king remained impassive to anything that was sensitive or to their desperate urge to run from the room.

Rowan now saw the inevitable danger staring him hard in the face, but it was not he who spoke. It was Lord Exihainn. "Sire, this is Faelan, a skilled physician from Ireland who was stolen from his home by corrupt merchant sailors. Rowan has vouched for him, and I fully trust Rowan. I also trust Faelan. He does not intend to cause trouble and travels with Rowan to help him find Warwick."

"Is this true?" bellowed the king at Faelan.

"Yes it is, sire. I saved Rowan's life when he was found floating unconscious in the waters off the coast of An t-Eilean Sgitheanach. In return, he saved mine by helping me to escape from the merchant ship. I have been his friend and have travelled with him ever since. I have no home to go back to now, and I would rather serve a good cause. I do not wish for hostility with you, sire."

The king's eyes turned and bored into Rowan. "Do you swear on your life, Rowan, that what he says is true?"

"I do, sire." As strong as Rowan tried to remain, he couldn't help but turn pale.

"Very well, you may stay, Faelan."

"Thank you, sire." He bowed low, doing his best to smile.

"Rowan, tell me about the dragons. It seems you have had a few encounters with them."

"I am not sure I can say much more than what you probably have already heard from Warwick. I survived the attacks because I was alert and luck was on my side. On An t-Eilean Sgitheanach, the dragon that hunted me whipped me across the back with its tail, and I was knocked deep into the water. The dragon didn't fly off straight away but looked into the water, waiting for me to surface. I held my breath for so long that I passed out, but eventually the dragon must have flown off. The dragon had picked up my scent from the sky caves, where it had made its lair deep inside the caverns. I am now all that's left of my order. There was another attack at An Garbh Criochan. We escaped then because I saw the clear signs of fear and panic all over the citizens' faces and could smell burning. We immediately bolted on our horses, and whilst the dragon attacked, we got clear of it. From the glimpse of that dragon I saw, it looked to be a different one than the one on An t-Eilean Sgitheanach. That's all I can tell you."

"Very well. It seems that you cannot tell me anymore than I already know. You may leave."

They bowed low and hastened for the door, with Lord Exihainn's servants going as fast as they could whilst carrying him to catch up to them.

"Wait!" Lord Exihainn shouted down the corridor outside of the throne room.

They stopped, and breathless and sweaty, his servants caught up with them. "Will you stay and dine with me as my guests for a while? You can't go without food and rest, and I have maps you can look at."

They looked at each other in silence, but neither could deny their bellies' cries. Besides, there was no question that having a map to look at would be a great help. They smiled in reply and followed behind Lord Exihainn to a large room with a banquet table in the centre. Lord Exihainn snapped his fingers, and servants began filling the table with hot, roasted meats, bowls of fruit, platters of bread and cheese, and giant jugs brimming with mead and wine. They piled their plates high and scoffed down as much as they could, but they were careful not to drink too much. The moment they had finished, they asked for a map, and Lord Exihainn could not deny them. A servant came into the room carrying a large rolled-up scroll. He passed it to Rowan, and Rowan rolled it out on the table, using bowls and plates to weigh down the edges. Lord Exihainn pointed on the map to where Srath Pheofhair was, and Rowan and Faelan traced a line back to Cill Chuimein. They noticed a road marked very small on the map leading over fairly flat ground all the way to Inbhir Nis on the south side of Loch Nis. It would save them from fighting through a labyrinth of valleys and save them time. As the map was taken away by the servant on Lord Exihainn's orders, he turned to look at them sympathetically. "I am sorry you cannot stay a few days more. It has been an honour to see you again. I understand you must make haste to find Warwick. So much weight sits upon his chest. Please, take these in friendship." He summoned two servants to run and bring two satchels and fill them with food from the table. By the time they were full, they were quite heavy.

It didn't matter that the daylight was ebbing away when they left the keep; their minds were set on finding Warwick, and nothing would stop them! Lord Exihainn was carried behind them as they made their way to the city gates. It proved to be beneficial, for when they reached the gates, the guard would not deny the lord's orders to open them. They loaded the satchels onto the horses and mounted. Lord Exihainn smiled at them. "Go with haste and my blessing. I hope that upon our next meeting you will stay longer. Farewell." Lord Exihainn watched them ride away with a raised hand till they were gone from sight.

CHAPTER 22

A DISTURBANCE ON THE ROAD

As soon as Warwick had left Cill Chuimein, he felt the heavy weight of the journey ahead of him. He was finding it hard to get used to his new, heavy clothing in the deep snow, clinking with every step. By no means was his pace fast, but at least he could say he was warm. As the distance between the shores rapidly widened, he made the choice to trudge round the north end of Loch Nis. He could see no end to the loch; it just looked like a great trench leading to the edge of the world. Dense pine forest lined both banks of the loch, rising high up into the slopes of the mountains. He knew his path was quite a way north of Loch Nis, but he could not see an easy way out of the glen—the snow-blanketed mountains that surrounded it were growing steeper with every mile that passed. He trekked along the cliff edges that abutted the loch to avoid the never-ending forest and the near-vertical walls of the mountain gullies. There was no way round the cliffs' rising and falling, but when he glanced down and saw the water smashing against the rough rocks thirty feet below, he really did wish for a way round.

By the end of the first day, he hadn't got far. The light failed, and the weight of his clothing got the better of him. He took some salted meat from his pack and chewed on that. It was as tough as old leather and tasted pretty similar too. It didn't do much to sate his hunger. He camped for the night at the edge of the trees on a small patch of soft, dry ground he found. He only stopped for a couple hours of sleep, though, and when he left, it was the middle of the night. His mind was set upon finding the sacred vale.

The cliffs descended onto slippery pebbled shores. His leather boots were the cause of many aches and bruises, as they kept slipping on the icy pebbles. He wondered what his parents would have thought if they could see him now. But did not linger on these thoughts for too long—he feared they would break his will. Still, he preferred these painful emotions over the fear growing at the back of his mind after not having seen a dragon in ages. Surely it had to be only a matter of time before one did come, since he wore a key containing a dragon soul round his neck. He was distracted from his thoughts when the clouds slowly cleared and the surface of the water became the most perfect mirror of the night sky. The stars gently rippled in the tame lapping of the water and looked like they could be fished from the shores. It was entrancing. He knelt down by the water's edge, sparing a moment of thought for Rowan. He touched the reflections and watched them dissipate in the ripples he caused. He continued on his way, staring hard into the darkness looking for the shadow of a valley to his left that would take him farther north.

Cill Chuimein was a long way from sight, lost behind the forests and mountains. The light had risen now, but not the temperature. By dawn, Warwick had made it past Inbhir Mhoireastain, and he was now walking round the headland. His means to head north was farther on, hidden behind the headland. By midday, he could still not see round the headland.

Something in the corner of his eye deep in the middle of the loch suddenly caught his attention. The waters had been very calm, almost like a mill pond, but now waves were rolling from the centre and crashing on the shores. He stopped still and turned to look right at the centre of the disturbance. What he saw shocked him. A giant, snaking trail of water was rapidly heading to shore. Something large was moving just below the surface. A deep dread filled his heart, and in his panic, he squashed up tight behind some rocks, well out of sight. He looked between a tiny gap in the rocks at the point on the shore where the thing or object seemed to be heading. He saw the huge back of something monstrous break the surface in the shallows before the thing crawled onto the bank. He could not believe what he was seeing. He could only describe it as a water dragon! From where he was, the dragon's scales shone in the sun with slime, and as he watched, it began to stretch its wings, which had been neatly folded at its side. Its eyes were still red, and it looked the same as the other dragons except that it had webbing between its talons and gills just behind its head. It sat on the bank for a while stretching, for it had been long since it had come above surface. Warwick hoped it could not smell him over its own stench, which could only be described as a smell of rotting fish mixed with that of rancid flesh. He looked back to the water for any more waves. How many could there be in the depths? He worried himself silly. Luckily, whilst he remained hidden, he was upwind of the dragon, and a couple of hours later, the dragon fully spread its wings and launched into the air, letting loose a deafening roar that cut through Warwick like a spear. It flew swiftly off to the north over the mountains. Warwick came out from his hiding place, and in his deep fear of the water, he ran as fast as he could. He kept going until he was tired and breathless and could go no farther. But whilst he had run, he hadn't realised that he had finally got round the headland. Not far ahead was the start of a long ridge rising from a glen to the mountain peaks. Knowing that his lochside journey was finally over, he found more strength, and within a couple of hours, he stood upon the top of the ridge. He looked back in the dying light towards the seemingly endless loch and was surprised to see it narrow in the far distance. When he looked ahead, he saw a mess of ridge lines and deep valleys, which would be impossible to navigate when it was dark. In a hollow sheltered by boulders, he made camp, tucking himself up as small as possible for warmth. That night, for the first time, he reflected on just how far he had come and just how much this journey had changed him. His old self seemed almost gone. For quite a while now, he hadn't felt compelled to stare at the key.

At first light, he made his descent into the maze to find the valley he needed. The first valley he came to ran northeast, and for a while he thought he had got lucky. The valley floors were littered with boulders, snow-covered peat bogs, and ice-cold mountain rivers. The rivers were fast flowing and very wide at points. Several times Warwick found his path blocked by them and tried to change his route, but this only led him to walk into boggy ground. Once he was left with no choice but to cross. As he crossed, the waters came up to his waist and stole his breath. The air in his lungs felt as if it had turned to razor sharp icicles. His whole body felt paralyzed as he came out the other side. To try to warm himself up, he ate a large piece of salted meat and then forced himself to run about. No matter how long he spent in this harsh environment, his body would not adjust. When he had dried out a little, he carried on to the end of the valley but only found a dead end. He was lost. Panic set in, and the fear that he would die here was growing with every minute. He looked all round at all the slopes, searching for anything that looked familiar as he turned through the valleys trying to follow back in his footsteps, but this just led him to become more lost. In the end, after trying to think for a fair while, he climbed the slope at the end of one valley, praying he wouldn't cause an avalanche. Hopefully from the top he would get a better view of which valleys ran in his direction. With his sword, he stabbed deep into the snow and ice to pull himself up the slope. He had been climbing slowly for ages, but the top was still a long way off. Big sheets of snow were breaking off all the time round him. Warwick was finding that he was sinking up to his knees in the snow. His speed was less than a crawl now, and the slope was growing steeper. He was using all the strength he had left in his body to anchor the sword into the snow. Several times the sword pulled out as he put weight on it to move, and he slipped a little way back, jabbing the sword into the snow to stop himself.

The sun was sinking when he reached the top, completely exhausted. He couldn't move any farther and collapsed in the snow. Getting lost had cost him a day in his journey, and he was greatly annoyed at it. His annoyance was replaced by a feeling of being very small as he looked across the mountain tops at the maze before him. He had no home or family, he was lost, and his spirit was cracking. There really did seem to be no end to the maze beyond. He wondered if he should ever feel freedom again. He could only see one ending to all of this, and that was his death. How was someone of his age meant to do all this alone?

When the light arose after what felt like an endless night, he moved on, but his pace wasn't much more than a drag. The entire night he had been plagued by visions of the water dragon and the fear of where it was now. He made his way along the arêtes, trying to avoid another big climb. Unfortunately, the ridge was slowly descending, and all he had to walk on was a very thin, icy rocky outcrop. The slopes on either side of him were sheer. He had soon descended below the other ridgelines, and all he could see was the web of routes below. He had no option but to enter them. From high up, he did have an idea of the direction he should head in, but lower down, the valleys looked nearly identical. It was the same for days.

It had been three days since he'd left Loch Nis, and he was becoming disorientated. Several of the valleys he walked through came to dead ends, and a lot of the valley walls were blocking the view of the sun. He could only look up at the sky in the hope that it remained clear and then look to see where the shadows were being cast to give himself a rough idea of his heading. When he was forced to climb to the ridges, he counted the valleys he needed to pass through as best he could, and then he counted them off in his head one by one as he passed through them.

The days seemed exceptionally short in the valleys, as the sun struggled to climb above the mountains. What made things worse was that it was clouding over, and by morning, the sky was a sheet of white. The snow came as the sky promised, and he struggled to see a hundred metres ahead of him. It was very difficult to distinguish between the sky and land, as they blended into one. The winds whipped up the snow into a massive blizzard that threatened his life. Warwick was tired, frozen, and sore; it was impossible to continue. Under the cliffs, he found a small crevice that was reasonably sheltered from the storm and hunkered down inside it, pulling some of the spare clothing from his satchel over him as a blanket. He had covered so little distance that day that when the storm eased he could still see the spot he had come from. It was another two days before the snow stopped and he arrived at Srath Pheofhair. The valleys had become bigger as he got closer and the mountains much, much higher. He, however, did not realise he was at Srath Pheofhair—there was no civilisation or roads or signs out here, just barren lands. All he saw was a vast range of valleys and mountains. Nothing looked like anything from the cave paintings. He passed by the valleys. From what he could remember from the map he'd seen at Cill Chuimein, a vast stretch of water was nearby at Inbhir Pheofharain. It was encountering this that brought him to realise that the valleys he had passed were Srath Pheofhair. He was now aware of a new problem: the valleys were so vast, and he had to find one small place within them. How was it possible? With this thought in his mind, he made camp in a valley as light was getting low, and by night he had formed a search plan. This was very hard, since he didn't know what he was looking for. He just hoped it would be obvious when he saw it. When morning hit, he stuck a large, broken stick in the ground by his campsite and wrapped a piece of spare clothing round it. From there he set out in all directions, always returning to the marker.

He explored valley after valley until light failed. He did not find anything. Rowan came into his thoughts, and Warwick hoped he had found his peace with his brother seers. This journey was costing Warwick all he held dear, and he'd had enough. He was angry and wanted revenge. The anger drove him on the next day, and he left no stone unturned. By mid-afternoon, he believed he had at least found the valley. Something about this valley felt different. Warwick could sense a weird silence about it, yet he didn't feel alone. Everything was as still as the stone round him. He moved his camp there and, while it was still light, started to search the valley's perimeter. A lot of trees had grown up the side of one of the banks and were very thick and tight together. He began his search amongst them. There wasn't a trace of wildlife under the trees. He was beginning to sense that a power was on the ground, and a very old one at that. He felt confident now that he was on the right path. With every minute he was there, his confidence in the fact that this was this valley he sought grew. He did hope, though, that he might get a better sign. He searched under the trees till the light became too low to see.

That night, he went to sleep with slightly more hope in his heart that it was all going to end shortly. He had gone past the point of caring how it ended, just as long as it did. The morning came, and Warwick was not slow to get started. He began by exploring the rest of the trees. He saw nothing till a faint glow started to emanate from the neckline of his clothing. He pulled out the key. When dragons had been near, it had shone with a blinding white light. But this was different; the light was a cool blue, like looking at the sun deep under clear water. The metal felt warm to the touch. He had learnt enough about the key to know it wouldn't glow without reason. After a while spent staring at the key, he began to climb a hill in a small clearing in the trees. It was the only bare patch in the forest, as far as he knew. From the top of the hill, he could see the whole valley. He turned his thoughts back to the cave paintings and closed his eyes, imaging the trees were not there. He swiftly realised that he was standing on the mound where the dragon was slain. It was also here that the key felt the warmest and shone the brightest. He could only guess that it meant he was near.

The mound was very slippery as well as rocky, and long tufts of grass poked through the snow. Warwick left the hilltop and walked round its base, but nothing obvious was visible. He sat down on a rock, staring hard at the key and looking round. Nothing he saw seemed out of the ordinary. In his anger, he kicked the rock on which he was seated, and to his shock, he could hear an echo behind it. The echo resonated for a long time, like there was a cave or tunnel concealed behind the rock. A brief moment of excitement came over him before he tried to move the rock. The rock would not move, no matter which way he tried. He even tried to jam a stick underneath and lift it out the way. He cleared the snow from round the base, looking for a seam. *Surely if there was something concealed behind it, there had to be a seam*, he thought to himself. But as hard as he tried to dig round the rock's base, he could find nothing. He felt sure it was an entrance—the feeling in his heart pointed to this rock—but why could he not move it?

For hours he sat on the ground looking at the stone. There were no markings, no handles, and no keyhole. He felt anger growing deep within him. As he gritted his teeth, he began to squeeze the key so hard that it cut into his hands. When he saw the blood, he chucked the key at the rock. He had expected to see the key just bounce off and nothing else, but it didn't. The key stuck to the side of the rock, and there was a loud cracking sound. A wide crack had opened at the base, and smoke rose through it. Reluctantly he touched it, not knowing what would happen.

CHAPTER 23

THE SACRED VALE

The cuts on Warwick's hands stung and dripped with blood. He numbed them and washed away the worst of the blood in the snow. His hands felt swollen, which prevented him from gripping anything for a while. He sat with his hands in his lap till he started to get feeling back. When he did, he stuck his hands into the crack, and with no great effort, he managed to move the rock. The key fell from the rock and he picked it up. Even though he knew there was something behind the rock, that didn't prepare him for what he saw. The rock had concealed a long, dark passage. Its walls were smooth; this was no natural tunnel! Without light, he could not go far inside. However, it was just light enough for him to make out an engraving on the left-hand wall. Squinting in the dim light made it no easier to see or read. It turned out that it was written in Latin. Even though he had seen the language quite a lot, he still did not understand any of it. It didn't surprise him that the engraving was in the old tongue. He at least knew by the carved, smooth walls of the tunnel and the Latin engraving that he had found the sacred vale. He spent a good while inside the cramped entrance looking at the engraving in case there was more to see. He gave up after a while. It read "Qui tenet Foekey ut tantum velociter transeamus", which meant "only the one who holds the Foekey may pass", but Warwick didn't know that. Warwick's shoulders brushed against the walls, and he had to walk doubled over, for the ceiling was really low. It was clear the tunnel had been designed to be small to conceal it better. He went in as far as the light would allow. He needed a torch, so he came back out into the open. He snapped off a good-sized piece of a fallen branch that felt dry, and then he tore some fabric from a piece of dry clothing in his satchel and wrapped it round the end of the branch. He struck his dagger against the rocks, sparks showered onto the material, and flames burst into life.

The air inside the tunnel felt thick, and with the flame next to his face, it was hard to breathe. He was becoming very sweaty. He would rather have not had to carry the flame so close to his face, but he had no option with how cramped the tunnel was. The heat was beginning to burn the side of his face. The wood must have been damp, too, for it filled the tunnel with thick smoke, making it even harder to breathe and see. Down and down the tunnel went, beyond the reach of the light. He could not see an ending, but surely it couldn't just keep on going down? He knew he must be deep under the hill. His head was full of crazy images of what might lay at the end. The one that stood out the clearest was of a giant underground temple. After a while more of going down, the passage levelled out, and the ending loomed within sight. He took a last look up the tunnel and could just see a faint pinprick of light from the entrance. At the end of the tunnel was a wall of stone. On closer inspection, he saw that it had a keyhole. All round the door, the walls and ceiling had been made wider and higher. There was enough room for him to stand up. He suddenly became aware of just how stiff he was, and it took him a while to straighten up properly. On the door were very old markings. The markings showed the sword being brought down upon the dragon's head, and at the top of the door was written "Hic iacet sacra valle, ut tantum electus transire..." This meant "here lies the sacred vale; only the chosen may pass." Warwick was starting to realise that should there be more writing, he would not have a chance. Even though it was deeply annoying him, he wasn't going to jump to conclusions till he saw what was inside. The lock on the door was a big, heavy, metal lock. It dwarfed even the locks of castle doors! As he inserted the key, there was a loud click of metal moving inside. He tried to turn the key, but the lock was stiff. It took a good deal of strength to get it to move, and by that time the cuts on his hands had opened up again. When the key eventually turned, an explosion of blinding white light burst from the lock, and the key melted into the lock. As shocked as Warwick was, he could not help but feel a little annoyed that the key that he had carried for so long and that had caused so much trouble was gone so quickly and simply. Now in the centre of the door where the lock had been there was a glittering ruby. That was all that was left of the key.

The door swung inwards as he pushed, disturbing a large dust cloud. The darkness before him was darker than dark itself. It seemed to be a living darkness that completely engulfed him as he stepped into it. It even seemed to choke the light of his torch. He daren't move for fear of tripping over something. The darkness soon aroused in him a feeling of being watched, and the more he stayed in the darkness, the stronger the feeling became. Seeing that he could do nothing without more light, he left the chamber and went back to his camp. He moved his camp to right outside the entrance of the tunnel. He thought about making lots of torches, but there were no torch brackets that he could see. The other option he had was to build a camp fire inside the chamber, but he feared he would smoke himself out. The rest of the day passed swiftly, and still he had no plan.

That night, he slept just inside the entrance to keep out of the strong, bitter wind. He woke stiff and saw that a small pile of snow had built up in front of the entrance overnight. After a light breakfast of a small piece of the leathery salted meat, he rekindled his torch and tried the darkness again. It was no different, but this time he went farther in and could feel lots of things brush against his hands. Even standing right next to them, he couldn't see anything of them. He could only tell by the rough grating on the back of his hand that most of it was stone. Then he felt something soft, like silk, brush against him. His curiosity got the better of him, and he overcame the feeling of being watched. Reaching out into the darkness, he felt again for the soft things that had touched his hands, but in the place he thought they had been he only found more stone. He stumbled on a bit farther and soon found a back wall. Under his fingertips, he could feel the grooves of engravings. Not even his torchlight

235

could highlight them. Once again, he felt something soft brush against him, and for a second, he thought he heard soft whispering right next to his ear. But he never heard a footstep. He shook it off, attributing the experience to the darkness playing tricks on his mind. He remained in there for hours and completely lost track of time. Something touched him again several times, making his heart race. He could not deny he was fearful.

Was it just his mind playing tricks, or could he hear footsteps echoing down the passage? He sat down in the darkness with his back against the wall and his eyes pinned to the spot where the door was. In the darkness, he could just see the entrance, which was slightly lighter than his surroundings. Suddenly he saw two tall figures standing silhouetted against the light from the blazing torches they carried. Warwick took a deep breath. He daren't move in case they heard him. He began to hear muffled words spoken between them.

"He is definitely here. The door's been opened."

"I cannot see him anywhere. If there weren't all those deep tracks in the snow and the remains of the camp outside, we should never have found this place."

Warwick listened closely but could not detect any clues as to who they were or where they had come from. He began to panic as they stepped into the darkness and were lost from sight. He could only track them by the sound of their footsteps, but everything echoed, so he could only be sure where they were when they got close. At the sound of someone close by, he moved to the side to avoid the person, hitting his knee on a rock and creating a loud bang. The sound of their voices instantly filled the chamber. They were moving towards the source of the sound. Warwick had moved a good few feet away and was now crammed into a small gap between two unidentifiable objects. He felt safer here. One of the voices sounded a little familiar to him, but the other was completely alien. He didn't expect it to be anyone he knew and put the familiarity of the first voice down to the darkness and the echo. Soon, as clear as day, he could hear his name being called softly. Although he still didn't want to move, his heart leapt, and yet he did not know why. He began feeling something brushing against him again, really frequently this time, and the voices were growing more distant. It was then that he realised who one of them was.

"Rowan, are you sure this is the right place. After all, there are many valleys, and we have no proof that he made it."

"We have all the proof we need, Faelan. The door has been opened. Only the Foekey could open this door!"

Warwick could not believe it, and just as they were about to step out of the door, he called out to them. The sound of his name being called followed straight after, and then there were the sounds of stumbling feet. Warwick moved to the doorway, and right before him stood Rowan.

"Let's go outside so we can see each other properly," said Rowan.

The moment they were outside, Rowan grabbed Warwick and hugged him like a father would hug a son. Tears streamed down their faces. When the tears stopped, Warwick couldn't help but gape at Rowan in confusion. So many questions ran through his head, but one stood out more prominently than the rest. Finding his voice was difficult. "Rowan ... why ... did ... you ... come ... back?"

Rowan had been waiting for the question, but nothing would destroy the ecstatic happiness he felt at seeing Warwick still alive. He wiped away his tears. "I came because I must. I was wrong to leave you. I wish I could tell you my full story, but it will have to wait for another time, as will yours. This is Faelan, a dear friend of mine." Warwick and Faelan smiled at each other. "I struggle to believe how far you have come by yourself. But now we must find the answers to all of our questions."

Rowan darted inside the tunnel, and Warwick and Faelan followed. They stepped into the chamber and were instantly swallowed by the darkness. While Warwick walked off, trying to find a wall again, Rowan and Faelan looked at the inscription round the door. As Rowan read the words, the smell of burning oil reached their noses, and as soon as he finished reading them, great flames leapt up from large troughs all round the room. As the room lit up and the smoke began to drift out through the door as if it were a great chimney, they saw for the first time the sheer beauty of the inscriptions round the walls. And there at the back of the chamber, floating a few inches above a plinth, was a two-handed great sword, its silver hilt encrusted with rubies. Snaking round the grip of the sword was a carved dragon. The blade's sheen in the light was enchanting. Warwick walked to it, drawn by its beauty, and on closer inspection, he could see ancient-looking runes engraved along the length of the blade. Warwick was about to touch the blade when a hand pulled him back. Rowan was staring at him intently with a warning look. Faelan, who'd had very little part in this, was standing, fixated by the door, with a look of shock across his face. Rowan decided it was best to read the inscriptions first before touching the sword. He moved round the walls, reading it all in Latin. As he did so, he became aware that they were words of power; he could feel the temperature in the room drop swiftly, and his breath began to fog before his eyes. A sound like a drum came from above them, and when they looked up to see what had caused it, they noticed that six hooded men had been carved into the ceiling. A pale blue mist was emanating from where each of their hearts would have been. Before they knew it, the mist had become six translucent figures standing and staring at Warwick. Rowan bravely moved a few steps closer to them, but they didn't even seem to notice him; it was almost as if they could only see Warwick. Warwick still stood by the altar where the sword floated. He was scared and at the same time felt a great desire to grab the sword. The spirits began to drift towards him. It was clear to see that they didn't quite touch the ground, and as quick as the sudden chime of a bell, Warwick realised what he had felt in the dark and why he hadn't heard footsteps. The spirits encircled the altar, trapping Warwick in the centre.

Rowan and Faelan moved swiftly towards them, afraid that they meant Warwick harm. They tried to move into the circle, breathing heavily and trembling, but found it to be like trying to get past an impassable shield wall. Though Rowan was scared that he couldn't enter, he realised that the power stopping him was similar to that of the power that had lingered over the mountain path back on Sgitheanach, only this time it was stronger. He called to Warwick trapped within the circle and found that not even his voice would penetrate. He could see Warwick, however, and he looked petrified. He was trying to watch all the figures at once. After a while of struggling to get through to Warwick, Rowan backed away slowly. The spirits began to chant in very low whispering voices, which echoed round the chamber. Rowan kept backing away, and before he knew it, he had backed into Faelan and almost fallen over. The chant lasted for what felt hours before the ghostly figures lowered their heads and fell silent again. The rubies on the sword were now glowing faintly.

Warwick had fallen to the floor when they had begun to chant. He wanted to speak, to tell them to stop, to ask who they were and what they wanted, but his voice failed him. Now that the chant was over, it seemed almost if they waited for him to talk. Warwick didn't even know if they would understand his tongue. He had listened intently to the chants, and none of it sounded like any language in existence. It had sounded more like it was lots of different languages. As the figures showed no sign of talking and almost looked like they were asleep, Warwick bit his lip and rose to his feet. As soon as he moved, one of the figures looked up, smiling at him. Oddly, though, Warwick didn't feel scared now, and finding his voice, he spoke. "W-who ... are ... you?"

"We are the guardians of the sacred vale. We have guarded this place since the prophecy was first written. We have waited for you and have spent the many long years of our lives here ... for we are the writers," spoke the figure.

"So, you do not mean harm?" Warwick spoke more confidently now, encouraged by their friendly nature.

"No, we only bring harm upon those who try defile this place!"

Warwick was instantly frightened and thought they wished harm upon Rowan and Faelan. "Please, don't hurt my friends." His voice was full of worry and almost sounded muffled in his panic. "They have only travelled with me to help me on my path!"

"We wish them no harm. We only wish harm to those that try defile this place."

Warwick relaxed a bit, even though his rapid heart rate still made him feel sick.

"The time has come for you to take the sword, but before you do, you must hear the full prophecy. It would be wise for your friends to hear it as well." For the first time, the spirits looked at Rowan and Faelan and beckoned them forward, allowing them to enter the circle. Once inside the circle they could hear the spirits' voices clearly, even though they still sounded like whispers. As Rowan and Faelan sat down by Warwick, the spirits moved to the carvings on the walls and pointed to each one as they began to speak. The first carving showed a dragon swooping upon many citizens. "It began in the year 2000 BC. The dragons were taking Scotland. Scotland's empire was all but destroyed." The spirits moved round to another carving of Scotland burning and a monarch sunken onto his throne, powerless. "It was because of this that the king was forced to make a rash decision, which undoubtedly cost many lives. The king sent his entire army to march upon the mountains in the valley of Srath Pheofhair where the dragons lived, and by mid-afternoon they stood upon the battlefield. It wasn't long before the dragons came."

The next wall that they pointed at showed an army the likes of which would probably never walk upon the earth again. They then swiftly moved on to another wall, which showed the swords being forged and enchanted before being handed to the dragon slayers. "We ancient seers created three weapons of power, which should have been strong enough to kill all the dragons, yet not all was well. The weapons were given to the three dragon slayers, Drake, Aillig, and Alec. The power within the swords came from deep within the mountain tunnels of Sgitheanach. We meditated on the words of power and poured that power into the hearts of the swords. We made a mistake, though. In our hurry to create a weapon that could harm a dragon, we overlooked the power of the words. The power was not strong enough to be able to destroy them all, and we had not foreseen that the ancient power released within those mountains would attract a dragon, which would then make its lair deep within the tunnels." They pointed to two different carvings while they spoke. The first was not an image but writing. It appeared they had carved the same words upon these walls as were in the cave on An t-Eilean Sgitheanach. The second image showed a dragon circling the top of a mountain. A tear trickled down Rowan's face, but Faelan and Warwick were too focused on the spirits and the carvings to notice. "We left a carving in the deepest chamber warning anyone who read it to get out."

The next carving was positioned between two stone columns. It showed the battle, but it was hard to tell what was happening from the carving, as it was just a mass of bodies and dragons. "We now move to the battle of Srath Pheofhair. The battle soon turned ill. The dragons did not understand mercy and took advantage of the fear that every man felt, but Drake held true, killing a dragon upon this hill. A feeling of triumph briefly surged through the men." The spirits pointed to a carving of a tall, heroic figure standing upon a blood-soaked hill holding his sword aloft, the dragon crumpled at his feet. "The dragons were greatly angered by this and came down upon the ground as the remaining army set a final charge upon them. Alec was killed." They pointed to a carving showing a mass of men charging at a wall of dragons and then a carving showing Alec the dragon slayer being struck by a dragon. "Drake and Aillig ran forward to avenge Alec's death. They swung both blades upon the dragon that killed him, but the dragon dodged the attack, and the swords struck the ground at the same time. When they hit the ground, the power within was released." They pointed to the largest of the carvings, which showed the swords hitting the ground and the dragons recoiling. "The dragons were hit by a great wall of energy, which was only strong enough to put them into a deep, enchanted sleep. The sleep was so powerful that they were presumed dead. Soon after the remaining soldiers left the battlefield, the stronger of the dragons began to waken and then raised the rest. The attack had greatly weakened them, so they went into hiding, where many died under the terrible conditions." The next carving they pointed to showed the dragons rising from the ground and heading into the dark places of the world. "They were forced to evolve and to take to living in the deepest lochs and caves. This is where they spent their lives till the time came to emerge and take to the skies again."

Warwick was shocked by the next carving, which showed an evolved dragon in water. It looked exactly the same as the one he'd seen with his own eyes. He let out a slight but audible gasp, which caused Rowan and Faelan to look at him briefly. The spirits continued, oblivious to the interruption. "Soon after the battle, we realised our great mistake. We understood that it was crucial mankind survived, and we knew the dragons would come back again. This was when we created the prophecy. We took the dead dragon's heart and soul and put them both into the Foekey and this weapon. We created this weapon from the three swords, and combined with the heart and soul, we created a power greater than all the dragons. We used our own power to make the weapon and key only useable by the champion chosen to triumph over the dragons." The spirits pointed to three carvings in rapid succession. The first was a carving showing the heart and soul of the dragon being extracted. Then the second showed the swords being melted down and the one sword rising from the molten metal, radiating beams of light. The third carving showed the ancient seers standing in a circle, putting their own powers into the sword and key. "Once it was all created, we built this chamber under the hill where the dragon was killed and sealed the sword inside until its time would come." They gestured towards a carving that showed the chamber being sealed and the Foekey being kept close to them. "We kept the key close to us and passed it on through the generations of seers until it found you. You will be wondering why it was you who was chosen. After we sealed the chamber, we started to have visions of the distant future, and we saw you. This was how we knew we had been right to make the prophecy. We knew now that the sword would work." They pointed to the last and grandest carving, which showed Warwick holding the sword at the ready and a dragon flying towards him. "Once we knew this, we went back to the mountains at Sgitheanach and created the clues to lead you here. The prophecy says that you are the one who will lead the armies one more time upon Srath Pheofhair and destroy the dragons with the weapon. However, you should not presume that just because the prophecy says this you will succeed!"

At these last words, Warwick felt a sense of dread creep into his heart. He was scared senseless by what he must do. How was he supposed to command an army? The spirits fell silent and turned back to the plinth that the sword floated above. Their heads were bowed, and once again they were as still as stone. Rowan, Faelan, and Warwick all turned to each other all with the same expression. It was clear they were all thinking the same thing, so none of them said anything. Warwick turned his attention back to the sword. The moment he looked at it, the spirits suddenly looked up. "It is time for you to take the sword, Warwick." Warwick stood up and moved towards it. Then the spirits spoke again. "The writing on the blade is its name. It is known in your tongue as Dragon's Bane. Take it and hold it aloft. You are ready!" Warwick closed his eyes, clenched his jaw, and reached out, wrapping his hand tightly round the hilt. With a jerk, he thrust the blade aloft. No sooner had he picked it up than the blade shone with a blinding white light, which filled the whole chamber. When the light finally faded from the sword, the room seemed dark for a while, even with the burning troughs. To Warwick's surprise, as well as Rowan's and Faelan's, the spirits had vanished without even a sound.

Warwick examined the sword in his hand. He couldn't help notice how light it felt. He'd expected it to feel like a dozen sacks of potatoes, but instead it was as if it were made of the finest, thinnest iron. He could not see how it was possible for it to feel this light— the blade itself was a good four feet long! He took a few swings with it and cut the air lighter than a feather. Now he smiled upon it. The detail upon the hilt was incredible. The dragon carved on it wrapped all the way round it and had a scarlet ruby for an eye.

There were two more rubies on either end of the cross guard. Upon closer examination, he saw that the stones were exactly the same as the one that had been in the centre of the Foekey. Again he held the sword aloft, watching it dazzle mystically in the light of the flames. The power of the sword was starting to seep into him. He suddenly felt confident and bold, and almost drunk on it. He turned back to Rowan and Faelan. They had remained silent this whole time, watching him examine the sword. Faelan didn't say anything. He was still lost for words. Rowan, however, had come to his senses. "This is it, Warwick. I don't think we need to talk about what we just heard, as I can't think how any of us could possibly have anything to say. I will say, though, that we will follow you whatever decision you make." Rowan wiped a tear from his eye. "I think you have proven to everyone that you are ready to be a man. If you like, I shall remove your plait. After what you have done, no one can say that you are too young or that you wouldn't be able to complete the test at the age of eighteen."

Warwick thought on in silence for a while before he answered. "I have come to like my plait, as it shows me for who I am. I will keep it in memory of my parents and my quest. Even if we do all die, at least then I will see my parents again." He wore a gleaming smile, and Rowan returned it.

"You are our leader now, Warwick. You must lead us, but we can still advise you."

Warwick did not reply but gave a slight smile in acknowledgement. Rowan now turned to Faelan. "You have done more than I could ever have asked of you. I will feel no anger and will not shame you if you want to avoid the coming war."

Faelan looked back, smiling. "I have come this far. I will fight and die at your side. I should think my skills will be needed for the wounded. And perhaps lending my aid may serve to bring peace between Scotland and Ireland."

Rowan had never felt more respect for Faelan than he did in that moment.

Warwick hugged Faelan. "I am glad to have you with us, but I think we should leave now. We should get back to Cill Chuimein. Let's hope there is no hostility!"

With a courteous nod to each other, they took one final look at the chamber and then left it behind. As they passed through the door, the flames inside were extinguished immediately. A whispering voice fell upon their ears saying, "Hail to thee, Dragon Slayer!" Then the door closed behind them and sealed shut, never to be opened again.

CHAPTER 24

ṢUMMONS TO WAR

Warwick rode on the back of Rowan's horse with the sword strapped to his back. "Rowan, don't we need to head to the southwest?" Warwick was very confused, as they were riding east towards the coast.

"You mean to say you came over the ridges behind us?" Rowan turned in his saddle with a look of shock on his face.

"Yes! Where did you come from?"

"There is a road on the south shore of Loch Nis that heads directly to Inbhir Nis. From there, it was a short journey north."

Warwick sat on the back of the horse feeling angry—his frightful day-to-day battle in the valleys had all been for nothing. "Where did you even get these horses from?"

Rowan glanced at Faelan out of the corner of his eye. "We traded our boat for them. I am afraid the rest of our business will have to wait till a better time."

The hardest part of the return journey was climbing out of the valley. The horses sunk in the deep snow and stamped impatiently at the weight on their backs. After many attempts, they dismounted, pulling the horses up the slopes instead. Faelan struggled so much that he was pulled clean off his feet and just managed to keep hold of his horse. He hung to the reins as tight as possible, as he knew the horse would bolt if he didn't. Warwick assisted Faelan with his horse, and together they pulled the beast to the top of the ridge. From the ridge they could see Inbhir Nis standing out clearly against the pure-white of the snow.

They passed by Inbhir Nis with no trouble and quickly found the road to Cill Chuimein. Progress was quick on the road, and within two days they were at the walls of the city.

At least this time they were able to pass into the city without too much trouble. They headed straight for the keep. The guards instantly recognised them as they got close enough to see and sent a runner into the keep. Moments later, a messenger appeared. It was one who served Lord Exihainn as well as the king. "Follow me quickly." They were taken straight to the throne room, and the moment the doors swung open, the entire room fell deathly silent. King Angus had been pacing round the room but stopped dead in his tracks to look directly at the three of them. To their relief, the king smiled, and by the relieved faces all round the room, it was clear that it was the first time the king had smiled in days. He sat down on his throne and beckoned them to step forward. Just then, the doors opened, and a beaming Lord Exihainn was carried into the room by two sweaty servants. He ordered his servants to bring three seats to the throne for Warwick, Rowan, and Faelan. As soon as they were seated the king spoke. "It pleases me to see you have returned and united again. I should like to hear about your journey, Warwick." The king nodded to Warwick with a courteous smile.

"My lord, if you would forgive me, it is most important that I tell you of the ill news I bring now!" The king gave him a nod, so Warwick continued. "This ancient sword is what I had to find. It is very powerful, and the dragons are most likely going to be drawn to its power now that it is discovered. So for fear of another attack, I must not linger here. It is vital that this council goes well!" He unsheathed the sword from his back and rested it across his lap for the king's hungry eyes.

"Very well, I have come to trust your word. Now, why do you seek a council?" The king looked longingly at the sword upon Warwick's lap, hoping that he would gain possession of it.

"The weapon was forged by the ancient seers to be used only by me—the powers within make it so," Warwick replied, noticing the desire in the king's eyes. "I seek a council with you now as I have learnt what I must do. The prophecy says I must ride at the head of your armies to the sacred home of the dragons, Srath Pheofhair. It is there that the last battle will be fought."

"So you want me to send forth my armies?" There was a hint of aggression in his voice.

"Yes, my lord."

The king clenched the arms of his throne tight, fighting his temper. "Before I even consider this ridiculous request, I want to know everything that happened at the sacred vale. I don't care how you got there."

Rowan and Faelan sat amazed at how well Warwick was handling the king. They looked at Warwick not as boy but as a lord.

"When I was in the chamber, I instantly felt the power that was concealed within. The sword was at the back of the chamber, floating a few inches above an altar. All round the chamber were Latin engravings, but I couldn't read any. Fortunately, Rowan could read the old tongue, and as soon as he began to read, it became clear they were words of power. The temperature plummeted, and six misty, blue spirits appeared. They formed a circle round me and the altar, shutting Rowan and Faelan out of the circle. The spirits started to chant in no language I had ever heard. When they finished chanting, the sword began to glow faintly. It was then that they spoke to me and I could understand them. They began to tell me the full prophecy, pointing to each engraving in turn. They spoke of the forging of the original weapons and of the battle that went wrong. After the battle, they said, the dragons crawled away into caves and deep lochs, where they evolved in to water dragons. The spirits then spoke of the forging of the Foekey and this sword, which they undertook after receiving visions of the distant future and me. The last thing they told me to do was to summon your army for the battle to come. These spirits were the ancient seers who had made the prophecy and built the sacred chamber, where they remained guardians. As we left the chamber, the spirits disappeared, and the door sealed itself behind us, never to be opened again."

"Tell me more about the dragons."

"I was told that after the battle, the crippled dragons crawled away into the dark places of the world. Some went into deep caverns and remained hidden, whilst others evolved and learnt to swim and breathe underwater in the deep lochs. I know this not to be false, as on my journey to Srath Pheofhair, I saw one emerge from Loch Nis." There was a gasp that echoed round the entire room.

The king sat deep in thought about everything he had just heard, especially the evolving dragons. "So this is the reason that you give me orders? With Scotland sitting upon the hilt of my sword, it would seem I have no choice, if the prophecy says it must be so. You have done well to convince me. If this is to be the last battle against these foul beasts, then you will need an army like none I have ever seen. But without An Gearasdan to call upon, such numbers may be hard to come by."

"So you will help, sire?" Warwick sat bolt upright in his seat with wide eyes.

"Well, you have made it clear that my power as king amounts to nothing in the face of prophecy. So I have no choice. In two days, we ride for war. You and your friends will ride at my side."

The king's messengers departed at once upon his orders to the great cities to summon the armies to hastily march to Cill Chuimein. The king then invited Warwick, Rowan, and Faelan to join him and his court in a banquet.

His banquet hall had been furnished with two extra-long tables to cope with the amount of food the kitchens were ordered to prepare. Whilst they dined, neither Rowan nor Faelan nor Warwick spoke of their journeys. Warwick, especially, felt very anxious about having to remain in the city for a further two days; the key wasn't nearly as powerful as the sword and yet that could still attract a dragon. He ate plenty nonetheless, but that was mostly to keep his mind busy. The feasting lasted into the early hours, by which time most of the lords were beyond the point of walking. Warwick, Rowan, and Faelan couldn't have felt more out of place, and hidden by the merriment, they slipped out once they felt full. They greatly desired to spend some time together in peace and quiet before the battle.

A large bed chamber in one of the towers with three big beds had been prepared for them. A servant took them to the bed chamber once they left the banquet hall. Not long after they reached the room, there was a knock on the door. It was one of the servants who served Lord Exihainn. "Lord Exihainn would like to see you."

Rowan could see the anger building on Warwick's face and quickly intervened. "Send our regards to Lord Exihainn. He shall have our presence tomorrow once we are rested." He pushed the servant out the door and shut it behind him. Even now that they were alone they didn't want to talk about their journeys, and for a while they sat in silence before falling fast asleep.

In the morning, they met a very impatient Lord Exihainn, who had ordered a servant to watch the bottom of the tower staircase for their appearance. They were taken straight to his chamber. Three high-backed wooden armchairs like the one Lord Exihainn sat on and a table with a jug of wine and goblets had already been set out in the room. "Please sit." He gestured to the three seats with a smile.

"I am sorry we did not come last night, my lord. We were tired and wanted some time to ourselves," said Warwick.

"Forgive me for my impatience. I was so excited to see all three of you together that I was too eager to wait to talk with you. You need not apologise." He smiled once more and gestured to the servant to pour the wine. "I should like to talk to you about your journeys, and Faelan, I should like to know you better."

It seemed they had no choice as to whether to talk about their journeys, and since he had addressed Faelan first, Faelan had no option but to speak. "I only shared a short portion of their journey, but I am glad I have been a part of it. My journey started when I was taken by force from my home in Ireland. I am a skilled physician, and the sailors took me as their prisoner and forced me to work for no wages. I had been captive for months before I met Rowan. Rowan was plucked from the water unconscious having been attacked by a dragon. I brought him back to health aboard the merchant ship. With his aid, it was possible to escape before we were both killed by the captain. We poisoned the crew, took a longboat, and sailed south. From then on, I accompanied Rowan on his journey to find Warwick. We couldn't have been happier to find Warwick alive, and we were amazed that he had almost completed his quest without aid."

Warwick turned, looking aghast, his mouth gaping slightly. His eyes flicked from Rowan to Faelan.

"This was the dragon attack you spoke of before, Rowan?"

"Yes, my lord," answered Rowan. "I was hunted from the moment I left the sky caves by the dragon, though I did not know it until I had nearly made the coast. I'd planned to build a raft, as I'd hoped Warwick would have taken the one we came across on." He turned and looked at Warwick. "It wasn't too long after you left, Warwick, that I tried to find you. After you went, I travelled back to the caves and found a dragon's lair in a different tunnel. I followed the tunnels to another exit, and there I found one of my brother seers, mortally wounded by the dragon. With his dying breath, he told me that I had made a big mistake leaving Warwick. So I went in search of you. I decided to head for An Gearasdan in the hope that you had retraced your steps. I feared I was looking for a body after a while. When we got to An Gearasdan and didn't find you, we ran out of plans and almost gave up. Then I thought of the cave paintings and your father serving under the king as a soldier, so we headed for Cill Chuimein. When we arrived, we were told you had left three days before. We set out immediately to find you. If it weren't for your tracks in the snow all along the valley, we wouldn't have."

"That is some tale you have told, Rowan. And if I remember correctly, you were nearly attacked again by a dragon on your journey," spoke Lord Exihainn.

"Yes, Faelan and I were nearly attacked on the journey south. Luckily we saw terror carved on people's faces and could smell burning, which gave us enough warning to get out of there. We hid for a long while in a forest to make sure it was safe to move."

The look upon Warwick's face could only be described as terror. "I wish I had turned round and come to find you. You were nearly killed several times. I thought my journey was hard."

Rowan looked back at him with a teary eye.

"Tell us about your journey, Warwick," said Lord Exihainn.

"I left Rowan never expecting to see him again. I had no plan on where to go, and for a while, I just headed back the way I came. I couldn't find the raft we'd come across on, so I made my own and sailed straight across. On the other side, I eventually came to a village with an inn quite a long way north of our original path. I couldn't stay, as it was full of sick and wounded people from the dragon attack at An Gearasdan. Then for days I navigated south by the glimpses of the sun. I feared I would die, but then I got lucky and managed to hunt a wolf one night when I made camp. I used every scrap of it. Eventually I did have a thought; I remembered my father serving the king. That directed me to head for Cill Chuimein. I wasn't quite sure how to get there, but then I met a messenger from the city heading north. He gave me directions. At Cill Chuimein, I had no idea where to start looking. The king gave me access to search his libraries and vaults that hadn't been opened in years. After a very long time, I found some scrolls—the only ones as old as the battle. They contained accounts of the battle and mentioned the place where I had to go to find my answers. The king then sent me on my way. I couldn't believe my eyes when I got to Loch Nis and saw something huge moving towards the shore. I hid and watched it reveal itself. It was a dragon! It had gills on its neck, and I don't think I will ever forget the smell of this slimy monster. It sat on the shore stretching for hours before it took flight to the north. The whole time I hid and watched, I hoped it wouldn't smell or see me. But that was far from the end of my problems. I became lost in the valleys for days, going from ridge to ridge with no idea where I was. I only knew I had passed my destination when eventually I came to the coast. When I finally found the hill, it was in one of the few places I hadn't looked. The key helped me find the entrance. It glowed blue and got brighter the closer I got. A solid, seamless rock blocked the entrance. I only managed to get past it when I lost faith and threw the key at it; I heard an echo of a long passage behind the rock, and then the rock cracked. I could move it to one side then. At the bottom of the passage was the door with a big lock in the centre.

The key melted into the lock when I turned it, and where the lock had been was now just the gemstone. The next day, we all met in the chamber."

"Your stories will be told for years to come. All three of you have faced such terror and heartache. It's a beautiful thing to see such friendship. I wish I could accompany you on the battlefield and share in your adventure. Can you tell me how you know the dragons will be there?"

"None of us really know. I think it will have a lot to do with the sword and the power that soaks the valley, but that is just a guess. The prophecy made it clear the battle would be there. We just have to trust to it," spoke Rowan.

"That sword is like no other I have ever seen. It must be heavy." Lord Exihainn's gleaming eyes fell on the blade resting at the side of Warwick's chair, since Warwick dared not leave it unattended.

"You would think so," said Warwick, "but when I handle it, it cuts through the air light as an arrow. It was made very clear that only I can wield it. Perhaps it is too heavy to lift for everyone else. I don't want to find out." Warwick lifted Dragon's Bane to eye level and admired its glint in the candlelight.

"I need not keep you here any longer should you wish to leave," said Lord Exihainn, "however I would be very honoured if you would join me tonight for a private feast. Consider it my gift of friendship to help you on the battlefield."

"We will join you," said Rowan.

The companions hastily got to their feet at a chance to leave, bowing low to Lord Exihainn. Back in their room, all three of them hugged each other tightly. Rowan could feel Warwick shaking like a leaf. The rest of the day they spent in the fresh air, trying to enjoy their last moments of peace, and when they went to the meal, they ate and drank much till they collapsed into their beds.

By the next day, news of the armies on the march had begun to spread, and Warwick's, Rowan's, and Faelan's fears became ever more real because of it. They spent most of the day outside, as the mood inside the keep had become very tense. Messengers and lords ran back and forth constantly for the king, and the king bellowed his orders. They went to bed early after a simple supper, but sleep that night was almost impossible, especially for Warwick. He lay on his bed staring out through the window, savouring the last rare moments of calm.

By morning, he was trembling and looked very pale. Rowan and Faelan weren't much better. They were disturbed very early by a knock at the door. It was a servant carrying their breakfast and orders to head to the armoury as soon as they had eaten. They ate their bread, cheese, and apples quickly. Then, with a trembling hand, Warwick grasped his sword so tightly that his knuckles turned white. They turned and hugged each other tightly before leaving the keep in silence.

The king's squire was waiting for them at the armoury. Their highly polished armour shone brightly laying on the table. The squire picked up an iron cuirass and fitted it with the help of servants over Warwick's vest of chainmail. Then an iron helmet was shoved forcefully upon Warwick's head. Since none other than Warwick could touch Dragon's Bane, he sheathed it himself in the straps fitted upon his back. He was given iron boots and his belt that contained his dagger. He stepped to one side as soon as the squire had finished with him, wondering how he would ever fight with all this ungainly weight. The squire proceeded to dress Rowan and then Faelan exactly the same. Then the servants took them to the stables. Three absolute giants amongst the horses were given to them. They were each a deep chestnut brown, and their immaculately muscled bodies made them look like lords. Each of them had an iron chest plate and chamfron, and the saddles bore the king's coat of arms. The size of the horses was a little intimidating; they seemed far too big for the three of them. Nevertheless, the servants shoved them up into the saddles. Warwick briefly looked into Rowan's and Faelan's eyes, and they looked back. Warwick did not need to say how he was feeling, as the look he bore was also upon Rowan's and Faelan's faces.

It was hard to believe that the time had come and these were the last few hours they may ever see each other again. Their hearts were in their mouths, and Warwick quickly leant over the side of his horse, as he was suddenly sick. A loud war horn was blown from the keep, and the king rode with his private guard through the city.

"Come on. We'd best go and meet the king," Rowan said hastily.

They rode out of the stables to find the king and his guard waiting for them. The king was so heavily armoured that barely any of his skin was visible. He looked the size of bear on his horse. He bowed towards Warwick. "Ride with me to the gates."

The three bowed back to the king, and before they knew it, the royal guard had boxed them in at the king's side. The king drew a beautiful short-sword with a golden hilt encrusted with sapphires and rubies and held it aloft. The war horn sounded again, and they trotted down to the gates. Rowan reached across and rested a comforting hand on Warwick's leg, giving him as much of an encouraging smile as he could muster. He then turned and did the same to Faelan. None of them dared to speak amongst the silent royal guard. The gates came into view from between the buildings, and Warwick felt a jolt go through his body. It seemed the entire city had come to offer their blessing. The majority of the women were dressed head to toe in white cloth and wept profusely, throwing heather at the horses' feet. The men were not dressed in white but had stopped whatever jobs they had busied themselves at and stood with their heads lowered. Warwick reached out a hand, caught a piece of heather, and attached it to his saddle. The woman who had chucked it blew him a kiss amongst her tears. The act of kindness gave him warmth, and he began to find some strength returning to him. He turned and smiled first to Rowan, then Faelan, and finally the king. In doing so, he brought some strength to them too. They rode slowly on, and the hinges of the gate groaned loudly as it opened. Warwick clenched the reins tight and locked his jaw as he saw what lay ahead—a solid wall of soldiers, armoured head to toe in heavy, iron armour with spears and the banners of many cities towering above their heads. The soldiers stood there looking completely unnerved and ready for battle. The three of them exhaled loudly enough for the whole company to hear. The army that had come was at least ten-thousand strong. The king rode forward, right to the head of the company, and Rowan, Warwick, and Faelan followed with his royal guard. The king seemed to grow in his saddle to a giant size and puffed out his chest. "My loyal friends, my proud warriors, people of Scotland," he bellowed like a roaring bear, "today we march like our ancestors once did to battle the dragons. We march not to defeat but to victory. Give them no quarter and show them the true might of Scotland. This is our land and our home. Their filth will be cleansed from the land like poison drawn from a wound. You go to battle as heroes with the love of all Scotland. No, we do not hide, and we do not run. *We fight*! We stand here united under one banner, tall and proud. Let this image blind the beasts. We have an advantage that even the dragons can't stand against." At this he pointed to Warwick with a look of hunger in his eyes. "This is Warwick who rides at my side. Yes, he is young, but he carries out hearts and gives us strength. He wields the mighty Dragon's Bane, a sword with the power to cut through the dragons as if they were made of sand. He is an almighty hero and has my full trust. Look to him with honour and strength and ride at his side to a glorious victory." The king gestured to Warwick to raise his sword. Warwick grabbed the hilt of the sword on his back and drew it, thrusting it high over the army, where it caught the early light and shone like the sun. As loud as an explosion, the entire army roared with pride, honour, and confidence. Although he could barely hear anything after the roaring, confidence surged from the hilt of his sword down through his fingertips and through the maze of veins snaking through his body. He had never felt strength like it. With his confidence, the rubies on the hilt burst with beams of red light, and the dazzled army roared even louder. Before he knew it, spears, swords, and bows all round were thrust sky high.

"March now to Srath Pheofhair," bellowed the king.

CHAPTER 25

THE BATTLE OF SCOTLAND

The march had begun. King Angus, Warwick, Rowan, and Faelan rode at the head along the old trading road that ran alongside the lochs. Every single marched footstep behind them sounded like thunder. As much as the icy wind tried to crush their spirits, it always failed against the warmth of the heavy armour. It seemed everything nature could throw at them would not dampen their spirits. After a little while, Warwick, Rowan, and Faelan began to master their temperamental horses. Still, it was hard work to stop them from galloping ahead.

Late morning on the following day, they marched upon the valley where the ancient battle had been fought. They had marched late into the night with very little rest; it showed in a few of the men, who looked far from their best. After a little food, they seemed to be a bit better. It was now on the battlefield that Warwick felt like he had stepped back in time to when Drake, Aillig, and Alec led the army. The only difference was Dragon's Bane. But after a while, there still wasn't a single sign of a dragon as the army stood like statues ready and waiting. A niggling doubt was creeping into the corners of Warwick's mind. *Where were they? What if the prophecy was wrong?* These and many more thoughts started to crush his spirits. He unsheathed his sword, thinking about its power, but nothing happened. The silence that now pressed on the valley felt heavy, almost like it had mass. They felt very small looking round at all the mountains surrounding them, expecting at any second to be engulfed in flames. It wasn't long before a few of the soldiers began to grow restless and the king's temper began to sour. Warwick thrust the sword again into the air, almost lifting himself out of the saddle. Still, nothing out of the ordinary seemed to happen. Then Warwick did something that left the king speechless. He dismounted from his horse and sent it on its way back to the city. "Against dragons the horses won't be of any use. We shouldn't needlessly kill our horses," said Warwick in response to the dazed looks he received from the king and the entire guard. They did the same but with far less will. Rowan and Faelan were the only ones not to hesitate. Warwick turned to King Angus with an idea. "Sire, will you summon a war cry and sound the war horns?"

The king turned to the waiting wall of soldiers, thinking very quickly. "It seems the dragons have been scared off already by our might. They are mere animals to a bow and arrow. To the greatest victory we have ever seen."

Like Warwick had asked, the roars erupted as swords were held aloft and the horns sounded in victory. Warwick thrust his sword into the air and felt the confidence come back. The sword all of a sudden burst forth with a blinding ray of white light, obscuring the valley from view for a short while. The bright light instantly silenced the army, and they all stood alert, shielding their eyes whilst trying to look at it. Warwick and Rowan were the only ones who looked away from the sword, looking instead from mountain top to sky. A sudden, ear-splitting roar echoed down through the valley, crushing the silence. Then like a huge earthquake, the ground trembled as something enormous landed on the mountainside. They looked up to the mountain ridge and saw a dragon that looked like a mountain itself. The whole army turned to face it. As they watched with their weapons clasped tightly in their hands, it tipped its head back and bellowed a twenty-foot high jet of flames into the air. Then, as if a bass drum the size of a mountain were playing quarter notes, more quaking thuds came from all round the valley. The wall of soldiers suddenly didn't look so impenetrable. The rocks of the mountainsides were beginning to slide, and the ground shook so much that it was hard to stand. The cause of the loud thuds became clear as one by one dragons clambered over the ridges all round them. Even the king recoiled in fear. Warwick and Rowan, at least, stood ready and tightened their grips on their swords.

So it was right here and now that the future of Scotland would be decided. At a quick count there were twenty-two dragons. The dragons showed no signs of attacking, but it seemed they were mocking the army. They sat on their mountains, black as night with those fierce, red eyes piercing everything that lived. Even while they were high up the slopes, Warwick could still smell the horrid stench of death they gave off. The battle hadn't even begun and Warwick could already see the army's faith crumbling. A lone dragon launched into the air, gliding with its wings fully spread and its head bowed. Many of the men turned and ran as it came straight for them. Now what had been a solid wall of soldiers was full of wide gaps. Warwick desperately thrust his sword into the air, as did the king, Rowan, and Faelan. Their refusal to move even when a dragon came straight at them showed the men strength, and their loyalty began to return. Warwick thrust the sword as high as possible now, and a flash of light shot from the sword straight into the dragon's eyes.

This was it, the battle had begun. Creating a mighty hurricane-force wind, all the dragons launched into the air and began to fly in rings above their heads. It rained fireballs the size of boulders, which exploded like bombs the moment they hit the ground. All round, wildfires spread rapidly and threatened to encircle the army. The heat from the fireballs melted metal, flesh, and bone. The number of soldiers that remained was still huge. The king ordered them into a circle to face all the dragons. Warwick could see that they were already trapped and looked to Rowan briefly. Rowan already looked dead, he was so pale. The only thing that was giving Warwick any strength was the power within Dragon's Bane. The dragons dived on the surrounded circle and whipped men with their tails thirty feet through the air in all directions. The men crashed down like all the bones in their bodies had been removed. It was no longer a circle.

"Shields!" cried King Angus. There was a sudden flurry of movement, and a canopy of tightly interlocked shields domed over the army. This did not hinder the dragons for a second; if they did not scorch the metal shields until they glowed white hot, they whipped the shields clean out of the soldiers' hands. Soldiers dived out the way to avoid the flames and the whipping tails, but most were not quick enough. Warwick was starting to learn that as long as his confidence remained, the sword would burst with light when thrust in the air. More than anything, he knew that if they were to stand a chance he needed to get the dragons to the ground. The only plan he had was to use the sword's light to draw the dragons away from the soldiers, and it did work briefly. He used his full strength and thrust Dragon's Bane sky high with a roar. The light shot from the sword dazzling the dragons, and the dragons turned away from it roaring in anger. Now they were too far away for their flames to reach the soldiers. Warwick's act had caught a lot of the army's attention, and they got to their feet and reformed a line. The king was right by his side.

Warwick shouted as loud as he possibly could with his sword still held aloft, commanding them to charge, but amongst the roars and beating of wings, his voice was lost. He turned to the king, Rowan, and Faelan and told them to run to the flanks of the army and order them to split into two units and charge down either side of the valley. The charge began in two long tails, Warwick and the king at the head of one, and Rowan and Faelan at the head of the other. But no sooner had it started than the dragons, like shepherds, herded the army into a panicked ball in the centre of the valley. The dragon's bodies were so vast above them that they blocked almost all the light as they soared overhead with the speed of an arrow.

The battle seemed to have only started moments ago, but thousands were already dead, scattered far and wide. Warwick stood powerless right in the centre of the soldiers, who were pushing in whichever way they could to try to escape. All round, the dead carpeted the ground. Warwick feared Rowan and Faelan were amongst them, as he couldn't see them anywhere. Tears spilled from his eyes, and he fell to his knees. All sound from the battle was lost to him, and all that existed were the dead and a red valley. He looked all round for Rowan and Faelan and caught a glimpse of the king on his knees surrounded by the few royal guardsmen that still lived. He had no sword in his hand, and he was covered in blood. He was not injury free himself. Cuts were all over him, and his hands were blistered. A deep gash on his left cheek poured blood, but the moment fire came close to him, it dried thick and sticky instantly.

With every second of the battle that passed, a hundred more joined the dead, and the dragons had not suffered a single scratch. The blade's glow had diminished with his hope, and it now looked no different from any other sword. Warwick pulled himself to his feet and pushed his way into the soldiers to find Rowan. Seeing Rowan would give him some courage. However, he was immediately bowled over in the stampede and struggled to get back on his feet. A short way ahead of him, between many legs, he could see Rowan on the ground trying to get up. Warwick pushed through with every bit of strength he had to get to him, shouting his name. Not even right in front of him could Rowan hear him. It was only when Warwick gripped his shoulder that Rowan realised who stood before him. With difficulty, Warwick pulled him to his feet. As he did so, he noticed that Rowan was having difficulty putting pressure on his left ankle and that it was twisted in a funny angle. It was broken. Warwick half-dragged, half-carried him to the edge of the battlefield. There he laid Rowan amongst the dead in the hope that it would protect him. As for Faelan, there was no sign of him. Thousands struggled back and forth, and half the army was gone. Some of the dragons had pulled away and landed on the slopes to watch with glee. Six dragons remained, diving vertically with their wings folded back against their bodies and pulling up just in time to slash, burn, and claw the soldiers.

The near death of Rowan had made Warwick very angry. As his anger grew, Dragon's Bane began to glow, getting brighter and brighter. He pushed his way into the middle of the frenzied panic and thrust it high above the soldiers so its blade could quite clearly be seen. There it shone like a beacon. It shone out as bright as the sun, and many of the soldiers stopped to look at it. All of a sudden, he felt much taller than the rest of the army. Warwick did not move, even with a dragon coming right for him. His bravery rallied a small number to his side with their swords and bows held at the ready. Someone close to Warwick sounded a war horn. Warwick turned to look and saw the king, helmetless, bloody, and burned, standing slightly hunched close to him. The air was full once more with all the dragons ready to make their final blow. Their blood-red eyes looked burning hot. They'd had had enough of toying with their prey; now they just were going to crush them. As a wall of dragons came diving with bared teeth towards them, Warwick cried the order to charge and broke not as a young boy but as a warrior into a furious charge. The dragons were on top of them in seconds, with their talons lowered ready to grab. One headed straight for Warwick, having eyes for no one else. At that moment, Warwick raised the sword in both hands high above his head with a cry of anger. The light blinded the dragon, and as it tried to pull away with the others from the light, it revealed its belly. In the few seconds that Warwick had, he leapt into the air with Dragon's Bane brought back behind his head and swung with such aggression and force that it cut through the belly of the dragon without any resistance. The sword wasn't even chipped! The sword had pierced several organs, and thick, black blood gushed over the army as the dragon nosedived into the ground. The dragon was dead! Everyone had seen it and heard the piercing cries as the blade cut through it; now everyone stood still looking at Warwick and the dragon. The brief silence that followed was shattered by the sudden war cry from the entire army. Killing the dragon had rekindled much hope, and at last, a wall of soldiers stood ready to fight with the mindset that the dragons could be killed. Warwick looked from his hands to the sword to the dead beast, dumbfounded by the fact that he had killed it. A tail swipe close by brought him back to his senses and not a moment too soon, as a ball of flames came rushing towards him. He dived out the way but only just made it. The heat from the flames blistered the side of his face. He gritted his teeth, scrabbling to his feet again.

The dragons attacked from farther away where the sword couldn't reach them. But this was worse; they seethed in anger and turned and dived in almost a blur. The first dragon's death had come as a great blow to them, and they were soon trying to make up for their mistake. At least three of the dragons now directed their attacks to Warwick. Warwick saw them coming and was ready for them with his sword constantly held high. His attackers came from all angles, one after the other. Balls of flames exploded all round him as he dodged and dived. He glanced rapidly all round for a sight of Faelan and Rowan. He could just make out Rowan where he'd left him, but Faelan had completely disappeared. Had he managed to escape? Warwick's will started to break again upon seeing how quickly the dragons killed the soldiers and flicked them as if they were match sticks right across the valley.

Only a quarter of the army still stood. But as much as his heart broke, Warwick's anger kept on building. Three hundred men stood by his side, refusing to break ranks. Their chance for victory depended upon the dragons fighting from the ground. Warwick thought hard as the dragons circled to make their next attack. An image of the cave paintings and the engravings in the chamber came to his mind, and it gave him an idea. He ran to the hill that concealed the sacred chamber, with the rest of the army following his lead. He raised the sword behind his head and swung with closed eyes upon the solid rock. It did not break and it did not blunt. It sliced through the rock and deep into the ground like butter. The rock exploded in all directions, and giant cracks that looked burnt at the edges ran through the earth. The force had sent a violent tremor through the ground and into the air. It bowled Warwick over with his sword in his hand and most of the soldiers too. It also hit the dragons but with a much greater force, as if the tremor knew who its enemy was. Their wings crumpled, broken and limp like tissue paper, and they fell like boulders out of the sky, crashing with an almighty thud all over the valley. Several attempted to take off again, but their wings were twisted and dragged on the ground. Warwick hoped it might have killed some of them, but they all stood up and started to charge towards them. They were almost as quick charging on foot as they were flying. Warwick felt confident that he knew what to do.

Rowan had watched from afar what Warwick had done and couldn't have been more proud. It brought back most of his strength, and he managed to stand, even with the pain from his ankle. Much to Warwick's surprise, he found Rowan standing at his side holding his sword. He looked like most of the surviving army—broken and beaten. Warwick put an arm round him. "I am glad you are with me one last time. For Helena and Deal." He turned to the king and the rest of the army. *"Charge!"* he roared, and the whole army echoed him in reply as they burst down the hillside towards the dragons. They split into many columns, ducking and diving under the dragons' legs but eventually forming a circle all round the dragons. The dragons were quick on the charge, but they couldn't turn nearly as quickly on the ground. The sea of swords and bows slashed, rebounded, splintered, and shattered no matter what part of the dragon they hit. The only blade that wouldn't break was Dragon's Bane. The dragons flicked their tails in wide arcs in retaliation. Many soldiers were sent flying, but they didn't fly as far now, so quite a few got back to their feet and came back to fight. Warwick ducked out of the way of a tail and swung his sword at the same time. It sliced deeply into a dragon's thigh. Blood splattered him, and the dragon, with wailing screams of pain, reared up on its hind legs, revealing its belly. Warwick dived underneath its belly before it crashed back to the earth and stuck his blade straight through its heart. He only managed to pull himself free of the dragon with moments to spare as the immense body slammed into the ground. The dragon blood did not seem to stain Dragon's Bane but just ran off as quickly as it had touched it.

The air was rent with the sounds of screaming and roaring, and it was filled with a stench like no other. The soldiers hemmed in the dragons as tight as possible so that it was hard for them to turn, and soon four dragons were dead. But the soldiers paid the price, keeping the dragons hemmed in with their lives. Soon the dragons were able to break through the ranks and move to the outside of the circle. Now the dragons had the advantage and fought from the centre and the outside. The men were outmatched. Warwick and about two hundred men that could manage to break from the trap retreated across the valley whilst the dragons crushed those remaining in the circle.

As much as Warwick did not want to watch from the opposite end of the valley, he could not help it, and the sounds of death burned inside him. Tears streaked his face, but not once did he lower his sword. He tried to muster his strength so the sword would blaze with light, but as hard as he tried, he couldn't do it. All he could do was watch as the sounds of the dying faded away. Many of the injured had started to rise from close by in support of him, and this comforted him. To Warwick's great relief, Rowan had somehow survived the massacre and hobbled over to him, with Faelan at his side looking very bloody and burnt. Faelan brought with him ill news: the king was dead! Warwick had wanted to greet him with a smile, but the news was too much. Fortunately, Faelan had only said it loud enough for Warwick and Rowan to hear. They suspected the rest of the army didn't know already, as they still stood ready to fight.

The dragons had turned to face them, and it was now that Warwick felt like he was Drake. They marched slowly towards the enemy, as this was about as fast as most of them could move, splitting round the outside of the dragons as best they could. But they were easy pickings at this speed and in such dwindling numbers. Warwick managed to dodge and weave his way close to the neck of a dragon and thought he had a clean shot, but out of nowhere, a tail struck him sharp in the back and threw him high above the soldiers. He crashed down not too far away. Rowan saw it happen and looked with horror in Warwick's direction, unable to get to him. Warwick's body soon became lost from view, trampled by many men.

Faelan was close to the outside of the circle and saw Dragon's Bane on the ground nearby. He had no idea of what had happened to Warwick. He staggered towards it in the hope of using it. In his heart, he knew something must be wrong for it to be lying there without Warwick. As he gripped the hilt, a sharp, burning pain jolted up the arm he held it in, and he dropped it at once. A black scorch mark was imprinted on his hand, and his whole arm felt paralyzed. He left the blade there and limped back into the battle. He was so exhausted that he could barely swing a blade in aggression. All round, soldiers scavenged weapons from the dead as their own broke.

Rowan staggered towards Faelan, knowing that defeat was moments away. But as he got closer, a tail swung and launched Faelan into the air. He fell lifeless to the ground. Rowan couldn't get to him, but he already knew he was dead by the way his body had crumpled. Faelan's death finally broke the will of the remaining soldiers. No man was attempting to fight anymore, and fear stalked the battlefield, locking the soldiers firmly in its talons until death came to collect them all. As the men tried to escape, the dragons immediately stopped it. Rowan stood in defeat, looking at all the dead spread out like a vast carpet, and then he saw Faelan, twisted and contorted. Rowan could only hope that he felt no pain where he was now. His heart bled with grief, and the last of his strength was leaving him. He stopped struggling, and his vision became unfocused as he looked back at the dragons. He closed his eyes as burning hot tears spilled down his cheeks. Then he fell to his knees. He was too tired to carry on fighting, and he knew he would not be able to touch Dragon's Bane after seeing the burns on Faelan's hand.

Warwick's fall had been cushioned by several dead bodies, and he was protected by the strength the sword had given him. The dragon's strike had knocked him unconscious. He started to come round, noticing that he was covered in blood. There were deep gashes upon his forehead and left shoulder slowly oozing blood. He cast his helmet aside, as it was broken and buckled. He felt for Dragon's Bane but couldn't find it anywhere. His vision started to clear, and he looked hard for it but couldn't see it anywhere. He was shocked to see how few remained and how many dead bodies had hidden him. He tried to stand, but his legs buckled, and he fell painfully back to the ground. He had enough strength to crawl, and so he did over the mounds of dead bodies, trying not to smell the putrid stench. Crawling had its advantages, as he could slip under the gaze of the dragons quite easily whilst they set about attacking the remaining standing survivors. Eventually he saw the hilt of Dragon's Bane glinting between a few dead bodies. The moment he held the sword, he felt the strength in him to stand. He was prepared to sacrifice his life to save the few that were left. It was going to be hard to fight with his injuries. Getting close enough would be hard enough with nothing to stop the dragons from turning.

The dragons had noticed Warwick's recovery, and they had learnt who he was by his blade. They wasted no time in trying to vanquish him quickly. The dragons wheeled round to focus on him. This allowed a few soldiers to flee towards the cover of the valleys. The dragons were only feet away when Warwick, with all his remaining strength, stabbed Dragon's Bane into a nearby boulder. The boulder exploded in all directions, and huge tremors charged towards the dragons. At the sound of the exploding rock, Rowan turned instantly with his eyes wide and his hope surging. He spotted Warwick right in front of the dragons with the sword in his hand, directing rays of light directly into their eyes. They both stood speechless as simultaneously the dragons' legs collapsed, followed by their bodies. Finally, those blood-red eyes turned a milky white. Like great mounds of earth, they lay on the ground, broken and dead. Warwick wasn't so quick to trust that they were actually dead and stabbed deep into each one. Satisfied that they were dead, he dropped to his knees with the sword limp at his side, its glow diminished. Rowan staggered over to Warwick and put his arms round him, hugging him whilst silent tears streamed down his face.

Thick black smoke rose up in columns, drifting over the battlefield, and with it came the stench of death. It did not feel like a victory when they looked at how many they had lost. Pain like this would never completely heal. Those who had managed to retreat started to return the moment they heard the cries of the dragons as they crashed to the floor. A deathly silence drifted over the battlefield, and they all stood staring in shock and exhaustion at the mass of dead dragons. When the shock passed, the surviving men began to move amongst the dead, calling out hopelessly for friends and family. The replies to their calls never came. This penetrated Warwick's and Rowan's hearts like an ice-cold spear. However, amongst all Warwick's pain and remorse, a feeling of overwhelming relief and success was bubbling its way to the surface. He had avenged his parents' untimely deaths like he had set out to do. His journey was finally finished. He staggered to look for Faelan with his arm round Rowan, supporting him. He soon found Faelan, and one look at him told him Faelan was dead. He did not weep or smile but just said two words: "thank you". Rowan looked at Faelan sadly, and Warwick patted him on the shoulder. "Faelan did not die in vain; his choices and death will create bonds of friendship between Ireland and Scotland. His story should be told and spread widely."

Rowan, for the first time, smiled and bent down to kiss Faelan on the forehead, muttering "goodbye".

All the men were starting to congregate together again. Only about two hundred of the soldiers remained and would return to Cill Chuimein, not with triumph in their hearts but with sadness for those who died. Now they had to find the strength to tell the city their king was dead. Warwick, with Rowan at his side, turned to face the army before the march started. To his great shock, the soldiers all sank down on one knee and hailed him as Warwick the Dragon Slayer. Then they stood and began to march away, with Rowan and Warwick following on behind.

CHAPTER 26

THE RETURN

They returned to Cill Chuimein, bitterly cold and exhausted, having barely rested. First there were cheers, and then those cheers turned to cries as the people swiftly realised how few returned. The soldiers kept looking straight ahead and didn't stop till they reached the keep.

The walls of the keep echoed with the sadness they all felt. The entire king's court seemed to be as silent as a breath of wind. While the king had been absent in battle, his steward had taken control of the throne and was sitting ready for the king to return. Warwick entered the king's chamber without the king and stood before the throne.

"How went the battle?"

"The dragons are dead but at great cost to our numbers. The king is dead!"

"This is grave news." The steward stood before the court and in a loud and very clear voice said, "The king is dead!" The whole room seemed to grow darker with the news. "We must honour his memory and the sacrifice he made to give us our freedom. Let us eat and drink to his memory and that of the victorious fallen. Warwick and Rowan, I would be greatly honoured if you would join us."

"We will join you, my lord."

Servants helped them to wash and dress to get ready for the meal. They feasted on fine meats, cheese, fruit, rich puddings, and the sweetest honeyed mead. The court toasted Warwick for his great deeds, and Rowan raised his goblet as well. Then they drank deeply to the king and the victorious dead. They feasted till dawn and then slept their aches and pains away, full to the brim with food and wine.

It was early when a knock came on Warwick and Rowan's chamber door. Warwick wasn't surprised to see Lord Exihainn's servant. The moment Lord Exihainn saw them covered in wounds, he turned white, and he slumped into his chair when he didn't see Faelan with them. A scribe waited at Lord Exihainn's side to write down everything. Together Warwick and Rowan told him the full account of the battle. By the end, Lord Exihainn smiled at them both and bowed to them. The scribe disappeared after the conversation had finished. Before they knew it, the story was being told right across the city.

Warwick was given a set of tailored, green, silken clothing and finest leather boots one morning and was told to put them on. They had been specially made for him. He took the gift but couldn't help feeling a bit confused. A bit later, a servant came and took him to the throne room. The steward was standing before the throne in his finest silks as well and holding the king's ceremonial sword. The whole court and remaining king's guard created a path for Warwick to walk up. When Warwick reached the throne, he noticed Lord Exihainn in his chair with Rowan standing next to him. Warwick bowed to the steward, who smiled in return. "You do not bow before this court, master Warwick. We bow to you for your services to the city and to all of Scotland. We have received the accounts of the war, and they shall be kept for anyone to read in the hope that no one forgets what you have done. The city would like to thank you and knight you, giving you titles fit for your service. On your knees, young Warwick."

Warwick sank to his knees, gritting his teeth; he still ached greatly and had slept very little, for his dreams were plagued by the screams of the battle. When he was on his knees, he felt the cold blade rest flatly on his shoulder.

"It is with my great honour that I pronounce you thane of Cill Chuimein and honour you with the title Warwick the Dragon Slayer. Now stand."

As Warwick stood, the whole room bowed, including Rowan.

Warwick did not like this responsibility and just wanted to be left in peace. That's not to say it didn't have its benefits. The rest of the week he spent resting in his new appointed home in the city with Rowan. It was very big: the ceilings were high and the rooms massive, with a log fire in nearly every room. The furnishings were fit for a king. Servants were sent to serve him. To Warwick, it seemed a palace. Many members of the court visited regularly for advice and to make sure everything was to his satisfaction. Warwick, however, wanted none of this, so he dismissed them quickly.

At the end of the week, when he felt strong enough, he made plans to leave. However, when it came to leaving, it was not easy. A young girl in his service called Freya, who was no older than himself, had been growing close to Warwick, and he had taken a liking to her. She was quite beautiful with her blue eyes and long, flowing brown hair, and fair skin. She always made sure he was warm and well fed and that his aches were well attended to, always blushing when in his company. Warwick did not punish her for obvious advances but welcomed them. Just before he planned to leave, he asked her to leave his service and live with him. She accepted but was also sad to find out he had plans to travel. The following day, Warwick and Rowan saddled up a couple of horses and filled a couple of satchels with food and water given to them by the servants. Warwick still didn't go anywhere without Dragon's Bane, and he fixed it to his saddle. Before they left, Warwick spoke alone with Freya. He told her that he would return and told her what it was he was going to do. At the door, before he mounted, she pulled him to one side and kissed him softly and then hugged him. With this new feeling of love beating in his heart, he smiled at her and mounted his horse. Then he rode down to the gates with Rowan and off into the wild.

They rode for his old home by Loch Domhain so that Warwick could say goodbye properly to his parents. With every day they rode, they noticed the temperature getting warmer and the snow thinner. Upon reaching An Gearasdan, they rested for a while and walked round the ruins. They both felt like they were travelling back in time to before their journey had begun, but Warwick knew in his heart that where he had once lived he could never live again. A few days' ride later, they were skirting the borders of Loch Domhain. They rode the last few miles, and as soon as Warwick saw the remains of his home, he froze and began to weep uncontrollably. Rowan took him to where he had buried Deal and Helena and left him alone for a while. Warwick knelt at their graves and rested a hand on the cairns. With a small smile, he kissed the top of each cairn and said his goodbyes for the last time.

THE END

ABOUT THE AUTHOR

Jamie Liquorish is a writer who lives in Loughborough, England. He walks all over Scotland, absorbing inspiration from its stunning culture, scenic vistas, and phenomenal wildlife, all of which he has laced into his short stories and now this, his first novel. For years, Jamie has investigated the paranormal, strongly believing that there is a lot more to this world. His research inspires his writing, adding a great sense of mystery and spirituality to his works. He writes both fiction and non-fiction stories and accounts of his findings. Jamie has been writing since he was a teenager, inspired by the great works of J. R. R. Tolkien.

Printed in Great Britain
by Amazon

74630013R00168